"Part noir throwback, part medical mystery, part comedy, and thoroughly, wonderfully entertaining. Highly recommended."
— *LIBRARY JOURNAL* (STARRED REVIEW)

"It's hard not to root for the loopy Genevich… [in this] promising debut."
— *BOOKLIST*

"Rejoice, Chandler fans … Paul Tremblay slices, dices and spins the neo-noir in his own strange way and delivers a fast, smart, and completely satisfying read."
— STEWART O'NAN

"Original and different, and yet somehow good kin folk to what has gone before in the tradition of Raymond Chandler."
— JOE R. LANSDALE

"*The Little Sleep* offers up an interesting gloss on the detective genre, in which the deepest and most profound mystery has less to do with any crime per se than with the enduring enigma of self."
— *LOS ANGELES TIMES*

"*The Little Sleep* is one of the most engaging reads I've come across in a good long while. Tremblay does the near impossible by giving us a new take on the traditional PI tale."
— TOM PICCIRILLI, AUTHOR OF *THE COLDEST MILE* AND *THE COLD SPOT*

"If Philip K. Dick and Ross Macdonald had collaborated on a mystery novel, they might have come up with something like *The Little Sleep*…"
— BILL CRIDER, AUTHOR OF THE SHERIFF DAN RHODES MYSTERY SERIES

THE LITTLE SLEEP

AND

NO SLEEP TILL WONDERLAND

PAUL TREMBLAY

THE
LITTLE
SLEEP
AND
NO
SLEEP
TILL
WONDER
LAND

TITAN BOOKS

The Little Sleep and No Sleep Till Wonderland
Print edition ISBN: 9781789096316
E-book edition ISBN: 9781789096323

Published by Titan Books
A division of Titan Publishing Group Ltd
144 Southwark Street, London SE1 0UP
www.titanbooks.com

First edition: April 2021
10 9 8 7 6 5 4 3 2 1

Printed and bound in Great Britain by CPI Group Ltd, Croydon CR0 4YY.

For Lisa, Cole, and Emma

I was more intrigued by a situation where the mystery is solved by the exposition and understanding of a single character, always well in advance, rather than by the slow and sometimes longwinded concatenation of circumstances.

—RAYMOND CHANDLER

ONE

It's about two o'clock in the afternoon, early March. In South Boston that means a cold hard rain that ruins any memories of the sun. Doesn't matter, because I'm in my office, wearing a twenty-year-old thrift-store wool suit. It's brown but not in the brown-is-the-new-black way. My shoes are Doc Martens, black like my socks. I'm not neat and clean or shaved. I am sober but don't feel sober.

There's a woman sitting on the opposite side of my desk. I don't remember her coming in, but I know who she is: Jennifer Times, a flavor-of-the-second local celebrity, singing contestant on *American Star,* daughter of the Suffolk County DA, and she might be older than my suit. Pretty and brunette, lips that are worked out, pumped up. She's tall and her legs go from the north of Maine all the way down to Boston, but she sits like she's small, all compact, a closed book. She wears a white T-shirt and a knee-length skirt. She looks too spring for March, not that I care.

I wear a fedora, trying too hard to be anachronistic or iconoclastic, not sure which. It's dark in my office. The door is closed, the blinds drawn over the bay window. Someone should turn on a light.

I say, "Shouldn't you be in Hollywood? Not that I watch, but the little birdies tell me you're a finalist, and the live competition starts tomorrow night."

She says, "They sent me home to do a promotional shoot at a mall and at my old high school." I like that she talks about her high school as if it were eons removed, instead of mere months.

"Lucky you."

She doesn't smile. Everything is serious. She says, "I need your help, Mr. Genevich," and she pulls her white-gloved hands out of her lap.

I say, "I don't trust hands that wear gloves."

She looks at me like I chose the worst possible words, like I missed the whole point of her story, the story I haven't heard yet. She takes off her right glove and her fingers are individually wrapped in bandages, but it's a bad wrap job, gauze coming undone and sticking out, Christmas presents wrapped in old tissue paper.

She says, "I need you to find out who has my fingers."

I think about opening the shades; maybe some light wouldn't be so bad. I think about clearing my desk of empty soda cans. I think about canceling the Southie lease, too many people double-parking in front of my office/apartment building. I think about the ever-expanding doomed universe. And all of it makes more sense than what she said.

"Say that again."

Her blue eyes stay fixed on me, like she's the one trying to figure out who is telling the truth. She says, "I woke up like this yesterday.

Someone stole my fingers and replaced them with these." She holds her hand out to me as if I can take it away from her and inspect it.

"May I?" I gently take her hand, and I lift up the bandage on her index finger and find a ring of angry red stitches. She takes her hand back from me quick, like if I hold on to it too long I might decide to keep those replacement digits of hers.

"Look, Ms. Times, circumstantial evidence to the contrary and all that, but I don't think what you described is exactly possible." I point at her hand. I'm telling her that her hand is impossible.

"Granted, my subscription to *Mad Scientist Weekly* did run out. Too many words, not enough pictures."

She says, "It doesn't matter what you think is possible, Mr. Genevich, because I'll only be paying you to find answers to my questions." Her voice is hard as pavement. I get the sense that she isn't used to people telling her no.

I gather the loose papers on my desk, stack them, and then push them over the edge and into the trash can. I want a cigarette but I don't know where I put my pack. "How and why did you find me?" I talk slow. Every letter and syllable has to be in its place.

"Does it matter?" She talks quick and to the point. She wants to tell me more, tell me everything about every thing, but she's holding something back. Or maybe she's just impatient with me, like everyone else.

I say, "I don't do much fieldwork anymore, Ms. Times. Early retirement, so early it happened almost before I got the job. See this computer?" I turn the flat-screen monitor toward her. An infinite network of Escheresque pipes fills the screen-saver pixels. "That's what I do. I research. I do genealogies, find abandoned properties, check the status of out-of-state warrants, and find lost addresses. I search databases and, when desperate, which is all the time, I troll Craigslist and eBay and want ads.

I'm no action hero. I find stuff in the Internet ether. Something tells me your fingers won't be in there."

She says, "I'll pay you ten thousand just for trying." She places a check on my desk. I assume it's a check. It's green and rectangular.

"What, no manila envelope bulging with unmarked bills?"

"I'll pay you another fifty thousand if you find out who has my fingers."

I am about to say something sharp and clever about her allowance from Daddy, but I blink my eyes and she is gone.

TWO

Right after I come to is always the worst, when the questions about dreams and reality seem fair game, when I don't know which is which. Jennifer Times is gone and my head is full of murk. I try to push the murk to the corners of my consciousness, but it squeezes out and leaks away, mercury in a closed fist. That murk, it's always there. It's both a threat and a promise. I am narcoleptic.

How long was I asleep? My office is dark, but it's always dark. I have the sense that a lot of time has passed. Or maybe just a little. I have no way of knowing. I generally don't remember to check and set my watch as I'm passing out. Time can't be measured anyway, only guessed at, and my guesses are usually wrong, which doesn't speak well for a guy in my line of work. But I get by.

I paw around my desk and find a pack of cigarettes behind the phone, right where I left them. I light one. It's warm, white, and lethal. I'd like to say that smoking keeps me awake, clears the head, all that good stuff normally associated with nicotine and carcinogens, but it doesn't. Smoking is just something I do to help pass the time in the dark, between sleeps.

On my desk there is no green and rectangular ten-thousand-dollar check. Too bad, I'd quickly grown fond of the little fella. There is a manila envelope, and on my notepad are gouges and scratches in ink, an EKG output of a faulty heart. My notepad is yellow like the warning traffic light.

I lean back in my chair, looking for a new vantage point, a different way to see. My chair complains. The squawking springs tease me and my sedentary existence. No one likes a wiseass. It might be time for a new chair.

Okay, Jennifer Times. I conclude the stuff about her missing fingers was part of a hypnogogic hallucination, which is one of the many pithy symptoms of narcolepsy. It's a vivid dream that occurs when my narcoleptic brain is partially awake, or partially asleep, as if there is a difference.

I pick up the manila envelope and remove its contents: two black-and-white photos, with accompanying negatives.

Photo 1: Jennifer Times sitting on a bed. Shoulder-length hair obscures most of her face. There's a close-lipped smile that peeks through, and it's wary of the camera and, by proxy, me. She's wearing a white T-shirt and a dark-colored pleated skirt. It's hiked above her knees. Her knees have scabs and bruises. Her arms are long and closed in tight, like a mantis.

Photo 2: Jennifer Times sitting on a bed. She's topless and wearing only white panties. She sits on her folded legs, feet under her buttocks, hands resting on her thighs. Her skin is bleached white, and she is folded. Origami. Arms are at her side and they push her small breasts together. Her eyes are closed and head tilted back. A light fixture shines directly above her head, washing her face in white light. Ligature in her neck is visible, as are more than a few ribs. The smile from the first photo has become something else, a grimace maybe.

The photos are curled, a bit washed and faded. They feel old and heavy with passed time. They're imperfect. These photos are like my memories.

I put the photos side by side on my desktop. On the lip of the Coke-can ashtray my cigarette is all ash, burnt down to the filter. I just lit it, but that's how time works for me. My constant enemy, it attacks whenever I'm not looking.

All right. Focus. It's a simple blackmail case. Some entrepreneur wants Jennifer to invest in his private cause or these photos go public and then she gets the gong, the hook, voted off the island on *American Star.*

But why would a blackmailer send the negatives? The photos have likely been digitized and reside on a hard drive or two somewhere. Still, her—and now me—being in possession of the negatives is troubling. There's more here, and less, of course, since I don't remember any of our conversation besides the finger stuff, so I light another cigarette.

The Jennifer in the photos doesn't look exactly like the Jennifer I've seen on TV or the one who visited my office. The difference is hard to describe, but it's there, like the difference in taste between butter and margarine. I look at the photos again. It could be her; the Jennifer from a few years ago, from high school, the Jennifer from before professional makeup teams and personal stylists. Or maybe the photo Jennifer is margarine instead of butter.

I pick up my notepad. There is writing only on that top page. I was dutifully taking notes while asleep. Automatic behavior. Like tying your shoes. Like driving and listening to the radio instead of actually driving, getting there without getting there. Not that I drive anymore.

During micro-sleeps, my narcoleptic brain will keep my body moving, keep it churning through some familiar task, and I won't have any memory of it. These acts belong to my secret life. I've woken up to find e-mails written and sent, soup cans stacked on my desk, peeled wallpaper in my bedroom, pantry items stuffed inside the refrigerator, magazines and books with their covers torn off.

Here's the top page of my notepad:

Most of it is likely junk, including my doodle arrows. The narcoleptic me is rarely accurate in his automatic behavior. The numbers don't add up to any type of phone number or contact information. But there's south shore plaza, Jennifer's public mall appearance. She and I need to talk. I get the hunch that this blackmail case is about as simple as quantum physics.

THREE

All my mornings disappear eventually. Today, some of it disappeared while I was on the phone. I tried to reach Times via her agency. No luck. I couldn't get past the secretary without disclosing too much information, not that I'm in possession of a bucketful of info, and I've always had a hard time with improv.

I did ferret out that my automatic self was wrong about the South Shore Plaza. There's just no trusting that guy. Times's mall meet-and-greet is at Copley Plaza, downtown Boston, this afternoon.

It's later than I wanted it to be, it's still raining, my black coffee is somehow hazelnut, and the line to see Times is longer than the Charles River. I hate hazelnut. The other coffee I'm carrying is loaded with cream and sugar. It's a cup of candy not fit for consumption, which is fine, because I don't intend to drink it.

Copley is cavernous, brightly lit in golden tones and ceramic tile, and caters to the high-end designer consumer. No Dollar Store here, but it's still just a mall, and its speakers pump out

American Star promo ads and tunes sung by Times. I think I prefer the old-school Muzak.

There are kids everywhere. They wait in line and they lean over the railings on the upper levels. Escalators are full in every direction. There's even a pint-sized pack of punks splashing in the fountain, taking other people's dimes and quarters. Everyone screams and waves and takes pictures. They hold up posters and signs, the *i*'s dotted with hearts, *love* spelled *luv*. Times is getting more mall worship than Santa and the Easter Bunny combined.

Because waiting in lines is detrimental to my tenuous conscious state, I walk toward the front. I growl some words that might sound like *Excuse me*.

I'm not a huge guy, but kids and their reluctant parents move out of my way. They do so because I walk with an obvious purpose, with authority. It's an easy trick. A person carrying two coffees has important places to go. Or, just as likely, people let me by because they're afraid of the hairy guy wearing a fedora and trench coat, the guy who's here without a kid and has a voice deeper than the pit of despair. Hey, whatever works.

I'm only ten or so people from the front of the line, far enough away not to be cutting in plain view of the cops and security guards circling Times and her entourage, but close enough that my wait will be mercifully brief. So I stop and step in front of a father-daughter tandem.

The father wears a Bruins hockey jersey and he's built like a puck, so the shirt works for him. His daughter is a mini-puck in jeans and a pink T plastered with Times's cheery face. This will be the greatest moment of her life until she forgets about it tomorrow.

I hold out the second coffee, my do-not-stop-at-go pass, and say, "Ms. Times wanted me to get her a coffee. Thanks, pal." My voice is a receding glacier.

The hockey puck nods and says, "Go ahead," and pulls his daughter against his hip, away from me. At least somebody is thinking of the children.

No one in our immediate vicinity questions my new existence at the front of the line. There are grumbles of disapproval from farther back, but nothing that needs to be addressed. Those grumblers only complain because they're far enough away from me to be safe, to be anonymous. If they were in the puck's shoes, they wouldn't say boo. Most people are cowards.

I sip my coffee and stain my mustache and smell hazelnut. Goddamn hazelnut. I want to light a cigarette and chew on the smoke, scorch that awful taste out of my mouth, but that's not going to fly here. At least the coffee is still hot.

The line moves with its regimented torpor, like all lines do, and my wait won't be long, but my lights are dimming a bit already, an encroaching numbness to the excitement and bustle around me. Thoughts about what I'm going to say to Times can't seem to find a foothold. I cradle the coffees in the crook of an arm, reach inside a pocket, and pinch my thigh. Then I regroup, shake my head, and take another sip of the 'nut. All keep-me-awake tricks that sometimes work and sometimes don't.

I scan the crowd, trying to find a focus. If I lock eyes with someone, they look away quick. Folks around me are thinking, *If he really got her coffee, why is he waiting in line at all?* It's too late for any kind of revolt, and I'm next. Two bodyguards, each with heads the size of Easter Island statues, flank Times, though they're set back a lunge or two. The background distance is there to encourage a ten-second intimate moment with every fan.

My turn. Maybe she'll John Hancock the brim of my hat, or my hand. I'll never wash it again.

Times sits at a table with stacks of glossy head shots, blue Sharpie in hand, her hair pulled back into a tight ponytail, showing off the crabapple cheekbones. She wears jeans, a long-sleeve Red Sox shirt, and very little makeup. All hints of sexuality have been neutralized; a nonthreatening just-a-sweet-young-American-girl-in-a-mall look.

She's probably not going to be wild about seeing me here. No probably about it. And I'm not exactly sure how I'm going to come out of this impromptu tête-à-tête in a positive light. She is my employer and I'll be admitting, in not so many words, that I was asleep on the job before it even started.

I step up to the plate and extend the candy coffee out to her, a gift from one of the magi, the defective one, the one who's broken. No frankincense or myrrh from this guy.

I say, "Thought you might need a coffee." A good opener for the uncomfortable revelations to come, and it reinforces that I'm willing to work for her.

She opens the curtain on her practiced, polished smile. One thousand watts. It's an egalitarian smile too. Everyone has been getting that flash of teeth and gums. There's not a hint of recognition in her face. Her smile says I'm faceless, like everyone else. She's already a pro at this. I'm the one who's amateur hour.

She says, "I don't drink coffee, but thank you, that's so nice." One of the Easter Island statues moves in and takes the coffee.

Maybe he'll analyze it, afraid of death by hazelnut and cream and sugar. I can't think of a worse way to go.

I try to be quiet and discreet, but my voice doesn't have those settings. Check the manual. "Sorry to do this here, you as conquering local hero and all that stuff, but I dropped by because I need your direct phone line. Your agency treated me like a refugee when I tried to call earlier." It isn't smooth. It's bumpy and full of potholes, but I'll explain if she asks.

"Why were you calling my agency?" She looks over both her shoulders. That twin-generator smile has gone, replaced with a help-me look. The giant heads stir, angry pagan gods, awake and looking to smite somebody's ass. They exchange nonverbal communication cues, signs that the muscle-bound and intellectually challenged understand by instinct: puffed-out chests, clenched jaws, tightened fists.

Is Times serious or putting on a public show, acting like she doesn't know me because she's not supposed to know me? Either way, this isn't good. This is already going worse than I imagined.

My head sweats under the hat. Beard and hazelnut mustache itch. Being stressed out won't exactly help me avoid some of my condition's less pleasant symptoms. But I sally forth.

I say, "I was trying to call you because I had some questions about your case, Ms. Times." I use her name in a formal but familiar way, reassuring and reestablishing my professional status.

"Case?"

"Yeah, the case. Your case."

She doesn't say anything.

22

I lean in to try a conspiratorial whisper, but she slides back in her seat, and it's too loud in here anyway, with all the chattering and screaming. Can't say I practice our culture's celebrity worship, and it's downright inconvenient right now. This place is the monkey house. I lose my cool. "Christ. You know, what was inside that manila envelope you left me certainly wasn't a set of Christmas cards."

All right, I'm not doing well here. Wrong line of questions, no tact. Okay, she clearly doesn't want to talk about it, or talk to me in public. I should've known that.

She says, "I don't understand."

I've been standing here too long. Everyone is staring at us, at me. Nothing is right. We're failing to communicate. It's only a matter of time before someone comes over to break up our verbal clinch.

"Fine. Just sign me a *picture*," I say, and pause, waiting to see if my pointed word has any effect on her. Nothing. She appears to be confused. She appears to be sincere in not knowing who I am. I add, "And I'll leave." It's weak. An after-afterthought.

Her mouth is open and she shrinks into a tightened defensive posture. She looks scared. She looks like the girl in the first photo, the clothed girl. Does she still have those bruises and scabs on her knees?

"My mistake. Sorry to bother you," I say, and reach into my coat for a business card. I'll just leave it on the table and walk away. Yeah, she contacted me first, which means she likely has my number, but I have to do something to save face, to make me feel like something other than a stalker.

I pull out the card between two nicotine-stained fingers and drop it on the table. The statues animate and land their heavy hands on each of my shoulders. There's too much weight and pressure, underlining the banner headline I'm already fucking this up completely. I've angered the pagan gods with my ineptitude. I don't blame them.

I guess I'm leaving now, and without an autograph. As the statues escort me toward one of Copley's many exits, I have enough leisure time to consider the case and what comes next. A cab ride to my office, more phone calls to Jennifer's agency, Internet searches. A multimedia plan B, whatever that is.

FOUR

Chapter 147: Section 24.
Applications; qualifications of applicants

An application for a license to engage in the private detective business or a license to engage in the business of watch, guard, or patrol agency shall be filed with the colonel of the state police on forms furnished by him, and statements of fact therein shall be under oath of the applicant.

George and I dropped out of Curry College together, each with three semesters of criminal justice under our belts. We didn't like where it was going. We spent our last weekend in the dorm skimming the yellow pages, fishing for do-it-yourself career advice. At the end of the weekend, we closed our eyes and made our choices.

I picked private investigation. I figured my mother, Ellen, who would not be pleased about my dropping out, might eventually be receptive given that a PI was somewhat related to my brief collegiate studies. I was right.

Eight years ago I got my license. According to Massachusetts law, having fulfilled the outlined requirements and submitted the fifty-dollar application fee makes me, officially, Mark Genevich, Private Detective.

Such application shall include a certification by each of three reputable citizens of the commonwealth residing in the community in which the applicant resides or has a place of business, or in which the applicant proposes to conduct his business—

Eight years ago I was sitting in the passenger seat of George's van, hurtling back to South Boston from Foxwoods, one of the Connecticut reservation casinos.

George was an upper-middle-class black kid from suburban New Jersey, but he pretended to be from Boston. He wore a Sox hat and talked with a fake accent when we were out at a bar. He played Keno and bought scratch tickets. He told bar patrons that he was from Southie and he was Black Irish. More often than not, people believed him.

George's yellow-pages career was a start-up rug cleaning business. I cleaned rugs for him on the weekends. He had only one machine and its exhaust smelled like wet dog. After getting my private detective's license, I was going to share my Southie office and charge him a ridiculously small rent. I could do that because Ellen owned the building. Still does.

The rug business name was Carpet Warriors. His white van had a pumped-up cartoon version of himself in standard superhero garb: tight red spandex, muscles bulging over other muscles, CW on his chest plate, and a yellow cape. Our buddy Juan-Miguel did the stenciling. George was not really a superhero. He was tall and lanky, his limbs like thin tree branches, always swaying in some breeze. Before getting into his Carpet Warrior van, George would strike a pose in front of his buff superhero doppelgänger and announce, "Never fear, the Carpet Warrior is here," reveling in the innuendo.

George was twenty-two years old. I was twenty-one. At Foxwoods, I played roulette and he played at the tables: blackjack and poker. We lost a shitload of money. In the van, we didn't talk until he said, "We blew ten rugs' worth." We laughed. His laugh was always louder than mine and more infectious. We might've been drunk, we might've been fine.

A tire blew out. I heard it go and felt the sudden drop. The van careened into a drainage ditch and rolled around like a dog trying to pick up a dead squirrel's musk. Everything was dark. I don't remember seeing anything. The seat belt wasn't tight against my chest because I wasn't wearing one. My face broke the passenger's side window and was messed up worse than a Picasso, everything exaggerated and in the wrong spots. Nose and septum pulverized, my flesh as remolded clay that didn't set where it was supposed to.

I broke the window but my body stayed in the van. George's didn't. He went out the windshield, ahead of the van, but he didn't fly far. Like I said, he wasn't a superhero. The van fishtailed sideways, then rolled right over him. George died. I miss him.

—that he has personally known the applicant for at least three years, that he has read the application and believes each of the statements made therein to be true, that he is not related to the applicant by blood or marriage—

After the accident and the surgeries, I grew a beard to hide my damaged face. My left eye is now a little lower than my right, and smaller. I'm always winking at you, but you don't know why. Too bad the beard never covers my eyes. The fedora—I wear it low—comes close.

Post-recovery, I lived with Juan-Miguel and another college buddy in the Southie apartment above my office. My narcolepsy symptoms started as soon as I got back from the hospital, a creeping crawling terror from a bad horror flick. I was Michael Landon turning into the teenage werewolf. I was always tired and had no energy, and I fell asleep while working on the computer or watching TV or eating breakfast or on the phone with potential clients. So I rarely answered the phone and tried to communicate solely by e-mail. I stopped going out unless it was to drink, which made everything worse. I know, hard to believe alcohol didn't make it all better.

Juan-Miguel came home one night to find me half inside the tub, pants down around my ankles, hairy ass in the air. I'd fallen asleep on the toilet and pitched into the tub. I told him I was passed out drunk. Might've been true.

When I was supposed to be sleeping, I didn't sleep well. I had paralyzing nightmares and waking dreams, or I wandered the apartment like the Phantom of the Opera, man turned monster. I emptied the fridge and lit cigarettes I didn't smoke. They left their marks.

Worst of all, I somnambulated into the TV room, freed myself from pants and underwear, lifted up a couch cushion, and let the urine flow. Apparently I wasn't even considerate enough to put the seat down after. I pissed on our couch every other week. I was worse than a goddamn cat.

—and that the applicant is honest and of good moral character.

I denied it all, of course. I wasn't asleep on the couch. If I was, it was because I drank too much. I wasn't doing any of those horrible, crazy things. It wasn't possible. That wasn't me even if my roommates saw me. They were lying to me. They were pulling cruel practical jokes that weren't at all practical. They were leaving lit cigarettes on the kitchen table and on my bedspread. One of them had a cat and they weren't admitting it. The cat was pissing on the couch, not me. I wasn't some animal that wasn't house trained, for chrissakes.

The kicker was that I believed my own denials. The truth was too embarrassing and devastating. I argued with my roommates all the time. Argument became part of my character. Nothing they said was true or right, even the mundane proclamations that had nothing to do with me or my narcoleptic actions. The only way I could consistently deny my new symptoms and odd behavior was to deny everything. I became even more of a recluse, holed up in my room until the asleep me would unleash himself, a midnight, couch-pissin' Kraken. My roommates moved out within the year.

Narcolepsy is not a behavioral disorder. It's neurological. It's physical. Routine helps, but it's no cure. Nothing is. There's no pattern to the symptoms. I tried prescription drugs, but the chemical stimulants resulted in paranoia and wild mood swings. My heart raced like a hummingbird's, and the insomnia worsened. So I stopped. Other than the coffee I'm not supposed to drink and the cigarettes I'm not supposed to smoke, I'm au naturel.

Eight years ago I got my private detective's license and narcolepsy. I now live alone with both.

That said, I'm waking up, and there's someone in my apartment, and that someone is yelling at me.

FIVE

Sleep is heavy. It has mass. Sometimes it has supreme mass. Sleep as a singularity. There's no moving or denying or escaping. Sometimes sleep is light too. I've been able to walk under its weight. It can be light enough to dream through, but more often than not it's the heavy kind. It's the ocean and you're pinned to the bottom of the seafloor.

". . . on fire? Jesus Christ! Wake the hell up, Mark!"

The impossible weight lifts away. I resurface too fast and get the bends. Muscles twitch and my heart pushes past my throat and into my head where it doesn't belong, making everything hurt.

It's Ellen, my mother. She stands in the doorway of the living room, wearing frilly blue oversized clown pants and a T that reads LITHUANIA. The shirt is an old favorite of hers, something she wears too often. The clown pants I've never seen before. I hope this means I'm having another hypnogogic hallucination.

I'm sitting on the couch. My mouth is still open because I was asleep with it that way. I blink and mash the back of my hand into my eyes, pushing and squeezing the sleep out. I have my cell phone in my right hand. On my left side is smoke and heat.

The couch is smoking, cigarette and everything. It's a nasty habit the couch can't seem to break. The couch doesn't heed surgeon generals' warnings. Maybe it should try the patch.

I lift my left leg and twist away from the smoke, but the cigarette butt rolls after me, leaving a trail of red ash. In the cushion there's a dime-sized hole, the circumference red and still burning. I'd say it's just one blemish, but the reality is my couch has acne.

I pick up the butt. It's too hot and I drop it on the floor. I pat the couch cushion. Red ashes go black and there's more smoke.

I say, "I wasn't sleeping. I wasn't smoking." Ellen knows what I mean when I'm lying: I don't want to talk about it, and even if I did want to talk about it nothing would change.

She shakes her head and says, "You're gonna burn yourself up one of these days, Mark. I don't know why I bother." Her admonishment is by rote, perfunctory. We can get on with our day, now that it's out of the way.

I make my greeting a subtle dig at her for no good reason other than I'm embarrassed. "Good to see you too, Ellen. Shut the door on the way out." At least this time she didn't find me asleep with my pants around my ankles and an Edward Penishands porno on the TV.

Ellen stays at my apartment a couple of nights a week. If pressed, she maintains she stays here because she wants to play Keno and eat at the Italian American and L Street Diner with her sister and friends. She won't admit to being my de facto caregiver. She's the underwriter of my less-than-successful private detecting business and the landlord who doesn't want her property, the brownstone she inherited from her parents, to burn to the ground. I can't blame her.

Ellen is Southie born and bred and, like every other lifelong resident, she knows everything about everybody. Gentrification has toned down the small-town we-are-Southie vibe a bit, but it's still here. She starts right in on some local dirt, mid-story, assuming I know what she's talking about when I don't.

"Davy T said he knew she was lying the whole time. He told me weeks ago. He could just tell she was lying. Do you know when someone's lying, Mark? They say you watch the eyes. Up and left means recall, down and right means they're making stuff up. Or it's the other way around. I don't know. You should take a class in that. You could find a class online, I bet."

Davy T is the centuries-old Greek who owns the pizza joint next door. That's the only part of her monologue that registers with me. I check my cell phone, no messages. It has been a full day since Jennifer's mall appearance.

Ellen says, "Anyway, Davy T knew. It'll be all over the news tonight. They found her out. She was making it all up: the cancer, her foundation, everything. What kind of person does that?" Ellen crosses the room as she talks, her clown pants merrily swishing away. She opens my windows and waves her hands. The smoke obeys and swirls in the fresh air. Magic. Must be the pants. "Maybe you should've been on that case, Mark. You could've solved that, don't you think? You could've saved folks a lot of money and aggravation."

To avoid discussing my condition or me burning up with the apartment, Ellen defaults into details of already solved cases that presumably I could've tackled; as if I've ever worked on a case that involved anything more than tapping keys in front of my computer or being a ghost at a library or a town hall registrar.

Still patting the couch like I can replace the burned and missing upholstery with my Midas touch, I say, "Sure thing, Ellen." Truth is, my confidence and self-esteem are fighting it out in the subbasement, seeing which can be lower.

Jennifer hasn't returned any of my calls to the agency. I fell asleep up here, waiting for a callback. Waiting for something to get me going, because I have nothing. I don't know how she was contacted by the blackmailer, if the pictures were mailed or left on a doorstop, if there had been earlier contact or contact since. It's kind of hard to start a case without a client, or at least a client that will talk to you.

I say, "So what's with the Bozo the Clown getup?"

Ellen walks into the kitchen. "I was shooting some kid's portrait today and the little bastard wouldn't stop crying until I put the pants on." When Ellen isn't her force-of-nature self in my apartment, she lives in the old family bungalow in Osterville, a small tourist haven on the Cape. In downtown Osterville she has a photography studio and antiques shop. She shoots kids, weddings, graduation pictures. Nothing fancy. She's been doing it since my father died.

"Wouldn't a red nose and a horn get the job done? Maybe one of those flowers that shoots out water. You need to rely on cliché a little more."

"What, you're an expert now? I got the shots." She plays with her clown pants, pulling them up at the knee, making mini circus tents. "I need to change." Ellen abruptly disappears into my bedroom and shuts the door.

I pick up the cigarette butt off the floor and try to tidy things up a bit, putting dirty glasses and dishes in the sink, stacking magazines, moving dust around. I eyeball the couch to make sure it's not still burning.

I check my cell phone again, even though I've already checked for messages. Why wouldn't she call me back? If this is supposed to be some super-special double-secret case, it's not going to work out. The sleeping me should've told her thanks-but-no-thanks when she dumped those pictures on me. The sleeping me is just so irresponsible on my behalf.

Earlier, I did a cursory Web search, reading blogs and message boards, finding no hint or threat of the existence of the photos, or a stalker, or a potential blackmailer. Everything from her camp seems as controlled and wholesome as can be. No one has even posted fake nudes of Jennifer yet, which is usually an instantaneous Internet occurrence once there's a new female celebrity. I don't get the lack of buzz. The irony is that if I posted the pictures, I'd likely be helping her career, but I'm not her agent.

Ellen emerges from the bedroom. Her shoulder-length gray hair is tied up and she has on her black-framed glasses, thick lenses that enlarge her eyes. She's still wearing the clown pants but has on a gray sweatshirt over LITHUANIA.

I say, "Are you going to take my picture later? Maybe tie me up some balloon animals? I want a giraffe, a blue one."

She says, "Everyone at the Lithuanian Club will get a kick out of the pants. And they are comfortable. Nice and roomy." She walks by and punches my shoulder. "So, should we do something for dinner?" Ellen never makes dinner a declarative statement. She's earnest in the illusion of a choice being offered. It's not that I can't say no. I never have a reason to do so.

I say, "Something sounds delicious, Ellen." I have a gut feeling the case is slipping away, and if I let it get away I'll be screwing up something important. This is my shot, my chance to be something more than Ellen's charity-case son who works on glorified have-you-seen-my-lost-puppy cases and sleeps his days away in front of his computer.

So let's skip from plan B down to plan X. I know that Jennifer's father, the DA, grew up in Southie and is around the same age as Ellen. Maybe, a long-shot maybe, she knows something about Jennifer, the first bread crumb in the trail.

I say, "Hey, do you still watch *American Star*?" Plan X: asking Ellen delicate no-I'm-not-working-on-anything-really questions to defibrillate my dying case. I don't have a plan Y or Z.

Ellen looks at me funny, like I stepped in something and she's not sure if she should admit she smells it. She says, "You're kidding, right? I don't miss a show. Never have missed a show in five seasons."

I know that, of course. She's obsessed with *American Star*. She watched the first two seasons from Osterville and still had me tape all the episodes here.

She says, "Why do you ask? Are you telling me that you're finally watching it too?"

I shrug. Shoulders don't lie. My fedora doesn't hide enough of my hairy face. It's the proverbial only-a-mother-could-love face because the mug was reshuffled partway through the game. Ellen hasn't once suggested that I shave. That means what it means.

I say, "The show is kind of hard to avoid now. I had it on the other night, but I fell asleep." Ellen is waiting for more, so I add, "Been hearing stuff about the local girl. She's the DA's kid right?"

Ellen smiles. "I might be crazy, but it sounds like you're pumping me for information. If you got something to ask, just come out and ask it. I'll help. You know I want to help."

I can't. I can't let her know that I'm working on a case that potentially involves extensive fieldwork. Leaving the apartment and going out by myself. There will be no dealing with any of that conversation. She wants to be supportive only as long as I'm safe in the apartment.

I say, "Nothing like that. Just having a conversation, Ellen. For someone who wears clown pants, you're tightly wound."

Ellen goes into the kitchen and roots around in the freezer. She says, "Yes, she's his daughter. She's—what, about ten years younger than you?"

Might as well be fifty years younger. "Yeah, I guess so."

Ellen says, "There's nothing good in there," and closes the freezer. "I didn't have time to pick up anything. We'll have to go out. At least I'm dressed for it, right?"

I stand in the kitchen doorway, holding up the frame. "Isn't DA Times from Southie originally?" A softball question, one I know she can't resist.

"Hell yeah, he's from Southie. He still owns a brownstone at the end of East Broadway. He doesn't stay there anymore though. He rents it out."

"Do you know him at all?"

"I know him well. Or knew him well, anyway. Billy Times and your father were close, used to pal around as kids. They lived in the same building in Harbor Point."

She hits the softball out of the park. Her answer isn't what I was expecting. Not at all. I talk even slower than normal, making sure I don't mess anything up, stacking the words on the kitchen table like bricks, making a wall; maybe it'll protect me. "Really? You never told me that before."

Ellen says, "Come on. I've told you that before."

"No. You haven't." I'm not offering subterfuge here. I'm more likely to find Spanish doubloons in a handful of loose change than get nuggets of info concerning my father, Tim, from Ellen. She's miserly with it, hoards it all for herself. I stopped asking questions a long time ago.

"That can't be right." Ellen is trying for a light, jovial, fluffy-banter tone, but it's faltering. "You just forgot." She adds that last bit as an afterthought, each word decreasing in volume. The sentence runs out of gas, sputters, and shuts off. The sentence goes to sleep. Everything goes to sleep if you wait long enough.

Now, what she said is not fair. Yeah, I forget stuff all the time, but she can't pass off years of silence and daddy awkwardness on the narcoleptic me like that. I'd call her on the cheap shot, but that's another argument I don't want right now. Need that primed pump to keep spilling. I say, "Cute. So Tim and the DA were BFFs and wore each other's varsity jackets?"

"Yes, actually, they were best friends but no jackets." Ellen laughs, but I'm not quite sure why. Nothing is that funny. "Those two used to be inseparable, always causing trouble. Nothing big, you know, typical Southie boys who thought they were tougher than they were."

She waves her hand, like she's clearing the air of more smoke. Further details won't be forthcoming unless I keep pecking away at her.

Okay. This goes a long way toward explaining how Jennifer Times landed in my office with her slide show. Her daddy can't take the case because people talk, word gets out, media sniffing around the DA, especially with his flavor-of-the-minute daughter smiling and primping all over the airwaves. So Daddy DA has Jennifer take her blackmail case, which is as sticky and messy as an ice cream cone on a summer Sunday, to an unknown lower-than-low profile investigator in South Boston, family friend and all that, a schlub willing to do all kinds of favors and keep things quiet with a capital Q, all in the name of his own dear old dad. This makes sense, but the only problem is I don't know any of this. I'm guessing. Maybe I was told a few days ago while the doctor wasn't in. Or maybe I wasn't told anything. Maybe . . .

"Hey, Mark!"

"What?" My body catches itself in mid-slide against the wall. Heavy feet move to get my weight back over them. They're neither graceful nor quiet. They kick a kitchen chair and clap against the hardwood floor. Don't know what my feet have against the floor, but they're always trying to get away.

Ellen is now sitting at the kitchen table, smoking one of my cigarettes. She says, "You were getting ready to go out, Mark." She won't say *sleep*. Not around me.

As difficult as it is to cobble together some dignity after almost falling asleep mid-conversation, I try to patch it up.

I've had a lot of practice. I say, "Would the DA recognize the Genevich name, you think?"

"Of course. There's no way he'd forget your father." Ellen leans forward fast, stubs out her cigarette like she's killing a pesky ant. She's adding everything together and doesn't like the sum. She's going to tell me about it too. "Why do you care? What's going on here, Mark? There's something you're not telling me. You better not be messing around with stuff that requires involvement with the DA. Leave that shit to the people who carry guns."

"Relax. There's nothing going on. It's just this all might be useful information. I'm supposed to ask questions for a living, right? Besides, a guy in my line of work having a potential family friend in the big office could help my cause."

Ellen stands up. Chair falls down. She's not buying any of it. "What cause?"

I like that she's so riled up, on edge. She doesn't know for sure I'm working on a case, but even she can sense something big is going on. It's real. It's legit. And thanks to her, I finally have my bread-crumb trail, or at least one crumb. I sit down at the table, take off my hat, run my fingers through my thinning hair.

"I was speaking figuratively, Ellen. My general cause. Or some-day, when I have a cause." I wink, which is a mistake. My face doesn't have a wink setting anymore.

"You're being awful strange tonight." She says it to the table. I'm supposed to hear her but not give anything back. Fair enough.

Worry lines march all around Ellen's face, and not in formation. She taps the all-but-empty pack of cigarettes with her wedding ring. Tim Genevich is twenty-five years dead, and Ellen still wears the ring. Does she wear it out of habit, superstition, or true indefinable loss, so the loss is right there in plain sight, her life's pain waving around for anyone to see? The ring as her dead husband, as Tim. My father on her hand.

I lean over and snatch the last cigarette out of the pack. Ellen stops tapping with Tim. I light up and inhale as much smoke as I can, then I take in a little more. Exhale, and then I do some reiterating, just to be clear in our communication.

I say, "Don't worry, Clowny. I have no cause. The DA and I are just gonna get acquainted."

SIX

Tim was a landscaper, caretaker, winterizer of summer cottages, and a handyman, and he died on the job. He was in the basement of someone else's summer home, fighting through cobwebs and checking fuses and the sump pump, when he had an explosion in his brain, an aneurysm. I guess us Genevich boys don't have a lot of luck in the brain department.

Three days passed and no one found him. He didn't keep an appointment book or anything like that, and he left his car at our house and rode his bike to work that morning, so Ellen had no idea where he was. He was an official missing person. Got his name in the paper, and for a few days everyone knew who Tim Genevich was.

The owners of the cottage found him when they came down to the Cape for Memorial Day weekend. The basement bulkhead was open. Tim was lying facedown on the dirt floor. He had a fuse in his hand. I was five years old, and while I'm told I was at the funeral and wake, I don't remember any of it.

I don't remember much of Tim. Memories of him have faded to the edges, where recollection and wish fulfillment blur, or they have been replaced, co-opted by images from pictures. I hate pictures.

Too much time has passed since my own brain-related accident, too many sleeps between. Every time I sleep—doesn't matter how long I'm out—puts more unconscious space between myself and the events I experienced, because every time I wake up it's a new day. Those fraudulent extra days, weeks, years add up. So while my everyday time shrinks, it also gets longer. I'm Billy Pilgrim and Rip Van Winkle at the same time, and Tim died one hundred years ago.

That said, I do have a recurring dream of my father. He's in our backyard in Osterville. He puts tools back in the shed, then emerges with a hand trowel. Tim was shorter than Ellen, a little bent, and he loved flannel. At least, that's what he looks like in my dreams.

Tim won't let me go in the shed. I'm too young. There are too many tools, too many ways to hurt myself. I need to be protected. He gives me a brown paper bag, grocery-sized, and a pat on the head. He encourages me to sing songs while we walk around the yard picking up dog shit. We don't have a dog, but all the neighborhood dogs congregate here. Tim guesses a dog's name every time he picks up some shit. The biggest poops apparently come from a dog named Cleo.

The song I always sing, in my dreams and my memories, is "Take Me Out to the Ball Game." Tim then sings it back to me with different lyrics, mixing in his dog names and poop and words that rhyme with poop. He doesn't say *shit* around the five-year-old me, at least not on purpose. The dream me, the memory me—that kid is the same even if he never really existed, and *that* kid laughs at the silly improvised song but then sings "Ball Game" correctly, restoring balance and harmony to the universe.

Our two-bedroom bungalow is on a hill and the front yard has a noticeable slant, so we have to stand lopsided to keep from falling. We clean the yard, then we walk behind the shed to the cyclone-fenced area of weeds, tall grass, and pricker bushes that gives way to a grove of trees between our property and the next summer home about half a block away. Tim takes the paper bag from me, it's heavy with shit, and he dumps it out, same spot every time. He says "Bombs away" or "Natural fertilizer" or something else that's supposed to make a five-year-old boy laugh.

Then we walk to the shed. Tim opens the doors. Inside are the shiny and sharp tools and machines, teeth everywhere, and I want to touch it all, want to feel the bite. He hangs up the trowel and folds the paper bag. We'll reuse both again, next weekend and in the next dream. Tim stands in the doorway and says, "So, kid, whaddaya think?"

Sometimes I ask for a lemonade or ice cream or soda. Sometimes, if I'm aware I'm in the dream again, I ask him questions. He always answers, and I remember the brief conversation after waking up, but that memory lasts only for a little while, an ice cube melting in a drink. Then it's utterly forgotten, crushed under the weight of all those little sleeps to come.

SEVEN

William "Billy" Times has been the Suffolk County DA for ten years. He's a wildly popular and visible favorite son. All the local news shows are doing spots featuring Billy and his *American Star* daughter. He hosts now-legendary bimonthly Sunday brunch fund-raisers—the proceeds going to homeless shelters—at a restaurant called Amrheins in South Boston. All the local celebs and politicians show their faces at least once a year at the brunches.

Although I am Tim Genevich's kid, I haven't been on the brunch guest list yet. That said, Tim's name did manage to get me a one-on-one audience with DA Times at his office today. What a pal, that Tim.

I fell asleep in the cab. It cost me an extra twenty bucks in drive-around time. I stayed awake long enough to be eventually dumped at 1 Bulfinch Place. Nice government digs for the DA. Location, location, location. It's between the ugly concrete slabs of Government Center and Haymarket T stop, but a short walk from cobble-stones, Faneuil Hall Marketplace, and the two-story granite columns and copper dome of Quincy Market, where you can eat at one of its seventeen overpriced restaurants. It's all very colonial.

Despite naptime, I'm here early when I can't ever be early. Early means being trapped in a waiting room, sitting in plush chairs or couches, anesthetizing Muzak tones washing over me, fluffing my pillow. An embarrassingly large selection of inane and soulless entertainment magazines, magazines filled with fraudulent and beautiful people, is the only proffered stimulus. That environment is enough to put a non-narcoleptic in a coma, so I don't stand a chance. I won't be early.

I stalk around the sidewalk and the pigeons hate me. I don't take it personally, thick skin and all that. I dump some more nicotine and caffeine into my bloodstream. The hope is that filling up with leaded will keep all my pistons firing while in the DA's office. Hope is a desperate man's currency.

I call the DA's secretary and tell her I'm outside the building, enjoying a rare March sunlight appearance, and I ask when the DA will be ready for me. Polite as pudding, she says he's ready for me now. Well, all right. A small victory. A coping adjustment actually working is enough to buoy my spirits. I am doing this. This is going to work, and I will solve this case.

But . . .

There's a swarm of *ifs,* peskier than a cloud of gnats. The ifs: If, as I'm assuming, the DA sent me his daughter and her case, why wouldn't he contact me directly? Again, am I dealing with the ultimate closed-lips case that can't have any of his involvement? If that's right, and I'm supposed to be Mr. Hush Hush, Mr. Not Seen and Not Heard, why am I so easily granted counsel with the public counsel? He certainly seemed eager to meet with me when I called, booking a next-day face-to-face appointment.

There are more ifs, and they're stressing my system. Stress, like time, is a mortal enemy. Stress can be one of my triggers, the grease in the wheel of my more disruptive narcoleptic symptoms. I could use another cigarette or three to choke myself awake, freshen up in the smoke.

I step out of the elevator and walk toward the DA's office. Bright hallways filled with suits of two types: bureaucrats and people carrying guns. The bullets and briefcases in the hallway make me a little edgy.

The DA's waiting area is stark and bright. Modern. Antiseptic. Very we-get-shit-done in its décor. Wooden chairs and glass-topped tables framed in silver metal, and all the window shades are up. No shadows here.

There are two men waiting in the room and they are linebacker big. They wear dark suits and talk on cell phones, the kind that sit inside the cup of your ear. The receiver is literally surrounded by the wearer's flesh; it's almost penetrative. The phones look like blood-swollen robot ticks.

The men are actively not looking at me. Sure, I'm paranoid, but when I enter a room people always look at me. They map out my lopsided features and bushy beard and anachronistic attire. Everyone is my cartographer. I'm not making this up. Even when I display narcoleptic symptoms in public and the cartographers are now truly frightened of me and try not to look, they still look. Furtive glances, stealing and storing final images, completing the map, fodder for their brush-with-unwashed-humanity dinner-party anecdotes. I'm always the punch line.

Instead of the direct path to the secretary's desk, I take the long cut, eyeing the framed citations on the walls, walking past the windows pretending to crane my neck for a better view of Haymarket. Those two guys won't look at me, which means they're here to watch me. I'm already sick of irony.

The secretary says, "Mr. Genevich?"

I've been identified. Tagged.

The two men still don't look up. One guy is shaved bald, though the stubble is thick enough to chew up a razor. The other guy has red hair, cut tight up against his moon-sized brain box. Freckles and craters all over his face. They talk into their phones and listen at alternating intervals like they're speaking to each other, kids with their twenty-first-century can-and-string act.

I say, "That's me." This doesn't bode well for my meeting with the DA. Why does he need Thunder and Thumper to get their eyeful of me?

The secretary says, "The DA is ready for you now." She stays seated behind her desk. She's Ellen's age and wears eye shadow the color of pool-cue chalk. I wonder if she wears clown pants too.

I say, "I guess that's what we'll find out." It feels like the thing to say, but the line lands like a dropped carton of eggs.

His secretary points me past her desk, and I head into an office with an open door. I walk in too fast.

DA William Times sits behind a buffet-style oak desk. The thing spans the width of the room. A twin-engine Cessna could land on top of it. He says, "Mark Genevich. Come on in. Wow, I can't believe it. Tim's kid all grown up. Pleasure to finally meet you." The DA walks out from behind his desk, hand thrust out like a bayonet.

I'm not quite sure of protocol here. How he's supposed to be greeted. What sort of verbal genuflection I'm supposed to give him. I try on, "Thanks for giving me the time, Mr. DA."

DA Times is as big as the two goons in the waiting room. I'm thinking he might've banged out a few hundred push-ups before I came in, just to complete his muscle-beach look. He has on gray slacks and a tight blue dress shirt; both have never seen a wrinkle. His hair is pepper-gray, cut tight and neat. White straight teeth. His whole look screams public opinion and pollsters and handlers. We have so much in common.

We cross the divide of his office and finally shake hands. His grip is a carnival strength test and he rings the bell. He says, "Please, call me Billy, and have a seat."

"Thanks." I don't take off my hat or coat, but I do pull out the manila envelope. I sit. The chair is a soft leather bog, and I sink to a full eye level below the DA and his island-nation desk. I wait as he positions himself. He might need a compass.

He says, "So, how's Ellen doing?"

He's not going to ask about my face, about what happened to me. He's polite and well mannered and makes me feel even more broken. We can play at the small talk, though. That's fine. Maybe it'll help me get a good foothold before we climb into the uncomfortable stuff. Daddy and his daughter.

I say, "Ellen's fine. She has a good time."

"Do you guys live in Southie again? She still owns that building on the corner of Dorchester and Broadway, right?"

I say, "Yeah, she owns it. I live there, but Ellen part-times Southie now."

"God, I haven't talked to her in years. I have to have you guys down at the next Sunday brunch. I'd love to chat with her."

I'm not quite sure what to say. I come up with, "That'd be just fine, Billy," real slow, and it sounds as awkward as I feel. I'm flummoxed. I was expecting anger on the DA's part, that he'd go all Hulk, you-wouldn't-like-me-when-I'm-angry, yell-scream-bite-scratch and bring in the goons because I wasn't doing my job, wasn't keeping things quiet by showing up at Jennifer's public appearance and now at his office.

He says, "So what can I help you with, Mark?"

Our meeting is young, the conversation still in we're-all-friends-here mode, but I already know he did not contact me. He did not suggest his daughter contact me. He has no idea why I'm here.

Need to play this straight, no funny stuff, no winks and nods. My winks tend to turn into fully shut eyes. "Not sure if you're aware, Billy, but I'm a private investigator."

The DA is still smiling. "Oh, yeah? How long have you been doing that?"

"Eight years, give or take." I pause because I don't know what to say next.

He jumps right in. "No kidding. I probably have a copy of your license somewhere in this building." He laughs. Is that a threat? A harmless attempt at humor? Humor is never harmless.

Maybe this was a mistake. Maybe I'm not ready for this and should've stayed in my apartment behind my desk and forgotten about everything. I'm getting a bad feeling. Not the gut this time. It's more tangible, physical. There's a small hum, a vibration building up, my hands tremble on the envelope a little bit. My system needle is twitching into the red. Danger Will Robinson. It's the same feeling I get before cataplectic attacks.

Cataplexy, like other narcolepsy symptoms, is REM sleep bullying its way into the awake state. Cataplexy is complete and total loss of bodily control. Muscles stop working, I can't even talk, and I melt to the floor, down for the count but not out.

I'm not asleep. I'm conscious but can't move and can't speak, paralyzed. Cataplexy is the worst part of my nightmare.

I don't have cataplexy often; the most recent event was that time after Ellen found me asleep in front of a porno. She walked into the apartment and I woke up with my pants around my ankles. She wasn't upset or hiding her face or anything like that, she was laughing. She could've walked in and found me playing with the world's cutest kitten and had the same response, which made it worse, made it seem like she was expecting to find me like that. I was so overwhelmingly embarrassed and ashamed, the emotions were a Category-5 hurricane on my system, and cataplexy hit while I was quickly trying to pull up my pants and put everything away. My strings cut and I dropped to the floor, heavier than a dead body, landing on my cheap came-in-a-box coffee table and smashing it, all my stuff still out and about. Ellen shut off the television without commenting upon a scene involving Edward Penishands and three of his most acrobatic female neighbors. She pulled up my underwear and pants, buttoned my fly, and prepared dinner in the kitchen while I recovered from the attack. Took about twenty minutes to come back completely, to be able to walk into the kitchen under my own power. We ate stir-fry. A little salty but decent, otherwise.

Too much time has passed since the DA last spoke, because his vote-for-me smile is gone and he's leaning on his desk. He says, "Did you bring me something? What's in the envelope, Mark?"

Okay, another new strategy, and yeah, I'm making all this up as I go. If this is going to work, I can't let myself think too much.

I'm going to read lines, play a part, and maybe it will keep the emotions from sabotage, keep those symptoms on the bench no matter how much the narcoleptic me wants in the game.

I say, "Your daughter, Jennifer, came into my office the other morning and hired me to solve a little problem." My hands sweat on the envelope, leaving wet marks.

The DA straightens and looks around the room briefly. He repeats my line back to me. "Jennifer came into your office with a problem." The line sounds good.

"Yup. Left me this package too. She didn't tell you anything about this?"

The DA holds up his hands. "You have me at a loss, Mark, because this is all news to me."

In concert with our everything-is-happy intro conversation, I think he's telling the truth, which complicates matters. Why would Jennifer not tell her DA daddy about the pictures and then come see me, of all PIs? Was it dumb blind luck that landed her in my office? I don't buy it. She and this case were dropped in my sleeping lap for a reason.

I say, "I came here because I had assumed you sent her to see me. To have me, a relation of an old family friend, deal with the situation away from prying public eyes."

"Jesus, Mark, just tell me what you're talking about. Is Jennifer in danger? What's going on?"

If he really hasn't sent Jennifer to me, then I've screwed up, big time. It's going to be very difficult to skip-to-my-Lou out of here without showing him the pictures, and I can't say too much, don't want to put any words into Jennifer's mouth. I don't want the case to be taken away from me.

I say, "I've made a mistake. If you didn't send Jennifer to me, I shouldn't be here. Client confidentiality and all that." I stand up. My legs are water-starved tree roots.

The DA stands and darts around his desk to stop me. He moves fast, and I'm no Artful Dodger. He says, "Wait! You can't come in here and drop a bomb about Jennifer and then just leave."

"Tell it to the goons you have waiting for me outside." I say it, even though I know it doesn't add up. One plus one is three.

"What?" He shakes his head, resetting. "Let's start again. Jennifer. What's wrong? You have to tell me if she's in any danger. You know, I can probably help here." He opens his arms, displaying his office, showing off his grand criminal justice empire.

My system-overload feeling is still there. My hands keep up with their tremors, twitching to some hidden beat, and my mouth is dry. This can't happen now. Not now, can't be now.

I say, "Let's sit again, and you can take a look." I have to sit. At least if I have an attack I'll be sitting.

We sit. The chair is a hug and my body reacts accordingly; the tremors cease but crushing fatigue rolls in like a tide. It's undeniable. New plan. I don't care that I'm breaking client confidentiality. Given the clientele, I doubt word of my etiquette breach will get out and ruin my little business, taint my street cred. I want to see the DA's reaction. I want to know why she'd drop these photos on my desk and not on Daddy's.

I yawn big, showing off the fillings, sucking in all the air. The DA looks at me like I pissed in the dinner wine. I shrug and say, "Sorry, it's not you, it's me."

I open the envelope and hand him the two photos. Definitely taking a chance on bringing him the originals. I didn't think to make copies; the negatives are in my desk. Anyway, I want to see what his reaction is to the real photos, not copies.

The DA takes the pictures, looks at them, and sinks into his chair. The pictures are a punch to his stonewall stomach. He loses all his air. I feel a little bad for him. Gotta be tough to have someone else's past walk in the door and drop nudie pictures of your kid in your lap.

He holds up both photos side by side and is careful to hold them so that they cover his face. He sees something.

The DA says, "Who gave you these pictures?"

"I told you. Jennifer. Try to stay with me, here."

"Who sent them to her?"

"I don't know yet. That's the case. I'm good, but I do need a little time to work my mojo." I meant to say magic, but it came out mojo.

He says, "Who else has seen these?"

"No idea." This is a rare occasion where telling the truth is easy as Sunday morning.

"Have you shown them to anyone?"

"No, of course not. What kind of private investigator do you think I am?"

He looks at the photos again, then me. The look is a fist cracking knuckles. He says, "I have no idea what's going on here, Mark, but the woman in these pictures is clearly not Jennifer."

Not the response I was looking for. I squirm in my seat, which is suddenly hot. I'm bacon and someone turned on the griddle. I fight off another yawn and push it down somewhere inside me, but it's still there and will find its way out eventually. I have bigger problems than a yawn. I ask, "What makes you say that?"

"It's not her, Mark." All hint of politics gone from his voice. He's accusing me of something. He's in attack mode, getting ready to lawyer me up. This isn't good.

I say, "It's her. Jennifer was the one who brought me the goddamn photos. Why would she need me if the photos aren't of her?" I'm getting mad, which is not the right response here. Shouldn't be ready to throw a tantrum because someone wants to tell me there's no Tooth Fairy.

The DA focuses. I'm his courtroom. He says, "There are physical inconsistencies. Jennifer has a mole on her collarbone, no mole here—"

I interrupt. "That's easy to Photoshop. You should know that."

He holds up a stop hand. "Her hair is all wrong. In the photo there's too much curl to it, and it doesn't look like a wig. That's not Jennifer's smile; the teeth are too big. This woman is smaller and skinnier than Jennifer. There's a resemblance, but it's clearly not Jennifer, Mark. I'm positive."

All right. What next? I say, "Can I have the photos back?" Christ, I'm asking permission. I'm a pathetic Oliver Twist, begging for table scraps.

The DA doesn't give them to me right away, and my insides drop into my shoes. I'm not getting the photos back—or my insides. I couldn't possibly have fucked things up any worse if I had a manual and followed the step-by-step instructions on how to screw the pooch.

He does hand the pictures over. I take an eyeful. The hair, her smile, all of it, all wrong. He's right. It's not her. My big mistake is getting bigger. I scratch my beard, then put the photos away. I need an exit strategy.

The DA stands again, walks to his window, then turns toward me, eyebrows arched. Maybe he's really seeing me, the broken man, for the first time. He says, "What are you up to, Mark?"

"I told you what was up, DA. Nothing funny on my end. Can't vouch for your daughter, though."

His hands go from inside his pockets to folded across his chest. He's a statue made of granite. I'm an abandoned rag doll.

"Maybe we should just call Jennifer, then, to straighten everything out," he says, pulling out his cell phone and poking at a few buttons before getting my permission.

"Let's. A fine idea." I yawn, my head getting murky, its natural state. I'm afraid of this phone call. I'll only get to hear his end of the conversation.

He says, "Hi, sweetie. It's Dad. . . . I know, but I need a quick honest answer to a potentially difficult question. . . . I know, great way to start a phone call. . . . So, did you hire a Mark Genevich? . . . Mark Genevich, he's a private detective. . . . He's here in my office, and he claims you went to his Southie office and hired him—says you gave him some photos. . . . What? . . . Oh, he did? . . . Okay, okay, no. . . . Don't worry, Jennifer. Nothing I can't take care of. I have to go. . . . Good luck tonight. You were great last night and I'm sure you'll make it through to next week. . . . Love you too."

I think I need to find my own attack mode. The problem is I'm toothless. I say, "You two have such a swell relationship and all, but if she said she's never met me, she's lying."

"Jennifer said you showed up in the autograph line at Copley the other day, claimed to be working on her case, and left your card."

"I sure did."

"She also said she'd never seen you before Copley."

I yawn again. The DA doesn't like it. There's nothing I can do about that. I say, "I have her signed contract back at my office." Complete bluff. He knows it too.

He walks around to the front of the desk and sits on the top. One leg on the floor, one leg off. A DA flamingo. He says, "Blackmail is a felony, Mark." He drops the hard-guy act momentarily and morphs into pity mode. He holds out his hands as if to say, *Look at you, you're a walking shipwreck, unsalvageable.* "If you need money or help, Mark, I can help you out, but this isn't the way to go about it."

I laugh. It's an ugly sound. "Thanks for the offer, DA, but I get by. And I'm not blackmailing anyone. If I were, would I be dumb enough to do it while sitting in your office? Give me a little credit."

"Okay, okay, but Mark, try to take my point of view here. You are presenting me an odd set of circumstances, to say the least. You come out of nowhere, telling me that my daughter hired you on the basis of photos that aren't of Jennifer. Are we on the same page so far?"

I nod. I yawn. The murk is getting used to my chair. The conversation is getting fuzzy. I need to move around, literally put myself on my toes. I stand up and wander behind the chair, pretending to stretch my back.

He says, "Jennifer denies having ever met you before you showed up at Copley. What is it exactly you want me to believe?"

Good question. I want to hear the answer too. I say, "I don't know what to tell you. Kids lie to their parents all the time, especially when they're in trouble. Maybe she's met some bad people. Maybe she's embarrassed, doesn't want Daddy to know that someone sent her a threat, some nude photos that look a lot like her, enough so that if released into the wild many folks would believe it's her in the pictures." I say it all, but I don't really believe it. There's something missing. What's missing is me. Why am I the one with these pictures?

He says, "No one would believe that woman was Jennifer."

I shrug. "Sure they would. Presented in the proper light; people want to believe the worst."

The DA has his chiseled face in hand, another pose, and says, "I'll have another talk with her later, but right now I believe her, not you."

It's not a shock, but it stings. To be dismissed so easily. I fire back with a double-barrel dose of healthy paranoia. "That's fine. I believe me over both of you. Tell me, DA, how do I know that Jennifer was really the person on the other end of that phone call?"

He rolls his eyes, gets up off the desk, and walks to his office door, holds it open. He says, "Okay, I think our meeting is done. If I hear or see anything more about these photos of yours, don't be surprised if you find me in your Southie office, warrant in hand."

"I guess this means no brunch." I adjust my hat and slip the envelope inside my coat. "I'm only looking out for your daughter's best interests because I was hired to."

There's nothing more to be said. We're all out of words. I walk out of the office. He shuts the door behind me. I tighten my coat, the envelope pressed up against my chest. The secretary has her head down, computer keys clicking.

The goons aren't in the waiting room. Maybe they were never here. Maybe, like Jennifer's mole, they've been Photoshopped out. The room is too empty. No chairs are askew, all the magazines are in a pile, nothing out of place, but it's staged, a crime scene without a body.

I'm alone again, with a client who denies such status and with photos that aren't of her. I'm alone again, with nothing, and I just want to sit and think, but my head is a mess, trying to put together a jigsaw puzzle that's suddenly missing all but a few pieces. I need to call a cab, go back to the office, begin at the beginning, focus on those few pieces I do have, and see if I can't force them to fit together.

EIGHT

After my DA meeting I sat at my office desk and looked at the photos again, searching for clues I might've missed. I didn't see any. In the first photo, the one with the fully clothed Jennifer, there was a bookcase that holds ten books. I couldn't read any of the slimmer titles, but there was one fat hardcover with LIT written big and white across the bottom of the spine. Library book probably. In the second photo, the camera is angled up, and I see only the ceiling and the wall and the topless Jennifer.

I locked the photos with the negatives in my office desk and slept the rest of the afternoon away on my apartment couch. I dreamed my usual Dad-in-the-backyard dream. There was still a lot of shit to clean up. No one called and woke me. No one missed my conscious presence. I'm used to it and don't take it personally anymore.

Now it's two o'clock in the morning. I've been wandering and haunting my own apartment, a ghost without the clanging chains. I can't sleep. I already said I was sick of irony, but it's a narcoleptic's lot.

I turn on the VCR and watch two taped *American Star* episodes, last night's and tonight's, the one I slept through. First show has a disco-night theme. Jennifer Times sings "I Will Survive." She sings well enough, right notes and right key, but she moves stiffly, her hips are rusty hinges and her feet don't want to stay in one spot, a colt walking in a field full of holes. The judges call her on it. The British guy says she was icy and robotic, a mannequin barely come to life. The people in the audience boo the judge even though he's correct. Truth is usually greeted with disdain.

Jennifer doesn't take the criticism well and fires back at the judges. She whines and is rude and short in dismissing the critiques. She turns and tilts her head, rolls her eyes, hands on her hips, stops just short of stomping a foot on the floor. She leaves the stage with, "I thought I was great and they did too," pointing to the audience. She gets a lukewarm cheer.

Jennifer forgot it's not about the song you sing or the words you have to say; it's always about the performance, how you present your public self. She could've come off as a hero if she argued with the judges correctly, mixing self-deprecation, humility, and humor with confidence and determination. Maybe she should've hired me as a coach instead of her PI.

As the vote-off show queues up next on my tape, I fire up my laptop and check out the Internet message boards and blogosphere reaction. Jennifer was universally ripped and often referred to as a privileged brat. There will be no recovering from that. The show's voters agreed with the brat tag, and Jennifer is the first finalist knocked out of *American Star*. A quick the end to that singing career, I guess. Jennifer doesn't take the news on the vote-off show well either. Instead of gracious smiles and hand-waving, we get the nationally televised equivalent of a kid storming out of her parents' room after a scolding. While I think Jennifer handled her fifteen minutes of fame poorly, I do sympathize with her. Sometimes you just can't win.

Maybe this means she'll return my calls when she gets back to Boston. Maybe she'll apologize for lying to her father, for making my public self appear to be a lunatic. My performance in her daddy's office needed her help, and she threw me tomatoes instead of roses. Or maybe she won't call me and the case is dead, now that she's off the show.

I shut off the VCR and laptop and wander back to bed. Insomnia is there waiting for me. The sheets and comforter feel all wrong, full of points and angles somehow. The pillow is not soft enough; it's too hard. I'm Goldilocks in my own house.

The awake me can't help but rerun everything in my mashed-up head. Yeah, I'm stubborn, but I have to try and see Jennifer one more time, somehow straighten out all that's been bent out of shape and put the case to bed, so to speak.

NINE

The phone rings; it sounds far away, in the next universe. I lift my head off my desk, an incredible feat of strength, and wipe my face. Leftover fried rice trapped in my beard and mustache fall onto the Styrofoam plate that had been my pillow. The rice bounces off and onto the desktop and on my lap. I need to make a note to vacuum later.

It has been two days since my meeting with the DA. My office phone has rung only once. It was Nanning Wok double-checking my order because the woman wasn't sure if I'd said General Gao or Kung Pao. The General, of course, as if there was any question.

I spent those two days getting nowhere with Jennifer's case. Her agency doesn't return my calls, and I don't know when her next public appearance is. I haven't looked at the photos since locking them in my desk. I wanted them to find their own way out, somehow, before I thought about them again. Doing nothing with them couldn't be any worse than my previous attempts at doing something.

The phone is still ringing. Someone insisting that we talk. Fine. Be that way. I pick it up.

I say, "Mark Genevich," my name bubbling up from the depths, sounding worse for the trip.

"Have you found it yet?" A male voice. He sounds older. His voice is deep, heavy with time, like mine.

I'm disappointed. I was really hoping it'd be Jennifer. Instead, it's a client that I've been shirking. I have two abandoned property searches that I've put on hold since the Times case came walking in my door.

I say, "No, I haven't found anything yet. Need more time." I should just hang up and put my face back into the leftover fried rice.

"I don't think we have more time, kid. There's a red car driving around my house. It's been by four times this afternoon already. Fuck!"

Maybe I'm dreaming and I'll wake up on my couch or reawake with my face in Chinese food to start it all over again. Maybe this is my old buddy Juan-Miguel putting me on, playing a joke. When we lived together he'd call in shit like this. I decide to play along with the caller a bit longer, gather more information before I make a hasty conclusion; it's how I have to live my everyday life. That said, this guy's voice has a kernel of sincerity that's undeniable.

I say, "Relax. Calm down. Red cars won't bother you if you don't bother them."

"There're two people in that red car. They know. They know about the pictures somehow. Shit! They're driving by again, and they slow down in front of my house every time. You didn't show anyone those pictures yet, did you? You can't until you find—"

I drop the phone, of course. It slides out of my greasy hands and bounces off my foot. Goddamn it! At least I know I'm awake. I'm awake because I'm usually competent in my dreams and hallucinations.

I pick up the phone. "Sorry, dropped you for a second. I'm still here." I stand up, walk across the room, and shut the door to my office. No one's in the hallway, of course, but Ellen could walk in unannounced at any time. "No. I didn't show anyone anything." It's easier to lie because I don't know who I'm talking to.

He says, "I shouldn't have given you those pictures. I don't know what I think I was doing, who I'd be helping. It was dumb. Now we're both fucked. Should've just kept sitting on it like the old hen that I am. This is so screwed up. Shouldn't have done anything. . . ." His words fall into odd rhythms, stops and starts mixed with letters that he holds too long. He slurs his *s*'s. He's been drinking. It's not helping his paranoia—or mine. His voice fades out as he's talking to either himself or someone else in the room with him; the phone must be dropping away from his mouth. I'm losing him. I have to keep him talking, even if it isn't to me.

I say, "Hey, pull it together. It'll be all right once I find"— yeah, find what?—"it." So I'm not so smooth on my end. I pace around my office and look for something that'll help me. Nothing's here. Hopefully he doesn't process my hesitation.

He says, "You need to hurry up. I don't want to say anything more. If they're driving around my house, it probably means they're listening in too, the fuckers."

He and I have seen too many of the same movies. I'm ready to agree with him. I have so many questions to ask this guy, starting with the introductory-level *Who are you?* but I have to pretend I know what's going on.

I say, "All right, all right. But before you hang up, I think we need to talk again. Face-to-face. It'll help us sort all this out, trust me. We'll both feel better about it."

"Not your office. I can't come to Southie again. I'm not going anywhere, not right now. I'm staying here, with my doors locked."

An espresso-like jolt rushes through my system. He's been here before. I say, "Okay, I'll come to you. Give me your address."

He does, but he doesn't give me his name. No matter. Address only. I write it down. Goddamn, he lives on the Cape, in Osterville, not far from where Ellen lives and where my childhood homestead still stands. Now pieces are fitting together where they shouldn't, square pegs in round holes.

I tell him I'll be there tomorrow. He hangs up, and that's it. The office and phone are quiet again. More old fried rice, looking like mouse turds, is on the desk and on the floor. I'm breathing heavy. I pull out a cigarette and start a fire.

I unlock my drawer and take out the photos. I try on a new set of eyes and look at the girl in the photos. Maybe she's not Times. And the photos: the matte and shading is faded and yellowing in spots. The photos are old, but how old?

Okay, slow down. I know now that Jennifer was never in my office. Even her presence was part and parcel of the whole hypnogogic hallucination. But why would I dream her into my office while asleep during phone guy's little visit? Did I conjure her solely because of the resemblance in the photos? Did her name come up in our initial meeting? Is he just some crazed fan of *American Star*? Maybe he's a would-be blackmailer, but that doesn't feel right. Is he telling the truth about being watched?

He didn't want me to show the pictures to anyone until I found something, and I already showed them to the DA. Oops. Why did phone guy, presumably from Osterville, choose me? Does he know me or Ellen? What am I supposed to find? My note about South Shore Plaza. Red car, Osterville, and a drunk on the Cape.

I think I've falsely harassed Jennifer Times and her DA father. I really don't know anything about this case, and there's still rice in my beard, but at least I have a client now. Yeah, tomorrow I'll make the little road trip to the Cape and then a house call, but I'm not getting paid enough for this.

TEN

I'm in Ellen's little green car. It's fifteen years old. The passenger seat is no longer conducive to my very particular posture, which is somewhere between question mark and Quasimodo. Lower back and legs report extreme discomfort. It's enough to keep me awake, which is miserable because I keep nodding off but not staying asleep.

We're cruising down Route 3 south, headed toward the Cape. It's off-season and the traffic isn't bad, but Ellen maintains a running monologue about how awful the traffic always is and how nobody knows how to drive. Meanwhile, she's tailgating the car in front of us and we're close enough that I can see what radio station he's tuned to.

I still have a driver's license but no car. Renewing the license isn't an issue for me. Driving is. I haven't driven in six years.

Last night I told Ellen that I needed to go to the Osterville library to help with a genealogical search and was pressed for time. She didn't ask for further details. She knew I wouldn't give any. When she picked me up this morning, she didn't ask questions about why all the toilet paper was unrolled and wrapped around my kitchen table—King Tut's table now—and why the apartment door was unlocked but my bedroom door was locked. She knew the narcoleptic me went for an evening stroll with the apartment to himself.

My eyes are closed; we're somewhere between Norwell and Marshfield, I think.

Ellen says, "Are you awake?"

I just want to sit and sleep, or think about what I'm going to say to the mystery client in Osterville. The names associated with the address are Brendan and Janice Sullivan. I was able to ferret out that much online.

I say, "No. I'm asleep and dreaming that you're wearing the clown pants again."

"Stop it. I just didn't want to stuff them into my night bag and get them all wrinkly. Those wrinkles don't come out. You'd think that wouldn't happen with polyester. Anyway, they're comfy driving pants."

I say, "I guess I'm awake then."

She says, "Good. You'll never guess who called me last night."

"You're right."

"Guess."

I pull my fedora farther over my eyes and grind around in my seat, trying to find an impossible position of comfort. I say, "A state lottery commission agent. You've been winning too much on scratch tickets."

"Hardly," she says, and slaps my thigh. "Your new pal Billy Times called."

She might as well have hit me in the groin instead of my thigh. I sit up and crush my fedora between forehead and car ceiling. I resettle and try to play off my fish-caught-on-a-line spasm as a posture adjustment. I say, "Never heard of him."

"Come on, Mark. I know you visited him earlier in the week. He told me."

"Since I'm awake-awake, I might as well be smoking. Mind?"

"Yes. I try not to smoke in the car."

"Good." I light up.

She sighs and opens her window a crack. "I'm a little impressed you went all the way in town to the DA's office." She says it like it was so far away I needed a passport. A condescending cheap shot, but I probably deserve it.

I say, "I had to hire a Sherpa, but I managed."

"I didn't think you were serious the other day with the whole DA-as-family-friend talk." She stops, waiting for me to fill in the blanks. I can't fill those blanks in, not even for myself. She thinks I have something going on. I do, but I'm not going to tell her about it. She wouldn't like it. She certainly wouldn't be transporting me down to the Cape to chat with Sullivan.

I say, "I'm always serious, Ellen." All right, I need to know it all. I need to know why the DA called my mommy. It'll hang over me the whole time I'm in Osterville if I don't ask. "So why'd he call you?"

"Actually, he invited me to one of his Sunday brunches. Isn't that neat?"

"How nice. I'm sure your friends will be excited to hear you've become a socialite. You'll be the talk of Thursday night bingo at the Lithuanian Club." Ellen doesn't say anything, so I add, "Come on, Ellen, you're as bad a liar as I am. What did he want?"

"I'm not lying."

"Ellen. Your clown pants puff out bigger when you're lying. Come on, spill it."

She hits me again. "He did invite me. And, he asked questions about you. Asked if you were okay. He said your meeting was very odd and he got the sense you were struggling."

"Struggling? More proof politicians have no sense."

"Yes, struggling. That's the exact word he used."

"So what'd you tell him?"

Ellen sighs and moves her hands around while talking. Someone should be driving. "I told him you were fine, but I mentioned the accident and how you had narcolepsy now. I stressed that you're doing fine, though." She lilts with each biographical phrase, singing the song of me. It's a dirge she's sung many times before. She performs it well.

"Jesus, Ellen. Thanks a lot. Did you tell him I don't like pickles or ketchup, I pick my nose, and I wet the bed as a kid?"

She says, "What's wrong with you? He was just concerned, that's all. Did you want me to lie or make something up?"

"No. Telling him I was fine would've been enough. He doesn't need to hear my sob story."

"I don't understand why this upsets you."

"If I ever need him for a case, he'll never take me seriously now."

"Of course he will. No one holds narcolepsy against you."

"Come on, Ellen. Everyone does. No one really believes I have anything medically wrong with me. They think I'm lazy or just *odd,* like the DA said." I stop talking but I could go on: most people think I really could keep from falling asleep if I wanted to, if I just focused, like narcolepsy is some algebraic equation I could solve if I worked at it hard enough, did all the homework. I'm a bad joke. A punch line. I'm Beetle Bailey, a cartoon character falling asleep at the switch for laughs. I might as well be wearing her goddamn clown pants.

"I don't think that about you, Mark." She's mad at me and my pity party. I don't blame her.

I inhale the cigarette down to the filter, more ash in my lap than in the ashtray. Yeah, I'm nervous about my meeting with Sullivan, and I'm taking it out on Ellen and myself.

I say, "You're right. I know you don't, Clowny. I'm your *American Star.*"

ELEVEN

Ellen drops me at the Osterville Free Library. It's a one-level brick building with white molding, trim, and columns. The Parthenon it's not. Ellen has a couple of family-portrait photo shoots and a meeting with a prospective wedding client, so I have three hours to myself.

I make an appearance inside the small library, wander the stacks for a bit, avoid story time and the children's wing, and check out a slim history of Osterville written and self-published by some local schmoe who probably has more cats than rooms in his house, not that I'm judging anyone. If Ellen comes back to the library before me, I can tell her I went for a read and a stroll. She might believe it or she might not.

The Sullivan house is two miles away from the library according to my Mapquest printout. The old Genevich homestead is on the other side of town, right off Route 28 and closer to downtown, so I'm not very familiar with this section of Osterville. This part of town has larger and pricier homes. No bungalows. No clapboard. These are summer homes for the well-well-to-do, mixed in with slightly more modest houses for folks who live here year-round. According to the map, most of my walk is down Wianno Avenue, left onto Crystal Lake Road, and then a quick right onto Rambler Road. Easy as A, B, and then C.

It's an overcast day with gusty ocean winds. The fedora quivers on my head, thinking about making a break for it. It's a quiet day otherwise. Only a handful of cars pass me on Wianno. None of them are red.

The exercise is good for my head, but the rest of my body thinks it's torture. Cranky knees and ankles carry the scars of the accident too. I walk as slowly as I talk.

While on my little hike, I try to focus on the case. On what it is I'm supposed to find. And it is a *what,* not a *who.* On the phone, Sullivan asked if I had found *it* yet.

Thoughts of the DA and Jennifer Times nag at me. I guess I should call the DA and apologize for the confusion, for thinking he was involved with sending me the photos. Apologize for my mistake. But it hasn't felt exactly like a mistake.

Sullivan's ringing question, *You didn't show the pictures to anyone, did you?,* was the same thing the DA asked me when he first saw the pictures. He didn't come right out with *It's not Jennifer.* He asked if anyone else had seen the pictures. I didn't think anything of it earlier because I'd assumed he didn't want his nude daughter subject to roving packs of prying eyes. Now, I'm not so sure.

Something's not right there. It's why he called Ellen too.

I turn onto Crystal Lake Road, and there are blue and red lights filtering through the trees ahead, and right there is Rambler Road. It's blocked to traffic by a police car. There are more flashing lights and the occasional chirp of a siren. Sullivan's house. I think the worst. It's easy to think the worst when it always happens. Crystal Lake Road loops around to the other end of Rambler via Barnard Road, but I bet that end is blocked off too.

I stuff my map into a pocket and walk toward the roadblock. There's one cop, leaning on the hood of the car, arms crossed over his chest. He's skinny, a straw that isn't stirring any drink. He wears sunglasses despite the overcast day. I tip my hat. Surprise, surprise, I get to pass without answering his questions three.

Fifty yards or so beyond the roadblock are two more police cars parked on the side of the road. The homes on Rambler don't crowd each other; groves of trees help everyone keep their distance.

The Rambler Road locals must all be at work. There are no rubbernecking neighbors on lawns, dressed in robes and slippers and sipping their home-brewed coffee. There's just me.

My left ankle is swelling up, rebelling against the sock, but I make it to the other cop cars. They're parked next to a black mailbox with *Sullivan* stenciled in golden cursive. The Sullivan home is set back from the road. If it were summer, the place would be difficult to see from the street because of the trees that surround it and flank its L-shaped gravel driveway, but it's March and there are no leaves or blooms. I see everything through the empty branches. The house is big and white, with a two-car garage. The exterior shows signs of wear, missing shingles and peeling paint.

There's a clearing and a small grassy patch at the end of the gravel driveway. Two more cop cars are parked on the grass. An ambulance cozies up to Sullivan's front door with its back doors open. A blue SUV sits in the driveway, the only civilian car on or around the property.

"Can I help you?" Another cop. He suddenly appears next to the mailbox and me. Neat trick. This one is my size and build, but no beard and no mangled face. Nobody's perfect.

I say, "Depends. Can you tell me if Brendan is okay?"

He says, "Sorry, I don't know anything. Move along." He's not wearing sunglasses. He doesn't look at me but past me. I've been dismissed, if considered at all.

He doesn't like me. I can tell. It's okay because the feeling is mutual. I say, "I guess you can't help me, then. I don't suppose you're going to let me walk up there and find someone who will actually, you know, help me?"

He sways on his feet, an impatient boxer listening to the referee's instructions, waiting for me to crawl out of my corner. He lets me get through my slow I'm-running-out-of-batteries spiel. He doesn't interrupt. I guess he deserves an iota of credit for that.

He says, "Why are you still here? Move along."

I hold up my hands. "Just a concerned acquaintance of the Sullivans out for a walk. I saw the lights and figured I'd check in and be neighborly."

Nothing from angry cop.

I say, "Well, you just keep on protecting the people, officer." I consider showing my PI ID and pushing back some more, but it would produce nothing but a migraine headache for me. Whatever happened at the Sullivan house isn't good, and I probably don't want to be connected to it. At least not right now. The last thing I need is to have to answer a bunch of Barney Fife questions *downtown,* and calling Mommy to pick me up at the police station would ruin the whole vibe for everyone involved. I'm more afraid of having to answer Ellen's questions than theirs. She's tougher.

My craven need for information will have to wait. I tell myself that patience will work best here and I'll find out what happened eventually. It's the only play I have right now.

I slowly walk away, exaggerate my limp, maybe give the cop some Keyser Söze thoughts. I'm aimed at the other end of Rambler, figuring to loop around to Wianno Avenue and back to the library. I have the time now, and not having to walk past the same set of cops is a good idea.

Then, through the trees, I see a stretcher brought out of the Sullivan house. It's holding a body with a white sheet over it. The stretcher's metallic legs are like the barren tree branches. They look dead, unfit to carry life and too flimsy to carry any weight.

TWELVE

Back on Wianno and getting physically fatigued fast. Joints tighten and demand that I stop moving. I don't walk this kind of distance regularly—or at all. This is my marathon.

Been waiting and listening for the ambulance and cop cars to pass. Nothing yet. They must've taken a different route.

I might be a half mile from the library now. A car approaches from behind. Its wheels grind salt and sand left over from the winter. The salt and sand have nowhere to go, I suppose. The car slows down and pulls onto the sidewalk ahead of me. It's in my path. It's a red car, something American and muscular, not at all practical, and that tells you all you need to know about the driver of such a thing. Whoever it is has to wait until I drag my limping-for-real ass up to them. Drama and tension happen naturally sometimes.

I mosey up to the car. The front windows are rolled down, engine still on, its idling is somewhere between a growl and a clearing throat. There's a thick arm hanging out the window, tapping the door, tapping to someone's favorite song. Not mine.

The driver says, "Hey there, Genevich. What's that you're carrying around?" The driver is the redheaded goon from the DA's office. The passenger is his bald buddy. It's sweet how they stick together, even this far from their natural habitat.

I say, "A book. Ever seen one before? Truth be known, I just look at the pictures." I hold it up. I don't have any secrets.

The passenger goon, Baldy, says, "Oh, he's a funny guy. I love funny guys. They make everything more fun."

I say, "That's quite the expressive vocabulary you got there. I can see why your buddy lets you talk." They both have their cell phones in their ears. Maybe they're surgical implants. I point and add, "Those phones will give you cancer. Be careful."

"Thanks for the tip," the redhead says. "What are you doing down on the Cape? For a retard who can't drive, you sure do get around." He laughs. It's forced and goofy.

I don't say anything. The goons go all sit-and-stare on me, dogs pointing at some dead animal floating in the water.

The library is in the visible distance. The clouds part a bit, a tear in the overcast fabric, and the sun shines on the library's white flagpole. I'm on a main road, middle of the day. I convince myself that I'm safe, so I decide to keep up the chatter.

I say, "I like the Cape this time of year. Think I'll play a little mini-golf later. Take advantage of the off-season touristy stuff. Want to play? Five bucks a hole until the windmill. Then it's ten."

Baldy says, "We'll pass, Mushface." He's breathing heavy, practically frothing. His chin juts out, a thick slab of granite, a section of the Great Wall of China. It seems to be growing bigger with each breath.

I say, "Now, now. No need to get personal, boys. This has been fun, but I think I'll continue on my afternoon constitutional, if you don't mind."

I resume my walk. I have goons from the DA's office tailing me in a red car, Sullivan's surveying red car. Nothing is coincidence.

Everything is connected.

They follow me. The engine revs, mechanical authority, a thousand angry voices. Clouds of exhaust punctuate the vehicular threats. The roars fill me, then pool in the back of my head. I want to turn to see how close they are, but I won't.

They pull up next to me again, but we all keep moving. Nobody is the leader. The car creeps farther onto the sidewalk, cutting into my path. There's a chest-high stone wall to my left. I might run out of space soon, sandwiched between metal and rock, that proverbial hard place.

Redhead says, "We weren't done talking yet. Leaving us like that was kind of rude, Genevich."

"Yeah, well, Miss Manners I ain't."

Their car edges closer. Heat from the engine block turns loose my sweat. I'm going to keep walking. I won't be the one to flinch in this game of chicken. No way. Not after that retard crack.

Redhead says, "I hope you didn't come all the way down here to talk to Brendan Sullivan."

Baldy finishes the thought. "Yeah, wasted trip, Genevich. He's got nothing to say. Never did."

I'm not safe. I never was. Safety is the big disguise. I keep walking. Straight line. That's what courage is: dumbass perseverance. The library flagpole is my bearing, my shining beacon. I'm done talking. Just walking.

Redhead says, "I can make this simple for you, Genevich. You can make us go away by giving us those photos."

My eyes stay on the flagpole. It's covered in white vines and white roses.

"Yeah, give us the photos, and then you can have a little nap."

"Or a big one."

"It's time to be smart, here."

"We don't play games."

"Ask Brendan."

Baldy says, "Oh, wait a minute, he can't ask Brendan."

The negatives are still in my desk but the manila envelope and photos are inside my jacket. I wanted to make Sullivan look at them again. I wanted to see his eyes seeing the photos. I can't explain what information it would've given me, but it would've been something. Maybe everything.

Redhead says, "Be a smart retard, Genevich. Give us the photos."

I can pretend the photos are inside my library book and, when

Redhead reaches for it, smack him in the face with it, knock him silly. Maybe it'll buy me enough time to get to the library. Maybe it won't. I wouldn't mind paying the missing book fee if it worked.

I don't give them anything, feet on pavement, playing it cool when everything is too hot. Their engine revs loud enough to crack the sidewalk under me but I just keep on going. My eyes are locked on the library and its flagpole, the flagpole with vines made of white roses, and those roses are now blooming and growing bigger, just like the smoking and growling threat next to me.

THIRTEEN

I'm falling but not falling. I'm not falling because I am sitting, but I am falling because I am leaning and sliding, sliding down. My right hand shoots out and slaps against wood. It wasn't expecting wood and I wasn't expecting any of this. Adrenaline. Fear. My heart is a trapped rabbit and it frantically kicks the walls with oversized hind legs. Disoriented is a brain comparing short-term memories to what the senses currently report and believing neither.

Goons, the DA's goons. Sitting on a bench. Surgical implants. A bench. Red car. Feet planted in grass. Walking. Falling, sliding. A stone wall. White flagpole on my direct left, and there are no vines or blooming roses. . . .

I blink and stare and look. If I was an owl I'd spin my head like a top and cover all 360 degrees, make sure there're no holes in what I see. Okay. I'm sitting on a bench, the lone bench in front of the library.

My legs hurt. They won't bend at the knee without complaining. I did the walk. Pain is my proof. My next thought is about time. How much I hate it, and how desperate I am to know how much of it has passed.

Here comes Ellen. Her little green car pulls into the library lot. I'll stay here, wait for her, and reboot from my latest system crash, but there'll be files missing. There always are.

I feel inside my jacket. The manila envelope. I peek inside and the photos are still there.

Ellen has mercifully changed out of her clown pants and into old carpenter jeans, faded, like my memories. She also has on a gray sweatshirt, part of her bingo attire. It makes her look older and tired, tired from all the extra years of hands-on mothering. I won't tell her that maybe the clown pants are the way to go.

Ellen says, "Have you been out here long?"

I wonder if she knows how awful a question that is to ask. I could say *not long* and be correct; it's relative. I haven't been out here asleep on this bench for long when you compare it to the amount of time I've existed with narcolepsy, if you compare it to the life span of a galaxy. Or I could say *not long, not long at all, just got here.*

I say, "I don't know."

Ellen ignores my response and its implications. She adjusts her monstrous bag on her right shoulder. She usually complains about that shoulder killing her, but she won't switch the bag over to her left. I don't know anyone else who exclusively uses her right shoulder for load bearing.

She says, "Did you get some work done? Get everything you need?"

I say, "Some work done. Still more to do." Still groggy. Speaking only in phrases is the ointment. For now, my words are too heavy for complex construction.

"That's good. Though you look a little empty-handed."

I had taken out the little Osterville history book. I check and pat the bench and my coat. It's gone.

Ellen says, "What's the matter?"

Maybe I hit the redheaded goon with the book after all, assuming there were real goons in the first place. I could verify some of my previous extracurricular activities. Go inside and ask if I had checked out that book, but I won't. An answer of *no* would do too much damage to me. I'd rather just believe what I want to believe. It's always easier that way.

I say, "Nothing. I think I left a book inside." I stand up and try not to wince. I'm going to have a hard time walking to the car.

She says, "What's wrong now, Mark?"

Everything. I need to go back to Southie, try to put distance between me, the maybe goons, and whatever happened at the Sullivan house. I also need to give Ellen an answer, an excuse, something that won't lead to a trip full of follow-up questions. "Nothing. My body is protesting another drive in your torture chamber."

"Want me to get your book?"

"No. It wasn't any good."

77

FOURTEEN

Back home. It's five o'clock. I've been gone for only half a day, but our little excursion to the Cape and back has left me with a weeklong family-vacation-type hangover. I just don't have a cheesy T-shirt, sunburn, and disposable camera full of disposable memories to show for it.

My office phone blinks. A red light. I have a voicemail message. Let's get right to it.

"Hello—um, Mr. Genevich? This is Jennifer Times. I got your number from your card that you left me?" Her statements are questions. She's unsure of what she's doing. That makes two of us. "I think we need to meet and talk. Please call me back as soon as you can." She leaves her number, and the message ends with a beep.

I won't call her right away. I need the meanings and possibilities to have their way with me for a bit. Just like I need a hot shower to untie my muscles; they're double-knotted.

First I'll check my e-mail. I turn on the computer. The hard drive makes its noises, its crude impersonation of life. The monitor glows, increasing in brightness until the desktop is visible. Same as it was yesterday and the day before. There's no e-mail. Then I do a quick search for any stories about Brendan Sullivan and Osterville and murder. Nothing comes up.

Maybe I should call Sullivan's house. Don't know if that's a good idea. Not sure if I'm ready to have my name popping up on police radar screens, if he was in fact murdered. There's still too much I don't know, too many questions I couldn't answer, but the call is the chance I probably have to take at some point.

I should call. Call his house now. Might not have been him I saw being taken out of the house. What I saw might not have even happened.

Screw it. I pick up the phone and dial Jennifer Times instead. Sullivan can wait. The shower can wait. It'll be good to have things to look forward to.

One ring. "Hello?"

"Jennifer, it's Mark Genevich returning your call." I'm all business, even if she's not the client and not in the photos anymore. Let her do the talking. I don't need her. She called me.

"Hi, yeah, thanks for calling me back. So, I was thinking we should meet and talk?" Still with statements that are questions. Maybe being forced from the spotlight has left her withered, without confidence. Maybe it's just my perception. For all I know she's a confident young woman, an aspiring celebrity, and she's only reflecting my constant state of insecurity because I want her to. It's what we all want from our celebrities. We want them to tell us something we don't know about ourselves when they can't.

Suddenly I'm Mr. Popular. I say, "I can do that. You pick the place." I assume that she doesn't want to come to my office. Otherwise, she would've offered.

"Can we meet for dinner at Amrheins later tonight? Seven p.m.?" Of course. The DA's pet restaurant. "I can do that too. But make it seven-thirty." I don't need the extra half hour. Sure, it'll give me a safety net, never know when that ever-elusive thief, lost time, might strike, but I said seven-thirty because I want to exert some of my own conscious will upon the situation. For once.

She says, "Okay."

There's silence. It's big enough to span the unknown distance between us. I say, "See you tonight, then, Jennifer." I'm not going to ask why she wants to meet with me or ask her what DA Daddy told her. There'll be plenty of time for the tough questions later. I'm not going to force this. I don't need to. I'm not used to the power position. I'll try not to let it go to my head.

FIFTEEN

A constant stream of traffic passes by like schools of fish, the sheer number of vehicles relentless and numbing. I'm standing on East Broadway, only a block from the Broadway Red Line T stop.

Seven-thirty has become seven-forty-five. It's all right. My cigarette is finished. Society always arrives late.

Amrheins is an Irish restaurant. Has its own parking lot, big enough for fifty-plus cars. The lot itself has to be worth a small for-tune in real estate. The restaurant is big. It has three sections. Bar section is the middle, dining areas on the left and right. The right side of the restaurant is elevated. Everything is kept suitably dark for the patrons.

I check in with the maître d'. He's a short young guy in a white dress shirt and black pants. The bright ink from his sleeve tattoos is visible through the shirt's thin cloth, their stories hinted at but hidden. He doesn't talk, only motions at the elevated section with his head.

Jennifer is alone, sitting at a table for two tucked away in a corner, as far from the entrance as possible. She sees me and nods. It takes me a dragonfly's life to limp across the restaurant to our table. She has on a jean jacket, open and rolled up to the elbows. Light blue shirt. Her hair is tied up, off her face, and she wears glasses. The glasses are enough to turn her into Clark Kent and successfully disguise her Superman, but I know it's her.

I say, "Sorry I'm late, Jennifer." I try to think of something witty to explain my lateness, but I figure my hangdog reappearance is enough. My clothes look slept in because they are. I never did take that hot shower. I can't even keep appointments with myself.

She says, "That's okay." The tablecloth is green. An unlit tea-light candle floats in a glass bowl. The melted wax makes tentacles. It's a floating inkblot I can't read, a portent for the evening. Maybe I should just sit my ass down. Jennifer sips from a glass of sparkling water, or maybe soda. A person can get lost trying to figure out all the details.

The place is half full, or half empty, the point of view hinging on how our meeting fares. I do sit. My back is turned to the rest of the restaurant. I'm not comfortable with my seating. Don't want my back to Southie because the place is full of goons. One such goon might have red hair, freckles, and a phone in his ear, and he might have a bald buddy. Yeah, it has occurred to me that this dinner could be a setup. I slide my heavy wooden chair loudly toward Jennifer's side of the table.

I say, "I like being able to see what I want to see, which is everything." I'm still fiddling with my chair and position. Jennifer makes a hand gesture and a waiter materializes instantly.

Jennifer orders mango turkey tips with pineapple salsa, then turns to me and says, "Sorry, but I can't stay long. He'll wait while you look at the menu, all right?"

The waiter nods at me. That's all I get from the staff. Head movements.

I suppose I deserve being put on the food spot for being late. I make it easy on everyone and order without looking at the menu. "Shepherd's pie and a coffee, and make sure my mug is always full."

The waiter has his errand, clicks his heels, and returns from whence he came. I say, "So, Ms. Times, here we are." Not exactly the best opening line, but it'll have to do, creepy-older-man vibe notwithstanding.

She says, "I have some questions," then stops. Her spine is telephone-pole straight. It makes me uncomfortable.

I say, "I have many answers. Ask me the questions and we'll see if any of my answers match up."

Her hands are on the table and folded over each other. She could be holding a firefly trapped in her hands or a coin she plans to make disappear. She has all her own fingers, no bandages or scars. Not that I expected differently, of course. She says, "I've never been to your office, Mr. Genevich. Why did you go to my father's office and tell him I hired you?" Her delivery is clinical, rehearsed. She must've practiced her questions with a mirror or with DA Daddy.

Doesn't matter. I tell her. I just flat out tell her everything, the truth along with my mistakes and lies. Can't have truth without lies. First I give an introduction to my wonderful world of narcolepsy. How it started. How it won't stop. Then fast-forward to our supposed meeting in my office. Her missing fingers and the hypnogogic hallucination. She's listening. I'm believing. Believing that if I open up and share my truths, maybe she'll share hers. It's the only chance I have of getting anything meaningful out of this meeting. I give her the highlights from the trip to the DA's minus the photos of her stand-in. She only needs to know I thought she was being blackmailed. Not over what. Finally, I tell her that the real client called me yesterday. I leave out the Cape, red car, and goons. I'm not going to give it all away.

She says, "Well, I'm glad you're admitting that I was never in your office." She unfolds her hands; the firefly is free to go. She reaches for her drink. "But do you know why you hallucinated me into your office?"

"You and *American Star* were impossible to avoid around here. Believe me, I tried. The local rags and news stations pumped out daily features and updates." I stop and Jennifer doesn't say anything. So I add, "That, and I'm your biggest fan. I never missed a show and called in to vote every night, unless I fell asleep first."

I laugh. She doesn't.

She says, "Is it because the woman in the pictures you showed to my father looks like me?"

The questions are piling up fast, adding up, stressing my system again. Not sure if I can keep up. I can keep telling myself I'm in control of this particular situation, but I know better. Luckily, the waiter picks the perfect time to return with my coffee. It's hot enough to melt skin. My belly fills with lava. Perfect.

I say, "So, your father told you about the pictures, I assume. It's nice that you guys can share like that."

She nods. "Did you bring them?"

I don't say anything right away because I don't know what I should say. Experience offers me nothing here because I have none. "I think I have those Kodak moments on me, yeah." The pictures never leave me now. They've taken root inside my coat.

"Will you show them to me?"

I say, "I don't think so. You're not my client." I say that, but I'm going to show them to her. Just want to know how much she'll push.

"I think you owe me. Don't you?" It's the first appearance of that privileged attitude I saw on TV. Can't say I like it. She says it with a face as straight as her spine, which is still as straight as a telephone pole. See, everything is connected.

I say, "No. I don't owe you anything other than a sorry-for-the-inconvenience." My coffee mug is empty despite my explicit instructions. That's inconvenient.

She says, "I want to see her. It's why I called you and it's why I'm here, Mr. Genevich. Nothing else. This is it. Our paths will never cross again after this." Jennifer takes off her glasses and wipes the lenses with her napkin, then puts them back on. Disguise intact. "I would like to see her. Please."

I know the DA put her up to this. It's too obvious. Now I just have to figure out the potential risk/reward of showing her the photos. I smile instead of yawning. It probably comes out all lopsided and crooked, a crack in a glass. I say, "Am I supposed to just pull out the photos here, in the middle of a restaurant?"

She says, "Yeah, why not? There's nobody over here. You're practically sitting in my lap, so it's not like anyone could see."

Hard to argue with that. I open my coat and produce the envelope, which has taken quite a beating. The manila is going all flaky on me, its structural integrity close to being compromised. Nothing lasts forever. I take out the pictures and hand the first one to her, the one with clothes.

Jennifer says, "Wow. She does look like me. Not exactly, but enough to be weird. Aren't there more?" She holds out a hand.

"I'll trade you. New for old."

She rolls her eyes but I don't care. Now I'm the spoiled brat who won't share. I make the international gimme-gimme-gimme sign with my hand and fingers. She gimmes. I put the second picture in her hand.

She says, "What did my father say when he saw these?"

"He said it wasn't you. I asked for proof. He said no mole. Hair and teeth were wrong." I leave out the part where he asked me if anyone else had seen the photos. I'm saving that for myself until I figure out what to do with it.

She says, "She's too skinny to be me. Her breasts are smaller too." Jennifer gives back the photo.

"My girlfriend used to say that all the time." I try to sound nonchalant but come off desperate instead. I rub my beard. It sounds awful loud. Awful and loud.

Jennifer says, "Your girlfriend sounds like a keeper," and gives me a pity smile. Thanks, but no thanks.

I say, "Nah, not really. Barely remember her." I reach for my cigarettes, but then I remember I can't smoke in here. Memory slower than the hand. Back to the beard.

Jennifer says, "But you remember she talked about her small breasts?"

I can't tell how much fun she's having at my expense. Doesn't matter, I suppose. I can pretend I'm out having a harmless conversation. Pretend that I didn't lose my face and then the last eight years of my life to little sleeps. I say, "Yeah. That, and I liked how she read books."

I'm sure Jennifer isn't expecting me to go here, a tangent running wildly into my personal territory, but she plays along. She says, "Should I be afraid to ask?"

"She wrote all over her books. She circled and highlighted words and phrases, drew pictures between the lines, and wrote down descriptions of the emotions she experienced in the margins. So when she went back to reread the book, she only looked at the pictures and the notes."

"That's odd. And certainly memorable."

I say, "I remember it because it's where I live now. In the margins." I don't think Jennifer realizes how honest I am being here. Maybe she does and finds it embarrassing. I'm like a friend admitting some reprehensible bit of behavior that forever warps and taints the relationship. Only I'm not a friend. I think I understand her obvious discomfort. Strangers are supposed to lie.

She steers the conversation back to her turf. "Do you swear no one is trying to use those to blackmail me? If those pictures end up on the Internet somehow, you'll have one pissed-off DA knocking on your door."

I tell her, "You're in the clear," though I don't really believe it. There's some connection. I mean, she's here, in front of me right now. That's more than I can say for any other aspect, potential or otherwise, of this case. An awkward silence has its way.

I say, "Glad we settled that. I can sleep now." I laugh at my own joke. I laugh too hard. It shakes our table. It's a laugh a prisoner might direct at the warden who just made a meal out of the cell key.

"Who do you think it is?" she says.

I stop myself from saying *If I knew, I wouldn't be here with you,* but I don't want her to take it personally. Yeah, that's a bad joke. I know this case is a lot more serious than blackmail and nudie pics, and it scares the hell out of me. I tell her, "Don't know yet."

"So you don't know who's in the pictures and you didn't know who sent the pictures?"

I say, "I know who sent them to me now."

"That's right. The convenient phone call."

"There was nothing convenient about the phone call."

"Still sounds like a tough case."

"Nothing's ever easy. But I'll figure it all out."

"Will you?"

"Yes."

The verbal volley is fast and everything gets returned. I manage to push out every one of my lead-heavy words.

She leans back in her chair, crosses her arms over her chest. "Those pictures felt old to me, like they were taken a long time ago."

"Probably just the black-and-white." She's right, but I don't want to admit it.

Our food arrives. My shepherd's pie is molten. We eat. Our silence becomes a part of the meal, a glass of wine that doesn't add any flavor but doesn't get in the way either.

Then I decide to get in the way. "Sorry you lost, Jennifer."

"Excuse me?"

"Lost. You know, *American Star.* I thought you got screwed, although you probably gave them too much attitude. Nothing wrong with attitude, but you gotta know, the peoples, they want their stars safe, smiling, and happy. At least until they get bored with them."

Oh, she's angry. It's all over her face. The emotion looks exterior, not belonging to her. It's a mask. It's not real. She's giving me what she thinks I expect or want. Maybe I'm projecting again. I don't know anything about this woman, but I did see her on TV surrounded by fans, and we're all conditioned to believe it's validation of her goodness, her worth, even if she was the first loser. Jennifer composes herself, takes off the anger mask.

"Thanks. It's been a tough few days, but I'll be fine. My agent says offers are already coming in."

Sure they are. More local mall appearances to be followed by national anthems at minor league baseball parks, and it only goes downhill from there. Her brief run as a celebrity was a mask too, or a full-body costume, one she rented instead of owned.

Seems the both of us are down, so I won't throw any more kicks her way. But I will throw her an off-speed pitch. "Did you tell your father you'd be meeting with me tonight?"

She says, "No." She doesn't use a knife, just mashes her fork into a turkey tip, splitting it in half. She's lying. That's my assumption until proven otherwise, private detective work as contrapositive.

I say, "Does your father think I'm making this all up? Does he think I'm dangerous? Should I be expecting him and a warrant at my door soon?"

Jennifer shrugs and destroys more turkey. "I don't know. He'll probably forget about it if he doesn't hear from you again. He was pretty pissed about your meeting, though."

"I have that effect on some people." A canned line, one that I regret instantly. "Did he tell you that he and my father were childhood friends?"

Jennifer tilts her head. "No, he didn't. Is that true?"

Could be the old man was just too angry to bother with the cozy nostalgia trip. Could be he didn't tell her for a reason. I say, "As true as eight o'clock." Not sure what that means, but I go with it. "I don't get into the DA's office without the Southie and family-friend bit. They grew up in the Harbor Point projects and palled around. Ask him about it."

Jennifer looks at her watch. I'm the appointment that's supposed to end soon. She says, "I will. Where is your father now?"

"He died when I was five."

"I'm sorry." She looks at me, puts me under glass, and says, "Tell me what narcolepsy is like."

"I can't tell you. I'm in it all the time. No basis for comparison. I might as well ask you what not having narcolepsy is like. I certainly don't remember what I felt like before I had it, before the accident." I stop. She doesn't say anything. She was supposed to. Some dance partner she is. I can't follow if she won't lead.

I say, "Do you remember what you felt like eight years ago?"

"No. I guess I don't."

"Neither do I." I'm getting mad. I shouldn't. If I could be rational for a moment, I should appreciate her interest in the state of the narcoleptic me. Very few people share this interest.

"How often do you fall asleep?"

"Depends on the day. Good days, I can make it through with one or two planned naps. Bad days, I'm falling in and out of sleep as often as some people change channels on their TV. And then bad days become bad nights."

"Is today a good day?"

"I don't have a lot of good days. I guess that makes me a pessimist. I'd care and try to change if I had the energy."

"You can't stop yourself from falling asleep?" Another statement question, one I know everyone thinks but doesn't have the guts to ask.

"Sometimes I can; if I recognize the feelings, I can try to change what I'm doing and fight it off. Coping strategies are hit-or-miss. Usually I'm so used to getting along with my gas tank needle hovering on empty that I don't realize I'm about to go out. And then I'm out. Caught in the little sleep."

"How do you feel right now?"

I say, "Tired. Tired of everything."

Jennifer puts down her fork and stands up slowly, as if afraid a sudden movement would spook me. I'm a frail bird she doesn't want to scare away. Or a cornered and wounded animal she's afraid might attack. She says, "Thanks again for meeting me here, Mr. Genevich. I'm sorry, but I really have to go now."

I make a move to stand up. She says, "Please, stay, finish your meal. It's all taken care of. I've already put it on my father's tab."

"He won't mind?"

"No. I do it all the time." She smiles. It's her first real smile of the evening. It's okay. I've seen worse. She edges away from the table, adjusts her jean jacket and her glasses, and leaves without looking back.

I finish my dinner. How do I feel right now? I feel like I missed something, something important. I always feel that way.

SIXTEEN

I should go straight home and try to find out what, if anything, happened to Brendan Sullivan. But I don't. I stay and take advantage of the tab. I drink three beers, a couple or three shots of whiskey, and two more coffees. At the bar, the townies are on one side and the trendies on the other, and both groups ignore me, use me as their barrier, their Thirty-eighth Parallel.

All right. It's time to go. I'm fine, and I'm taking half the shepherd's pie home with me. It'll make a good breakfast or midnight snack. There's no difference for me.

There's a cabstand down by the Red Line stop, but I'll try and flag a ride in front of the restaurant. It's dark, late, and raining: my perpetual state. I pull up my collar, but that only redirects wind and water into my face and inside my shirt.

I raise the hand that isn't holding a cigarette at a cab, but a black limo cuts it off and pulls into the Amrheins lot, angled, an angry cross-out on a piece of paper, black limo takes the square. Droplets of water on the windshield shine under the streetlamp, making little white holes. Maybe the whiskey shots were overkill.

A rear door opens and the DA thrusts his head out. "I can give you a ride home, Genevich. Jump in."

I know there's no such thing as a free ride, but I take the invite anyway. The door closes and I'm inside the limo with the DA. So are my two friends the goons. I'm not surprised, but it's crowded in here. There are no ashtrays.

I say, "Evening, boys. Have a safe trip up from the Cape?" I blow smoke, smoke and words.

Redhead says, "Hey, retard, remember me?" He's grinning like a manic comic-strip villain, all teeth and split face, flip-top head, a talking Pez dispenser. Ellen still stuffs my Christmas stockings with Pez dispensers, usually superheroes like Spider-Man and the Hulk.

I say, "I missed you most of all." The three of them wear matching blue suits, no wrinkles, and the creases are sharp, dangerous. "Hey, you guys gonna be catering somewhere later? Or maybe you're starting a band. I got a name for you: The Dickheads. Best of luck with that." My anger feels good.

The DA has his legs crossed and hands folded over his knees. If he was any more relaxed he'd be narcoleptic. He says, "I trust you had a nice dinner with Jennifer."

Like I told Jennifer, I'm tired of everything. I knew she was lying to me. There was no appointment she had to keep. Her dinner with the sideshow freak was a little job for Daddy. She set me up, put me on a platter. The only thing missing is an apple in my mouth.

All right. I'm through playing the nice guy, the clueless schmuck. I'm nobody's fall guy. I'm nobody's cliché. I say, "Nah, the food sucked and she talked too much. I'm glad she lost. The Limey judge was right about her."

The bald goon punches me in the stomach, one for flinching. It doesn't hurt. He says, "Watch your mouth."

"Need to work on that uppercut. Saw it coming from last block," I say. The cigarette hangs off my bottom lip and I'm not controlling it anymore. Whether it's sticking around during a tough time or getting ready to abandon ship, I don't know. "Don't get me wrong, DA. The free beer was great. It'll help me sleep tonight."

Redhead laughs. "We can help you with sleep." His eyes are popping out of his head, showing too much white. He's on something serious. I get the sense that if he throws me a punch, I'll break like a porcelain doll.

The DA furrows his brow. He's so concerned. He says, "You have an odd way of expressing appreciation, Genevich."

I'm not nervous. I'm still on my first ball and nowhere near tilting. I should be nervous, though. The momentum of the evening is not in my favor. Must be the beers and booze helping me out.

I say, "I'll thank you for the ride home if I get there. Unless you're expecting something more. Sorry, but I don't put out on a first date." The interior light is on in the limo but everything is still dark. I think we're headed toward West Broadway.

The DA says, "You should be expressing appreciation for my patience. It wouldn't take more than a phone call and a few computer keystrokes to have you locked up. Or worse." He uncrosses his legs and leans toward me, a spider uncurling itself and readying to sprint down the web.

The goons sitting across from me, they're in the heel position but twitching. Hackles up. Ready to go.

The DA is bluffing. He's all talk and no chalk. Otherwise his threatening little scenario would've already happened. Nothing is going to happen. They're going to drop me at my apartment with another tough-guy act and another warning. Warnings. I'm collecting them now like stamps, or butterflies.

Then again, that's not to say that the DA can't do what he said. It'd be suicide to assume otherwise. I'm going to try this out: "Sounds like you're putting me on double-secret probation. What would my dear old dad say about you harassing his son like this? It's not very Southie of you."

He squints, eyelids putting on a mighty squeeze. I got to him. Not sure how. Can't be just the memory of my father, can it? He says, through a mouthful of teeth, "Your dad isn't around anymore, is he? Hasn't been around for a long time, not sure if you're aware."

"I'm always aware." I sound stupid. He gives me threats and doom, and I give him a self-help life-affirmation aphorism.

He says, "And don't tell me what's Southie, Genevich. You have no idea."

I hold up my hands. The DA is getting too hot. No telling what his goons might do if he starts to smoke. I say, "If you say so. Still not sure why all the fuss here. I'm not in your way now, and I haven't done anything wrong. I'm clean, as in squeaky."

He smiles. "When has that ever mattered?" His regained polished tone and delivery is a gun pointed in my face. It holds that much potential for damage. I have no chance.

The bald goon says, "Let's hurt him."

I say, "Jeez, DA, do your constituents know that you run with this kind of crowd? I'm shocked and more than a little disappointed."

He doesn't go for it. He says, "What do you say you just give me the photos, Genevich. The negatives—and don't look surprised, I know there are negatives—and any copies you might've made, digital or otherwise. Give me everything, and that'll be the end of this and any further unpleasantries."

"Or what? You'll call my mommy again?" Things are happening too fast. I add, "You don't need the photos. I've said my mea culpas. They're not of Jennifer. I told her as much during dinner. She's out of the picture, so to speak. And she's fine with it. You should be too."

The DA and the goons laugh. Apparently I'm funny. He says, "The photos, Genevich. I want them. Now is not soon enough. We can take them by force if necessary. It wouldn't bother me. The funny part is we could hold your hand and take you home, sit on your couch, and just wait for you to fall asleep."

I say nothing. His last line robs me of both cool and machismo. Not that I have any.

The DA says, "Tell our driver to turn left onto D Street, and we'll all just enjoy the ride." Redhead follows through on the instructions.

Might as well lay it all out right here. "So how is our friend Brendan Sullivan these days?"

The goons laugh. I've said something incredibly smart or stupid. Likely both.

Baldy says, "He ain't doing too good right now."

Redhead says, "He did answer our questions though, poor guy."

The DA says, "You don't even know what you're saying half the time, do you, Genevich? I suggest you cut the tough-guy PI act, leave the big-boy stuff to us big boys, and give me the photos."

The limo slows and stops. I look out the tinted window and see a Burger King. We're at the D Street intersection. The D Street projects are on the other side of the street. The buildings look like gravestones.

Baldy slaps my face. I hang on to the cigarette but things go fuzzy. I might just go out now, but I pull it together.

"The patty-cake shit is getting old, goon." I fill my lungs with smoke and it stokes a fire in my chest. I exhale a smoke ring that haloes Baldy's head, and I say, "I buried the photos on Boston Common, under the roots of a sapling. The tree will sprout pictures instead of leaves. Harvest in the fall. Good luck with that."

Baldy tries to slap me again but I catch him by the wrist and stub out my cigarette on the back of his hand. He yells. I pull him into my knee, right in the balls, and then push him over, into Redhead. The DA does nothing. He barely looks interested.

I try the limo door, expecting it to be locked, but it opens and I spill out onto the wet pavement and the other lane. Just ahead is a double-parked and idling cab. It's white with some black checkers on the panels. No driver. He must be inside the fast-food joint taking a leak. I look over my shoulder. Redhead crawls out of the limo after me. A gun is in his hand, big as a smokestack.

There's isn't much time. I scuttle around the cab and jump into the driver's seat. The steering wheel is warm and too big.

There're too many places for my hands to go. They don't know what to do. The instruments in the dashboard are all in Japanese.

A bullet spiderwebs the rear passenger window. The glass bleeds and screams. Didn't think they'd shoot at me out in the open like this. Must be a mistake, but one that can't be reversed. A chain of events now set into motion until there's one conclusion: me with extra holes. I fumble for the automatic transmission shift. Goddamn it, it's on the steering wheel. It shouldn't be there. I pull on it but it doesn't move. I don't know its secret.

There are loud and fast footsteps on the pavement. Two footsteps become four and multiply rapidly until there's a whole city of footsteps running at me. Redhead appears at my window. He's yelling some crazy stuff, doesn't make any sense. Maybe he's reading the dashboard labels. The gun barrel snug against the glass doesn't have any problems communicating its message.

I'm pulling as hard as I can and the gearshift finally gives in to my demands, which weren't all that unreasonable. I drop the transmission into drive and squeal the wheels. I'm moving forward and I duck, down beneath the dash; there's another gunshot, this one sending glass snowflakes falling onto my head, and there's . . .

SEVENTEEN

"We're here."

I come to in the back of a cab. I'm still buzzed and my mouth tastes of vomit. I bolt upright like a rake getting stepped on. The

Johnny Rotten of headaches lurches and struts around my brain. God save my head.

The cab and me, we're at the corner of Dorchester and Broadway, idling in front of my office and apartment building. I want to go digging back under, into the brine, find me some real sleep, the kind that makes my body glad it's there to support me. But I won't find any in here, and I probably won't find any upstairs in my apartment.

"Don't be sleeping on me now," the cabbie says. His voice is full of *fuck you,* but he really cares about me. I can tell.

I'm awake now. I have no idea how much of the DA, the limo ride, and the goons happened. My left cheek, where Redhead slapped me, is sore and puffy. Maybe I did escape their limo and jump into this cab and then dreamed the rest. I don't know.

The cab's heat is on furnace blast. The muscles in my hands feel week. I open and close shaky fists. They're empty and tired, like me. The little sleep was and is too hard.

I pull a crumpled bill out of my pocket and throw it at the cabbie. It's not a good throw. "Keep the change." Don't know if it's enough, and don't care. Neither does he apparently.

I open a door, leave without a further exchange, and manage to land standing on the curb. The cab leaves. It was white and had black checkers on the panels. It's late. There aren't any black limos or red cars on the street. It's still dark and raining.

I need time to process the evening: what happened, what didn't happen, what any of it means. I have my keys out, but the front door to my office is open. The door is thick and heavy, probably as old as the brownstone building, and it sways in the wind and rain.

I step inside the front entryway. The stacks of local restaurant menus are all wet and turning to pulp under my feet. This isn't good. I walk into my office. I don't need to turn on a light to see that everything is all wrong, but I turn it on anyway. Never did like surprises.

Someone picked up my office and shook it around like Daddy needed a new pair of shoes and rolled snake eyes. And then the shaker took out his frustration with the undesired result on my fucking office.

Flat-screen computer monitor is not quite flat anymore and is on the floor, where my client chair used to be. That chair is huddled in the corner of the room, licking its wounds. It saw everything and is traumatized. It'll never be the same.

My file cabinet has been stripped of its contents. Its drawers are open, metal tongues saying ah, and the files spread out on the floor. My desk drawers are open and empty too. They didn't want to feel left out. I step on paper and walk over to my desk. My phone is gone. So is the hard drive and backup flash drive. I don't see my yellow notepad, the one with the narcoleptic me notes. It could be buried in here somewhere, but I doubt it. Good goddamn mercy. And Christ, the negatives, they're not in the empty drawers.

I leave the office and walk upstairs in the dark. It occurs to me that the ransackers could still be here, maybe in my apartment, waiting for me, the ransackee, to come home. I don't care. I have no weapons and I'm no brawler, but if there really are goons and they're upstairs, I'll hit as hard as I can give. And then hit them harder.

My apartment got the same treatment. Door is open. This entry was rougher. The door is splintered by the knob and hangs by one hinge. I knock it off its last thread, put it out of its misery. I turn on the lights. I'm alone, I can tell. The TV is gone and so is my laptop. CD towers, bookcases, pictures, lamps, and everything else flipped, kicked, or stomped over. Into the kitchen, and all those drawers are turned out on the floor. The dish didn't run away with the spoon.

I can't face the crime scene waiting for me in the bedroom, so I stumble back to the living room and my couch. I brush off the debris of my life and sit. Cigarette comes out next. Guess I can just use the floor for an ashtray.

I still have the pictures in my coat. I still have my cell phone. I'm going to make one personal call before letting the police know about the sledgehammer tap dance through my building.

I call Jennifer's number. Yeah, I still have that too. She doesn't answer. I wasn't expecting her to. I get her voice mail.

I say, "Hey, thanks for the setup tonight, Jennifer. I hope your dad and his boys had a great time tearing through my place. I knew that was the only reason why you'd eat dinner with me. Tell those guys sorry I didn't have anything good in the fridge for them, and that they had to leave empty-handed."

My voice sounds drunker than I thought. I'm crying too. Practically in full blubber mode, but there's no stopping my message from a bottle.

"So, yeah, I know you were lying to me the whole night. That's okay, because I lied to you too. I said I didn't remember what I felt like before my accident, before I became the narcoleptic me. I remember what it felt like. I was awake, always awake. I didn't miss anything. I could read books for more than a few pages at a time. I didn't smoke. I watched movies from start to finish in real goddamn theaters. Wouldn't even leave my seat to go to the bathroom. I stayed up late on purpose. Woke up and went to sleep when I wanted. Sleep was my pet, something I controlled, scheduled, took for walks. Sit up, roll over, lie down, stay down, give me your fucking paw. Not now. Now there's only me and everything else is on the periphery, just slightly out of reach or out of touch or out of time. I don't have a real career or a real life. Ellen supports me and I sleepwalk through the rest. I'm telling you this because I want you to know who you set up tonight. And there's more. Not done. Not yet. I remember what it was like to have a regular face, one that folks just glanced at and forgot. There's more. I remember everything I lost. That's what I remember. The loss and loss and loss. . . ."

I stop talking. Too much self-pity, even for me. I'm sure her voice mail stopped recording a long time ago. Who knows how much she got? Who knows what I actually said out loud?

I slouch onto the arm of the couch, cell phone balanced on my head. I'm listening to the digitized silence and it brings an odd comfort. My cigarette slips out of my hand. Hopefully it'll land on something that doesn't take fire personally.

The sleep is coming. I feel it. At least this time, I want it.

EIGHTEEN

The sun shines bright, just like the ones on cereal boxes. Tim and I are in our backyard in Osterville. He's putting tools back in the shed, then emerges with a hand trowel. It's the specialized hand trowel. He locks the shed. I'm still too young to go inside.

I wait by the door and receive my brown paper bag and the pat on my head. Good boy. It's time to clean up the yard again. The grass is green but there's more shit than usual to clean up.

The sky is such a light shade of blue, it looks thin, like it could tear at the slightest scratch. I don't feel like singing for Tim today, but I will. I'm a trouper. I give him a round of "Take Me Out to the Ball Game." My bag gets heavy with deposits. He names the dogs. We've all been here before.

We fill three bags' worth of crap and dump it all in the woods behind our property. Each time he dumps the bag, Tim says, "Don't come back."

We walk back to the shed and Tim opens the doors. He says, "So, kid, whaddaya think?"

I twist my foot in the grass and look down. The five-year-old me has something uncomfortable to say. "That friend of yours, Billy Times, he's been a real douche bag to me, Tim."

Tim laughs, bends to one knee, and chucks my chin with his fist. Aw shucks, Dad.

He says, "He's not all bad." He gets up and locks the shed doors. Tim picks me up and puts me on his shoulders. I'm closer to the cereal-box sun and the paper-thin sky now, close enough to destroy everything if I wanted to.

NINETEEN

The South Boston Police know of me like the residents of Sesame Street know of Aloysius Snuffleupagus. They know my name and they tell exaggerated stories of my woe and comic-tragic circumstance, but only some big yellow dope believes I'm real. And I am real.

It's about 11 a.m. The morning after. Two officers, one female and one male, cop A and cop B, walk around my apartment and office. They take notes. They're dressed in their spotless blue uniforms, hats, guns, cuffs, shiny badges, the works.

I wear a hangover. It's three sizes too big. I'd take it back if I could, but it matches my rusty joints and blindingly sore muscles so well.

Okay, I'm still in my own rumpled slept-in-again uniform: work clothes doubling as a lounge-about bathrobe. Everyone should be so lucky.

I sit on home base, the couch, a coffee cup in one hand, a lit cigarette in the other. There's sunlight coming through the naked windows, trapping dust in the rays. I watch the pieces of my apartment floating there in the light. I can't float. I have to squint. I can't squint and think at the same time.

Think, Genevich. First, I decide that yesterday really was only one day. My aching and quivering muscles are proof of my yellow-brick-road jaunt to Sullivan's house. No idea who the body was or, if I'm willing to be completely honest with myself today, if there even was a body. No computer or laptop means, for now, no way to find out what happened. I could call Sullivan's number, but I'm not ready to call yet. I think I can be patient. Play it a little slow, given the current set of circumstances, which is my already broken world breaking at my feet.

Cop A asks for my written statement. I give it to her. It has some stray ashes on it but no burn holes. I grope for the little victories. I told them what's missing and now they have it in writing too. They didn't ask if I thought the break-in was related to one of my cases, which is fine, because I haven't decided how I would answer that question.

More from yesterday's log: The shepherd's-pie doggie bag is on the floor, in front of my bedroom door. It's safe there. My cell phone has my dialed numbers and incoming call history. Proof of my chats with Jennifer right there on the glowing LCD screen, including my late-night soliloquy. She hasn't called back. I don't expect her to.

The police haven't been very chatty or sympathetic. They didn't like that my distress call occurred more than ten hours after the actual break-in. And I think they believed the puke next to the couch and puddle of urine in the corner of the kitchen was somehow my fault. I told them it wasn't. Cop B said I smelled drunk. I said I was drunk, but the puke and piss weren't mine.

The cops leave, finally. My cigarette is dead. I'm left with a trashed office and apartment and more than a few choice items stolen. None of this is circumstantial or coincidence. The DA has a good reason to want those pictures, something more than their chance resemblance to his daughter.

Right about now I'm starting to feel a boulder of guilt roll up onto my shoulders when thinking about Sullivan and his possible or likely fate. Sullivan asked me in a panic if I had shown anyone the pictures yet without finding *it*. I did show them, and I certainly don't have *it*. I took the photos to the DA and then everything that was yesterday happened. I'm that portable Kraken again. Point me in a direction and I unleash my destruction.

"Jesus H. Christ, what happened? Mark, are you in here?"

Ellen. I haven't called her yet. Her voice is on a three-alarm pitch and frequency. It rockets up the stairwell and into my apartment. My hangover appreciates the nuances in its swells of volume.

I shout, "I'm okay and I'm up here, Ellen." I shouldn't be talking, never mind yelling.

Ellen pounds up the stairs, repeating her What-happeneds and sprinkling in some Are-you-all-rights. Maybe I should go into the kitchen and cover the urine puddle with something, but I don't think I can get up.

Ellen stands in the doorway. Her mouth is open as wide as her eyes.

I say, "I know. Friggin' unbelievable mess, isn't it?"

"My God, Mark, what happened? Why the hell didn't you call me?" She looks and sounds hurt. It's not a look I see on her often. I don't like it. It turns that maybe boulder of guilt for Sullivan into the real deal.

I still can't tell her the truth about the case, though. Telling her anything might infect her, put her in more danger than she already is just for being around me. I'm her dark cloud. I'm her walk under a ladder and her broken mirror all in one.

I say, "I went out last night, treated myself to a meal and a few drinks at Amrheins, and found the place like this when I came home. I was a little tipsy and fell asleep on the couch before I could call you or the police. For what it's worth, the police weren't too happy that I didn't call them earlier either."

"You should've called as soon as you woke up." She stands in the doorway with her arms folded across her chest.

"I'm sorry, Ellen. Really, I am." This is getting to be a little too much for me. The edges are blurring again. I put my head in my hands and let slip: "I don't know what I'm going to do."

She says, "About what? Are you in some kind of trouble?" She hikes over the rubble of my existence. There's no path and she has to climb. She makes it, though, sits next to me on the couch, and puts an arm around my shoulder.

I breathe loudly. She waits for me to stop. I say, "No, I'm fine. You know, just how am I going to clean up and get everything going again?"

She says, "We have insurance. I'll get an adjuster here within the hour. We'll get everything fixed up."

We let silence do its thing for a bit. Then I tell her what was stolen. She pulls out a cigarette for both of us. Time passes, whether I want it to or not.

Ellen gets up and says, "I'll call the insurance company, and I'll get somebody to clean this up. You go pack a bag while I make a few phone calls."

I say, "Bag? I'm not going anywhere."

Ellen knows I don't mean it. She says, "You'll stay with me while the place is fixed up. Just a couple of days, right?"

Living at home again for a couple of days. Yeah, Ellen owns this building but it's still my apartment, my place. I promised myself after the accident I'd never live in Osterville, not for day one, because Thomas Wolfe had the whole you-can't-go-home-again thing right.

"Nah, I can stay in a hotel or something."

"Don't be ridiculous, Mark."

I want to say: Look at this place. Look at me. I am ridiculous.

I say, "Couple of days. Okay. Thanks, Ellen. I owe you."

Ellen shakes her head and says, "You don't owe me anything." Her voice is real quiet, not a whisper, but the words have lost all conviction and they are empty.

I get up real slow, then groan and grumble my way to the kitchen. Ellen already has someone on her cell phone. She's a hummingbird of chatter.

Now that I'm up and semimoving, I realize a trip back to the Cape won't be all bad. Not at all. A couple of days out of Southie might turn down the heat. Maybe I can make another trip to the Sullivan house via the Osterville library. Maybe I'll be safer down there too. Regardless of the maybe goons sighting I had down there, at least I'll be out of the DA's jurisdiction.

Instead of packing a bag, I try to be real quiet while filling the sink with hot water and prying the mop out from under my banana tree, spice rack, and wooden cutlery block. Discreet and mopping up piss generally aren't partners, but I give it my best shot. The job doesn't take long. The puke can be someone else's gig.

Ellen is still on the phone. I go into my bedroom and pack the proverbial bag. When I come out of the room, she's off the phone. I say, "Who were you calling?"

She tells me. Ellen has already rallied the local restaurateurs and some fellow members of the Lithuania Club to set up a nightly neighborhood watch, just like that. Her buddy Sean is going to print T-shirts and window stickers.

I tell her I feel safer already.

She says, "I just have to run to the bank and check in with Millie before we go south, okay?"

I hold out a be-my-guest hand and say, "That's fine. No rush." I'm so magnanimous.

Ellen studies me. I'm the lesson that never gets learned. She says, "Who do you think did this?"

"Terrorists." I adjust the duffel bag on my shoulder, but it's for show. There isn't much in it.

She lights another cigarette but doesn't offer me one. That means I'm in trouble. She says, "When I first came in here I assumed it was local punks. Vandalism and grab-the-new-TV-and-computer type of thing. I know it happens all the time. There was a break-in like this a couple of weeks ago on Gold Street, remember?"

I say, "Yeah," even though I don't.

Ellen walks toward the apartment door but doesn't take her eyes off me.

I say, "I told the police I thought it was vandals."

She says, "Did you?"

"Yeah, Ellen. I did."

She taps the broken front door gently with her foot. The door doesn't move. It's dead. "Is there anything going on that I need to know about, Mark?"

"I got absolutely nothing for you, Ellen." I say it with conviction.

TWENTY

Ellen has been in my apartment twice a week every week for the past eight years, but I don't remember the last time I set foot in the old family bungalow. Was it at Christmas two years ago maybe? No, she had me down for a cookout last summer, I think. I helped her set up her new grill. Isn't that right?

Doesn't matter, the place is the same. It's stuck in time, like me.

There're only five rooms: living room, dining room, kitchen, and two bedrooms with a shared bathroom. There isn't a lot of furniture, and none of it is permanent. Everything is an antique that's in rotation with other unsold antiques from Ellen's store. The rotation usually lasts about six months. Right now, in the dining room there's a waist-high hutch and a wooden table with only two chairs, both pushed in tight, afraid to lose track of the table. A rocking chair sits in the living room with a white wicker couch, its cushion faded and flat. Everything is too hard to sit on, nothing just right.

The most notable aspect of chez Genevich is the army of old black-and-white photos that cover the walls and sit on the hutch and the windowsills and almost anything above the floor with a flat, stable surface. There are photos of buildings in Southie and landscapes from Osterville. There are photos of obscure relatives and friends, or relatives and friends who've become obscure. Those are photos that belonged to Ellen's mother or that Ellen took herself, and mixed in—and likely more than half now—are photos of complete strangers. Ellen continually adds to her photo collection by snatching up random black-and-whites from yard sales and antiques shops.

Whenever I'm here, Ellen gives me a tour of the photos, telling me all their names, or stories if they have no names, and if no stories then where she bought them. I don't remember any of it.

None of the pictures are labeled. I don't know how she remembers who are our relatives and who are the strangers. Everyone has similar mustaches or hairstyles and they wear the same hats and jackets, T-shirts and skirts. Maybe Ellen forgets everyone and just makes up the stories on the spot, giving them all new secret histories.

I think she moves and switches the pictures around too, just like the rotating furniture. I think the picture of my apartment building was in the kitchen the last time I was here. Now it's in the living room.

Me? I'm in the kitchen. So is Ellen. It's late but not late enough.

I smoke. She sits and thinks. We drink tea, and we're surrounded by those old photos and old faces, everyone anonymous to me, everyone probably dead, maybe like Brendan Sullivan.

Ellen stirs her tea with a finger. She's quite the charming hostess. She says, "Feeling okay?"

"I'm peachy." I'm not peachy. I'm not feeling any fruit in particular. The narcoleptic me is taking over more often. The symptoms are getting worse. Dr. Heal-Thyself thinks it's the case and the face-to-faces with the Times clan, the stress of confrontation, that's setting me off. Before the photos landed on my desk like some terrorizing band of Cossacks, I had a hypnogogic hallucination maybe once a month. Now it's daily. I can't go on like this much longer. I need a vacation from the case I don't have.

Ellen adds more honey to her tea and stirs counterclockwise, as if she could reset the tea to its beginning. She licks her finger, and it sounds downright messy.

"Ever hear of a spoon, Ellen? Newest gadget going. Not too expensive, user-friendly too." I shoot smoke at her.

She wipes her hand on a napkin and says, "You don't sound peachy. You seem a little extra frazzled."

"Other than my home and office being put in a blender and set to puree, I'm just fine."

I'm growing more desperate. I'm actually contemplating telling Ellen everything. I'll tell her to avoid the DA and large men with cell phones in their ears. Maybe she could inspect my photos. She's the expert. She'd be able to tease and wiggle something out of the pictures, something I'm not seeing, or at least tell me when the photos were shot, how old they are.

She gets up from the kitchen table. Her chair's legs argue with the hardwood floors. "There's a picture I want to show you."

"Anyone who had the under on five-minutes-before-the-picture-tour is a winner," I say.

"Don't be a jerk. Come on. It's in the living room."

We walk through the dining room, past the collection of little bits of history, someone else's lost moments. All those forgotten eyes are staring at me, a houseful of Mona Lisas giving me the eye. Christ, I'm a mess. I need some sleep. Some real sleep.

Living room. We walk to one of the front windows. She plucks a photo from the windowsill. She says, "It's the only one I could find with both of them in it," and hands it to me.

Three preteen kids sit on the front stoop of an apartment building, presumably from the Harbor Point projects. It's summer in Southie. The boys have buzz cuts and gaps in their smiles and skinned knees. They all wear white socks and dark-colored sneakers, shoelaces with floppy loops.

The kid in the middle is the biggest, and he has his arms wrapped roughly around the necks of the other two boys. The kid on the right has his head craned away, trying to break out of the hug turned headlock. The kid on the left has his rabbit ears out but didn't get his hand up over his friend quick enough. The one trying to break away is my father, Tim.

I say, "I've probably seen this a hundred times but never really looked at it. That's Tim there, right?"

"That's him. He was a cutie." Ellen is talking about Tim. A Halley's Comet rare occurrence. "You looked just like him when you were a kid."

That's not true. I looked more like Ellen. Now I look like nobody.

Tim has dark brown hair, almost black. The other two kids have much lighter whiffle stubble and skin. I say, "So that's DA Times in the middle, right?"

"Yup."

Smack in the middle. The ringleader. The hierarchy of neighborhood authority is clear. The other two boys might as well have deputy badges on their T-shirts. Even back then he had his two goons.

The Tim in the picture, the kid so obviously owned by Times, does not jibe with the Tim of my dreams. Tim is a large, confident man in my dreams who can take care of himself and everyone else, especially the kid me, maybe even the narcoleptic me.

I'm embarrassed for this Tim. This is like seeing him with his pants down. This is like finding him sitting and crying in a room by himself. I don't want any part of this Tim, the Tim that DA Times obviously still remembers, given his strong-arm tactics with me.

I say, "Who's the third kid?"

Ellen says, "Brendan Sullivan. For a while there, those boys were never apart. They were practically brothers."

My stomach fills with mutant-sized butterflies. Their wings cut and slash my stomach. Neurons and synapses sputter and fire, and I can actually feel the electricity my body generates amping too high, pumping out too much wattage too soon, and the circuit breaker flips, shutting me off and down. Not a blackout, though. This is worse. I'll be awake and I'll know what's going on. This is cataplexy. I crumble toward the floor, my head pitching forward and into Ellen's legs. She falls back into the window and sits on the sill, knocking pictures to the floor. I'm going to join them. Nothing works except my thoughts. I can't move or speak. My bulk slides down her legs and I land facedown, my nose pinned against the frame of a picture.

Ellen isn't panicking; she's seen this before. She says, "Are you all right, Mark?" repeatedly, a mantra, something to help her through my attack.

I'm not all right. I'm paralyzed. Maybe this time I won't recover. I'll be stuck like this forever, lying in Ellen's bungalow, facedown, on a photo.

She lifts my head and shoulders off the ground. One of the pictures below my face is of an old guy in a bait-and-tackle shop. I have no idea who it is or if I'm supposed to know. He's likely someone she picked up antiquing. He's been collected by Ellen. He wears a dark-colored winter hat, a turtleneck stretched tight across his chest, suspenders, and hip waders. Maybe he's going clamming, or he already went. He's looking at the camera, looking at me, and holding up something, some bit of unidentifiable fishing gear. It's pointed toward his temple, and from my prone vantage point it looks like a gun. The other picture is the one of my father, DA Times, and Brendan Sullivan, and I can't look at it without new, cresting waves of panic crashing. I'm in big trouble.

Ellen kicks the pictures away and rolls me onto my back. She feels my cheeks and snaps her fingers in front of my eyes. I see them and hear them, but I can't do anything about them.

All I can do is lie here until the circuits cool and I reboot. Thinking about Tackle Man might help. Why not? He's a ghost, and he can't hurt me or Ellen.

Tim Genevich or Billy Times or Brendan Sullivan, on the other hand? They can hurt us, and they are here now, in the bungalow and in my case.

TWENTY-ONE

Recovery. I'm sitting in the rocking chair, holding the same cup of tea I left in the kitchen. It's warm. Maybe Ellen stirred mine counterclockwise. I hope she used a spoon.

I say, "Can I see that picture of Tim again?" My voice is a cicada's first call after its seventeen-year slumber. After cicadas wake up, they live for only a day or two and then are usually eaten by something.

Ellen sits on the wicker couch with the picture pressed into her lap, protecting it from disaster. She can't protect them. She nods and hands it to me.

I get another good look at the three friends. Tim is part of the case. He has to be. He's why Sullivan sent me the pictures. Times is why Sullivan didn't want me to show the pictures to anyone without finding the *it* first, and yeah, I screwed up that part, just a wee bit. I owe it to Sullivan to see this thing through to the bitter end, probably my own bitter end. I'm going to keep swinging, keep fighting those windmills.

I say, "When did you meet Tim?" I wiggle my toes as a reassurance. For the moment, I'm back behind the controls.

Ellen and I are going to chat about Tim and the boys tonight. We never talk about Tim. He's never been the elephant in our room. He's always been bigger.

Ellen smiles. The smile is lost and far away, lips unsure of their positions. She says, "When he was twelve. Tim and his friends hung around Kelleys on Castle Island, bugging me for free ice cream. I only gave it to Tim. He wasn't as obnoxious as the other two, which wasn't saying much. The three of them were such pains in the ass back then. Hard to believe Billy became a DA."

"Can't disagree with you there." I look at the picture and focus on the Brendan Sullivan kid. Never mind Tackle Man, here's the real ghost—or, at least, the latest model. "These guys all lived in Harbor Point together, right?"

"That's right." Ellen isn't looking at me. Her arms are wound tightly around her chest, a life jacket of arms. I'm interviewing a hostile witness.

I say, "That was a rough neighborhood, right?"

"Roughest in Southie. It's where Whitey Bulger and his boys got their start."

Whitey Bulger. Not crazy about hearing Boston's most notorious—and still on the lam—gangster name getting dropped. I'm not crazy about any of this. Especially since the early-to-mid-seventies time line for Bulger's rise coincides with Tim's teen days. I say, "Did Tim know Whitey at all?"

"Everyone knew of Whitey back then, but no, Tim never talked or bragged about knowing him. Billy, though, he would talk big to all us neighborhood kids, stuff about him helping out and doing little jobs for Bulger. Tim always told me he just liked to talk. He probably hasn't changed a bit," Ellen says, and laughs, but the laugh is sad. It has pity for everyone in it, including herself. She sits on the edge of the couch. She might fall off. She wants the picture back. She's afraid of what I might do to it.

I say, "Was Times really all talk? He wasn't connected at all to Bulger? You know that for sure?"

To her credit, Ellen thinks about it. She doesn't give me the quick, pat answer. "Yes, I'm sure," she says. "There's no way he messed around with Bulger. Tim would've told me. What, you think Billy Times is dirty?" Ellen scowls at me, the idea apparently less believable to her than the shooter on the grassy knoll.

"No. I don't think anything like that."

Whitey Bulger took over the Winter Hill Gang in the mid-to-late seventies. He was smart. He didn't sell the drugs or make the loans or bankroll the bookies. He charged the local urban entrepreneurial types a Bulger fee to stay in business. He later took advantage of FBI protection and contacts to get away with everything, including murder, for decades. The Whitey Bulger name still echoes in South Boston. He's our bogeyman, which means we all know his stories.

This isn't going where I wanted it to. This isn't about Bulger. Ellen still isn't giving me any real information about Tim and his friends.

Then this question bubbles up out of nowhere. I don't like it. The answer might hurt. I say, "Wait a minute. Was this picture taken before you met Tim?"

"Oh, yeah. The boys are like nine or ten, maybe eleven. This is actually the first picture your father ever took. He used a tripod, a timer, and the whole bit. Then his uncle taught him how to develop it."

"Wait, wait, wait." This story is wrong. Ellen is the one with the uncle who taught her to develop pictures, not Tim. I rub my face. My beard resists my fingers. It has grown a year's worth in a matter of days. I feel the house of pictures around me, ready to fall. "You've always told me that you took these pictures, except for the antique buys." I manage a weak gesture at the legion of black-and-white photos that surround us.

There's this look I get all the time from other people, people who don't know me and haven't come close to earning the goddamn right to give me that look. The look is why I stopped talking to Juan-Miguel or any of my old roommates, even when they tried to keep in contact with me.

Ellen has never given me that look, even when seeing or finding me at my worst, but she's giving me that look now. Eyebrows pull down hard like they're planning on taking over her eyelids. Her mouth opens, lip curls. The goddamn look:

concern trying to mask or hide scorn. Mashed potatoes spread over the lima beans. You can't hide scorn. Ellen looks at me like I'm wrong, like I'm broken. And nothing will ever be the same.

She says, "You're pulling my leg, right, Mark? Tim took those pictures—"

I jump in, a cannonball dive that'll get everyone wet. "It has been a long day, a long week, a long year, a long goddamn lifetime. I'm not pulling your leg."

She says, "I know, I know. But—"

"What do you mean, Tim took most of these? Tim didn't take pictures. He was a handyman, an odd-job guy, not a photographer. That's you. It's your job. You're the shutterbug. And goddamn it, stop fucking looking at me like that."

It's her turn to put her face in her hands, maybe try to wipe that look off her face. She must feel it. I do. She backs off. "Calm down, Mark, you're just a little confused. Tim was the photographer first, remember? When he died, I took his equipment and started my business. You know all this, Mark, don't you?"

"No. I don't know all this. You assume I know everything about Tim when you never talk about him. You tell me more about these photographs than you do about my father. That's all he is to me, an image. There's nothing there, and it's your fault for not telling me. You've never talked about Tim. Never." It all comes out and it's a mess, just like me. I know it's not fair. It's more likely that me and my broken brain have jumbled everything around, putting the bits and pieces of the past into the wrong but convenient boxes, but I'm not giving in.

I say, "This is not my fault. I did not fuck up my father's past. No one has told me anything. This is not something you can pin on me. No one told me any of this. No one. Not you." Even if it isn't true, repeat the lie enough times and it becomes true.

Ellen holds steady, battens down the hatches, and makes it through my storm. She says, "Okay, okay. I'm sorry. I just assumed you know everything about Tim. You're right, I haven't told you enough about him." She stops short, brakes squealing and coffee spilling. She doesn't believe her own words. We're both liars, trying to get our stories straight.

She lights two cigarettes and gives me one. We're tired and old. She says, "So ask away. What do you want to know?"

"Let's start with telling me about him and you and photography."

She tells me. Despite having no money and living in a project, Tim had a surprising amount of photo and film equipment. Yeah, he might've stolen some of it, but most of it came from locals who swapped their old projectors and cameras for Tim's odd jobs, and he'd scour flea markets and moving sales. He would sell pictures to locals and store owners, not charging much, just enough to buy more film, always black-and-white because it was cheaper, and Tim always insisted it looked nicer. Their first kiss happened in a makeshift darkroom. She only got into photography after they were married. She still has all of Tim's equipment and displays it in her shop. She talked through both of our cigarettes.

I say, "Let's look at more of Tim's pictures." I stand up and my legs are foal-unsteady. I'm learning to walk again.

We go on yet another tour of the pictures, but with a different road map and guide this time. We're walking through Tim's history, which has always been a secret. Ellen starts the tour subdued but gains enthusiasm as we progress. We are progressing. She shows me an aunt who lost a foot and three fingers to diabetes. There's Tackle Man again; he was a great-uncle of Tim's, a fisherman who died at sea. Almost everyone I meet is dead, but they have names.

Ellen keeps going, but I stop and hover at Great-uncle Tackle Man's photo. There's something else there. Three letters: LIT, in the photo's background, written on a small square of paper taped to the glass counter. I've seen those letters before, I think, in another photo, written on the spine of a book.

I'm still holding the photo of Tim and the gang. They're all still there, on the stairs, waiting for me patiently. I look and I look and I look, and there, on the stairs, under Tim's string-skinny legs, written in chalk, the letters are two or three inches high. LIT. I want to open the frame and run my fingers over the scene, feel the chalk.

Ellen stops in the hallway just ahead of me and walks back. "What's up, Mark?"

Trying to remain calm is difficult when my heart is an exploding grenade in my chest. I say, "Just noticing the letters LIT in these two pictures." I should've noticed them earlier. It's a scratch on a new car. It's the mole on somebody's face.

Ellen laughs and says, "That's Tim's signature. He'd hide the letters LIT, for Lithuania, somewhere in the background of almost all his pictures. Your father was never subtle."

I smile. I'm going to check all the pictures, every picture in the house, maybe every picture in Osterville, before I recheck the photos that are burning inside their manila envelope.

I pick up the next picture. It's a shot of a tall-grass meadow with one tree set back, not quite center in framing. I don't see the letters anywhere. I'm frantic looking for them. Maybe in the bark of the tree but the tree is too far away. Time as distance.

Ellen says, "Tim didn't take that one. I bought this last summer. I like how the tree isn't quite centered. Initially it has an amateur look to it, but I think the photographer did it on purpose. Gives it an eccentric feel. I like it."

"Why do you buy these antique pictures, Ellen?"

She doesn't answer right away. She pulls out her lighter but only flips it open and then closed. There's no fire. Ellen isn't comfortable because I'm asking her to be vulnerable.

She gives me time to make up her answer. Either she can't bring herself to throw away or pack up Tim's pictures so she mixes them in with antiques, hiding Tim's work in plain sight, distance by numbers instead of time; or she's pretending that Tim is still around, taking photos, the new ones she buys continuing their silent, unspoken conversation.

Ellen shrugs. "It's hard to explain. It's just a hobby, I guess. I like the way the black-and-white photos look. Aren't most hobbies hard to explain? Can a stamp collector tell you why she collects stamps?"

I say, "I don't know any stamp collectors."

It's all I can do to keep myself from pulling out the manila envelope in front of Ellen, ripping it open, and checking the photos for Tim's signature. I can't do that. I'll have to wait until she goes to bed. The less she knows, the better off she'll be. This case is getting too dangerous; or, to be more accurate, it already was dangerous and I didn't know any better.

Still, my hands vibrate with want. So instead, I snatch the lighter out of her fist and light up a cigarette. The smoke isn't black or white, but gray.

TWENTY-TWO

I'm in my bedroom, sitting at the edge of my bed, manila envelope on the bedspread. The door is shut. Ellen is watching TV. I'd check my closet for monsters, but I'm afraid I'd find one.

I open the envelope. No more monster talk. Now I'm thinking about letters, the molecules of sentences and songs, the bricks of words. Letters, man, letters. They might mean everything or nothing at all.

Letters are everywhere: the DA's waiting room with stacks of magazines and newspapers; the Osterville library, filled with dusty volumes that haven't been read in generations; Southie with its bill-boards and their screaming ten-feet-tall words; with stenciled script and cursive etchings on pub windows and convenience-store signage; on the unending stream of bills and circulars filling my PO box, and the computer and the Internet and all those sites and search engines and databases and spam e-mails; television; lost pet signs; the tags on my clothing; my yellow notepad that ran away from home.

How many letters are in the whole bungalow, or the town, or the state, or the country? An infinite sum of letters forming words in every language. Someone at one time or another wrote all those letters but, unlike their bodies, their armies of letters live on, like swarms of locusts bearing long-dead messages of happiness or doom or silliness. And hell, I've only been thinking about print letters. How many letters do I speak in a day, then multiply that by a lifetime of days, then by billions of lifetimes, and add that to our written-letter count and we're drowning in an uncountable number. We're the billions of monkeys typing at the billions of typewriters.

Okay. I'm stalling when I don't have time to stall. Let's cut the infinite number down to three. I'm afraid of three letters. LIT. I'm afraid I'll see them and afraid that I won't.

First up, the topless photo. I need to reacquaint myself. I haven't looked at the pictures in days, but with all the little sleeps between viewings it feels like months. The woman looks less like Jennifer Times. The photo is now clearly over thirty-five years old. Perspective makes detective work easy. It's a hard-earned perspective.

I look. I don't find any letters. The camera is angled up, shot from a vantage point slightly below the subject. There isn't much background to the photo. Ceiling, empty wall, tips of bedposts, the top of the bookcase. The white light above the woman washes out everything that isn't the woman. I keep looking, keep staring into the light.

When I come to, I'm horizontal on the bed, legs hanging off like loose thread on clothing. The photos are on the floor. I go to the floor, crawl on my hands and knees. Maybe I should check for monsters under my bed, but I'm afraid I'd find one. I'm starting this all over again.

I pick up the fully clothed photo. She's wearing her white T-shirt and skirt. The camera angle is played straight. No ceiling light. There is nothing on the walls behind her, nothing on the bed. There's the bookcase in the left background. It holds books like a good bookcase should.

LIT is there, written on that book, across the bottom of its spine. Tim's signature. Tim's photograph.

The bungalow is quiet, the TV dead. Ellen must be asleep. I don't have a clock in my room. There are no pictures on the walls, only small shelves with assorted knickknacks. I put both photos back in the envelope and go to bed. I shut the light off but I probably won't be able to sleep. There's no one to tuck me in, and there are too many monsters in this room.

TWENTY-THREE

It's morning, I think. The sun is out. Good for the sun. I'm walking down the hallway, the corridor of photos, Tim's memories, everything adding up to a story with some twist ending.

I can't stay here today or for the days after. I have to get out soon, back to Southie. Despite everything I learned last night, agreeing to stay here for the rest of the week is a mistake. I'd rather sleep on the rubble of my life back in Southie than spend another night here. At least then I can be a failure in my own home. And I am going to solve this case if for nothing more than to prove to myself that I can do something, something real, something that has effects, repercussions, something to leave a mark. Mark Genevich was here.

Ellen is in the kitchen sitting with what looks like a week's worth of local newspapers spread out on the table, splashy circulars all mixed in with the black-and-white text. She cradles one steaming coffee mug in her hands, and there're two more full mugs on the counter. I hope one of them is mine.

There's sunlight everywhere in the kitchen, and not enough shadow. Ellen doesn't look up. "You're not going to believe this."

I say, "Someone is having a sale on clown pants." The coffee is scalding hot, as if it knew exactly when I would be awake. That makes one of us.

Ellen throws a bit of folded-up newspaper at me. I don't catch it and it bounces off my chest.

"Hey! Watch the coffee, crazy lady." The microwave's digital clock has green digits that flash the wrong time. Ellen never sets the thing. Told you she was crazy.

She says, "I was just catching up, reading yesterday's newspaper, and found that."

I pick up the front page of the local rag. Headline: osterville man commits suicide. Included is a head shot, and the article identifies the man as Brendan Sullivan, age fifty. I don't see that twelve-year-old I was introduced to last night inside the head shot. This Brendan Sullivan is bald, has jowls a Saint Bernard would envy, and thick glasses, thicker than Ellen's. Apparently, he put a handgun under his chin and pulled the trigger. He leaves behind his wife, Janice; no children. He was an upstanding citizen. Neighbors said he kept to himself, drove tractor trailers, and did a little gardening. Sad story. One that's impossible to believe.

I wish I had a shocked reaction at the ready for Ellen, something I kept like a pet and could let out on command. Instead, I give my honest reaction, a big sigh of relief. Yeah, my buffoonery in the DA's office probably killed this man, but now I have confirmation that Sullivan was the body I saw. And what I saw was what I saw, not a hallucination. That counts for something, right?

I say, "Isn't that odd." I've never been very smooth.

Ellen puts down the rest of her newspaper, the afterthought folded and stacked neatly. This might be her moment of epiphany, bells ringing and seraphim floating in her head. Ellen knows there's something going on. She might even think I know more than I know. I'll have to get her on her heels, put some questions out there, keep her from grilling me like a hot dog. I'd crack in record time under her interrogation lamp.

I say, "Did you know that Sullivan was living in Osterville?"

Ellen blinks, loses her train of thought, at least for the moment, and says, "What? No, no. I had no idea. The article says he'd bounced around the Cape, but I never ran into him."

"Strange."

"It gets stranger. I called Aunt Millie to tell her about poor Brendan, and she told me she saw him in Southie last week."

I squeeze the coffee mug and it doesn't squeeze back. "No kidding. Where?"

"She saw him in CVS on West Broadway. She said, 'Hi, Brendan,' and he just said a quick 'Hi' back, but he was in a hurry, left the store, and headed out into that terrible rain last week, remember? She said he started off toward East Broadway."

He was walking toward my office. He was coming to meet me but got the narcoleptic me instead. The narcoleptic me accepted his pictures and wrote down notes on a yellow pad but didn't forward any other pertinent information, especially the promise to not show anyone the photos until I'd found *it*.

I make some toast. Ellen has an old two-slice toaster that burns the sides unevenly. The bell rings and the bread smokes. In the fridge is margarine instead of butter. I hate margarine.

Ellen says, "I'm actually leaving soon because I have a kiddie shoot at eleven. I was going to let you sleep, but now that you're awake, what do you want to do today? Feel like manning the antiques section for a while? I'll open it up if you want."

I haven't been here twenty-four hours and she's already trying to get me to work for her. At least these questions are ones I can answer. I say, "I'll pass on antiquing." Don't know if she noticed, but I have the Sullivan account folded under my arm. I'm taking it with me. "You can drop me at the library again. I've got work I can do there."

She says, "I didn't know you brought any work."

I down the rest of the coffee, scalding my gullet. A ball of warmth radiates in my stomach; it shifts and moves stuff around. "I'm not on vacation, Ellen, and this isn't Disney World. I do have clients who depend on me." I'm so earnest I almost believe it myself, at least until I drop the newspaper. It lands heads with the blazing headline facing up.

Ellen peers over the table. We both stare at the newspaper on the floor as if waiting for it to speak. Maybe it already has. She says, "I think you can take a few days off. Your clients would understand." It sounds angry, accusatory. She knows I'm keeping something from her.

"Sorry, the work—I just can't escape it." I take the toast on a tour of the bungalow. The tour ends where it should, with the photo of Tim, the DA, and Sullivan. Ellen is still inside her newspapers so she doesn't see me lift the photo, frame and all, and slide it inside my coat.

Finally, I have a plan. No more screwing around. The toast approves.

TWENTY-FOUR

I'm tired. I'm always tired; it's part of being me. But this tired is going radioactive. It's being down here in the Cape away from the city. Even when I'm doing nothing in Boston, there's the noise of action, of stuff happening, which helps me push through the tired. Down here, there's nothing but boxes and walls of lost memories.

I don't give Ellen a time to pick me up at the library. I tell her I'm a big boy and I'll make my way downtown eventually. She doesn't argue. Either the fight has momentarily left her or she's relieved to be free of my company. I have that effect on people.

I do an obligatory walk-and-yawn through the library stacks to make sure that I'm seen by the staff, all two of them. It's a weekday, and only moms and their preschoolers are here. The kids stare at me, but their moms won't look.

My cell phone feels like a baseball in my hand, all inert possibility. I have no messages; I knew that before I checked. Then I call Osterville's only off-season cabbie, Steve Brill. He's in the library parking lot two minutes later.

Brill is older than a sand dune and has been eroding for years. His knuckles are unrolled dice on his fuzzy steering wheel. The cab is an old white station wagon with brown panels and rust, I'm not sure which is which. Duct tape holds together the upholstery, and the interior smells like an egg and cheese sandwich, hold the cheese. A first-class ride.

I say, "Brill, I want you to drive like I'm a tourist."

Although Brill is a regular in Ellen's antiques store and he's met me on a couple of occasions, he isn't much for small talk and gives me nothing but a grunt. Maybe he doesn't like me. Don't know why, as I haven't done anything to him. Yet.

First, we make a quick trip to a florist. Brill waits in the cab with the meter running. I go small and purchase something called the At Peace Bouquet, which is yellow flowers mixed with greens, the sympathy concoction in a small purple vase I can hold in one hand. Me and the peace bouquet hop into the cab.

In the rearview mirror, Brill's eyes are rocks sitting inside a wrinkly bag of skin. The rocks disapprove of something. He says, "What, the big-city PI has a hot date tonight?" Then he cackles. His laughter shakes loose heavy gobs of phlegm in his chest, or maybe chunks of lung. Serves the old bastard right.

I'm nobody's joke. I say, "I have a hot date with your mother."

Brill shuts off the engine but doesn't turn around, just gives me those rocks in the rearview. He says, "I don't care who you think you are, I'm the only one allowed to be an asshole in my cab."

"You're doing a damn fine job of it, Brill. Kudos." I have a fistful of flowers in my hand and I'm talking tough to Rumpelstiltzkin. Who am I kidding? I'm everyone's joke.

He says, "I'll throw your ugly ass out of my cab. Don't think I won't. I don't need to give you a ride anywhere."

He's pissing me off, but at least he's getting my juices flowing. I stare at the back of his bald and liver-spotted head. There are wisps of white hair clinging to his scalp, pieces of elderly cotton candy.

I guess he's not going to apply for my personal-driver gig. I have to keep this from escalating. I need his wheels today. "Yeah, I know you can. But you'll give me a ride. Corner of Crystal Lake and Rambler, please."

Brill says nothing. I pull out two cigarettes and offer him one. His nicotine-stained hand snakes behind him, those dice knuckles shaking. He takes the stick and sets it aglow with the dash lighter. He inhales quietly, and the expelled smoke hangs around his head, stays personal.

I say, "Do you know how to get to where I want to go?" I pull out my lighter, flip open the top, and produce my one-inch flame.

Brill says, "I heard you the first time. And no smoking in my cab."

Brill starts up the cab and pulls out of the parking lot. I pocket my cigarette. I won't argue with him. I'm happy to be going somewhere.

Our ride from the florist to Sullivan's house should be short enough that falling asleep isn't really a worry. Knock on wood. The flowers are bothering my eyes and sinuses, though. I try to inhale the secondhand smoke instead. It's stale and spent, just like me and Brill.

He pulls over at the end of Rambler Road, the passenger side of the cab flush up against some bushes. I have to get out on the driver's side, which doesn't feel natural. The old man is screwing with me. He doesn't realize I don't need this shit.

Brill still doesn't turn around. He doesn't have to. He says, "Sad end for that Sullivan fella."

That's interesting. He could be just making small talk, but Brill doesn't do small talk. I'm going to play a hunch here. It sounds like Brill has something to say.

"Ends usually are sad. You know anything about Sullivan?"

Brill shrugs and says, "Maybe."

Even more interesting. I take out a twenty and throw it into the front seat. Brill picks it up quick and stuffs the bill into his front shirt pocket. The shirt is pink. I say, "Talk to me."

Brill says, "He was a quiet, normal guy. I gave him a ride a couple weeks ago to and from Lucky's Auto when his car was on the fritz. He tipped well." He stops. The silence is long enough to communicate some things.

"That's it? That's all you got?" I say it real slow for him, to let him try on the idea that I'm not amused.

He says, "Yeah, that's all I know," then laughs. "It's not my fault if you're playing Mickey Mouse detective."

There's no way this small-town pile of bones is pulling that on me. I may be amateur hour, but I'm not an easy mark. I reach over the bench seat and into his front pocket with my ham-sized fist. It comes back to me with my twenty and interest. I toss the interest back over the seat.

"You motherfucker, stealing from an old man." He still hasn't turned around.

"You know the language, but you wouldn't last a day driving a cab in Boston." It's mean, but it's also true. I add, "You can have the twenty back if you earn it."

He loses some air, deflates behind the wheel. He's a small, shrinking old man, and I don't care. He says, "The day before Sullivan killed himself, he had me pick him up and we just drove around town. I asked him about his car because it was sitting in his driveway, but he brushed me off, seemed agitated, spent most of the time looking out the windows and behind us."

Brill stops again, and he's staring at me. He needs another prompt. I'll provide. "Yeah, and where'd you go?"

"He had me drive by your mother's house. Twice. Second pass he told me to stop, so I did. He was talking low, mumbling stuff."

"What kind of stuff?"

" 'Gotta do it yourself, Sullivan,' that kind of thing. He always talked to himself so I didn't pay much attention. He never got out of the cab. I thought he was going to, though. Finally, he told me to take him home. He was all spooked and mumbling the whole way back."

I say, "Did you tell the police any of this?"

"No."

"How about Ellen?"

"No."

"Why not?"

"They didn't ask."

I say, "You mean they didn't gild your lily for the info."

He doesn't say anything. Looking for more bang from my buck, I say, "Kind of strange that he'd be casing her house the day before he offs himself."

Brill shrugs. "I figured Sullivan was cheating on his wife with Ellen. He was acting all paranoid, like a cheat. You know, the cheats are most of my off-season income. I cart them around to their secret lunches and goddamn by-the-hour motels."

Brill paints an alternate scenario in my head, one where Ellen did know Sullivan was living in Osterville and knew him well; secret lunches and other rendezvous. No. That isn't what happened. I dismiss it.

Ellen was genuine in her reaction this morning to the news of Sullivan's Osterville residency and suicide. She has had no contact with him. She wouldn't have shown me the picture of Tim, the DA, and Sullivan if she was playing the other woman with him. Right? I suppose her motivation behind showing me the photo could be a way to introduce me to her new fling, but that's not how it happened, did it? No.

No. The picture was part of her tour, coincidence only. Sullivan came by the bungalow to do his own looking for the fabled *it* because I hadn't come through yet. I have to go on that assumption. It's the only one that fits my case. I don't have the patience or time for curve balls and red herrings.

Still, Brill's cheats spiel shakes me up enough that I'll lie to him. I say, "Ellen doesn't know who Sullivan was. I promise you."

He says, "Maybe. Maybe not. It doesn't matter to me. I don't care what people are up to. I give rides wherever they want to go, and that's it, and everyone knows it. Now give me my twenty bucks, you motherfucker."

I give it to him. Twenty dollars very well spent. I say, "Don't go driving off too far, Brill. I might not be here all that long." I slide across the bench seat and get out. The road is narrow and I'm in its middle, exposed and unprotected.

Brill says, "Are you paying me to wait?"

"No." I pay the fare and add a tip. There's an insistent breeze coming off the nearby water. The individual flowers point in differing directions; they can't agree on anything.

Brill takes my money and doesn't stop to count it. He says, "Then call me later, fuzz face. Maybe I'll answer." Brill spins his rear tires and the station wagon cab speeds away, weaving down Rambler Road. Maybe I didn't tip him enough.

Sullivan's neighborhood is quiet. No one is out. The sun is shining, but it's cold and there are no signs of approaching spring. It's still the long cold winter here. I walk the one hundred feet to Sullivan's house. I have a plan, but I haven't decided what I'm going to do if his wife isn't home.

Looks like I don't have to worry about that. There are three cars in the driveway. One of them is the blue SUV I saw last time. The other two cars are small and of some Japanese make. Neither of them is red.

Okay, Sullivan's wife, Janice, is home but not alone. Alone would've been preferable, but I know such a state isn't likely, given hubby just died. I'm guessing the cars belong to members of the grief squad who swooped in to support her, friends in need and all that.

I walk down the gravel driveway and my feet sound woolly-mammoth heavy. Stones crunch and earth moves under my rumbling weight. I'm the last of some primitive line of prehistoric creatures on his final migration, the one where he dies at the end of the journey, that circle-of-life bullshit that's catchy as a Disney song but ultimately meaningless. Yeah, I'm in a mood.

The house is still white and needs a paint job. I'll try not to bring that up in conversation. I make it to the front door, which is red, and ring the bell. Two chimes. I hold the flowers tight to my chest, playing them close to the vest. This needs to be done right if I'm to learn anything.

When she opens the door, though, I won't take off my hat. No one wants to see that.

TWENTY-FIVE

An old woman answers the door. She might be the same age as Brill the happy cabbie. She's short and hunched, which maximizes her potential for shortness. Her hair is curly and white, so thick it could be a wig.

She says, "Can I help you?" After getting an eyeful of me, she closes the front door a bit, hiding behind the slab of wood. I don't blame her. I don't exactly have a face for the door-to-door gig.

I say, "Yes, hi—um, are you Mrs. Sullivan?"

"No, I'm her Aunt Patty." She wears a light blue dress with white quarter-sized polka dots, and a faux-pearl necklace hangs around her neck. I know the pearls are fake because they're almost as big as cue balls.

Aunt Patty. Doesn't everyone have an Aunty Patty? I give her my best opening statement. "My late father was an old friend of Brendan's. He grew up with Brendan in Southie. When I heard of his passing and the arrangements, saw I wouldn't be able to attend the wake or the funeral, I felt compelled to come down and give my family's condolences in person."

I hope that's enough to win over the jury. I look at her and see conflict. Aunt Patty doesn't know what to do. Aunt Patty keeps looking behind her but there's no one there to talk to, no one to make the decision for her. She's here to cook and clean and help keep the grieving widow safe from interlopers and unwanted distractions. She's here to make sure that grief happens correctly and according to schedule.

I know, because Ellen has been part of so many grief squads in Southie that she might as well register as a professional and rent herself out. Maybe Ellen does it to remember Tim and grieve for him all over again or she's trying to add distance, going through a bunch of little grievings to get over the big one.

I say, "I've come a long way. I won't stay too long, I promise."

That cinches it. Aunt Patty gives me a warm milk smile and says, "Oh, all right, come in. Thank you for coming." She opens the door wide behind her.

I'm in. I say, "You're welcome. Thanks for letting me in. Means a lot. Is Janice doing okay?"

"About as well as can be imagined. She's been very brave." Aunt Patty shuffle-leads me through the dining room, our feet making an odd rhythm on the hardwood floor.

It's dark in here. The shades are drawn over the bay windows. The house is in mourning. It's something I can feel. Sullivan died somewhere in this house. Maybe even the front room. Gun under his chin, bullet into his brain. Coerced or set up or neither, this is serious stuff. I can't screw any of it up.

There are pictures and decorations on the walls, but it's too dark to see them. There are also cardboard boxes on the dining room table. The boxes are brown and sad, both temporary and final.

Aunt Patty limps, favoring her left side, probably a hip. When her hip breaks, she won't make it out of the hospital alive. Yeah, like I said, I'm in a mood.

She says, "What's your name?"

"Mark. Mark Genevich. Nice to meet you, Aunt Patty."

"What nationality?"

"Lithuanian." Maybe I should tell her what I really am: narcoleptic. We narcoleptics have no country and we don't participate in the Olympics. Our status supersedes all notion of nationality. We're neutral, like the Swiss, but they don't trust us with army knives.

She says, "That's nice." My cataloging is a comfort to her. I'm not a stranger anymore; I'm Lithuanian.

The kitchen is big and clean, and bright. The white wallpaper and tile trim has wattage. Flowers fill the island counter. I fight off a sneeze. There are voices, speaking softly to our right. Just off the kitchen is a four-season porch, modestly decorated with a table for four and a large swing seat. Two women sit on the swing seat. The hinges and springs creak faintly in time with the pendulum. One of the women looks just like Aunt Patty, same dress and pool-cue necklace. The other woman does not make three of a kind with the pair of queens.

Patty and I walk onto the porch. The swingers stop swinging; someone turns off the music. The vase of flowers is a dumbbell in my hand.

Aunt Patty says, "That's my twin sister Margaret and, of course, the other beautiful woman is Janice. This is Mark Genevich?" I'm a name and a question. She doesn't remember my opening statement or my purpose. I need to fill in the blanks and fast. I've never been good under pressure.

I open with, "I'm so very sorry for your loss." And then I tell Janice and Aunt Margaret what I told Aunt Patty. Janice is attentive but has a faraway smile. Aunt Margaret seems a bit rougher around the edges than her sister. She sits with her thick arms folded across her chest, nostrils flared. She smells something.

Janice is of medium build and has long straight hair, worn down, parted in the middle, a path through a forest. She looks younger than her front-page husband but has dark, almost purple circles under her eyes. Her recent sleeping habits leaving their scarlet letters. Most people don't like to think about how much damage sleep can do, evidence be damned.

Janice says, "Thank you for coming and for the flowers. It's very thoughtful of you." The dark circles shrink her nose and give it a point.

I give Janice the flowers and nod my head, going for the humble silent exchange of pleasantries. Immediately, I regret the choice. I want her to talk about Brendan but she's not saying anything. Everyone has gone statue and we sit and stare, waiting for the birds to come land on our shoulders and shit all over us.

My heart ratchets its rate up a notch and things are getting tingly, my not-so-subtle spider sense telling me that things aren't good and could quickly become worse. Then I remember I brought the picture, the picture of Brendan and the boys. I focus my forever-dwindling energies on it.

I ask, "Did Brendan ever talk about my father?" For a moment, I panic and think I said something about Brendan and my mother instead. But I didn't say that. I'm fine. I shake it off, rub dirt on it, stay in the game. I reach inside my coat and pull out the photo of Tim, the DA, and Sullivan on the stairs. It's still in the frame. Its spot on Ellen's windowsill is empty. "That's Brendan on the left, my father on the right."

Patty squeezes onto the swing seat, sitting on the outside of her sister. I'm the only one standing now. It's noticeable.

Janice says, "I don't remember your father's name coming up. Brendan and I had only been married for ten years, and he never really talked much about growing up in Southie."

It's getting harder not to be thinking about Ellen and Sullivan sitting in a tree as a slight and gaining maybe. Goddamn Brill. I say, "I understand," even if I don't. It's what I'm supposed to say; a nice-to-see-you after the hello.

Janice sighs heavily; it says, *What am I supposed to do now?* I feel terrible for her. I don't know exactly what happened here with Sullivan, but it was my fault. And this case is far from over. She doesn't know that things could get worse.

Janice fills herself up with air after the devastating sigh, which is admirable but just as sad, and says, "I wish Brendan kept more stuff like this around. Could I ask you for a copy of this picture?"

"Of course, consider it done," I say.

Janice smiles, but it's sad; goddamn it, everything is sad. We both know she's trying to regain something that has already been lost forever.

Aunt Margaret grabs the picture with both hands, and says, "Who's that boy in the middle?"

I say, "That's William Times. Currently he's the Suffolk County district attorney."

Patty clasps her hands together and says, "Oh, his daughter is the singer, right? She's very cute."

"Nah, she's a loser," Margaret says, waving her hand. Case dismissed.

Patty says, "She's not a loser. She sang on national TV. I thought she sang beautifully too."

"She stunk and she was a spoiled brat. That's why they voted her off the show," Margaret says.

Janice, who I assume has been acting as referee for the sisters for as long as they've been at her house, says, "She was a finalist on *American Star*. She's hardly a loser."

Margaret shrugs. "She lost, right? We'll never hear from her again."

The volley between family members is quick, ends quicker, and is more than a little disorienting. It also seems to be the end of the small talk. We're back to staring at each other, looking for an answer that isn't here.

I'm not leaving this house empty-handed, without knowing what the next step is, without having to grill Ellen about a tryst with Sullivan. Hopefully, the photo of the boys has bought me some familiarity chips that I can cash.

I say, "I'm sorry, there's no good way to say this, so I'm just going to come out with it."

Margaret says, "Come out with it already and be done then."

"Good advice." I pull out a business card and my PI ID and hand them to Janice, but Margaret takes them instead. "I'm a small-time, very small-time, private detective in South Boston."

Patty's eyes go saucer-wide and she says, "How exciting!"

It's not warm in here but my head sweats under my hat. I nod at Patty, acknowledging her enthusiasm. At least I'll have one of the three on my side. I say, "Last week your husband, Brendan, came to my office in Southie and hired me."

Janice sinks into her swing seat. Patty covers her mouth. Margaret still has her arms crossed. Janice says, "Hired you? Hired you for what?"

Christ, I probably could've come up with a better way to introduce the subject, but there's no turning back now. As uncomfortable as this is, asking the questions that will haunt

Janice for years to come, I owe it to Sullivan to see this through. I owe it to myself too.

I say, "Mind if I sit?" No one says anything. I grab a fold-up chair that's leaning against a wall and wrestle with it for a bit; the wood clacks and bites my fingers. I'm sure I look clumsy, but I'm buying some time so I can figure out what I can and can't tell her. It doesn't work.

I say, "The hard part is that I don't think I can tell you much until I figure it all out for myself."

Margaret says, "He's a crock. This guy is a phony. He's trying to get something out of you, probably money. Let's call the police."

Patty says, "Stop it, he's a real detective."

"How do we know that? How do we know anything about this man? That picture doesn't prove anything. Might not even be Brendan in the picture," Margaret says, building up steam, and a convincing case against me.

Patty is horrified. She says, "Look at his card and ID. He's going to tell us something important, right?" Patty leans out toward me. To her I have the answers to life somewhere inside my coat. I only keep questions in here.

Margaret ignores her sister, points a worn-tree-branch finger at me, and says, "Shame on you, whatever it is you're up to. Janice is a good woman and doesn't deserve to be put through anything by the likes of you. I'm calling."

I say, "Whoa, take it easy, Auntie Margaret. I'm telling the truth and I'm not here to hide things from Janice, just the opposite. I don't know how everything fits together yet, and I don't have all the puzzle pieces either. What I'm hoping is that you"—I turn to Janice—"can help me."

The sisters argue with each other. They have their considerable arms folded over their chests and they bump into each other like rams battling over territory. The swing seat complains and sways side to side, not in the direction the swing was intended to go. I yawn and hope nobody sees it.

Janice says, "Wait, wait. Stop!" Her aunts stop. "Are you really the son of Brendan's friend?"

"Yes. And what I'm working on, what Brendan wanted me to figure out, is something from the past, the long past but not gone, and I think it involves both men in that picture, my father and the DA."

Janice says, "I already told you, I don't know anything about Brendan's past, never mind anything about your father and the DA."

I resist telling her that I know very little about my father's past and less about my own mother's present. I say, "That's okay. I think you'll still be able to help."

Margaret is shaking her head, silently *tsk-tsk* ing the proceedings. Patty has wide eyes and nods her head, yes. Janice is stoic, unreadable as a tabloid.

I say, "Janice, may I ask you some questions? Then I promise to tell you and show you what I know."

Janice nods. "Okay."

"How did you meet Brendan?" I start off with an easy question, get her used to talking about her and him, get her used to being honest and thinking about Brendan as past, maybe as something that can't hurt her, or can't hurt her much.

Janice cooperates. She gives a summary of their too-brief history. Her voice is low and calm, soothing, as if I'm the one who needs cheering up. Brendan was a truck driver and they met at a diner in New Hampshire. They sat next to each other at the counter. Janice worked at a local park, part of an environmental conservation and preservation team. They were married two months later, moved to Provincetown shortly thereafter, spent the last bunch of years bouncing around the Cape in accordance with Janice's varied environmental gigs. They loved the Cape and were going to stay forever, grow old, would you still need me, feed me, and the rest of the tune, happily ever after. . . .

Margaret is slapping me in the face, shouting. "What's wrong with you? Are you asleep? Wake up."

Patty hangs on her sister's arm, the nonslapping arm. "Stop it, Margaret, you'll hurt him!"

"I'm awake. I wasn't asleep. Jesus! Stop hitting me!" The old and familiar embarrassments swell, filling me with anger and hate for everyone, myself included. Makes me want to lash out, lie, share my poison with anyone around me. God help the person who finds my continued degradations and humiliations funny.

The twin aunts retreat to the kitchen, arm in arm, their cranky-hipped limps fitted together like the gears in a dying perpetual motion machine. Janice crouches at my feet. She says, "Are you okay? You just slumped in your chair. It looked like you passed out."

"I'm fine, I'm fine." I stand up, stumble a bit, but get my legs under me. I rub my face with my hands. If I could take my face off, I would.

Janice stands next to me, her hand on my elbow. It's a light touch, and comforting, but it's all I can do not to flinch and pull myself away. The twins come back. Margaret sits on the swing and has the cordless phone in her hand. Patty has a glass of water, which I assume is for me, until she takes a sip.

I swallow some air, willing the oxygen to do its goddamn job and keep me working right. "Sorry, I'm narcoleptic." I say it under my breath, the words cower and hide, and hope that only Janice hears my quick and unexpected confession.

Margaret says, "What?" Of course she heard me. She says it loud, like she's responding to a lie. This is not a lie.

I say, "I have narcolepsy." That's it. No explanation.

Patty appears at my left side like a spirit. "You poor dear. Drink this." There's lipstick on the glass. My job is so glamorous.

I say, "Please, everyone sit back down. I'm fine. It happens all the time and I know how to deal with it. I know how to live with it." I give back the community water. The women stare and investigate me. My status changing from potentially dangerous intruder to vulnerable afflicted person might just help my cause here.

I say, "Look. My narcolepsy is why I need to ask you questions, Janice. When Brendan came to my Southie office I fell asleep, like I did here, but not exactly like I did here because I probably looked awake to Brendan, did some sleep-talking and -walking like I do sometimes: automatic behavior, they call it." I stop talking and wave my hands in front of my own face, cleaning up the mess of words. "Anyway, I was out when he was in and all I've been able to piece together is that Brendan wanted me to find something, something that relates to my father and the DA." I pause and point at the picture again. It pays to have props. "I don't know what it is I'm supposed to find because I was asleep, and Brendan died before I could find out."

There. It's out. The truth as I know it and I feel fine. Everyone blinks at me a few times and I hear their eyelids opening and closing.

Margaret talks first. She says, "He's faking. Be careful, Janice."

Patty slaps her sister's hand.

Janice curls up her face and says, "Oh, be quiet, Margaret."

Margaret looks at me and shrugs, like we're commiserating, like I'm supposed to agree with her can-you-believe-these-knuckleheads-are-buying-what-you're-selling look. Can't say I'm all that fond of Aunt Margaret.

I say, "So, Janice, I assume you didn't know Brendan came to South Boston and hired me."

She says, "I knew he made a day trip to Boston, but I didn't know anything about you."

I nod. "I did talk with Brendan one other time. Is this a smoke-free house? Do you mind if I smoke?" My timing has always been impeccable.

Janice shakes her head and is now exasperated with me. "Yes. I mean, no, you can't smoke in here. When did you talk to Brendan?"

I can't tell her it was the day before he died. It won't help anyone, especially me. I say, "A couple of days after his visit he called to check on my progress. Because I'm stubborn, I didn't come right out and admit to him that I slept through our face-to-face. I didn't ask him what I was supposed to find. I hoped during our phone conversation that those details of the case would just, you know, present themselves."

Margaret says, "I take it back. He's not faking. He's just a buffoon." She sets off another family brouhaha. Yeah, all this because of little old me. Janice clears the room of the battling aunts, banishing them to the kitchen.

When Janice returns to her seat on the swing, I say, "The important or odd part of our phone conversation was that Brendan seemed agitated, even paranoid. Does that mean anything to you?"

Janice turns on me quick and says, "No, that's not the important part." She leans closer to me and enunciates her words, sharpening them to a cutting point. "Brendan, my husband, killed himself, shot himself in the face with a gun. He was downstairs, in our basement just a few days ago when he pulled the trigger. Your saying he was agitated and paranoid on the phone is not a surprise and certainly not the important part to me."

"I'm sorry. You're right. I'm sorry." I cannot say I'm sorry to her enough. I reach inside my coat and pull out the envelope. I'm careful to remove only one of the photos, the one with clothes. "While Brendan was there, the narcoleptic me managed to take some notes. Those are gone. Most of it was gibberish, but I'd written down South Shore Plaza. Do you know what that means? Brendan left me with this photograph, and I'm supposed to find something else, but obviously I haven't found it yet."

"South Shore Plaza means nothing to me. Brendan hated malls, wouldn't go in them if he could help it." Janice takes the picture, looks at it quick, and then looks away, like the photo might burn. "Who is she?"

"I don't know."

Janice looks at it again. "She looks a little like the *American Star* girl. The DA's daughter, right?"

I smile, and it doesn't feel right on my face. "It does look like her. But it's not her."

"No. I know. The photo is clearly older than she is."

I say, "Yes. Of course. Clearly. There was never any doubt."

"It does look a lot like her. Kind of spooky, in a way."

"Uncanny." I'm just going to agree with everything she says.

"Why did Brendan have this? Why did he give this to you?"

"I don't know, Janice. Like I said, he came to me to find something else. Not a person. An *it*."

She nods, even though I'm only answering her rhetorical questions, questions about her husband that will haunt her for the rest of her life because there might be no answers forthcoming. I don't know if she realizes that yet. Or maybe she does, and she's tolerating my presence with a staggering amount of dignity. Maybe she can share some dignity with me.

I say, "I'm sorry, but I have to ask this, Janice. Did Brendan act strangely, do anything out of character, say anything odd in the days before he died?"

"You mean besides going to South Boston and hiring a private investigator?"

I don't say anything or do anything. I know that much, at least. Janice loses herself again in the photo, the piece of her husband's past that has no place here, even though I'm trying to find it.

Finally, Janice says, "That girl on *American Star*. What's her name?"

"Jennifer Times."

"Right. Jennifer Times." Another pause, drinking in more of the photo; then she gives it back. "Brendan and I both watched the show together when this season started, but he stopped watching once they started picking the finalists. I feel like I remember him leaving the room when that local girl, Jennifer, was performing." Janice isn't looking at me but off into some corner of the porch, seeing those final days she shared with her husband. She's not talking to me now, either. She's talking to herself, trying to find her own answers.

"There was a night when Brendan came into the room with two glasses of wine, sat down next to me on the couch, but stood up and left as soon as he saw the show was on. He said something about how dumb it was, and that was strange because up until a week or two before, he was watching with me. We liked to make fun of the really bad singers.

"But I remember when he left the room it was Jennifer on the TV; she was singing. Brendan went into the kitchen, still talking to himself. He talked to himself quite a bit. He was a truck driver, and he said truck drivers talked to themselves a lot, even when they were talking to other people. I never told him, but I loved that about him and eavesdropped on him whenever I could. I'd feel guilty after, like I was reading a diary, but I still did it.

"He was in the kitchen, talking away." Janice pauses. "Sorry, but this is hard. I've been thinking about nothing but him for days now, and it's not getting any easier."

"Perfectly understandable."

Janice nods. Her eyes are wide and she's still not here. She's back at that night with Brendan, listening to him in the kitchen. Maybe this is what it was like for Brendan that day in the office, when he was talking to me and I wasn't there.

I say, "Did you hear what Brendan was saying in the kitchen?" I keep still, don't move in my seat, not even a wiggled pinky.

Janice says, "He was muttering and wasn't very loud. I didn't hear much. I got up and tiptoed to the doorway, like I usually did when I caught him talking to himself." She stops and smiles, but it falls apart, and I think she might start crying and never stop but she doesn't. She goes on. "I didn't hear much, just snippets, nothing that made a whole lot of sense, so I walked into the kitchen. He was leaning on the kitchen island, talking and sipping his wine. When he saw me he smiled. I don't think he expected me to be there, but he smiled anyway. I walked over to him, gave him a kiss on the cheek, and thanked him for the wine. He said, 'Anytime,' squeezed my shoulder real quick, and I left him there, in the kitchen."

Janice sinks into the swing seat, slouching into the large green cushion. She's probably done, but I'm not moving. I won't move until I get what I need. I say, "When he was talking to himself, do you remember any phrases or words? Anything?"

Janice looks at me and covers her face with her hands. I know the feeling. She is done. She's going to tell me she doesn't remember anything else and that's it. She'll ask me, politely, to leave.

Then she sits upright again, her hands drop, and she says, "Yes. I think he said something about film, or more film."

My leg shakes, bobs up and down, tries to walk out of the room on its own. Is it more photos, then? An undeveloped roll, or more negatives, the rest of Tim's bedroom shoot? Maybe the rest of the pictorial includes more nudes, maybe the same girl, maybe a different girl, and I bet this missing portfolio includes some juicy eight-by-tens of Brendan and Billy Times, juicy enough to make the DA dangerously cranky. I say, "More film."

Janice nods. She wraps her arms around her chest, looks out the window, sits back in the swing seat, and sways. She says, "I have your card, Mark. I'll call you in a few days or a week. I need to know how this ends up."

I don't have to say anything, but I do. "Call me anytime. Thank you, Janice, you've been very helpful. And again, I'm so incredibly sorry about Brendan." I'm not going to tell her about the DA and his goons. I can't tell her it might be my fault that Brendan is dead. Not now, anyway. I need to finish this case first. There'll be time for the recriminations later.

Janice says, "Thanks. So am I."

It's past time to go. I get up and walk out of the porch, and I walk out fast, or as fast as I can handle. The twin aunts sit in the kitchen, huddled in two chairs they positioned near the breezeway entrance into the porch. They're whispering and they don't stop whispering as I walk by. Margaret has the phone in her hand, fingers hovering over buttons that spell 9-1-1. I'm sure they heard everything.

I say, "The pleasure was all mine. Don't get up, I can find the front door." I touch the brim of my hat for a faux tip, but the lid doesn't move, not for anyone.

Patty says, "Good luck." At least, I think it's Patty. I'm already out of the kitchen and through the dining room, where it's dark, so dark I can't really see, and I walk into the table shins first. Ow. The hutch and its china shakes. Nothing broken.

I right the ship, feel my way past the table, and find the front hallway and door. There are small curtained windows in the doorframe. My bull's charge through the dining room notwithstanding, I'm going to be as careful and cautious as I can the rest of the way. I know I'm close. I pull back the curtains for a little peek-a-boo.

The red car is outside. Can't say I'm surprised.

TWENTY-SIX

The red car idles in front of the gravel driveway. No, it's not idling, it's crawling, and it crawls by the house and down the road.

They know I'm here. Maybe they planted some sort of homing device on me. I'm the endangered animal that needs to be tagged and tracked. Or it's possible they don't know I'm here and they're just checking to see who's hanging at chez Sullivan. I didn't see the red car when I was in Brill's cab. Of course Brill could've spilled my beans for their twenty bucks. He strikes me as an equal opportunity kind of guy.

I take out my cell phone and dial. One ring and Brill answers. "Town Taxi, how can I help you?"

"Brill, it's me, Genevich. Can you pick me up on Rambler Road?"

He sighs. It doesn't sound nervous or guilty, just that he's pissed off to have to do his job. "Christ, where do you want to go now?"

The red car drives by again, in the opposite direction. It's moving faster, almost but not quite a normal, leisurely, obey-the-suburban-speed-limit pace. Then it's gone. I say with a mock British accent, "Home, James. Where else? Home."

Brill hangs up. I choose to believe that means he's coming to get me.

Voices from the kitchen: "Everything okay, Mark? Who are you talking to?"

I say, "I'm fine. Just calling a cab. He'll be here any minute. 'Bye and thanks." The weather is tolerable, it'd be hard to explain me standing inside, nose buried in the curtains by the front door, so I go outside, close the door gently behind me. Thinking better of sitting on the steps, in plain view of Rambler Road, I walk down the gravel driveway and conceal myself behind the blue SUV. Hopefully no one in the house is watching.

I go fishing for a cigarette and find one. It lights like it has been waiting for this moment all its life. I think about the red car and the goons. Are they planning another drive-by? Maybe they're getting the jump on my next destination. They'll be sitting in Ellen's kitchen when I get there, keeping the light on for me. They trashed my office and apartment, what's to say they won't do the same to the bungalow or to me? Nothing, far as I can tell.

Maybe I'm asking the wrong questions. I should be asking why haven't they ransacked the bungalow already? Would it look too fishy for break-ins and house-trashings to be following me around? Maybe they're not on such comfortable footing down here, away from the DA's stomping grounds. Didn't seem to bother them in Brendan's case, though. Maybe they're tired of looking for *it,* whether *it* is an undeveloped roll or a set of incriminating pictures, and they'll be happy just to deal with me after I do the grunt work for them.

Either or any way, doesn't matter to me anymore. What matters is that I have to find the goods before they find me again.

A car horn blasts two reports. That, or someone is trying to ride a goose sidesaddle. Brill's here. He beeps again. I step out from behind the SUV. He rolls down the passenger-side window and yells, "Come on, get in the goddamn car. We ain't got all day."

I say, "Ain't it the truth."

He says, "Did you get what you needed?"

"I was only offering my condolences and my flowers to the widow." I shouldn't be smug, but I am.

"Right. You didn't find shit."

I sit in Brill's backseat, and my ass picks up a strip of duct tape, which is just what my ass needs. I say, "The Genevich bungalow, Brill. You know where that is, right?"

He does. He drives down Rambler Road. According to my cell phone it's only 12:30. My cell phone doesn't tell lies. Ellen won't be home for another four hours, at least.

Brill pulls out onto the main drag. The library is just ahead. I try to turn around to see if anyone is tailing. I shift my weight in the seat and there's a loud and long ripping sound.

Brill says, "Goddamn it, you're tearing my seat apart!"

"Don't get your Depends in a bunch. It's your duct tape sticking to my ass like it's in love." I keep turning around, looking for the red car, and the duct tape keeps stripping off and clamping onto me.

He says, "Jesus Christ, stop moving around! What do you think you're doing back there anyway? It's going to take me the rest of the afternoon to fix that up right."

"Nothing. Just admiring the scenery." I stop moving, mostly because my legs are practically taped together. "Hey, did you see a red car today, earlier, when you were driving around?"

Brill's eyes get big. The wrinkles animate and release the hounds of his eyes. He says, "Yeah. It followed me to Rambler Road."

"No kidding." This isn't good. This—

Brill blows air through his lips, spitting laughter. Then it's out full. It's a belly laugh, a thigh-slapper. I'm not so amused.

He says, "You are one sad sack, Genevich. Oooh, a red car, watch out for the red car! Ha! That's quite a gift for description you got there. You must solve all kinds of cases with those detailed detective powers of yours."

"All right, all right. Forget it."

"No, no, it's a good question. Except for holidays and a week off here and there, I've been driving around town ten hours a day, seven days a week for forty years, but I have never, ever, seen a red car on the road, not a one, until today. Man, I'm so glad you're on the case."

Brill laughs it up some more. I just might introduce my knuckles to the back of his head. He wheezes and chuckles until he drops me off at the bungalow. I don't tip. Let's see if he finds that funny.

He drives away. I'm here. I'm at the bungalow. And I know it's here. The rest of the film has to be here, if it's anywhere.

The sky has gone gray, the color of old newspapers. There's no red car in the driveway or anywhere on the block, but that doesn't mean the goons aren't inside. I have no weapon, no protection. I could grab something out of the shed, I suppose, but I don't know the finer points of Zen combat with pruning shears, and in the tale of the tape, trowels and shovels don't measure favorably when going against guns.

Play it straight, then. The front door is locked and intact. All the windows are closed. I peek inside a few, cupping my hands around my face. It's dark inside, but nothing seems out of place. I walk around to the backyard. It doesn't take me long. The house could fit inside my jacket. I hear the rain landing on my hat before I feel it.

I backdoor it into the kitchen. Everything is how we left it this morning: newspapers on the table, coffee mugs and toast crumbs on the counter. It's quiet, and I hope it stays that way. I won't turn on any lights, pretend I'm not here. It'll be easy.

Start at the beginning, the kitchen. I'll be thorough and check everything and everywhere: under the sink, between and behind pipes, the utensil and utility drawers. Maybe the film is hiding in plain view, just like Tim's photos on the walls, I don't know. There's a finite amount of space here in the old homestead; those family secrets can't stay hidden forever.

I look in the cabinets below the sink, past the pots and pans, the small pair of cabinets above the refrigerator that Ellen can't reach without a stool and neither can I. There's nothing but old phone books, a dusty bottle of whiskey, and books of matches, but I still push on the panels and wooden backings, seeing if anything will pop out or away, secret passages and hiding spots. I don't find any. The kitchen is clear.

The dining room and living room are next. Closets full of winter coats and dresses in plastic bags. No film. I move furniture and throw rugs, test for loose slats by rapping my foot on the floor. I go to my hands and knees and feel along the perimeters of the baseboards. Nothing and nothing. It's getting warm in here. My coat comes off, and the picture of Tim, Sullivan, and the DA goes back in its spot on the windowsill. It wasn't missed.

The guest room is next. There's only one closet and all it holds are two wooden tennis racquets, my old baseball glove— the one I pretend-signed with Carney Lansford's signature— four misshapen wire hangers, outdated board games that I open and rifle through, and empty luggage. The white suitcase and bag are as old as I am. I move the bed and bureau out, repeat my floor-and-baseboard checks, and find nothing.

It's all right. The nothing, that is. The first three rooms are only preludes, dry runs, practice searches for the real test. Ellen's room and the basement.

Ellen's room was their room. There are black-and-white photos on the walls, and they look to be half-and-half Tim pictures and antique finds. The Tim pictures are all of me, ranging in age from newborn to five years old. I'm in the pictures, but they're all someone else's memories, not mine. There's only one picture where Ellen shares the scene with me. It's a close-up and our faces are pressed together with Ellen in profile, hiding her smile behind one of my perfect chubby cheeks. My cheeks are still chubby.

No time for that. I do the bed and rug/floor check first, then the baseboard. I have a system, and I am systematically finding nothing. Then comes the nightstand, and I find her address book and flip through it. Nothing sinister, everything organized, all the numbers have a name. None of the names are Sullivan. Take that, Brill.

Next up, her antique wooden trunk that holds sweaters and sweatshirts, then her dresser, and, yes, I'm going through her dresser, and I have to admit that I fear finding personal items that I don't want to find, but I can't and won't stop now. Underwear drawer, shirt drawer, pants and slacks, bras, and all clear.

Her closet is a big one, the biggest one in the house. It must be in the closet somewhere. I remove all the hanging clothes and place them on the bed. Then I pull out all the shoes from the floor and the shelves, along with hatboxes and shoeboxes, most of them empty, some of them trapping belts and scarves, tacky lapel pins and brooches, general shit Ellen never wears. No clown pants in here.

The back of the closet is paneled and some of the panels hang loose. I pull up a few but find only plaster. To the left, the closet goes deeper, until the ceiling tapers down, into the floor. There are stacks of cardboard boxes and I pull those out. One box holds tax and financial information, the other boxes are assorted memorabilia: high school yearbook, plaques, track-meet ribbons, unframed pictures, postcards. No rolls of film, no pictures.

I put everything back. It's 2:25. My back hurts and my legs are stiffening up, revolting against further bending against their will.

On the way to the basement, I do a quick run through the bathroom. I look inside the toilet tank, leaving no porcelain cover unturned. Then back to the kitchen, and it's grab a flashlight and pound the stairs down into the basement.

The basement, like the house, is small, seemingly smaller than the bungalow's footprint, though I don't know how that's possible.

The furnace, washer, and dryer fill up an alcove. There's less clutter than I expected down here. There's a pair of rusty bed frames leaning against the foundation walls, a set of metal shelves that hold a mish-mash of forgotten tokens of home ownership, and an old hutch with empty drawers. It looks like Ellen was down here recently, organizing or cleaning. I check the exposed ceiling beams and struts; the take-home prizes are spiderwebs and dead bugs, but no film.

A tip, an edge, of panic is starting to poke me in the back of the head, now that I haven't found it yet. The bungalow doesn't want to let go of its secrets.

Back to the alcove. Behind and above the washer and dryer is a crawl space with a dirt floor. I climb up and inside I have to duck-walk. Not wild about this. Dark, dirt floor, enclosed space: there's a large creepiness factor, and it's very easy to imagine there are more than metaphorical skeletons stuffed or buried here.

I find a Christmas-tree stand, boxes of ornaments and tablecloths, and one of my old kiddie Halloween costumes, a pirate. Christ. Everywhere I turn in the damn house is stuff that doesn't need to be saved, but it's there, like a collection of regrets, jettisoned and almost but not quite forgotten.

I use the flashlight to trace the length of the dirt floor into the corners and then, above me, on the beams and pipes. The film is not here. Is it buried? I could check, get a shovel and move some dirt around, like some penny-ante archaeologist or grave robber. Indiana Jones, I'm not. Goddamn, that would take too long. Time is my enemy and always will be.

Maybe the missing film isn't here. Maybe the DA and his

goons already found it in my apartment or the office with their quaint search-and-seizure operation; it would explain why they haven't torn this place apart. But that doesn't work. Ellen's parents were still alive and living in the building when Tim died. He wouldn't have hidden film at their place. Even if he did hide it there, too much work and change has happened to the interior of the building in the intervening years. The years always intervene. It would've been found.

It could be anywhere. It could've been destroyed long ago, purposefully or accidentally. It could be nowhere. Or it's here but it's lost, like me. Being lost isn't the same as being nowhere. Being lost is worse because there's the false hope that you might be found.

I crawl out onto the washing machine ass first. I'm a large load, wash in warm water. Brush myself off and back upstairs to the kitchen. I sit heavily at the table with the newspapers. I want a cigarette but the pack is in my coat and my coat is way over in the other room. My legs are too heavy. My arms and hands are too heavy. If I could only get around without them, conserve energy, throw the extra weight overboard so I could stay afloat. Can't get myself out of the chair. You never get used to the total fatigue that rules your narcoleptic life, and it only gets more difficult to overcome. Practice doesn't make perfect.

TWENTY-SEVEN

The sun shines bright, just like the ones in cartoons. Cartoon suns sing and wink and have toothy smiles. Do we really need to make an impossibly massive ball of fire and radiation into our cute little friend?

Tim and I are in our backyard. Everything is green. It's the weekend again. Tools go back in the shed, but he keeps the hand trowel, the special one. We've all done this before.

Tim is still in the shed putting things away. I take a peek inside. Along with the sharp and toothy tools are bottles of cleaners and chemical fertilizers, their labels have cartoon figures on them, and they wink at me, ask me to come play. I remember their commercials, the smiley-faced chemical suds that scrub and sing their way down a drain and into our groundwater. Oh, happy days.

Tim closes the shed doors and locks them, even though he'll just have to unlock them again later. A loop of inefficiency. The doors are newly white, like my baby teeth. I can't go inside. He tells me I'm too young, but maybe I just don't know the secret password. There are so many secrets we can't keep track of them. We forget them and shed them like dead skin.

I stand next to the doors. The doors are too white. Brown paper bag. Pat on my head. Good boy. It's time to clean up the yard, again and again and again.

The sky is such a light shade of blue, it looks like water, and it shimmers. I don't much feel like singing for Tim today, but I will. He'd be devastated if I didn't.

I sing the old standard, "Take Me Out to the Ball Game." Tim switches the lyrics around and I put them back where they belong. It makes me tired. It's hot and the poop bag gets full. Tim never runs out of names for the dogs, the sources of the poop. We never see the dogs, so he might as well be naming the dog shit, but that wouldn't be a fun or appropriate game.

We dump the poop in its designated and delineated area, over the cyclone fence and into the woods behind the shed. It smells back here. As he dumps the bag, Tim says, "Shoo, fly, shoo."

We walk around to the front of the shed and Tim opens the doors. It's dark inside and my eyes need time to adjust. Tim says, "So, kid, whaddaya think?"

My hands ball up into tiny fists, no bigger than hummingbirds' nests. The five-year-old me is pissed off and more than a little depressed that Tim was the photographer for those pictures, and for more pictures I can't find, some film that is a terrible secret and resulted in the death of his friend Brendan. Say it ain't so, Tim.

I say, "Where's the film? Who is she, Tim?"

Tim laughs, he loves to laugh, and he bends to one knee and chucks my chin with his fist, so fucking condescending. I should bite his knuckle or punch him in the groin, but I'm not strong enough.

Tim says, "I don't know and I don't know." He gets up and moves to lock the shed doors, but I make my own move. I jam my foot between the doors so they can't shut. I'm my own five-year-old goon, and my will is larger than the foot in the doors.

I say, "Who are you?"

Tim looks around, as if making sure the coast of our yard is clear, and says, "You don't know, and you never will."

He lifts me up when I'm not looking. I am all bluff and so very easy to remove from the doors. There's always next time. Tim puts me on his shoulders. I land roughly; my little body slams onto his stone figure. A sting runs up my spine and makes my extremities tingle. It hurts enough to bring tears.

I'm too high up, too close to that cartoon sun, which doesn't look or feel all that friendly anymore. My skin burns and my eyes hide in a squint that isn't getting the job done. The five-year-old has an epiphany. The cartoon sun is why everything sucks.

Tim walks with me on his shoulders. I'm still too high up. I wonder if he knows that I could fall and die from up here.

TWENTY-EIGHT

Full body twitch. A spasm sends my foot into the kitchen table leg. The table disapproves of being treated so shabbily and groans as it slides a few inches along the linoleum. My toes aren't crazy about the treatment either. Can't please anyone.

I'm in the kitchen and I'm awake. Two states of being that are not constant and should probably not be taken for granted. As a kid, I thought the expression was *taken for granite,* as in the rock. I still think that makes more sense.

All right. Get up. I go to the fridge and keep my head down because I do not want to look out the kitchen window, out in the backyard. I need to let the murk clear from my latest and greatest little sleep, to burn the murk away like morning fog before I'll allow a eureka moment. I don't want to jinx anything, not just yet. It's 3:36.

I make a ham and cheese on some whole-grain bread that looks like cardboard with poppy seeds. Tastes like it too. Everything sticks to the roof of my mouth. I eat one half of the sandwich and start the other half before I let myself look out into the backyard.

There it is, the answer as plain as my crooked face. Down at the bottom of the slanted yard: the shed. The missing film is hidden in the shed. It has to be.

I finish the sandwich and gulp some soda straight from the two-liter bottle. What Ellen doesn't know won't gross her out. Then I go into the living room for my jacket, my trusty exterior skin, and then to the great outdoors.

The sun is shining. I won't look at it because it might be the cartoon sun. I light a cigarette instead. Take that, cartoon sun. I ease down the backyard's pitch.

The shed has gone to seed. It's falling apart. Because of the uneven and pitched land, the shed, at each corner, sits on four stacks of cinder blocks of varying heights. The back end is up a couple of feet off the ground. The shed sags and tilts to the left. A mosquito fart could knock it to the ground. My ham-and-cheese sandwich rearranges itself in my stomach.

The roof is missing shingles, a diseased dragon losing its scales, tar paper and plywood exposed in spots. The walls need to be painted. The doors are yellowed, no longer newly white, just like my teeth. Looks like the doors took up smoking. The one window is covered with dust and spiderwebs. It's all still standing, though. Something to be said for that.

The shed was solely Tim's domain. Ellen is a stubborn city dweller with no interest in dirt or growing things, other than the cosmetic value live grass supposedly gives to her property. Ellen does not mow or rake or dig or plant. Even when I was a kid and we had no money, she hired landscapers to take care of the yard and they used their own equipment, not the stuff that has been locked in the shed for twenty-five years. After Tim died, the shed stayed locked. It was always just a part of the yard, a quirk of property that you over-looked, like some mound left by the long-ago glacial retreat.

The shed doors have a rusted padlock as their neglected sentinel. It has done the job and now it's time to retire. I wrap my hand around the padlock and it paints my hand with orange, dead metal. The lock itself is tight, but the latch mechanism that holds the doors closed hangs by loose and rusted screws. Two quick yanks and it all comes apart in my hand. The doors open and their hinges complain loudly. Crybabies.

Might as well be opening a sarcophagus, with all the dust and decay billowing into my face. One who dares disturb this tomb is cursed with a lungful of the stuff. I stagger back and cough a cough that I refuse to blame on my cigarettes.

I take a step inside. The floorboards are warped, forming wooden waves, but they feel solid enough to hold me. There's clutter. The years have gathered here. Time to empty the sucker. Like I said before, I'm not screwing around anymore.

I pull out rakes and a push mower, which seems to be in decent shape despite the long layoff. Ellen could probably sell it in her antiques store. Shovels, a charcoal grill, a wheelbarrow with a flat tire, extra cyclone fencing, bags of seed, fertilizer, beach toys, a toddler-sized sled, a metal gas can, an extra water hose, empty paint cans and brushes. Everything comes off the floor and into the yard. There's a lot of stuff, but it doesn't take long to carry it outside. The debris is spread over the grass; it looks like someone is reconstructing a Tim airplane after it crashed.

Shelves on the side walls hold coffee cans full of oily rags, old nails, washers, and screws. There's nothing taped underneath those shelves. The shed has no ceiling struts like the basement did, but I do check the frame, the beams above the door. Empty.

The rear of the shed has one long shelf with all but empty bottles of windshield washer fluid, antifreeze, and motor oil. Underneath the long plank of wood is a section of the rear wall that was reinforced with a big piece of plywood. There are nails and hooks in the plywood. The nails and hooks are empty, nothing hangs, but it looks like there's some space or a buffer between the plywood and the actual rear wall of the shed, certainly room enough for a little roll of film, says me.

How much space is there? I knock hard on the plywood, wanting to hear a hollow sound, and my fist punches through its rotten surface, out the rear wall of the shed, and into the sunlight. Whoops. I pull my bullying fist back inside unscathed. There's less space between the plywood and wall than I thought, and it's all wet and rotted back there, the wall as soft as a pancake from L Street Diner.

Ellen won't notice the fist hole in the wall, I don't think. When does she ever go behind the shed? I try to pry off more of the plywood, but another chunk of the back wall comes with it.

Dammit. I'll demolish the shed looking for the film, if I have to. Can't say I have any ready-made excuses to explain such a home improvement project to Ellen, though.

Take a step back. The floorboards squeak and rattle. Something is loose somewhere. I back up some more, pressing my feet down hard, and in the rear left corner of the shed, where I was just standing and punching a second ago, the flooring rises up and off the frame a little bit and bites into the crumbling plywood above it. Maybe X marks the spot.

I go back out onto the lawn and fetch a hand trowel. It might be the poop-scooping shovel of yore, it might not. It ain't Excalibur. I use the thing like a crowbar and pry up that rear corner until I can grab it with my hands. The floorboard isn't rotted; the wood is tougher and fights back. I have a tight grip on the corner, and I pull and yank and lean all my weight into it. There's a clank and the hand trowel is gone, falling into the gap and beneath the floor, making a suitable time capsule.

The wood snaps and I fall on my ass. The shed shakes and groans, and for a second I think it's going to come down on my head, and maybe that wouldn't be a bad thing. Maybe another knock on my head will set me straight, fix me up as good as new.

The shed doesn't come down. The shaking and groaning stops and everything settles back. My fingers are red, raw, and screaming, but no splinters. I squeeze my hands in and out of fists and walk toward the hole in the floor. The sun goes behind a cloud and everything gets dark in the shed.

I go into snake mode, crawl on my belly, and hover my face above the hole. I look down and see the ground and the hand shovel. Fuck it. Leave the shovel under the shed where it belongs. I don't need it to tear up more of the floorboards. My hands will do just fine.

Wait. There's a dark lump attached to one floor joint, a black barnacle, adjacent to the corner. I reach out a hand. I touch it: plastic. Two different kinds of plastic; parts feel like a bag and other parts feel more solid but still malleable. I jack my knees underneath my weight and the floorboard buckles and bows out toward the ground under the pressure, but I don't care. I need the leverage and both hands.

I lean over the dark lump; it's something wrapped in a garbage bag and duct-taped to the frame. My fingers get underneath, and it comes off with a quick yank. On cue, the sun comes out again. Maybe that cartoon sun is my friend after all.

Things get brighter and hotter in the shed. I move away from the hole and stand up. There's duct tape wound all around the plastic bag. I apply some even pressure and the inside of the package feels hard, maybe metal. Jesus Christ, my heart is beating, and—yeah, I'll say it—I am goddamn Indiana Jones, only I'm not afraid of snakes. If this thing were a football I'd spike it and do a little dance, make a little love. But I'm a professional. It's all about composure.

Through the plastic, I trace its perimeter. I'm Helen Keller, begging my fingers to give me the answers. It's shaped like a wheel, and it's too big to be a roll of film. It's a tin, or a canister, or a reel of film. A movie.

It gets darker inside the shed again, but the sunlight is still coming in through the punched-out hole in the back wall. My back is to the door and I feel their shadows brushing up against my legs. I've been able to feel their shadows on me since the first trip to Sullivan's house.

"Whaddaya say, Genevich?" says one goon.

"Jackpot!" says the other.

TWENTY-NINE

Looks like I was right about them choosing to wait me out, let me do all the heavy lifting. Seems to have worked out for them too. They get the gold stars, but I can't let them have the parting gift.

I turn around slowly, a shadow moving around a sundial. The two goons fill the doorway. They replace the open doors. They are mobile walls. The sun might as well be setting right behind them, or maybe one of them has the sun in his back pocket. I can't see their faces. They are shadows too.

One of them is holding a handgun, a handgun in silhouette, which doesn't make it look any prettier or any less dangerous. Its barrel is the proboscis of some giant bloodsucking insect. Its bite will do more than leave an itchy welt, and baking soda won't help.

I say, "If you're a couple of Jehovah's Witnesses, God isn't in the shed and I'm a druid."

"Looks like you're having a little yard sale. We thought we'd drop by, see what hunk of worthless junk I can get for two bucks," says Redhead. "Whaddaya say, Genevich? What can I get for my two bucks?" He's on the right. He's the one with the gun and it threatens to overload my overloaded systems. Things are getting fuzzy at the edges, sounds are getting tinny. Or it could be just the echoes and shadows in a small empty shed.

Even in silhouette, Redhead's freckles are visible, glowing future melanomas. Maybe if I keep him talking long enough he'll die of skin cancer. A man can hope.

Baldy joins in, he always does, the punch line to a joke that everyone sees coming. He says, "Two bucks? Nah, he'll ask for ten. He looks like a price gouger. Or maybe he's selling his stuff to raise money for charity, for other retards like him."

I'm not sure what to do with the plastic-wrapped package in my hands. They've seen it already. Hell, I'm holding it in front of my stomach, so I nonchalantly put it and my hands behind my back. Nothing up my sleeves.

I say, "What, you two pieces of shit can't read the keep off the grass sign out there?"

They take a step inside the shed and have to duck under the doorframe to enter. The wood complains under their feet. I empathize with the wood. I did say I was a druid.

The goons take up all the space and air and light in the shed. Redhead says, "We're gonna cut the banter short, Genevich. You have two choices: we shoot you and take the movie or we just take the movie."

"And maybe we shoot you anyway," Baldy says.

I do register that they're confirming my find is in fact a movie, which is a plus, but I'm getting tingly again and the dark spots in my vision are growing bigger, ink leaking into a white shirt pocket. Come on, Genevich. Keep it together. I can't go out now, not now.

I shake my head and say, "That's no way to treat the gracious host. Bringing over a bottle of wine would've sufficed."

Redhead says, "We don't have manners. Sometimes I'm embarrassed for us. This isn't one of those times."

I say, "There's no way I'm giving you the flick. You two would just blab-blab-blab and ruin the ending for me." I don't think they appreciate how honest I'm being with them. I'm baring my soul here.

Baldy says, "Sorry, Genevich. We get the private screening."

They take another step forward; I go backward. We're doing a shed dance. I go back until the rear wall shelf hits me across the shoulders.

Redhead raises the gun to between-my-eyes level and says, "We do appreciate you clearing out a nice, clean, private space for your body. The way I see it, we shoot you, put all that crap back inside the shed, and no one will find you for days. Maybe even a week, depending on how bad the smell gets."

I say, "I didn't shower this morning and I sweat a lot."

Baldy says, "Give us the movie. Now."

That's right, I have the film, and until they get it, I have the upper hand. At least, that's what I have to fool myself into believing. I am a fool.

I can't move any farther backward, so I slide toward the right, to the corner, to where I found my prize and to the hole I punched through the back wall. The rotted plywood and wall are right behind me.

I say, "All right, all right. No need for hostilities, gentlemen. I'll give it to you." I pretend to slip into the floorboard hole, flail my arms around like I'm getting electrocuted. Save me, somebody save me! The movement and action feels good and clears my head some. I might be hamming it up too much, hopefully not enough to get me shot, but I don't want them watching my sleight of hand with the package, so I scuff and bang my feet on the floor, the sounds are percussive and hard, and then, as I fall to my knees in a heap, I jam the film inside my jacket, right next to the manila envelope. The photos and film reunited and it feels so good.

Redhead traces my lack of progress with his gun. He says, "Knock off whatever it is you're doing, Genevich, and stand up."

I say, "Sorry. Tripped. Always been clumsy, you know?" I hold out my empty hands. "Shit, I dropped the movie. I'll get it." I turn around slowly. I'm that shadow on the sundial again.

Baldy says, "Get away from there, I'll get it," but it sounds tired, has no muscle or threat behind it because I'm trapped in the corner of the shed with nowhere to go, right? Redhead hesitates, doesn't say anything, doesn't do anything to stop me from turning around.

My legs coil under me. My knees have one good spring in them. I'm aimed at the fist-sized hole in the wall and ready to be fired. I'm a piston. I'm a catapult.

I jump and launch shoulder first toward the plywood and the rear wall underneath the shelf, but my knees don't have one good spring in them. My feet fall into in the hole, lodge between the floor and the frame, and then I hit the plywood face first. The plywood is soft, but it's still strong enough to give me a good shot to the chops. There's enough momentum behind me and I bust through the shed and into the fading afternoon light. I'm a semisuccessful battering ram.

There's a gunshot and the bullet passes overhead; its sound is ugly and could never be confused with the buzz of a wasp or any living thing. The grass is more than a couple of feet below me. I tuck my chin into my chest, my hat falls off, and I dip a shoulder, hoping to land in some kind of roll. While dipping my shoulder, my body twists and turns, putting a tremendous amount of pressure on my feet and ankles; they're going to be yanked out of their respective sockets, but they come out of the corner. Upon release I snap forward, and land awkwardly on my right shoulder, planting it into the ground. There's no roll, no tens from the judges. My bottom half comes up and over my head into a half-assed headstand, only I'm standing on my shoulder and neck. I slide on the grass in this position, then fall.

There are two loud snaps, one right after the other. Breaking wood. I'm on my stomach and I chance a look back at the shed, instead of getting up and fleeing for my life. Most of the rear wall is gone, punched through, and the hole is a mouth that's closing. The roof is falling, Chicken Little says so. Yet despite the sagging roof, the shed is growing bigger, a deflating balloon somehow taking in more air and taking up more of my view. Wait, it's moving, coming right at me. The cinder blocks are toppling, and so is the propped-up shed.

The goons. They're yelling and there's a burst of frantic footsteps but those end suddenly. The curtain drops on their show. I might meet a similarly sudden fate if I don't move. The shed falls and roars and aims for me. I roll left, out of the way, but I go back for my hat. I reach out and grab the brim right as that mass of rotted wood and rusty nails crash-lands on the hat and my fingers are flea lengths away from being crushed. More stale dust billows into my face. All four walls have collapsed, the doors broken and unhinged. Just like that, the shed that stood forever is no more.

I yank my hat out from beneath the rubble. It has nine lives. I stand up and put the hat on. It's still good.

Most of my body parts seem to be functioning, though my face is wet. My fingers report back from the bridge of my nose; they're red with blood. No biggie. Just a scratch, a ding, otherwise good to go.

I have the film. The goons don't and they're under a pile of suburban rubble. I step over the cyclone fence and remake myself into a woodland creature. I give one last look behind me.

The backyard of the Genevich family plot has the appearance of utter devastation and calamity, the debris of Tim's life destroyed and strewn everywhere, spread out for everyone to see, should they care to. Secrets no more. Tim's stuff, the stuff that defined Tim for the entirety of my life, is nothing but so much rusted and collapsed junk, those memories made material are asleep or dead, powerless and meaningless, but not harmless.

I walk away from the damage into the woods, thinking that Ellen won't be pleased when she finds the shed. Hopefully, I'll be around long enough to improvise a story.

THIRTY

I walk a mile, maybe two. Keep to the woods when I can, stay off the streets. When there aren't any woods, I cut through people's yards, stomp through bushes, trample on lawns, cross over driveways. I hide behind fences meant to keep riffraff like me out. I walk past their pools and swing sets. People are home, or coming home from work. They yell at me and threaten to call the police. But they don't, and I keep walking. Small children run away; the older ones point and laugh. I don't care. I wave them off, shooing away flies. I'm carrying the big secret. It gives me provenance to go where I need to go.

I'm hungry, thirsty, and tired. Not the same tired as usual, but more, with a little extra spice, a little kick. Buffalo tired, General Gao tired. I can't do much more walking. The aches and minor injuries from the rumble and tumble with the shed are building, combining into a larger pain. They aren't inert.

I have no immediate destination in mind other than away from the goons and my house, just to go somewhere they won't find me. That's it. No more walking. I find two homes that have an acre or more of woods between them. I go back into hiding, but get the street name and address numbers first.

I call Brill, tell him where to pick me up. He says he'll be there in ten minutes. That's a good Brill.

Being the only cab in town during the off-season, this is a risk. Assuming the goons have emerged from the woodpile, they'll do all they can to get back on my trail. They'll figure out he's the only way around town for me, if they don't know that already. I have to chance it. I need one more ride from him.

I sit on a tree stump. The street is twenty yards away, far enough away that I can see the road, but I'll only be seen if someone stops and searches for me. I won't be seen from a quick drive-by.

I take the film—what I presume to be the film—out of my coat. The wrap job is tight. After an initial struggle to get the unraveling started, the layers of tape and plastic come off easy and fast, the way I like it. It's a canister of film, maybe six inches in diameter. I open the canister and there's a reel of celluloid. I lift it out like a doctor extracting shrapnel, or like I'm playing operation, careful with that funny bone, can't touch the sides.

The film is tan and silky and beautiful, and probably horrible.

It holds thousands of pictures, thousands of moments in time that fit together like the points in a line. It's getting dark in the woods and I try holding the film up to the vanishing light. There are shapes, but I can't make out much of anything.

I need equipment. Luckily, I know a film expert. She wears clown pants sometimes.

My cell rings. I dig it out of my pocket. I don't recognize the number, but it's the Boston area code.

"Hello."

"Hi, Mr. Genevich? It's me, Jennifer."

I look around the woods like she might pop out from behind a maple. I say, "What's wrong? Daddy doesn't know where I am?"

There's a beat or two of silence on the phone, long enough to make me think the call was dropped or she hung up. She says, "I'm sorry about what happened. I just thought my father was going to watch you, make sure you weren't dangerous or up to some crazy blackmail scam. That's all. I got your message and today I saw the break-in of your office and apartment in the paper. And I'm sorry, Mr. Genevich. Really, I didn't know he was going to do anything like that."

I'm in the middle of the woods, and I'm too tired to breathe. I want to sit down but I'm already sitting down. Not sure what to believe or who to believe, not sure if I should believe in myself.

I say, "On the obscure chance you're telling it straight, thanks."

"Why would my father do that?"

"No *would* about it. Did. He did it."

"Why did he break into your apartment? Was he looking for those pictures?"

I say, "Your father was looking for a film to go along with those pictures I showed you. The pictures are meaningless; they can't hurt anyone. But the film. The film is dangerous. The film can do damage."

"Do you have it?"

"Oh, yeah. I have it. I'm getting copies made right now. Going to send them to the local stations as soon as I get off the phone with you." Dressing up the truth with some bluff can't hurt, especially if she's trying to play me on behalf of DA Daddy again.

"Oh, my God! Seriously, what's on it?"

"Bad stuff. It's no Sesame Street video."

"Is it that girl who looks like me?"

"What do you think, Jennifer?"

"How bad is it?"

"One man is already dead because of it."

There's a beat of silence. "What? Who's dead?" Her voice is a funeral, and I know she believes me, every word.

"Brendan Sullivan. Police report says he shot himself in his Osterville home. He was the one who hired me, sent me the pictures, and wanted me to find the film. I found the film. Sullivan was a childhood friend of my father and your father. We're all in this together. We should all hold hands and sing songs about buying the world a Coke."

More silence. Then: "Mr. Genevich, I want to see it. Will you meet me and show it to me?"

"Now that sounds like crazy talk. Even assuming that I don't think you're trying to set me up again, I don't know why I would show you the film."

"I know and I'm sorry. Just listen to me for a sec. After our dinner, I couldn't stop thinking about those photos, and then when I heard about your apartment, it got worse, and I have such a bad feeling about all this, you know? I just need to know what happened. I promise I'll help you in any way I can. I need to see this. I'll come to your office and watch it. I can come right now. It won't take me long to get there."

Jennifer talks fast, begging and pleading. She might be sincere, but probably not. With the goons having lost my trail, the timing of her call just plain sucks. That said, the DA can't go to her well too often. She'll know too much.

How about I keep the possibilities open? I say, "We'll see. Need to finish getting copies made. Maybe I can offer you a late-night showing. I'll call you later." I hang up.

The cell phone goes back in my pocket. I need to chew on this for a bit. For such a simple action, watching a film, there are suddenly too many forks and branches and off-ramps and roadblocks and . . .

Three loud beeps shake me off my tree stump. I land in a crouch. A white car crawls along my stretch of woods, stops, then beeps again. It's my man Brill.

I try to gather myself quickly, but it's like chasing a dropped bundle of papers in a windy parking lot. I come crashing through the woods. The film is back inside my coat pocket. There's a moment of panic when I expect the goons to be in the backseat waiting for me, but it's empty. I open the door and slide in. The seat's been retaped, just for me.

Brill says, "I'm not even gonna ask how you got out here."

"That's mighty fine of you."

"I won't ask what happened to your face, either. But I hope it hurt like hell because it's killing me."

"Just a scratch. The perils of hiking through the woods, my man."

"All right. Where to, Sasquatch?"

I say, "That's actually funny. Congrats."

Let's try a change of destinations. I can't rely on Brill anymore, too risky. I say, "Take me to the nearest and dearest car rental agency. One that's open."

THIRTY-ONE

I'm leaned back into the seat, relaxed. I feel magnanimous in my latest small victory. Let Brill have his cheap shots. Let the people have cake. At least I feel magnanimous until I wake up, not on a sleepy Osterville road but in the parking lot of a car rental agency.

Brill is turned around. The old bastard has been watching me. His skeleton arm is looped around the back of his seat, and he shows me his wooden teeth. I suppose it's a smile. I didn't need to see that. I'll have nightmares the next time I pass out.

I say, "What are you smiling at?"

He says, "Your little nap made me an extra ten bucks. If I had any kids, you'd be putting them through college one z at a time."

I say, "I wasn't asleep. Making sure the lot and inside was all clear. Sitting here thinking. You should try it."

"You must've been doing some hard thinking with all that twitching and snoring." He laughs and coughs. Can't imagine he has much lung left.

I don't have a comeback for him, so I change the thrust of our departure conversation. "Nice tape job on the seats, Brill. You're first class all the way." I'm running low on cash. I have just enough to pay the grinning bag of bones.

Brill takes the bills. He says, "You here to rent a car?"

"No, I'm going to get my shoes shined and then maybe a foot massage. All that walking and my dogs are barking."

Brill turns back around, faces front, assumes the cabbie position. "You driving on my roads, any roads? That can't be legal."

I open my door. I don't have to explain anything to him, but I do. I say, "I have a driver's license and a credit card. I can drive a car. I'm sure the transaction will be quite easy. Wait for me here, we'll drag-race out of the lot. I'll let you be James Dean. You got the looks."

"No, thanks. I'm turning in early if you're going to be on the road." He revs the tiny four-cylinder engine. My cue to leave.

I get out. The lot is small and practically empty. The sun-bleached pavement is cracked and the same color as the overcast sky. Brill drives away. He's no fun.

Inside the rental agency, everything is bright yellow and shitty brown. There are cheery poster-sized ads hanging on the walls featuring madly grinning rental agents. Those madly grinning rental agents are at their desks but outside with a bright blue sky as their background. Apparently renting a car should be some sort of conversion experience for me. We'll see.

Before docking my weary ass at the service counter, I make a side trip to a small ATM tucked away between two mini–palm trees. I need to replenish the cash supply. First I do a balance check: $35.16.

Been spending too much and it's been weeks since I had a paying client. I'll take out twenty. While patiently waiting to add the exorbitant transaction fee to my ledger, I check my reflection in the handy-dandy mirror above the ATM. There's dried blood on the right side of my nose and cheek. The shed hit me with a pretty good shot but I won by TKO in the fifth.

No other customers in the joint, so I'm up next at the counter.

The agent says, "Can I help you?" He's a kid, skinnier than a junkie. Greasy hair parted all wrong, shadow of a mustache under his nose.

I say, "I need a car. Nothing fancy. But if you have something that has bumpers, real bumpers with rubber and reinforced, I don't know, metal. Not those cheap plastic panels they put on the front and back of most cars now. Real bumpers."

The kid stares at me. I know, I'm pretty. The dried blood adds character to a face already overburdened with character. He probably thinks I'm drunk with my slow, deep voice and my sudden bumper obsession. I suppose I should've cleaned myself up in the bathroom first. Can't do much about my voice, though. I am what I am.

He snaps out of his trance and types fast, too fast. There's no way he's hitting the keys in any sort of correct order. He says, "The only vehicles we have with what you described are a couple of small pickup trucks and three SUVs."

"Nah, I hate trucks and SUVs. Too big." I don't want to hurt anyone more than I already might. "I want something compact, easy to drive." I know enough not to add, *Won't cause a lot of collateral damage.*

"Okay. We have plenty of compacts." He types again at warp

speed. It's actually kind of impressive. Good for him for finding his niche at such a young age.

I say, "A compact, but something safe. Air bags and all that stuff, and maybe with bumpers."

"I'm sorry, sir, but we don't have any compacts or sedans with the bumpers you described."

"Right, right, you already told me that. Sorry. Oh, and it should have one of those GPS thingies for directions."

"Our vehicles all come equipped with GPS."

Fantastic. I give him my license and credit card. All is well. We will complete our vehicular transaction and there will be joy.

I look outside the bay windows. No sign of the goons. There's a slowly creeping thought, bubbling its way up through the murk, the remnants of my cab nap. And here it is: I forgot to ask Brill where he dumped me. I was asleep and have no idea if we're still in Osterville or not. There's a nondescript strip mall across the street from the agency. It looks like every strip mall on the Cape. It has a pharmacy, bank, breakfast joint, gift shop, and water sports store. Maybe we're in Hyannis.

Wait. I find a life jacket. There's a stack of business cards on the counter; I paw at a couple and spy the address. Okay, still in Osterville, at its edge, but I know where I am now.

I say, "Oh, if you haven't picked me a car already, can I get one that has a lot of distracting stuff going on inside?"

He doesn't look up from his computer. He knows that won't help him. "You mean like a CD player?"

I say, "That's okay too, but I'm thinking more along the lines of a car that has a busy dashboard, tons of digital readings, lights, and blinking stuff."

"You want to be distracted?"

"When you say it like that, it sounds a little silly, but yeah, that'd be swell."

"I think we can accommodate you, Mr. Genevich."

"You're a pro's pro, kid."

I relax. I know I'm making a fool of myself, but the looming situation of me behind a steering wheel has me all hot and bothered. I know it's irresponsible and dangerous, reckless, and selfish. Me behind the wheel of a car is putting Mr. and Mrs. Q. Public and their extended families in danger. But I'm doing it anyway. I can't wait to drive again.

I'm done with Brill. Renting a car is the only way I'm going to get around without further endangering Ellen, and hopefully it'll be less likely the goons will pick up my scent again. They know my condition, they've been following me around; they won't be expecting me to rent a car.

I tell the kid I want the car for two days. He quotes me the price and terms. I cross my fingers and hope there's enough room on my credit card. Then he says, "Will you be buying renter's insurance for the vehicle?"

I laugh. Can't remember the last time I laughed like this. This could be a problem. For many narcoleptics, laughter is a trigger for the Godzilla symptoms, the ones that flatten Tokyo. But I know where I am and I know what I'm doing and I know where to go next. I feel damn good even if my contorted face reopens the cut along my nose.

I say, "Oh, yeah, kid. I'll take as much insurance as you'll give me. Then double the order."

THIRTY-TWO

My car is blue and looks like a space car. Meet George Jetson.

The kid has to show me how to start the thing, as it has no ignition key. Insert the black keyless lock/alarm box into a portal in the dash, push another dash button, and we're ready to go. Simple. The car is one of those gas-electric hybrids. At least I'll be helping out the environment as I'm crashing into shit. Hopefully I don't damage any wetlands or run over endangered owls or something similarly cute and near extinction.

Okay, I start the car up. My hands grip the wheel hard enough to remold the plastic, turn it into clay. White knuckles, dry mouth, the whole bit. I wonder what the air bag tastes like. Probably not marshmallow fluff.

I roll to the edge of the lot and onto the street, and I don't hit anything, don't pass out asleep, and the wheels don't fall off, so I relax a little bit. I join the flow of traffic, become part of the mass, the great unending migration, the river of vehicles, everyone anonymous but for a set of numbers and letters on their plates. My foot is a little heavy on the brake pedal, otherwise I'm doing fine. If millions of privileged stunted American lunkheads can operate heavy machinery, I can too. Driving is the easy part. It's staying awake that'll take some doing.

Yeah, I'm an accident waiting to happen, but I should be all right on a short jaunt into town. This first trip is only to downtown Osterville. It's the later excursion back to Southie that'll be my gauntlet.

I'm driving at the speed limit. I check all my mirrors, creating a little rotation of left sideview, rearview, right sideview, while sprinkling in the eyes-on-the-road bit. The OCD pattern might lull me to sleep so I change it up, go from right to left. I forgot how much you have to look at while driving, the proverbial everywhere-at-once. It's making me tired.

Of course, the roads are congested all of a sudden and out of nowhere. Did I run over a hive or something? Cars swarming and stopping and going and stopping. The town has been deader than the dinosaurs since I've been here, and all of a sudden it's downtown LA.

No signs of the red car, or at least one particular red car and its goons. I should've asked for a car with tinted windows so nobody could see me. I wasn't thinking. My windshield is a big bubble and I'm on display, behind glass; don't break in case of emergency.

Traffic stretches the ride out to fifteen minutes before I penetrate the downtown area. There's Ellen's photography studio/antiques store. The antiques side is dark. During the off-season, she only opens on Fridays and weekends. There are lights on in her studio, though, so she's still here. Not sure if that's a good thing or bad thing.

I take a left onto a one-lane strip of pavement that runs between Ellen's building and the clothing boutique next door, and I tuck me and my rental behind the building. There's no public parking back here, only Ellen's car, a Dumpster, and the back doors.

I get out and try the antiques shop first. There are two large wooden doors that when open serve as a mini-bay for larger deliveries. The doors are loose and bang around in the frame as I yank on them, but they're locked. Damn. It's where I need to go and I don't have any keys.

Door number 2, then, the one I wanted to avoid. Up three wooden stairs to a small landing and a single door, a composite and newer than the antique doors, which is how nature intended. That's locked too. I'm not walking around out front on the off-chance the goons do a drive-by. I ring the bell. It doesn't ring. It buzzes like I just gave the wrong answer to the hundred-dollar question.

Footsteps approach the door and I panic. Ellen can't know that I drove here. I'm parked behind the Dumpster, my shiny space car in plain view. Crap. I try to fill the doorway with my bulk, but Ellen will be half a step above me, elevated. The door opens.

Ellen's wearing her clown pants again. She says, "Hey. What are you doing back here?"

I yawn and stretch my arms over my head, trying to block her view. For once, me being tired is schtick. I say, "I don't know. There was a lot of traffic out front and Brill came back here to drop me off. He's kind of a surly guy."

"Stop it. He's a sweetheart." Ellen is whispering and throwing looks over her shoulder. "I've got a client and I'm in the middle of a shoot. Go around front."

I say, "Come on, I'm here, my knees have rusted up, and I'm dead tired. Let me in. Your client won't even notice me limp through." I lay it on thick but leave out the pretty please.

She says, "Yeah, right," but steps aside, holds the door open, and adds, "Just be quick."

"Like a bunny," I say. I shimmy inside the door, crowding her space purposefully so she has a harder time seeing over me and into the lot. I compress and crumple her clown pants. It's not easy being a clown.

She says, "What the hell is that car doing back here?"

My hands go into my pockets. Instead of balls of lint and thread, maybe I'll find a plausible excuse. I say, "Oh, some guy asked if he could park there real quick. Said he was just returning something next door. I told him it was fine." Lame story, but should be good enough for now.

Ellen lets out an exasperated sigh. "If he's not out in five minutes, I'm calling a tow truck. I can't have people parking back here." She's all talk. She'll forget about the car as soon as the door is shut. I bet.

Ellen leads me through a small back hallway and into the studio. The background overlay is a desert and tumbleweeds, huge ones, bigger than my car. A little kid is dressed up as a cowboy with hat, vest, chaps, six-shooters, spurs, the whole bit. He must've just heard the saddest campfire song ever because he's bawling his eyes out while rocking on a plastic horse.

Those UFO-sized photographer spot lamps are everywhere, warming the kid up like he's a fast-food burger that's been sitting out since the joint opened. I don't blame him for being a little cranky.

His mom yaks on her cell phone, sniping at someone, wears sunglasses and lip gloss shinier than mica, and has a purse bigger than Ellen's mural tumbleweed. It ain't the OK Corral in here.

I say, "Sorry to interrupt. As you were."

The little kid jumps at the sound of my voice, cries harder, and rocks the wooden pony faster, like he's trying to make a break for it.

I say, "Remember the Alamo, kid."

Ellen apologizes, puts on a happy face like it's part of her professional garb, something that hangs on a coatrack after work is over. She ducks behind her camera. "Come on, Danny boy, you can smile for me, right? Look at my pants!"

Yikes. I'm out of the studio, door closed behind me, and into her nondescript reception area. Ellen has a desk with a phone, computer, printer, and a buzzer. Next to that is a door to the antiques store. That's locked too. The doorknob turns but there's a dead bolt about chest high. I need me some keys. Don't want to have to see the clown pants and cowboy-tantrum show again. I go behind her desk and let my fingers do the walking through her drawers. I find a ring of ten or so keys.

Guess and check, and eventually the right key. I don't turn on the lights, as the store's bay window is large and I could easily be seen from outside. The afternoon is dying, but there's enough light in here that I can see where I'm going.

The antiques store is packed tight with weekend treasures: wooden barrels filled with barely recognizable tools that might've come from the dawn of the Bronze Age, or at least the 1940s; home and lawn furniture; kitschy lamps, one shaped like a hula girl with the shade as the grass skirt; fishing gear; a shelf full of dusty hardcover books; tin advertising placards. Piles of useless junk everywhere. If it's old, it's in here somewhere. I never understood the appeal of antiques. Some things are meant to be thrown away and forgotten.

The photography and film stuff has its own corner in the rear of the store. There's a display counter with three projectors under glass. Short stacks of film reels separate the projectors. Nice presentation. No price tags, but the specs and names of the projectors are written on pieces of masking tape that are stuck to the counters. The curling and peeling tape is in much worse condition than the projectors, which look to be mint.

All right. I assume the film is 8 millimeter, but I'm not exactly sure what projector I need to play it, and even if I had the right projector I don't know how to use it. I need Ellen's help. Again.

Out of the dusty store and back into the reception area, I stick my head inside the studio. Glamour Mom is still on the phone, talking directly to a Prada handbag maybe. The kid continues to wail. Ellen dances some crazed jig that pendulums back and forth behind her tripod. She makes odd noises with her mouth. A professional at work.

I say, "Hey, Bozo. I need your expertise for a second."

Under normal circumstances (maybe these are her normal circumstances, I don't know), I'd assume she'd be pissed at me for interrupting. She mumbles something under her breath that I don't quite hear, but it might be *Thank Christ.*

Ellen has to say, "Excuse me," three times before the woman puts down her phone. "Maybe we should try something else. I don't think Danny likes being a cowboy. Why don't we change him, let him pick something else out of that bin over there, and I'll be right back?"

The brat has worked her over pretty good, softened her up, and hopefully made her head mushy enough so she can't add one and one together. I need to take advantage and throw stuff at her quick.

Ellen has only one foot in the reception area and I'm sticking the film canister in her face. I say, "I just need a little help. This is eight-millimeter film, right? Or super eight? Or something else?"

Ellen blinks a few times, clearly stunned after trying to wrangle Danny the Kid into an image. She says, "Let me see."

I open the can and let a six-inch tail grow from the spool. She reaches for it. I say, "Don't get your grubby fingerprints on it."

"I need to see the damn thing if I'm going to tell you what it is." I give it to her, ready to snatch it back out of her hands should she hold it up to the light and see something bad. "This isn't super eight, it's too dark. Eight millimeter." She gives it back, yawns, and stretches. "My back is killing me. Where'd you get that?"

I don't answer. I say, "I need a projector. I need to watch this. Got anything I can borrow?"

"Yeah, I have projectors. Silent or sound?"

"I don't know. Do you have one that plays both?"

I take her by the arm and lead her into the store. She doesn't turn on the lights. What a good clown.

Small key goes into small lock, and the glass slides open to the left. "This one will play your movie, sound or no sound. It's easy to use too."

I read the tape: Eumig Mark-S Zoom 8mm magnetic sound projector.

She picks it up, shuts the glass case, and rests it on the counter. It's a mini-robot out of a 1950s sci-fi flick, only the earth isn't standing still.

She says, "Let me finish up the shoot and I can set up the projector in here. I've got a screen in the closet."

"No, I can't watch it here. This film, it's for a client. Just need to make sure what's in the can is the real deal, that it's what I think it is. No one else but me can see it."

"Why? Where did you get it?"

"Sorry. Secrets of state. I can't tell you."

"Wait. What client? How have you had any contact with a client since we've been down here?"

I think about the backyard and demolished shed. She'll know where I found it.

I hold out my cell phone, wave it around like it's Wonka's golden ticket. "I've been on the phone with my clients all day. I'm not gonna just sit on my ass the whole time I'm down here. That wouldn't be very professional, would it? Don't worry. It's no big deal. I watch the flick for simple verification, then stick it in a FedEx box, case closed. You go. Go finish up with that little cherub in there. I'm all set."

Ellen folds her arms across her chest. She's not having any of it. She digs in, entrenches, a tick in a mutt's ear. She says, "I think you're lying to me."

"Frankly, I'm nonplussed. Would I lie to you, Clowny?"

"Yes. You do, all the time."

"True. But this time everything is kosher." I spread the word *everything* out like it's smooth peanut butter.

Ellen sighs and throws up her hands. "I don't know what to do with you, and I don't have time to argue. I'll set up the projector, then go back into the studio, and you can watch it in here by yourself."

Okay, I'm by one hurdle, now on to the next. I talk as fast as I can, which isn't very. "No good. I need someplace private. Not rush-hour downtown Osterville in an antiques store with a huge bay friggin' window. Let me borrow it. I promise to return it in one piece. I'll set it up and watch it at the house before you come home."

"You're a giant pain in my butt, you know that, right?"

I say, "I'll have a bowl of popcorn ready for you when you get back. Extra butter."

"Fine. Let me see if the bulbs still work." Ellen plugs it in, turns it on. A beam of light shines out of the projection bulb and onto a bearskin rug and its matted fur. I resist the urge for a shadow puppet show. She turns off the projection bulb and two small lights come on within the body of the projector.

I say, "What are those lights?"

"You could thread the film in the dark, if you needed to."

"Good to know."

"This projector will automatically thread through the film gate, which is nice. If you think it's a sound film, you'll have to thread it manually through the sound head and then to the take-up reel. It's easy, though." Ellen points out the heads, loops, and hot spots. I should be taking notes, drawing diagrams.

She says, "The instruction manual is taped underneath the projector if you want to mess around with it. If you can figure out how to do it yourself, great, or just wait until I get home. I won't be long. This kid is my last shoot of the day." She shuts off the projector and unplugs it.

I say, "Thanks. I think I can handle it from here."

Ellen walks to the other side of the counter, then ducks down and disappears. Momentarily inspired, I take one of the display case's stacked film reels and tuck it inside my coat. The reel is black, not gray, but about the same size as the one I found. I'm a collector now.

Ellen emerges with a carrying case. "This was Tim's projector. If you break it, you're a dead man." The little robot disappears into the case. I hope it won't be lonely, separated from its friends.

Tim's projector for Tim's film that was in Tim's shed. I've opened one of those sets of nested Russian dolls, and I don't know when the dolls will stop coming out or how to stop them. I grab the case by the handle and let the projector hang by my hip. It's heavy. It's all heavy.

"How come you don't sell these projectors, or the cameras on the wall?"

"What? We don't have time for this."

"You're right, we don't, but I want to know. Maybe the answer is important. Give me your gut-shot answer. Quick. Don't think about it. Don't think about what I'd want to hear or don't want to hear. Just tell me."

She says, "Because no one else should be using Tim's stuff."

I want to take the question back because she can't answer it. It wasn't fair to try and distill something as complex as her twenty-five-plus years of being a widow into a reaction. She gave it an honest try. Don't know what I was expecting, maybe something that would make Tim seem like a real person, not a collection of secrets, clues, and consequences. Something that helps me to get through tonight.

I say, "Fair enough. There will be no breaking of the projector. I'm a gentle soul."

Ellen puts her hands in her hair. "You've got me all frazzled. I need to go back. There's a stand-alone screen in that closet over there. Take it with you."

I scoot down to the end of the display cabinet, boxing her in while I root through the closet for the screen. I hold up a long heavy cardboard box. "Is it in the box?"

"Yes! Now get out of the way. Shoo!"

I hustle after Ellen, my arms full of film equipment. Let's all go to the lobby. I follow her into the reception area, to the studio. Ellen stops at the door.

"Where are you going?"

I say, "I'm going out the way I came in. Brill is going to meet me out back. He went to get a coffee and a pack of smokes and a *Playboy*. I'm telling you, he's a sick old man."

Ellen ignores me and walks into the studio. "Okay, so sorry for the interruption. He's leaving, finally."

It's true.

Ellen breaks into a fake-cheery voice. She's a pro at it, which makes me wonder how many years she used that voice on the kid me: everything is great and happy and there's nothing wrong here, nothing can hurt you.

She says, "How's Danny doing? Is he ready? You're going to look so cool in the pictures, Danny. Picture time!"

The movie-show equipment is cumbersome. I flip the screen up onto my left shoulder, lugging it like a log. Balancing and carrying it is not easy.

Glamour Mom couldn't care less about the goings-on and continues to talk on the phone. Danny is still crying, and is now dressed like a duck; yellow feathers and orange bill split wide open over his face, the suit swallows him. His wings flap around as Ellen changes the desert scene to a sunset lake.

I'm no duck. I am the guy waddling out, away from the sunset lake and into a back alley.

THIRTY-THREE

The sun is setting but there's no lake back here. I buckle the projector into the passenger seat. It could be a bumpy ride and I don't want it rolling around the trunk or backseat. It needs to survive the trip.

Before I climb behind the wheel, I take out the cell phone. No messages. I consider calling Brill, but I won't. There's no way he'd give me a ride to Southie, even if I did have enough cash, which I don't. I turn off the cell phone. I'm sure Ellen will be calling me as soon as she gets home.

Yeah, Southie. I've made a decision. Don't know if I'm going to call Jennifer, but I'm going back to Southie and my apartment. This is the only way to finish the case. My case. I don't think I have the cash or credit card balance left to hole up in a local motel, or any motel on the way to Southie, and watch the film. Besides, this isn't about hiding anymore. That skulking-around shit I went through today is not for me. It makes me irritable and fatigued. This is about doing it my way. I'm going to go back to my office and my apartment, where I will watch this film and solve this case. It's going to end there, one way or the other, because I say so.

Okay, the drive. The downtown traffic has decreased considerably. The townies are all home, eating dinner, watching the local news. I wonder what Janice Sullivan is doing tonight. I don't remember if Brendan's wake was today or not. I wonder how long her twin aunts are staying at the house. I think about Janice's first day alone, and then the next one, and the next one. Will I be able to tell her, when all this is over, about the death of her husband?

Stop. I can't lose myself in runaway trains of thought. Those are nonstop bullets to Sleep Town.

Motoring through the outskirts of Osterville and I need to make a pit stop before the big ride. I pull into a convenience store. Mine is the only car in the lot. If this was Southie, the townie kids would be hanging out here, driving around and buzzing the lot because there's no other place to go. They'd spike their slurpies and drink hidden beers. But this isn't Southie. I'm not there yet, not even close.

Inside, a quick supply run: supersized black coffee, a box of powdered donuts, and a pack of smokes. Dinner of champions. Let's hope it brings on a spell of insomnia.

Back behind the wheel with my supplies, I check the seat belt rig on my copilot. I apologize for not getting it a Danish. I'm so inconsiderate.

I turn on the space car. The dashboard is a touch-screen computer with settings for the radio, CD player, climate control, fuel efficiency ratings for the trip, and a screen that displays an animated diagram of the hybrid engine and when the power shifts from gas to electric. Have to hand it to the rental agent, I wanted distracting and the kid gave it to me.

Next is the GPS. I plug in the convenience store's address, then the destination, my apartment. I choose avoid highways instead of fastest trip. Driving on the highway, especially the expressway when I get closer to Boston, would be too dangerous for everyone. I know the drive, normally ninety minutes, will take twice, maybe even three times as long by sticking to back roads, but there's always congestion on the highways and the likelihood of me killing myself and someone else with my car at highway speeds is too great. I'll take it slow and steady and win the race on the back roads.

The GPS estimates driving time to be three hours and twenty-two minutes. I pat the projector, say, "Road trip," and pull out of the lot. The GPS has a female voice. She tells me to turn left. "You're the boss."

I drive. Osterville becomes Centerville becomes Barnstable becomes Sandwich. My coffee is hot enough to burn enamel, the way I like it. The combination of excitement, fear, and caffeine has me wired. I feel awake. I know it's the calm before the storm. I still could go out at any minute, but I feel good. That's until I remember there's only two ways off the Cape. Both include a spot of highway driving and a huge bridge.

It's past dusk and there's no turning back. The sun is gone-daddy-gone and might never come up again if I'm not careful, as if careful ever has anything to do with narcolepsy. I'm in Sandwich when the GPS tells me to get on Route 6. She's too calm. She doesn't realize what she's telling me to do.

The on-ramp to the highway winds around itself and spits me onto a too-small runway to merge into the two-lane traffic. I jump on with both feet and all four tires, eyes forward, afraid to check my mirror. A hulking SUV comes right up my behind and beeps. The horn is loud enough to be an air raid siren. I jerk and swerve right but keep space car on the road. Goddamn highway, got to get off sooner than soon.

The Sagamore Bridge is ahead, a behemoth, seventy-plus years old. That can't be safe for anyone. It spans the Cape Cod Canal and is at least 150 feet above the water. Its slope is too steep, the two northbound lanes too narrow. No cement dividers, just double yellow lines keep northbound and southbound separated. They need more than lines. North and south don't like each other and don't play well together. Doesn't anyone know their history anymore?

There are too many cars and trucks squeezing over the towering Cape entrance and exit. I stay in the right lane. I'm so scared I'm literally shaking. White powder from a donut I stuff in my mouth sprinkles all over my pants. I probably shouldn't be eating now, but I'm trying for some sort of harmless everyday action while driving, just like the other slob motorists on the death bridge.

The steel girders whisper at my car doors. I'm on an old rickety roller coaster. The car is ticking its way up the big hill, still going up, and I'm anticipating the drop. My hands are empty of donut and back on the wheel, still shaking. This is a mistake. I can't manage my narcolepsy and I can't manage who or what I'll hit with the space car when I go to sleep. No if. When. I don't know when an attack will happen. There's no pattern. There's no reason.

I try to drink the coffee but my tremors are too violent and I get my lips and chin scalded for the trouble. The swell of traffic moves at a steady 45 miles per hour. There are other vehicles on the front, back, and left of me. I can't slow down and can't switch lanes. I won't look right and down, to the water. I'm not afraid of the bridge or the fall. I'm afraid of me, of that curtain that'll just go down over my eyes.

I crest the top of the bridge. A blast of wind voices its displeasure and pushes me left a few inches. I correct course, but it's not a smooth correction. The car jerks. The wind keeps blowing, whistling around the car's frame. My hands want to cry on the steering wheel. They're doing their best. They need a drink and a cigarette.

After the crest is down. The down is as steep as the up, and almost worse. The speed of the surrounding traffic increases. We have this incredible group forward momentum and nothing at the bottom of the hill to slow us down. I tap my brakes for no reason. I chance a look in the rearview mirror and the bulk of the bridge is behind me. Thank Christ. I'm over the canal and off the Cape. I breathe for the first time since Sandwich. The breath is too clean. Need a smoke, but that will have to wait until I get off the highway.

I'm finally off the bridge. Ms. GPS says she wants world peace and Route 6 is now Route 3 north, and I need to take the first exit to get with the back-roads plan again. Easy for her to say. I still have some highway to traverse.

I'm putting along Route 3 in the right lane, going fifty while everyone else passes me. The flat two lanes of highway stretch out into darkness, and the red taillights of the passing cars fade out of sight. I think about staying on the highway, taking it slow, pulling over when I get real tired and getting to Southie quicker, but I can't chance it. I crash here, I'm a dead man, and I'll probably take someone with me.

I'm already yawning by the time the first Plymouth exit shows up on my radar screen. Maybe I'll show my movie on Plymouth Rock. I take the exit and pull over in a gully soon after the off-ramp. Need to reset my bearings, take a breather. My hands and fingers are sore from vise-gripping the wheel.

I light a cigarette and turn on my cell phone. It rings and vibrates as soon as it powers up. It's Ellen. I let it ring out, then

I call her back. My timing is good. She's still leaving a message for me so my call is directly shuffled off to her voice mail.

Talk after the beep. "I'm okay, Ellen. No worries. Just so you know, the DA is crooked, can't be trusted. You stay put and call the police if you see a couple of mountain-sized goons on your doorstep, or if any red cars pull into the driveway. Or if that doesn't make you feel safe, go to a motel. I'm being serious. I'd offer to treat but I'm just about out of cash. I've almost solved my case. I'll call you back later, when it's over."

It is possible the goons are in the house, have Ellen tied to a chair, gun to her head, the whole mustache-twisting bit, and are making her call me under the threat of pain. Possible but not likely. Sure, it's getting late and the DA and his squad are desperate to get the film, but they also have to be careful about how many people know what they're doing. They start harassing too many folks, the cleanup gets too big and messy. Then again, maybe I shouldn't underestimate their desperation.

I can't turn back now. If the goons want me, they can call from their own phone.

The cell rings. It's Ellen and I don't answer it. She must've heard my message. I'll make it up to her later, if there is a later. I turn on the car, and it's back on the road again for me.

Plymouth is its own state. The biggest city in Massachusetts by square mileage, and I'm feeling it. Drive, drive, drive. Lefts and rights. Quiet back roads that range from the heart of suburbia to the heart of darkness, country roads with no streetlamps and houses that don't have any neighbors.

It's a weeknight and it's cold, so no one is out walking or riding their bikes. Mostly, it's just me and the road. When another car approaches in the opposite lane, I tense up, a microwave panic; it's instant and the same feeling I had on the highway. I think about what would happen if I suddenly veered into that lane, into those headlights, and I'm the Tin Man with no heart and everything starts to rust. Then the car passes me and I relax a little, but the whole process is draining.

I pull over and eat a few donuts. I pull over and take a leak, stretch my legs. I pull over and light another fire in my mouth. I pull over and try to take a quick nap, but as soon as I park the car, shut everything off, I'm awake again. The almost-asleep feeling is gone. I close my eyes, it's lost, and for once I can't find it.

Drive, drive, drive. The GPS says I'm in Kingston, but I don't remember leaving Plymouth. That's not good. My stomach fills with acid, but that's what I get for medicating with black coffee and powdered donuts.

I think about calling someone, just to shoot the shit. Talking can help keep me awake, but there's no one to call. I try to focus on the GPS, its voice, maps, and beeps. I learn the digital pattern, how soon before a turn she'll tell me to turn. This isn't good either. The whole trip is becoming a routine. I've been in the car long enough that driving is once again automatic behavior.

I sing. I play with the touch screen, changing the background colors. Kingston becomes Pembroke. Pembroke becomes Hanover.

More than ninety minutes have passed since the start. I'd be in Southie by now if I could've driven on the highway. That kind thinking isn't helping. Stay on the sunny side of the street, Genevich.

The road. The road is in Hanover, for now. I flick the projector's latches up and down. The projector doesn't complain. The road. How many roads are there in Massachusetts? Truth is, you can get they-uh from hee-uh. You can even find roads to the past. Everything and everyone is connected. It's more than a little depressing. I flick the latches harder; apparently I'm sadistic when it comes to inanimate objects. The road. Flick. Then everything is noise. The engine revs and the space car fills a ditch. My teeth knock and jam into each other with the jolt. The car careens left into bushes and woods. Budding branches scratch the windshield and side panels. I cut the wheel hard right and stomp on the brake pedal. The car slows some, but the back end skids out, and it wants to roll. I know the feeling. The car goes up and I'm pitched toward the passenger seat and the projector. The space car is going to go over and just ahead is the trunk of a huge tree.

Then the car stops. Everything is quiet. The GPS beeps, tells me to turn right.

I climb out. The car is beached on a swale, a foot away from the big tree. It's pitch dark and I can't see all that much, but the driver's-side door feels dented and scratched. I crossed over the right lane and into some woods. There's a house maybe two hundred yards ahead. I walk around to the passenger side and check the projector, and it seems to be in one piece.

"Now that we've got that out of the way."

I climb back in the car and roll off the hill; the frame and wheel wells groan but I make it back to the road and go a half mile before I pull over again. The space car's wounds seem superficial. Tires still inflated. No cracked glass, and I have no cracked bones.

The GPS and distracting dashboard aren't enough to keep me conscious. I need another stay-awake strategy. I dig a notepad and pencil out of my coat and put it in the passenger seat. It's worth a shot.

Hanover becomes Norwell. I'm keeping a running tally of yellow street signs. Whenever I pass one, I make a slash on the notepad, a little task to keep me focused and awake. Norwell becomes Hingham. I'm driving with more confidence. I know it's a false confidence, the belief that the disaster has already happened, lightning struck once, and it won't happen again. I know that isn't true but after a night spent in a car, by myself, it's easy to cling to my own lies.

I keep up with the tally marks. I play with the dashboard some more. I still get sleepy. I push on. Hingham becomes Weymouth. I pull over twice and try to sleep. Again, no dice. I walk around, take deep breaths, alternating filling up my lungs with hot smoke and with the cold March air. I pee on someone's rosebushes.

It's almost midnight, but as I creep closer to the city there are more lights, a neon and halogen path. Things are getting brighter. Weymouth becomes Quincy. Despite the late hour, there are more cars around. I let them box me in and go where the currents take me. Quincy becomes the outskirts of Dorchester. I pass the JFK library and UMass Boston and BC High School. Dorchester becomes Southie.

I've made it. Bumped and bruised, scratched, damaged, more than a little weary, but I'm here.

THIRTY-FOUR

I drive by my building three times, approaching it from different angles and streets. I'm circling, only I'm not the buzzard. I watch the local traffic and eyeball the parked cars. No sign of the goon car. My office and apartment windows are darkened. No one left the light on for me.

Time to end the magical mystery tour. I park on West Broadway, a block away from my building, across from an empty bank parking lot. I wait and watch the corner, my corner. There's nothing happening around my apartment. Cabs trolling the streets, homeless sinking inside their upturned collars and sitting on benches, and pub crawlers are the only ones out.

I take out my cell and flip it around in my hands, giving the fingers something to hold besides the steering wheel. I'm not going to call Jennifer right now. Maybe later. Maybe after I watch the film. Maybe not at all. I don't care all that much about what happens after the film. I just need to see it before everything falls apart and on top of me.

Phone goes back inside the jacket and the manila envelope comes out. I check that the photos are still inside, that they haven't run and hid anywhere. The photos are still there, so are the young woman and those three letters. LIT, Tim's signature. I tuck the envelope under the driver's seat, a pirate hiding his booty. I don't know if I'll be able to reclaim the pictures later, but I want to keep the film and the photos separate, just in case.

I get out of the car and remove a small branch that was pinned under a wiper blade. That's better. Here, under the streetlights, the damage to the space car looks severe and permanent, more a bite from a pit bull than a bee sting. Bumpers wouldn't have helped, either.

I unload the screen and projector, the precious cargo. My muscles are stiff and the joints ache from the drive. They don't want to move and they liked it in the car. Sorry, fellas. There's work to do.

Screen lying across my shoulders and the projector dangling from my left hand, I hike up the street. I'm some limping and bent documentary director about to see my life's work for the first time. I have no idea what kind of story, what kind of truth I've discovered, documented, even created. I'm afraid of that truth and wish I could hide from it, but I can't. Won't. Yeah, I'm a kind of hero, but the worst kind; the one acting heroic only by accident and because of circumstance.

There's a cold breeze coming off the bay. It's insistent and gets trapped and passed between the rows of buildings, bouncing around like a ricocheting bullet, hitting me with multiple shots. No tumbleweeds, but wisps of paper wrappers and crushed cans roll on the sidewalks. West Broadway isn't deserted, but it might as well be. There's a distinct last-person-on-earth vibe going on. I'm alone and have been for a long time.

I make it to my front door and put my burdens down on the welcome mat. The door is locked, both knob and dead bolt. I feel so protected. My keys fit into their assigned slots and Open Sesame. I should have a flashlight. I should have a lot of things. I lump the equipment inside and I turn on the hall and office lights for a quick peek.

The office and hallway have been cleared and cleaned out,

the carcass picked over and stripped. Only the file cabinet and the desk remain in the office. The desk is missing a leg and leans crookedly toward a corner of the room. It's almost like I was never there. I'm a ghost in a ghost office. I don't bother to check if any of my files survived the purge. I don't want to advertise my triumphant return, the not-so-prodigal son, so I shut the lights off. The darkness comes back, slides right in, settles over everything, a favorite blanket.

The ascent up the stairs to the second-floor landing isn't quite blind, since leftover streetlight spills through the landing window. I huff and puff up the stairs, then put down the equipment next to my door. It's shut. Ellen's peeps have already fixed it. I take out my lighter and the half-inch flame is enough to guide my entry into the apartment. Unlike the office, my apartment has yet to be cleaned or even touched. The shambles and wreckage of my personal life are right where I left them, which is nice. Seems an appropriate scene as any for this little movie.

I scavenge some scraps of paper, find an ashtray, and light a small fire. The fire burns long enough for me to find two small candles in the kitchen. I light those. Don't know if their orange glow can be seen from the street, so I get a couple of wool blankets out of my bedroom and hang them over the windows, tucking and tying their corners into the curtain framing. A makeshift darkroom.

I set the screen up in front of my bedroom door, which is opposite the blanket-covered windows. Next up, quietly as I can, because anyone could be listening, I clear out some space and bring in the kitchen table. Two legs are broken. I experiment with varied hunks of the living room flotsam and jetsam and manage to jury-rig a flat stable surface for the projector. It'll hold the weight even if I can't.

I take the projector out of its case, careful, reverential, a jeweler plucking a diamond from the setting of an antique ring. The projector goes on the table. Its dual arms are stubby and upright. I plug it in, turn it on. Out spits a ray of blinding light, a spotlight that enlarges to a rectangle that's half on and half off the screen. I shut off the projection bulb and small pilot lights glow around the feeds. I read the manual. It has directions in English and French. It seems like straightforward stuff, but then I think I should try the other film I nabbed from Ellen's store first, just a little film-threading practice. Never mind. I don't have the time. I make adjustments to the height of the projector. I place the film on the front reel and thread it through the sound head like Ellen showed me. It's working.

I fear I might do something to tear or snap the tape, this collection of lost memories is so fragile its impossible thinness passes between my fingers, but the film feeds smooth and the take-up reel gathers frames. A quick adjustment to the lens and everything is in focus. I stand next to the projector and the table with its two legs. The projector is doing its projecting. I'm standing and watching. The film is playing.

THIRTY-FIVE

White empty frames are accompanied by a loud hiss, a loud nothingness. Then the white explodes into sound and color.

The projector's speaker crackles with off-camera laughter, laughter that momentarily precedes any clear images. It's the laughter of boys, full of bravado and mischief and oh-shit-what-have-we-got-ourselves-into? The bedroom is drab with its green bedspread and off-white paint-chipped walls; nightstand and bookcase are splintering and warped. A neglected, dying bedroom in a Southie project. The scene is fixed; the camera is on a tripod.

She sits on the bed wearing her white T-shirt and short denim skirt, but also wearing big purple bruises and rusty scrapes. In color, she looks even more like Jennifer, but an anorexic version. Her arms are thinner than the film running past the projector's lens, skin washed with bleach. Her eyes are half open, or half closed. I want her to have a name because she doesn't have one yet. She sways on her knees and pitches in her own two cents of laughter. It's slurred and messy, a spilled drink, a broken cigarette. She's not Jennifer.

Off camera, the boys speak. Their voices are boxed in, tinny, trapped in the projector's speaker.

"Let me take a couple of quick shots."

"What the fuck for?"

"So he can beat off to 'em later."

"Fuck off. For cover shots, or promos. It'll help sell the movie, find buyers. What, am I the only one here with any business sense?"

"You ain't got no fuckin' sense."

"And you ain't got no fuckin' dick."

More of that boy laughter, plus the clinking of bottles, then Tim appears on-screen, backside first. He turns around, sticks his mug into the camera and travels through decades. He fills the frame, fills the screen in my apartment. He's a kid. Fifteen tops. Dark hair, pinched eyes, a crooked smile.

Ellen was right. He does look like me, like I used to look. No, that isn't it. He looks like how I imagined my own appearance, my old appearance in all the daydreams I've had of the pre-accident me. He is the idealized Mark Genevich, the one lost forever, if he ever existed in the first place. He's young, whole, not broken. He's not the monster me on that screen. He's there just for a second, but he's there. I could spend the next month wearing this scene out, rewinding and watching and rewinding, staring into that broken mirror.

Then Tim winks and says, "Sorry. I'll be quick, just like the boys will."

Off camera: a round of *fuck you* s and *you pussy* s mixes in with laughter. Tim turns away from the camera and snaps a picture. He says, "One more. How 'bout a money shot. Take the shirt and skirt off." The chorus shouts their approval this time. The camera only sees Tim's back. He completely obscures her. She mumbles something and then the sound of clothes being removed, cloth rubbing against itself and against skin. T-shirt flutters off the bed, a flag falling to the ground. Tim snaps a second picture, then hides behind the movie camera.

No one says anything and the camera just stares. She's shirtless and skirtless. She opens her eyes, or at least tries to, and says, "Someone gimme a drink."

Off camera. "When are we gonna start this shit?"

Tim says, "Whenever you're ready. Start now. I'll edit out your fuckups later."

Two bare-chested teens enter the scene, both wearing jeans. Their skin is painfully white and spotted with freckles and pimples. These guys are only a couple of years removed from Ellen's keepsake picture on the stairs, boys in men's bodies. Sullivan is on the right and Times on the left; both have wide eyes and cocksure sneers. Unlike in the stair picture from Ellen's house, Sullivan is now the bigger of the two, thick arms and broad shoulders. He's the muscle, the heavy lifter, the mover, the shaker. Times has a wiry build, looks leaner, quicker, and meaner. Here's your leader. He's holding a bottle of clear liquid, takes a swig.

Times kneels on the bed beside the woman and says, "You ready for a good time?" No one responds to or laughs at the porn cliché, which probably isn't a cliché to them yet. It's painfully earnest in this flick.

The new silence in the room is another character. Times looks around to his boys, and it's a moment when the whole thing could get called off, shut down. Sullivan and Tim would be all right with a last-second cancellation of this pilot. I can't know this but I do. The moment passes, like all moments must pass, and it makes everything worse, implicates them further, because they had a chance to stop and they didn't.

Times says, "Here." He gives her the bottle and she drinks deep, so deep I'm not sure she'll be able to come back up for a breath. But she does, and hands back the bottle and melts out of her sitting position and onto her back. Sullivan grabs a handful of her left breast and frantically works at the button and fly of his pants with his free hand.

Her right hand and arm float up in front her face slowly, like an old cobra going through the motions for some two-bit snake charmer, and her hand eventually lands on Times's thigh. She's like them, only a kid. And she's a junkie. I wonder if those three amigos could see that and were banking on it, or if they were too busy with their collective tough-guy routine to see anything.

Times says, "Lights, camera, action."

The sex is fast, rough, and clumsy. With its grim and bleak bedroom setting, drunk, high, and uninterested female star, and two boys who are awkward but feral and relentless, it's a scene that is both pathetic and frightening at the same time. The vibe has flipped 180 degrees, from should-we-do-this to where the potential for violence is an ogre in the room. Like someone watching a scary movie through his fingers, I cringe because I know the violence is coming.

The camera stays in one spot and only pans and scans. There's never a good clear shot of the woman's face. We see her collection of body parts in assorted states of motion but never her face. She's not supposed to matter, and even if nothing else were to happen, this is enough to make me hate the boy behind the camera and the man he became. Tim says nothing throughout the carnal gymnastics. He's the silent but complicit eye.

Sullivan finishes first and stumbles out of the scene. He gives Tim—not the camera—a look, one that might haunt me for the rest of my little sleeps and short days. When that kid's middle-aged version killed himself in the basement of his Cape house, I imagine he had the same look on his face when he pulled the trigger. A look one might have when the truth, the hidden and ugly truth of the world, that we're all complicit, has been revealed.

Times is still going at her. He's on top and he speeds up his thrusts for the big finish. Then there's a horrible choking cough. It's wet and desperate and loud, practically tears through the projector's speaker, and makes Brill's lung-ejecting hacks sound like a prim and proper clearing of the throat.

"Jesus, fuck!" Times jumps off the bed like it's electrified.

It's her. She's choking. I still can't see enough of her face; she's lying down and the camera isn't up high enough. She coughs but isn't breathing in. Out with the bad but no in with the good. Yellow vomit leaks out of her nose and mouth and into her hair. Her hands try to cover her face but fall back onto the bed. She shakes all over, the convulsions increasing in speed and violence. I think maybe I accidentally sped up the film but I didn't; it's all her. Maybe the bed is electrified.

From behind the camera, and it sounds like he's behind me, talking over my shoulder, Tim says, "What's fuckin' happening?" He doesn't lose the shot, though, that son of a bitch. The camera stays focused on her.

"Oh, fuck, her fucking eyes, they're all white. Fuck! Fuck!"

Sullivan says, "She's freaking out. What do we do?"

The camera gets knocked to the floor, but it still runs, records its images. A skewed, tilted shot of under the bed fills the screen. There's nothing there but dust and cobwebs and darkness.

The bed shakes and the springs complain. The choking noises are gone. The boys are all shouting at the same time. I can only make out snippets, swears, phrases. It's a mess. I lean closer to the screen, trying to hide under that bed, trying to hear what they're saying. Their voices are one voice, high-pitched and scared.

Then the three voices become only two. One is screaming. I think it's Times. He's says, "Shut the fucking camera off!" He shouts it repeatedly, his increased mania exploding in the room.

And I hear Tim—I think it's Tim. He's whispering and getting closer to the camera. He's going to shut it off, taking orders like a good little boy. He's repeating himself too, has his own mantra. Tim is saying, "Is she dead? Is she dead?"

The screen goes white. The End. *Fin.*

The take-up reel rattles with a lose piece of film slapping against the projector. My hands are sweating and I'm breathing heavy. I shut off the projector, the screen goes black, the take-up reel slows, and I stop it with my hand. The used engine gives a whiff of ozone and waves of dying heat. Everything should be quiet, but it isn't.

"Who is she?" A voice from my left, from the front door.

I say, "Don't you mean, who was she?"

THIRTY-SIX

Jennifer Times stands in the front doorway. She looks like she did at the mall autograph session. Sweatpants, jean jacket over a Red Sox T, hair tied up into a tight ponytail. It might be the weak candlelight, shadows dampening her cheekbones and eyes, but she looks a generation older than when we were at the restaurant. We're both older now.

I say, "I don't remember calling and inviting you over. I would've cleaned up a bit first. Maybe even baked a cake."

She walks in, shuts the door behind her. Someone raised her

right. She says, "Who was she? Do you know?"

I say, "No idea. No clue, as it was. How much did you see?"

"Enough."

I nod. It was enough.

She says, "What are you going to do now?"

"Me? I'm done. I'm taking myself out of the game, making my own call to the bullpen. I'm wrapping this all up in a pretty red bow and dumping into the state police's lap. Or the FBI. No local cops, no one who knows your dad, no offense. I was hired to find it. I found it."

Jennifer carefully steps over the rubble and crouches next to me, next to the projector. She stares at it like she might lay hands on it, wanting to heal or be healed, I don't know. "What do you think happened to her after?"

I say, "How did you get in here?"

"I checked the welcome mat and there were keys duct-taped underneath."

Keys? I never left any keys. I don't even have spares. Ellen wouldn't do that either. Yeah, she's the de facto mayor of Southie, friends with everyone, but she's also a pragmatist. She knows better than to leave keys under a welcome mat on one of the busiest corners of South Boston. All of which means Jennifer is lying and also means I'm screwed, as I'm sure other unexpected guests are likely to arrive shortly.

Jennifer holds up a ring of two keys on a Lithuanian-flag key chain.

Shit. Those are Ellen's keys. I say, "How did you know I was here?"

"Why are you interrogating me?"

"I'm only asking simple questions, and here you go trying to rush everything to the interrogation level."

She says, "I was parked outside of your apartment and saw you. I waited a few minutes and let myself in, then I sat outside your door listening. I came in when I heard them yelling."

I fold up and break down the projector as she talks. I don't rewind the film but, instead, slip the take-up reel into my coat pocket, next to the other film. I wrap up the cord and slide the projector into its case, latch the latches twice for luck. I say, "Why are you here?" and walk past her to the screen.

"I needed to see if you were telling me the truth on the phone. I had to know."

The screen recoils quickly and slides into its box nice and easy. I say, "And now that you know, what are you going to do?"

Jennifer walks past the table and sits on the couch. "How about answering my question?"

"What question was that? I tend to lose track of things, you know?"

"What do you think happened after? After the movie? What did they do?"

My turn to play the strong silent type. I lean on the screen, thinking about giving an answer, my theory on everything, life, death, the ever-expanding doomed universe. Then there's a short bang downstairs. Not loud enough to wake up neighbors, a newspaper hitting the door.

Jennifer whispers, "What was that?"

"It ain't no newspaper," I say. "Expecting company, Jennifer? It's awful rude to invite your friends over without asking me."

"I didn't tell anyone where I was going or what I was doing."

She gets up off the couch, calm as a kiddie pool, and tiptoes into my bedroom. She gestures and I lean in close to hear. She whispers, "See if you can find out who that woman was and what they did with her after. You know, do your job. And if things get hairy, I'll come out and save you." Jennifer shuts the door.

No way. I'm going to pull her out of the room and use her as a human shield should the need arise. I turn the knob but it's locked. Didn't know it had a lock.

If things get hairy. I'm already hairy and so are the things. Yeah, another goddamn setup, but a bizarre one that makes no sense. Doesn't matter. Prioritize. I need to hide the equipment, or at least bury it in junk so it doesn't look like I'd just watched the film for the first time. I lay the screen behind the couch, unzip a cushion and stuff the film inside, then go to work with the projector and case, putting it under the kitchen table, incorporating it into one of the makeshift legs. I move the candles to the center of the table.

Maybe my priorities are all out of whack. I give thought to the back exit and the fire escape off the kitchen, but the front door to my apartment is currently under assault. I'm not much of a runner or climber, and I'd need one hell of a head start. I could call the police, but they'd be the DA's police, and even if they weren't, they wouldn't get here in time. No sense in prolonging this. I walk over to the front windows and pull down the blankets. I lean against the wall between the windows, light a cigarette, shine the tops of my Doc Martens on the backs of my calves, adjust my hat, pretend I have style.

The door flies open and crashes into the wall. The knob sinks into the plaster. The insurance bill just got a little bigger.

As inevitable as the tides, the two goons are in my doorway.

I say, "That ain't the secret knock, so I'm going to have to ask you gentlemen to leave."

Redhead says, "Candles. How romantic."

Yeah, even with the added ambience of streetlamps and assorted background neon, the light quality isn't great, but it's enough to see a hell of a shiner under his right eye, scratches on his face, and the gun in his hand. He holds it like he's King Kong clutching a Fay Wray imposter and can't wait to squeeze.

Can't focus on the gun. It gets my panic juices flowing. This time with the goons, it feels different already, like how the air smells different before a thunderstorm, before all the action. My legs get a jump on the jellification process.

Baldy says, "Romancing yourself there, retard? You're fuckin' ugly enough that your right hand would reject you."

I blow some smoke, don't say anything, and try to give them smug, give them confidence. My bluff will work only if I get the attitude right. And even then, it still might not work.

Redhead is a totem to violence. He wears threat like cologne. He says, "I wouldn't be standing there fucking smiling like you know something. Smiling like you aren't never gonna feel pain again, Genevich."

I say, "Can't help myself, boys. I'm a happy guy. Don't mean to rub your noses in it."

Baldy says, "We're gonna rub your nose all over our fists and the fuckin' walls." He cracks his knuckles, grinding bone against bone.

They walk toward me, necks retracted into their shoulders, and I can just about hear their muscles bulging against their dress shirts and suit coats. Dust and sparks fall out of their mouths. Oh, and the gun is still pointed at me.

Can't say I've thought my Hail Mary bluff all the way through, but I'm going with it. I open my jacket and pull out the dummy film, the black one, the one from Ellen's store. Only what I'm holding isn't the dummy film. Apparently I put that one inside the couch cushion. What I'm waving around in front of the goons is the take-up reel, half full with Tim's film.

Oh, boy. Need to regroup, and fast. I say, "Have you boys seen this yet? Some of the performances are uneven, but two thumbs way up. You know, you two fellas remind me of the shit-talking boys that star in the movie. Same intensity and all that. I'm sure the reviews will be just as good when it gets a wide release. Twelve thousand theaters, red-carpet premiere somewhere, Golden Globes, then the Oscars, the works."

The goons stop their advance, share a look. My cigarette is almost dead. I know the feeling well.

Redhead laughs, a car's engine dying. He says, "You trying to tell us you made a copy?"

Baldy's head is black with stubble. I guess, with all the *mishegas*, he hasn't had time for a shave. He should lighten his schedule. He says, "You haven't had time to make any copies."

"Says you. I had it digitized. Didn't take long, boys. Didn't even cost that much. Oh, I tipped well for the rush and all. But it got done, and done quick. Even made a few hard copies for the hell of it. You know, for the retro-vibe. The kids love all the old stuff."

Baldy breaks from formation and takes a jab step toward me. I think he's grown bigger since he first walked into the room.

His nostrils flare out, the openings as wide as exhaust pipes. I'm in big trouble. He says, "You're fuckin' lying."

I don't know if that's just a standard reply, maybe Baldy's default setting. The goons creep closer. My heart does laps around my chest cavity and its pace is too fast, it'll never make it to the end of the race. Appearing calm is going to be as easy as looking pretty.

I say, "Nope. This one here is one of the copies. You don't think I'd wave the original around, do you? I figure I can make a quick buck or two by putting that puppy on eBay."

It's their turn to talk, to give me a break, a chance to catch my breath, but my breath won't be caught. It's going too fast and hard, a dog with a broken leash sprinting after a squirrel. Black spots in my vision now. They're not buying any of this, and I'm in a barrel full of shit. I move back, away from the window. My legs have gone cold spaghetti on me and I almost go down, stumbling on my twisted and bent CD tower. Muscles tingle and my skin suddenly gets very heavy.

I say, "If my video guy doesn't see me on his doorstep tomorrow morning, alone and in one piece, he uploads the video onto YouTube and drops a couple of DVDs into FedEx boxes, and the boxes have addresses, important addresses, on them, just in case you were wondering."

The goons laugh, split up, and circle me, one goon on each side. I'll be the meat in the goon sandwich. Looks like I should've gone with a frantic fire-escape escape. There isn't always a next time.

Redhead scratches his nose with the gun barrel and says, "You're bullshitting the wrong guys, Genevich. We don't believe you, and we don't really care. We're getting paid to find the film, take that film, copy or not, and then knock the snot out of you."

Things are getting more than hairy. Things are going black and fuzzy and not just at the edges. I say, "Don't make me drop another shed on your asses."

Baldy lunges, his coat billowing behind him like giant bat wings. The wings beat once, twice, he hangs in the air, and I feel the wind, it's hot and humid, an exhaled breath on glass that lifts the hat off my head. Then he takes a swing, but he doesn't land the blow because I'm already falling, already going down.

THIRTY-SEVEN

I open my eyes and everything is wrong. Cataplexy. My waking coma. The wires are all crossed, the circuit breakers flipped. I can't move and won't be able to for a while.

DA Times sits in front of me. He's wearing black gloves and holds a gun. Maybe I should get me one of those; seems like everyone else is buying. I'm always the last one in the latest trends. I'm the rotten egg.

"Mark? You there?"

I try to say, "Yeah," but it's only loosened air, don't know if he hears it so I blink a few times. Yeah, I'm here, and here is wrong. Here is my couch. The projector is on the kitchen table, the take-up reel and the film hang off the rear arm. The candles are two fingers from burning out, white melted wax pools around the holders. The screen is set up in front of my bedroom door. The blankets are over the windows.

The DA is dressed all in black: tight turtleneck and pants. He says, "I never realized how awful narcolepsy was, Mark. Are you currently experiencing cataplexy?" He shakes his head, his faux pity the answer to his own question. "These symptoms of yours are just dreadful. I feel for you, I really do. I don't know how you make it through the day."

"Positive thinking," I say. "I'm fine. I could get up and pin your nose to the back of your head if I wanted to, but it'd be rude." The murk is still in my head and wants me to go back under, back down. It'd be so easy just to close my eyes.

He frowns and talks real quiet. He's a dad talking to a screwup kid, the one he still loves despite everything. "From what Ellen tells me, you've had a real tough go of it."

"Ellen likes to worry." Luckily, I'm in no condition to present a state of shock or agitation at the mention of Ellen's name.

"I'd say she has reason to. Look at the couch you're sitting on, Mark. It's absolutely riddled with cigarette holes. Ellen mentioned the couch to me, but I thought she was exaggerating. It's a minor miracle you haven't burned this place to the ground. Yet."

I say, "Those aren't cigarette burns. I have a moth problem." My voice is weak, watery. It usually takes me twenty minutes to fully recover from cataplexy. I need to keep the chatter going. Despite his daddy-knows-best schtick, the gun and black gloves broadcast loud and clear what his real plan is for the evening. The DA gets up and fishes around in my pockets. I could breathe on him real heavy, but that's about the only resistance I can offer. The DA takes my lighter out. No fair, I didn't say he could have it. Then he finds my pack of smokes, pulls one out, sticks it in my mouth, and lights it. It tastes good even though I know it's going to kill me.

Time to talk. Just talk. Talking as currency to buy me time. I hate time. I say, "Don't know why you and the goons bothered setting the equipment back up. But who am I to critique your work?" The cigarette falls out of my mouth, rolls down my chest and onto the floor between my feet. I hope it's on the hardwood floor, not on rug or debris.

The DA pulls out another cigarette and fills my mouth with it. He says, "Goons?"

I concentrate on the balancing act of talking and keeping the butt in my mouth. I'll smoke this one down to the filter if I have to. "Yeah, your boys, your goons. Redhead and Baldy. I'd like to make an official complaint to their supervisor when all this is over."

The DA leans in and hovers the gun's snub nose between my eyes. It's close enough that I smell the gun oil. The DA waving that thing in my face isn't going to speed up my recovery any.

He says, "Are these the same imaginary goons you warned Ellen about in a voice mail? You said something about a red car and a crooked DA too."

An upper cut to my glass chin. He really did talk to Ellen. I say, "If you did anything to Ellen, I'll—"

"She called me, Mark. Tonight. She was distraught, didn't know where you were. She said you had destroyed the shed today, emptied your bank account, and maxed out your credit cards in the last week. She told me how strangely you'd been behaving and said your symptoms seemed to have been worsening.

"We had a nice long chat. Ellen is a wonderful and brave person. She told me everything about you and your narcolepsy, Mark. She told me that stress triggers the worst of your symptoms." He moves the gun all around my face, tracing the damaged features but not touching me. "I told her I'd check up on you. And here I am." He switches hands with the gun.

I can't think about Ellen and her motivations for calling the DA despite my pointed instructions to the contrary. It would ruin what little resolve I have left.

I say, "Gee, thanks. You're like a warm blanket and cup of hot chocolate, even if you are lying about the goons through your capped and whitened teeth." Despite my apartment being made to appear that I didn't break down all the film equipment before everyone showed up, I know he's lying.

He leans in and says, "For what it's worth, and that's not much because it has no bearing on what will happen here tonight, I'm telling the truth. No goons. You hallucinated or dreamed them up. This is all about me and you." His voice goes completely cold, can be measured only in the Kelvin scale.

I say, "And a woman. You know, the one who looks like your daughter? Except dead."

The DA doesn't say anything but leans back into his chair.

Need to keep the chatter going. I say, "What about your old pal Brendan? He's dead too."

The DA pushes the gun into my face again and says, "Are you stressed, Mark?" He looks down toward the floor, to something between my feet. "That cigarette has already caught on something. Can you smell the smoke? You need to be more careful and take care of yourself. No one else will."

He's bluffing about a fire, I hope. The paranoid part of me feels the temperature rising around my ankles, a fledgling fire starting right under my feet, a hotfoot joke that isn't so funny.

I try to move the feet—and nothing. Might as well be trying to move the kitchen table with my mind.

I wiggle my fingers a little bit but can't make a fist, wouldn't even be able to hitchhike. But they'll be back soon. My legs are another matter. Those won't be able to hold me up for at least fifteen minutes, maybe longer. My second cigarette is burning away like lost time.

I say, "Jennifer is here."

"Mark, I really am sorry about all of this. I know you don't want to hear it, but at least your suffering will be over. You won't be a burden to Ellen or yourself anymore. It's really going to be for the best." Now I'm getting mad. The fucker is talking to me like I'm some drooling vegetable and should pull my own plug.

I say, "Jennifer is hiding in my bedroom. Go take a look. I apologize if my bed isn't made. I've been a little busy." My cigarette jumps up and down, performing carcinogenic calisthenics as my volume rises. This is desperation time. I need him to go into that bedroom.

He says, "Mark, enough, really."

"Listen to me! If she isn't in there, you win, and I'll close my eyes and you can burn me up and stub me out like the rest of my cigarettes. But go fucking look, right now!" My voice breaks on the last line.

The DA stands up, puts his gun down on the projector table and his hands in his pockets. Then he leans forward, sticking his face in mine, our noses a fly hair away from touching. His eyes line up with mine and I don't see anything there that I recognize or understand. Anyone who tells you they can read someone's eyes is lying.

I blow smoke in his face and say, "Be careful, that secondhand smoke is a killer."

He hits me in the arms, chest, stomach, and the groin, looking for reactions, movement. I'm the dead snake and he's poking me with a stick.

I feel it all, but I don't move. I say, "Stop it, I'm ticklish."

He backs off, picks up the gun. "All right, Mark, but only because you're Tim's kid. I shouldn't be an enabler, but I'll go look in your bedroom, and then we'll be done."

"Say hi to Jennifer for me."

The DA backs away from the couch, moves the screen out from the front of my bedroom door. Still watching me, he turns the knob and pushes the door open. Yeah, I know now that Jennifer and the goons were a hallucination, but part of me is still surprised that the door is unlocked. Times ducks inside my bedroom.

My right hand is heavier than a mountain and moves like a continent, but it moves, aiming inside my jacket pocket. I don't need more smokes, but I do need my cell phone. I'm moving too slow. I have only moments, moments that can't be defined or measured in seconds, not by me anyway. My fingers are clumsy and thick, but they find the hunk of plastic, hold on, and pull it out. I can't hold the phone up in front of my face, so I flip it open and rest my hand, arm, and phone on my stomach. The LCD screen glows brightly in the dark room.

The DA says, "Drop the phone, Mark." Gun held out like he means it, but he won't shoot me unless he absolutely has to. I'm banking that it would be too messy to cover up. Here's hoping there isn't a run on the bank.

I say, "No need to get your tassels in a twirl, DA, I just wanted to show you I had a little phone chat of my own, earlier."

Goddamn it, the buttons are so small and my thumb isn't ready for the minute motor coordination test. I hit the wrong buttons. The DA lunges across the room. My thumb cooperates, I select incoming calls from the main menu, scroll down, and there it is. The magic number. Phew. It's actually there.

The DA grabs the cell phone, but he's too late.

I'm breathing heavy. Ash floats onto my chest. Cigarette two is getting low. I say, "Take a gander at the screen. That's a list of incoming calls, not outgoing. See that menu heading, DA? Tell me, what does it say?"

He complies without looking up. Good DA. "Incoming calls."

I say, "Oh, I lied about Jennifer being here. Sorry about that. If I had told you to check the incoming calls of my cell phone, you either wouldn't have or would've lied about what you saw. That, and it was nice to have a few seconds of me time."

The DA doesn't say anything, just stares at the phone and then up at me.

I say, "I think you recognize Jennifer's number, unless that's some secret line you don't know about. Nah, you know that number. I can tell. Note the time too. She called me this afternoon. Hours and hours ago. And now I'm wondering: have you talked to her since she called me? I'm guessing not. I'm guessing that if she was home, she avoided you like herpes."

He says, "Why would she call you?"

I say, "I'm also guessing she didn't really tell you about our date at Amrheins either. Did she tell you I showed her the pictures? No? Fancy that. Tell me, are you stressed now, Billy?"

He yells, "What did you tell her?"

Cigarette number two is a bullet between my teeth, and I'm chomping the hell out of it. I say, "I told her everything. I told her that once upon a time there were three musketeers, you, my father, and Brendan Sullivan, the lords of Southie—or lords of their project at least—and they decided to try their hand at an amateur porno. Tim was the director, Brendan an actor, and everyone's local hero, Billy, was costar and producer. They found and bribed some young barely-there junkie, and a star was born. Only she OD'd, or was just so drunk she choked on her own vomit, and died on camera as you guys just sat and watched with your thumbs up your asses.

"Some bad luck there, I guess, but you three of Southie's finest never reported the death. No. You see, Billy Times used to go around bragging about mob and Whitey Bulger contacts to whoever would listen. Yeah, you had a big mouth and it was always running, but maybe it wasn't all talk, maybe you weren't just full of shit. So the junkie died in your bedroom, you called in a favor, and the body magically disappeared. But what you weren't expecting was that two of your musketeers, your pals, Tim especially, didn't trust you. Not one goddamn bit. He didn't destroy the pictures or the film. He split them up with Brendan, a two-man tontine of your former musketeers. That's gotta hurt a little, eh, DA?"

While I'm talking, the DA drops my cell phone and it disappears into the rubble. He jams the gun in his waistband, by his left hip, and slumps over to the projector. He plucks the take-up reel and film from the rear arm.

I say, "Fast forward to last week. Brendan saw Jennifer

performing on *American Star,* and she looked so much like the junkie, like the dead girl, and your name was being bandied about on fluff news pieces all over the state, Brendan had a belated attack of conscience. He brought me the photos and hired me to find the film. Of course I was, shall we say, indisposed when he was in my office and I thought it was Jennifer who gave me the pics. This is where you come in again. Yeah, this Monday morning quarterback knows taking the pictures to you was a full ten on the Richter scale of mistakes, which resulted in my apartment and office being torn apart and your goons putting the lean on me and making sure Brendan Sullivan was out of the picture, so to speak, or dead if you prefer I speak plainly. But I found the film.

"Oh—and this last bit is pure conjecture, but Jennifer thought it sounded plausible—the narcoleptic me had taken some notes when Brendan was here. The only piece of automatic writing that wasn't gibberish was *South Shore Plaza,* and that notepad was stolen from my office. Haven't had a chance to check dates yet, but I'll bet more than two bits there was some heavy construction going on at that mall back in your day, and Dead Girl has herself a cement plot, maybe parking-garage Level Three?

"That's what I told Jennifer. All of it. She found it to be riveting stuff. Begged me to show her the film and told me she'd help me if I needed it. So, Billy boy, what do you think? How'd I do? Did I get it right?"

He says, "Not perfect. But you're more right than wrong."

He doesn't accuse me of bluffing, doesn't deny the goons, either. I nailed it. Perfect dismount. I broke him down. I'm the one with all the hand. In the midst of the mental back pat, cigarette number two falls out of my mouth and onto my chest. My arms are tree trunks, but I slowly manage to brush the glowing stub off onto the couch—but still too close to me. Wasn't thinking right. Should've flicked it across the room with my fingers.

I still smell smoke, and now I see it. It's coming up from the floor, from between my legs. Unless my floor has taken up smoking, there's a fire down below. I try to move my legs; still no go. I don't have much time.

The DA has gone all quiet. He's the secret that everyone knows. He passes the film from hand to hand. He says, "Jennifer wouldn't believe you."

I try to move, but all I manage is some feeble twisting of my torso and some hip movement. It's not the Twist and I'm no Chubby Checker. The dummy film inside the couch cushion digs into my ass as I move. It's not helping. I say, "Why wouldn't she believe me? Especially after I wind up quote *accidentally dead* unquote."

The DA looks at me, his wheels turning, but they aren't taking him anywhere. He says, "She'll believe me over you. Time will pass, and she'll believe me." He says it, but I don't think he buys it, not even at discount. He stands in the dark of my ruined apartment.

Need to keep those wheels a-spinnin'. I say, "Who was Dead Girl? Tell me."

He says, "I don't know, Mark. I really don't."

The couch on my too-close left is smoking now. Maybe it's my imagination but the apartment is getting brighter. The heat down by my feet is no longer a phantom heat. It's real.

I say, "Come on. It's over, Times. Just cross the Ts for me."

The DA pulls his gun out. I might've pushed him too far into desperation mode. "I can't tell you what I don't know. We found her in Dorchester. Tim had seen her wandering the streets for days, bumming smokes and offering five-dollar blowjobs. We didn't even know her name, and after—after, no one missed her. No one asked about her."

I say, "That's not good enough—" and then a searing pain wraps around my left ankle, worse then anything I've ever felt, worse than anything I've ever imagined. I scream and it's enough of a jolt to bend me in half, send my arms down to the emergency scene. My left pant leg is engulfed in flame; so is most of the floor beneath my feet. I beat frantically at my pant leg, each swipe of my paw like mashing a nest full of yellow jackets into my ankle. I quickly and without thinking or planning try to stand, and manage a somewhat upright position but fall immediately to the left, crash-landing on shards of broken coffee table. That hurts too. The high-intense pain of my actively burning flesh is gone, replaced by a slow, throbbing, and building ache. I belly-crawl away from the flames, but things are getting hotter and brighter in the apartment.

I look up. Times is still there, looking down, watching me, gun in one hand, film in the other. I say, "Burning me up isn't gonna solve anything. You'll still have questions to answer." The flames are speaking now, the greedy crackle of its expanding mouth.

He says, "I'm sorry it has to be this way. I'm not a good guy." He bends down, knocks my hat off, grabs a handful of my hair, and yanks my head up. Can't say I'm thrilled with this by-the-scruff treatment. He says, "Your father wasn't a good guy either, Mark. But I liked him anyway."

The pain in my leg starts to subside and this isn't a good sign, because it likely means I'm going out again, and this time the sleep won't be a little one. I yell, and scream, and bang my forehead on the floor, anything to keep myself awake.

The fire races up the blankets over the windows, throwing an orange spotlight on the room and waves of powerful heat. The DA stands up, coughs, and takes a step toward the front door.

I reach out with my right hand and clamp down on his ankle. I'm a leech, a barnacle, and I'm not letting go. I yell, "Go ahead, shoot me!" He won't. If he's careful, he won't even step on my hand to break it, or mark me up with bruises. He can't chance ruining his quaint narcoleptic-burned-himself-up-smoking setup.

The DA halfheartedly tries to pull his leg out of my hand, and it gives me time and an opening to pull my torso close and wrap myself around his leg. Now I'm an anchor, a tree root, and he isn't going anywhere.

Apparently my apartment isn't very flame retardant, because a full-on blaze is roaring now. I curl up into a tighter ball, trying to keep my assorted parts out of the fire. The DA is yelling, getting more violent and desperate.

I turn my head and pin my face to his leg, trying to protect it. I close my eyes, waiting for a bullet that doesn't come. Instead, he kicks me in the back of the head and kicks me in the ribs, but I'm not letting go. No way.

The DA drags me and his leg behind him, toward the front door. He gives me a few more kicks, then pulls us out into the hallway. My legs are weak, but they have something in them, they have to.

He sticks the gun barrel in my ear, jams it inside, trying to poke at my brain. The pain is like that pressure-point pain where your whole body involuntary gives up. He yells, "Fucking let go! Right now!"

I twist and load my legs under my weight, like I did in preparation for my ill-fated shed leap. Then I lift his leg off the ground and I'm in a crouch. The gun hand goes away with the sudden shift and he stands and waves his arms like a kid on a balance beam. I throw his leg left, which spins the DA around, away from me and facing the stairs.

I jump up, my burned leg erupting into new pain, but I get into a standing position right behind the DA. I grab handfuls of his turtleneck first, fixing to twist his gun arm and pin it behind his back, disarm him, and be the hero, but my legs go out like they were never there. My momentum takes me forward into the DA's back and my legs tangle and twine in his, knocking out his knees. He can't hold us and we pitch down the wooden stairs.

The DA lands almost halfway down the flight, face first, with me on his back, clinging, hands still full of turtleneck, and I'm driving, forcing all my weight down, not that I have a choice. We land hard. There's a crack and I bounce up and manage to stay on his back, riding him like a sled, until we hit the first-floor landing. I involuntarily roll off him, crashing back first into the outside door. The glass window rattles hard in the frame but holds together.

The DA comes to a stop at my feet, sprawled and boneless, his head bent back, too far back, a broken doll. The gun is still in one gloved hand. The take-up reel of film sits on the bottom step, between the DA's feet.

I think about sitting here and just closing my eyes, letting that orange warmth above rock me to sleep. I think about crawling into my office, maybe that bottle of whiskey is still in the bottom drawer of my file cabinet. Those scenarios have a nice captain-going-down-with-the-ship appeal to them, but that's not me.

I grab the film, open the front door, and crawl out onto the sidewalk, the gritty and cold sidewalk, and the door shuts behind me. Everything goes quiet, but below the quiet, if my ears dig hard enough, is the not-so-subtle rumble of flames doing their thing inside the building.

I crawl the first fifty feet down the street, then struggle onto unsteady feet. I use the facades of apartment buildings and pizza joints and convenience stores to rappel down West Broadway and to my rental car.

Inside. I start the car. The dash lights up and I have plenty of gas, enough for another road trip. Beneath my seat, the manila envelope is still there, the pictures still inside, the girl still dead and anonymous. The film goes inside the envelope. It fits.

The sound of flames has disappeared but there are sirens now. One fire truck roars up Broadway past me. I watch it go by; its sound and fury stops at the corner, my corner. Maybe they're in time to save the building and some of my stuff, like the projector. I know better. They won't be able to save anything or anyone.

It's the wee hours of someone's morning. I'm all out of cigarettes, but my leg feels like a used one. Hands on the wheel at two and ten. I check my mirrors. No one is double-parked. My U-turn is legal and easy, and I drive away.

THIRTY-EIGHT

I'm back at the bungalow. Ellen isn't home and she didn't leave the lights on for me. I'm used to it. I limp inside the back door and into the kitchen. First I grab that dusty bottle of whiskey from the cabinets above the refrigerator, take a couple of pulls, and then head to the bathroom to check out my leg. Priorities, man, priorities.

I took the back roads to the Cape, made a pit stop or two, pulled over and napped a couple of times. The sun was coming up as I white-knuckled it over the Sagamore Bridge again, but I made it here. And I made it here without another car accident, although I think I ran over a squirrel when I found myself two-wheeling it up a sidewalk. Sorry, fella.

Bathroom. I roll my pants up and the burned parts stick to my leg. I clean it up best as I can in the tub, but the water hurts. The whiskey doesn't help as much as it should. The skin on my ankle and about halfway up my calf is burned pretty good. I have no idea of the degree scale, but the skin is red and has oozing blisters. I squeeze some Vaseline onto gauze pads and wrap things up tight, but not too tight. It's a bad wrap job, gauze coming undone and sticking out, Christmas presents wrapped in old tissue paper. But it'll have to do.

Me and the bottle of whiskey, we hobble into the living room and I sit on the couch like a dropped piano. I take out the manila envelope and one of the pictures, the picture of Dead Girl wearing the white T-shirt and skirt. The photo is black-and-white but I'll remember her in color, like in the film. She seems a little more alive in this picture, as if the second picture, taken moments later, wears that spent time instead of clothes. The girl in the second photo is that much closer to death, and you can see it.

The living room is getting brighter and my eyes are getting heavier, but I can't go to sleep just yet. I walk to the front windowsill and grab the picture of the old fisherman holding whatever it is next to his head, and I still think it looks like a gun. I also take the picture of the three musketeers: Tim, Billy, and Brendan, those clean-looking carefree preteens sitting on the stairs. I escort the pictures back to the couch and put them on the coffee table, whiskey bottle between them.

I pick up the old fisherman, flip it around to the back, undo the golden clasp, and remove the photo from the frame. I put the picture facedown on the table. Don't mean any disrespect to the guy.

I stick the first picture of the girl into the frame. Don't need to trim the edges or margins. It's a perfect fit. I spit-polish the glass. Looks good as new. I put her down next to the boys. LIT in the lower left of both pictures.

The boys. Those goddamn buzz cuts and soda-pop smiles. That picture might as well be of anyone. I don't know them, any of them, never did, never will, and don't really want to, but I know their lies.

I think about taking down all the photos off the walls, making a pile, mixing these two in, then reshuffling the deck and hanging everything back up. Maybe I could forget that way and no one would ever find them again.

I think about Jennifer, Ellen, Janice, and me and of how, because of them, our lives will always be about lies and lost time, just like my little sleeps. I think about the dead girl, the stubborn memory that everyone has forgotten. Maybe tomorrow someone will remember.

I gather up my cargo and walk into the hallway. Framed black-and-white pictures hang on the walls on both sides of my bedroom doorway. Faux-lantern lamps hang on either side of the doorway and beneath the lamps are two pictures. I take those two frames down and stack them on the floor.

I double-check that the manila envelope with the other photo and the film is still inside my jacket. It is. I'm holding on to that sucker like a mama bird with a wing around her egg.

The other photos, those I hang on the wall. The girl and the boys fit the nails and fill those glowing empty spots on the walls, one picture on each side of my door for all the world to see.

I open the bedroom door. Unlike the hallway, it's dark inside. I won't open the curtains or pull the shade. I won't turn on the light. I know where I am and I know where I'm going.

Tomorrow, if there is one, will be for remembering. Now? I'm going to sleep, even if it's just a little one.

THIRTY-NINE

The sun shines bright and hot, too hot. It's a remorseless desert sun, a sun completely indifferent to the effect of its heat and radiation. It's the real sun, not a cartoon. Can't even be bothered to say *fuck you*.

It's the weekend. Tim and I are in our backyard. I'm five years old. Not everything is green. Debris and old equipment cover the yard. Someone's life has exploded. The shed has been destroyed and is nothing but a pile of sharp and splintered pieces. All the king's men can't put it back together again. The shed is dead.

Tim and I stand in front of the fallen shed, hand in hand. His big hand sweats around my little one and I want to let go. I really want to let go, but I can't.

He pats me on the head, hands me the brown paper bag, and says, "Come on. Let's clean up all this shit." I follow Tim around the yard. He picks up his old lawn mower along with the sharp and toothy tools that used to wink and gleam at me from inside the shed. They go inside my little brown paper bag. Next into the bag are the bottles of cleaners and bags of fertilizer. There's no game today and Tim doesn't name dogs after the stuff we pick up.

He says, "You can still sing your song, buddy."

I don't. And I won't.

Some of the stuff we find lying on the grass is charred and smoking. He picks up a projector, a screen, and a film can, all empty secrets, and they go into the bag. There are other bits and pieces burned beyond recognition, and I get the sense that this is a good thing. Everything goes into the bag. The bag is getting heavy.

We still have much more to pick up, haven't made a dent with our cleanup effort, but Tim leads me behind the fallen shed, takes the brown bag, and tips it upside down behind the fence. Nothing comes out. Tim says, "Goodbye," as he shakes out the empty bag.

We walk around to where the front of the shed used to be. He kicks at the fallen cinder blocks, gray as tombstones, and paces in the rectangular dirt spot left by the shed. I stay where the shed's front doors used to be, like a good boy.

Tim stops walking and stands in the middle of the dirt spot. He says, "So, kid, whaddaya think?"

The five-year-old me is tired, tired of the cleanup and the questions, tired of everything. I say, "I think you're a coward." It has no ring of authenticity to it, not one bit, because I think I'm a coward too. Like father, like son.

Tim doesn't offer me any apologies, recriminations, or excuses. He doesn't tell me what I know already, that I have to clean up the mess by myself. He doesn't even say goodbye. He turns, walks over the pile of wood and glass and tar, and disappears into the woods behind our house.

FORTY

The real sun shines bright and hot. It has some bite to it. Spring has become summer. I guess there was a tomorrow after all. Fancy that.

Ellen and I are in the bungalow's backyard. It's my first time in Osterville since I was allowed back into my apartment and office just over a week ago.

Ellen cooks chicken and hot dogs on the small charcoal grill, the grill from the old shed. I think it's the only piece of the lost treasure she kept. The shed is long gone and she hasn't put up a new one. Landscapers spread topsoil and planted grass over the site. Grass grows, but the footprint of the shed is still visible. It's the backyard's scar.

Ellen wears black gym shorts that go past her knees and a green sleeveless T-shirt that's too small. She has a cigarette in one hand, spatula in the other.

She says, "The hot dogs will be ready first." It might be the longest sentence offered to me since arriving at the bungalow.

"Great. I'm starving." A cigarette rolls over my teeth. I'm sitting on a chaise longue, protected by the shade of the house while I wrestle with a newspaper. There are cigarette ashes in my coffee cup. I don't mind.

Almost four full months have passed since the night of the fire in my apartment. Newspaper articles and TV exposés about the DA and the repercussions of my case are still almost a daily occurrence. Today's page 2 of the *Boston Globe* details the complexities associated with the planned exhumation of the body from the foundation of the South Shore Plaza's parking garage.

We know her name now too. Kelly Bishop. An octogenarian aunt, her only living relative, recognized Kelly in the photos, but very little is known or has been reported about Kelly's life. Other than the photos and film, the evidence of their shared time, no further link between Kelly and the boys from Southie has been unearthed.

I don't think the DA was lying to me when he said they didn't know who she was. She was already an anonymous victim, which is why the press drops her story and sticks with the headliners, the DA and his daughter. Kelly's story is too sad and all too real. No glamour or intrigue in the death of the unwanted and anonymous. I remember her name, though, and I'll make it a point not to forget.

I flip through the paper. There's a bit about Jennifer Times in the entertainment section.

I say, "Looks like somebody is cashing in, and it isn't me."

Ellen gives me a hot dog and bun, no ketchup or mustard. She says, "Who are you talking about?"

I say, "Jennifer Times is forging an alternate path back to celebrity land. She's due to be interviewed on national TV again. Tonight and prime time. She has plans to announce that a book and a CD are in the works."

Ellen shrugs, finishes her cigarette, and grinds it under her heel. Her heel means business. It's the exclamation point on the months of stilted conversations and awkward silences. I probably shouldn't be mentioning Times around her. She clearly doesn't want to talk about that.

Then Ellen hits me with a knockout punch. She says, "I saw Tim with her."

I drop the hot dog and ash-filled coffee cup to the grass. I say, "Who?" but I know the answer.

Ellen says, "Kelly Bishop."

I struggle out of the chaise longue. I need to stand and pace or run away. I need to do something with the adrenaline dump into my system. I'm still in the shade but everything is hot again. I repeat what Ellen said, just to get the facts straight like a good detective should. "You saw Kelly with Tim."

Ellen opens the grill's lid, and gray smoke escapes and makes a run for it. She crosses her arms, knotting them into a life jacket. Then she takes off her glasses and hides her eyes. I might not be able to find them.

She says, "It was early evening, and it was already dark. I

was leaving Harbor Point to meet my friends on Carson Beach. I'd stolen a quarter bottle of gin from the top of our refrigerator. I got busted later, when I came home drunk.

"I was fourteen. I remember running down the front steps, hiding the bottle in my fat winter coat even though it was summer. I was so proud of myself and thought I was so smart. Well, there was Tim and the girl, arm in arm, walking through the parking lot. He was holding her up, really. She was obviously drunk or high and couldn't walk. I had no idea who she was. She was so skinny and pale.

"Tim said, 'Hey, Ellen.' Then he smiled. It wasn't a good smile. It was a smile I used to get from the boys who snapped my bra strap or grabbed my ass when I wasn't looking. I didn't say anything back to him. That Kelly looked at me but she couldn't focus. She giggled and rested her head on Tim's shoulder. Then they just stumbled away, into the building.

"I invited you down today to tell you this, Mark." Ellen closes the lid on the grill and the smoke goes back into hiding.

I don't know what to think, but I'm angry. I probably shouldn't be. "Why didn't you tell anybody else?"

"I told the police. I told them as soon as I saw the pictures of her. I just didn't tell you."

My anger evaporates instantly and leaves only sadness. Sadness for us and for everything. The truth is sadness. I walk over toward Ellen and the grill and say, "Why didn't you tell me?"

Ellen isn't hiding her eyes anymore. I get the double barrel. "You kept that case a secret from me. You kept everything he did from me."

"I told you everything I knew once I'd solved the case."

"Only because you had to, Mark. Would you have told me anything if you managed to solve your case without destroying the shed and setting my building on fire?"

I take off my hat and scratch my head. "Yeah, Ellen. Of course I would've told you."

Ellen turns away and opens the grill again. The chicken hisses and steams. It's done. She plucks the meat off the grill with tongs, then dumps on the barbecue sauce. She says, "I know, Mark. I'm sorry. I'm not being fair. But I'm still so angry. I wish you'd told me about what was going on earlier."

"I didn't want to say anything until I knew exactly what had happened. There was no guarantee I was going to figure it all out. Giving you the bits and pieces and then living with the doubt would've been worse."

Ellen breathes in sharp, ready to go on offense again, but then she exhales slowly and shakes her head. She says, "I've tried telling myself that it wasn't Kelly I saw with Tim that night. Maybe I'm just putting that face from those pictures onto someone else's body. It's possible, right?" She pauses and fiddles with the burner knobs. "I do know that just a few days after I saw him with that girl, Tim stopped hanging around with Times and Sullivan and started chasing after me. He was a different kid. He wasn't obnoxious and loud and cocky like the rest of them. He got real quiet, listened way more than he talked. At the time, I thought it was because of some puppy-love crush he had on me. Jesus Christ, I thought he was acting like that because of me. Ridiculous, right?"

Ellen talks just above a whisper but waves the spatula over her head and scrapes the blue sky. "Now, I don't know what to think. Did he only start pursuing me and dating me because of what happened, because of what he did? Was he using me to hide his guilt, to try and somehow make up for that night, to try and become some person that he wasn't? What do you think, Mark? I want to know. I have to know. Can you answer any of those questions for me, Mr. Private Detective?"

I could tell her that maybe it was her and that she somehow saved Tim, redeemed him. But she knows the truth; I can't answer any of those questions. No one can. I don't even try.

I say, "I'm sorry, Ellen," and I give her a hug. She accepts it grudgingly. It's the best I can do.

Ellen releases me quick. "Let's eat before the flies and yellow jackets find us."

So we sit outside, next to each other on adjacent chaise longues, and eat our barbecued chicken and hot dogs. We don't talk because we don't know what to say anymore. When we finish eating we each smoke a cigarette. The filters are pinched tight between our fingers. We're afraid to let go.

Eventually, I get up and say, "Thanks for dinner, Ellen. It was great. I'm getting tired. Should probably move around a bit or I'm gonna go out." I get up and gather the dirty dishes and makeshift ashtrays.

Ellen says, "Thank you, Mark." She doesn't look up at me. She starts in on another cigarette and stares out to where the shed used to be, to where the grass isn't growing fast enough.

I say, "You're welcome."

I walk through the back door, dump the dishes in the sink, then mosey down the hallway and into the living room. I dock myself on the couch as the murk and fatigue come rolling in.

My eyelids are as heavy and thick as Dostoyevsky novels and my world is getting dim again, but I see all the black-and-white pictures are still on the walls. Ellen hasn't taken any of them down. Not a one. Maybe it means that, despite everything, Ellen is determined not to forget, determined to keep her collected memories exactly where they were before, determined to fight against her very own version of the little sleep.

I don't think she'll succeed, but I admire the effort.

ACKNOWLEDGMENTS

There are so many people who need proper thanks that I won't be able to thank them all, but I'll give it a try. If I've forgotten anyone, it wasn't intentional and mea culpa.

Gargantuan thanks to Lisa, Cole, Emma, Rascal, Kathleen M., Paul N. T., Erin, Dan, Jennifer, the Carroll and Genevich clan, and to the rest of my family and friends for their love and support and for putting up with my panics, mood swings, and egotistical ramblings. Special acknowledgment to Michael, Rob, and Mary (along with the tireless and wonderful Lisa and Dad) for acting enthusiastically as my first readers way back when I wrote just awful, terrible stuff.

Giant, sloppy, and unending thanks and admiration to Poppy Z. "I love Steve Nash, really" Brite, Steve "Big Brother" Eller, and Stewart "Don't hate me because I root for the Raiders" O'Nan. They have been and continue to be invaluable mentors, supporters, and friends. I will never be able to thank them enough.

Big, aw-shucks, punch-you-in-the-shoulder thanks to the following who have shared their talent and helped me along the way: assorted Arrows, Laird "Imago" Barron, Mairi "seismic" Beacon, Hannah Wolf "da Bulls" Bowen, Michael "The Kid" Cisco, Brett "They call me F" Cox, JoAnn "He's not related to me" Cox, Ellen "Owned by cats" Datlow, dgk "kelly" goldberg (you are missed), Jack "I know Chandler better than you" Haringa, John "Don't call me Paul" Harvey, and the rest of the Providence critique crew, Brian "bah" Hopkins, Nick "I hate TV" Kaufmann, Mike "Blame Canada" Kelly, Dan "Samurai" Keohane, Greg "Hardest working man in horrah" Lamberson, John "Purple flower" Langan, Sarah "He's not related to me" Langan, Seth "I'm taller than you" Lindberg, Simon "IO" Logan, Louis "A guy called me Louie . . . once" Maistros and his family, Nick "nihilistic kid" Mamatas, Dallas "They call me . . ." Mayr, Sandra "I can whup Chuck Norris" McDonald, Kris "Mudd" Meyer, Kurt "Fig" Newton, Brett "el Presidente" Savory, Kathy "I played Mafia before you" Sedia, Jeffrey and Scott "But not Kristen" Thomas, M. "Not related to them" Thomas, and Sean "Cower as I crush you" Wallace.

Special thanks to my agent, Stephen "They're coming to get you" Barbara, who understands my work and tolerates my occasional tantrums and delusions.

More special thanks to the entire Henry Holt team, and especially to Sarah "The Dark" Knight for her thousand-watt enthusiasm and for believing in *The Little Sleep* and in Mark Genevich.

Thanks to (give yourself a nickname) for reading *The Little Sleep*. Now, go tell your friends and neighbors or blog about it. Blogging would be good.

Cheers!

NO
SLEEP
TILL
WONDER
LAND

For Lisa, Cole, and Emma, always

ONE

It's too hot, even for mid-July. The mercury pushes past ninety degrees even as the sun stuffs its hands in its pockets, turns its back, and walks away for another night. I feel the same way.

We're inside, though, momentarily away from the heat. Tan carpeting, blue wallpaper, white ceiling with track lighting. Six of us are in chairs, sitting in a circle, an obedient shape. We're quiet. We're trained. The hum of the central air conditioner is enough to keep us occupied while we wait for further instructions. No one wants to look at the other, or engage in conversation, not before the designated time. Normally, it's the kind of situation I wouldn't mind tweaking, but I'm still exhausted and overheated from my walk over here. Besides, we've all been tweaked enough.

This guy named Gus sits next to me. He's been coming here as long as I have. He's short and wiry, and he wears black horn-rimmed glasses. He has thick beard stubble that has been cultivated and encouraged and colorful tattoos on his pale, thin arms. Behind one less-than-impressive bicep is the face of a green cartoon dog that winks and chomps on a cigarette. The dog has the right idea.

Gus is around my age, early-but-aging thirties, and like me he's dressed in vintage clothes: black leisure pants, black wingtips, a white, skin-tight V-neck T-shirt tucked in and underneath his unbuttoned powder blue guayabera, a canary yellow porkpie hat that struggles to hold down purposefully greasy tufts of black hair. He pulls off the look better than me. I look like I stumbled out of your grandfather's closet, mothballs and all.

Gus is done with his drawing, and it rests on his lap. He taps his pen on the metal chair, working out something in double time. I sneak a peek at his picture. He took up an entire page. His head and hat are detailed and accurate. His body is a cartoonish mess. Legs and arms are broken, twisted. His forearms, hands, shins, knees, and feet and other unidentifiable pieces of himself break off and fall away, toward the bottom of the page. It's a good picture.

Gus catches me looking and says, "Don't judge me," but then he winks, just like his tattoo dog. That's supposed to be a joke. I don't find anything funny.

Here's my drawing:

It's a smaller, doodle version of my head. It's all anyone ever need see of me. Rembrandt, I'm not. I'm not even that paint-the-happy-tree-there guy.

Gus leans in and gets an eyeful. I say, "I did better when I tried drawing that turtle and the pirate for those art tests in the backs of magazines."

Doctor Who announces his return to the circle. "Okay, everyone," he says, and that's it. It's enough for us to know what to do next. He hands out bonus smiles while collecting the pens and our composition notebooks, the kind I used in elementary school. My notebook has chunks of paper torn out. The black-and-white cover is warped and cracked. Our assignment was to draw a self-portrait, but we're not going to talk about it until next week. This is my sixth group therapy session at the Wellness Center, and I'm feeling well-er every day.

If I sound skeptical, I don't mean to. I'm just practical. My landlord and mother, Ellen, made my weekly visits to the center compulsory if I was to continue running my little private detective business rent free in her building. We're at a point where she thinks my narcolepsy is some kind of social disorder, not physical. It's all depressing enough to make me want to attend group therapy.

The doctor pulls a chair into our circle. He's not British or into science fiction, but he tolerates me calling him Dr. Who. He'd tell you that my naming him is an attempt at asserting some control in my life. He'd tell you that my everyday existence is usually about naming and piecing together my reality even if the pieces don't fit. I'd tell you that I just like calling a tall, skinny, bald guy Dr. Who.

The doc, he's nice, plenty enthusiastic, and obviously means well the ultimate backhanded compliment. There've been times when I wanted to tell him everything, tell him more than I know. But there are other times when I'm ready to take a vow of silence, like now, as I look at his faded khaki pants with the belt cinched well above the Canadian border and his white too-tight polo shirt. That shouldn't bother me, but it does.

He swoops the drawings up and away. Now it's story time. Everyone is to spill their tales in a regimented, predetermined order. I think that's what I hate most about this whole setup. It's disrespectful to stories. Stories don't happen that way. There's no order, no beginning, middle, or end; no one simply gets a turn. Stories are messy, unpredictable, and usually cruel. I try not to listen. I'm not being selfish. It's not that I don't empathize, because I empathize too much, and I can't help them.

I say I try not to listen, but it doesn't work. The man across from me goes on about how his cats are trying to sabotage the fragile relationship he has with his third ex-wife. Or maybe I'm asleep and dreaming it.

It's Gus's turn. He has a smile that's wholly inappropriate for the setting. I kind of like it. He talks about how his mother who died two years ago used to make her own saltwater taffy when he was a kid. He tells us that since her death, he craves social settings and has become a compulsive joiner. If you have a club or group or association, he'll join it. He pulls out a wallet full of membership IDs. He gives me two cards: one for the Libertarian Party and the other belonging to some anarchist group that's clearly fraudulent because anarchists don't make ID cards. He seems particularly proud of that one.

Dr. Who holds up his clutched hands, like he's arm wrestling himself, and says, "You're always welcome in our group, Gus."

Gus tips his hat and sags in his chair, clearly at ease in the group setting, a junky getting his fix. Despite his earlier protest, I'm judging him. I don't feel guilty. I never promised him anything.

Dr. Who asks, "Mark, do you have anything to share with us today?"

Last week he phrased the question differently: *Do you feel up to joining our conversation this week?* I answered with a rant concerning his poorly phrased question, about how it was domineering and patronizing and made me feel more damaged than I already was. It was a solid rant, an 8 out of 10. But I don't know how much of the rant I let loose. I woke up with my circle mates out of their chairs, standing, and staring at me like I was a frog pinned up for dissection.

Gus wiggles his fingers at me, a reverse hand wave, the international *Let's have it* sign.

All right. Let's have it.

TWO

Here's what I don't tell them:

I don't state the obvious; things are not going well for Mark Genevich. About a year and a half has passed since I broke a case that involved the Suffolk County DA and his dirty secret: the disappearance of a girl more than thirty years ago. My personal not so dirty secret was that my business had never been profitable, had never been anything more than a hobby, something to occupy my time and mind; private investigation as babysitter. But after the DA case went public, I had my fifteen minutes. Everyone in South Boston knew who I was, and my kitten-weak business experienced a bump.

Initially, I handled the bump okay. I had this one lucrative gig where I ran background checks for a contractor who was hiring locals to build the nursing home going up on D Street. I verified income and places of previous employment and the like for his applicants. My shining moment was ferreting out one guy who was illegally collecting disability on the side. But soon enough I started getting small-time cases a popular subset of which were complaints of Facebook harassment and other online misdeeds from people who'd read about the DA and only wanted to rubberneck, collect anecdotes for their friends. Because the money was good, I had an impossible time saying no, which means I didn't play it smart. I played it desperate, like I always do. I took on too many cases, and I flamed out on most of them. I even tried taking an online course from some Private Investigating Training School, thinking it would help me organize and prioritize my schedule, identify my investigative strengths. Six months into the three-month course I identified only my growing stack of bills.

Narcolepsy was and is my only constant. It did not improve during the business bump despite renewed attempts at lifestyle changes and adaptations. I quit coffee, smoking, and booze for almost two months. Okay, maybe two weeks. I tried new and aggressive drug therapies, but it didn't help and it left me washed out and washed up, and with a list of dissatisfied clients and an ever-growing monster named Debt.

Oh, what else?

I don't tell the group that my business is just about dead, kept barely breathing in a monetary iron lung only because Ellen continues to begrudgingly fund it.

I don't tell them about Ellen's version of desperation, her Hail

Mary: the humiliating group therapy deal. She even had me sign a contract. It was pathetic. I was asleep on my couch, and I woke up with her standing above me, the contract on my chest like a scarlet letter, and a pen in my hand, which leaked black ink onto my fingertips. After she sprang the deal on me, we had an argument that went atomic. We're still in its nuclear winter. I avoid talking to her, and she does the same. She used to come to Southie and crash at my place two nights a week, but Ellen has quarantined herself on the Cape for the entire summer.

I don't tell them the irony is that I should be the one sequestered and tucked away on the Cape and Ellen should be living here in Southie. Ellen is of this place and is only happy when she's here, and I've never understood why she continues to stay on the Cape and not relocate her photography business. We're both too stubborn to swap out. I've lived and worked in Southie for ten years, but I grew up on the Cape, where neighbors lived too far away and tourists were a necessary evil, a commodity. I grew up in a vacation spot, transient, by its very definition and purpose, so I do not understand identity by proximity, by place. I do not understand the want and will of a community, which is so insular at times, even after growing up in the considerably long shadow thrown by Ellen and her Southie, the Southie she always told me about. It is hers, not mine, will never be mine, and that's okay. Granted, my South Boston years have been influenced, shall we say, by narcolepsy. Who am I kidding? It's been ten years of me as Hermit T. Crab.

I don't tell the members of my group therapy circle that I hate ketchup and pickles. I don't tell them that I think the *Godfather* movies are overrated.

I don't tell them the hallowed members of our kumbaya circle that I hate them and their cats and their problems and their we-can-stay-awake-on-command asses.

THREE

Here's what I do tell them:

Last week I tailed Madison Hall, wife of Wilkie Barrack, the local CEO of one of the Northeast's largest investment firms, Financier. Mr. December thought his May bride was cheating on him. Standard kind of job. I usually don't take on infidelity cases. Not because of some moral high ground I don't have. I'm just not well suited for surveillance gigs. That said, the payday was too big to turn down.

Barrack's lawyer was my contact, and he e-mailed me Madison's photo and their Commonwealth Ave address, some high-priced in-town apartment they rented but rarely used. Apparently she used it more often than hubby thought.

Madison left her apartment building at seven each evening. I spent the two nights tailing her from a safe distance. She was easy to spot: a Marilyn Monroe–style platinum blonde wearing big Jackie O sunglasses, a white scarf, and a yellow sundress. She spent her evenings wandering over to Newbury Street and window-shopped all those overpriced fashion boutiques, exotic restaurants, and cafés.

The only place she entered was Trident Booksellers & Cafe. It looked like the perfect place for a rendezvous. Inside, she swapped out her Jackie Os for wire rims and wandered the stacks. She wasn't meeting anyone there. She didn't stop to talk to anyone, not even the staff. She bought a book on both nights, set herself down in the café section, ordered a coffee and tiramisu, and then read by herself until the place closed at midnight.

I spent my surveillance time hunkered in the stacks or across the street smoking cigarettes, and managed to stay mostly awake the entire time. Mostly. The second night I ventured into the café and sat as far away from her as I could, she with her back to me. It was a slow night, and there was only one other person in the café. He nursed his coffee, newspaper, and considerable thoughts. The three of us spent a solid hour in silence. It was like I'd walked into that *Boulevard of Broken Dreams* painting. Would it be too self-indulgent of me to say my dreams have always been broken?

After closing time she took a cab back to her apartment. I hung around in front of her building until about 2:00 a.m., waiting to see if anyone rang her bell; no one did. A handful of men entered the building with keys but never the same guy on consecutive nights. She wasn't cheating on her husband, at least not while I watched her.

After that second night, I e-mailed the lawyer an update, reporting her so-far chaste activities. That same morning, the *Boston Herald*'s gossip section, Inside Track, ran shots of Madison leaving some flashy and splashy nightclub, arm in arm with a professional indoor lacrosse player. I didn't know we had a team. The woman in the paper wasn't the same woman that I'd spent two nights following. Oops.

In the retelling for my fellow circle freaks, I leave out the names and Financier details, of course. If any of them really want to figure out who I am taking about, it won't be difficult. I don't really care. Timothy Carter, the CEO's lawyer, is already threatening me with a lawsuit. Haven't told Ellen about that yet. Don't think it will go over well.

Dr. Who quickly thanks me for sharing, reminds us that our conversations are to be held in confidence even if we don't have any and dismisses us. I closed the show.

Everyone is fixed and saved, at least for another night, and the circle disintegrates into its disparate points, everyone but Gus standing and slowly ambling away. He's still in his seat, next to me, and he has his inked arms folded behind his head. I think about his picture and hope his arms don't break off and into pieces. He sees me looking at him, laughs, and says, "Man, great story. You talk slower than a sloth on Quaaludes, though."

What are you supposed to say to something like that?

He says, "Come on. Let's go get a drink. I know a place. I've got the first round."

I think I know what to say to that, even if I'm out of practice.

FOUR

Gus does most of the talking during our trudge down D Street and onto West Broadway. I'm not keeping up my end of the conversational bargain. He doesn't seem to mind. He also seems to know half the city, nodding or semisaluting at the scores of pedestrians we pass. Everyone knows his name and they're glad he came. It's goddamn irritating. Me? I'm like my home base brownstone. People know I'm there, but I'm just part of the scenery.

Me and the humidity are going to duke it out to see who will be the bigger wet blanket tonight. I loosen my tie, unbutton my cuffs, and roll the sleeves to my elbows. I say, "Do we keep passing your fellow anarchists? Did you miss a meeting tonight?"

He laughs. It's big and fake, a show laugh. "Anarchists don't wave, my good man. They give each other the finger. Don't give out our secret handshake, now."

I limp and struggle to keep up with him. My gears aren't fitting together right. Hard breaths leak out, and my muffler and exhaust system are shot. So I light a cigarette. Gus glides gracefully over the pavement, like he's spent his prime years rigorously training how to walk. Another reason to despise my new drinking buddy.

We pass the Lithuanian Club, and its never-ending sign crawls along the brick in yellow letters, reading: SOUTH BOSTON LITHUANIAN CITIZENS ASSOCIATION. I point to it and say, "I might be able to get you in the Lit Club if you want." I say it with spite.

I say it to tweak him, although I have no reason to do so.

Gus stops and adjusts his hat. It's a good move. He says, "Doth I offend you somehow, Mark? Look, man, you don't have to come out for a drink if you don't want to. I'll shed no tears, and my heart will go on."

He's right. I don't have to, but I want to, even if I'm not acting like it. I'm so complex. I say, "Don't mind me. I don't get out much, and walking makes me cranky and tired."

"I understand. If you don't feel up to it, we can do it again some other time, maybe next week."

He doesn't understand, but I'm not going to argue the point. I say, "I'm always tired." I offer him a cigarette, and he takes two out of the pack, one for his mouth and one behind his ear. He's earned it.

He lights up, points at the Lit Club, then says, "I'm already a member. I'm actually part Lithuanian."

I won't call his bluff, if it is a bluff. I say, "Which part?"

"We're going to get along fine." He pats me on the shoulder. Way to go, sport.

Not crazy about the physical contact. He's too easy with it. Not crazy about everything. It has been too many years since my friends and roommates fled the apartment and the narcoleptic me, and seemingly longer since anyone other than Ellen has willingly made me, the self-styled narcoleptic monk, a social call. I can admit I'm drowning-man desperate for some companionship, even the most fleeting and temporary. I know, a real breakthrough. If only Dr. Who could see me now.

We traverse the remainder of West Broadway without further incident. He talks about being a kid and his family coming up from Hull once a month to go to St. Peter's, a Lithuanian Catholic church. I sweat through my shirt and into my black necktie.

At the corner of West Broadway and Dorchester Street is the brownstone where I live and work. I make a show of checking the front door, to see if it's locked. The window with my stenciled name and job description rattles in the frame.

Gus steps back to the edge of the sidewalk, looks the building up and down like he wants to ask it to dance, and says, "Nice digs."

I shrug. I don't take compliments well. Besides, it's Ellen's brownstone, not mine.

"Did you have an accident up there?" Gus points above, presumably to the stubborn soot stains on the bricks around the second-floor windows.

"Fire did a couple of laps around the apartment. Hazards of my thrilling glamourrama job."

"You sure you weren't just smoking in bed or something?" He takes the shot at me and combines it with a smile. Fair enough, and he pulls it off with the charm I don't have.

I say, "I'm never sure."

We cross Broadway and turn left onto Dorchester. I know where we're going, but I don't think I'll like it. Two blocks, then left onto West Third Street, and we're here. Here is a bar called the Abbey, which is as run-down as its reputation. Off the beaten Broadway path, the Abbey is stuck between abandoned or failing industrial buildings and a congested residential section of Southie. The two-and three-family homes are on the wrong side of Dorchester Street. They can see East Broadway and the houses and brownstones that have become high-rent apartments or high-priced condos, but they're not quite there.

The Abbey's front bay window runs almost the full length of the bar. The window is tinted black with only a neon Guinness sign peeking through, and it sits inside a weather-beaten wooden frame that could use a coat or three of stain. There's a guy sitting on a bar stool next to the front door. He's tall, thin, wearing a white sleeveless undershirt and baggy black shorts. His tattooed arms are wrapped around one of his propped-up legs. He's a coiled snake, and he doesn't like the look of me. No one does. He nods at Gus and says, "Who's this you bringin' in here?"

Gus's voice goes performance loud. A bad actor reading worse lines, he says, "Mark, this is the ever-charming Eddie Ryan: bouncer extraordinaire, raconteur . . ."

I hold out my paw. Eddie reluctantly unfolds an arm and takes my hand like it's a rock he's going to use at a stoning. He says, "I don't want no fuckin' pretend cop in my bar."

Always nice to be recognized by the little people. I say, "And I don't like people with two first names."

Gus laughs even though we all know this isn't a joke. "Come now, Eddie. Mark's not a pretend cop. He doesn't even have any handcuffs, and he's not working right now. Relax."

"I know what he is." Eddie rubs his buzz cut and rolls his shoulders, a boxer getting ready in his corner. I'd be intimidated if it wasn't so typical. He points a finger at me and says, "No snooping around or buggin' the customers with your shit, all right, or I'll throw your ugly ass to the curb."

I'd love to keep the witty repartee going, but I keep my tongue in a bear hug. I guess this means I'm serious about drinking with Gus, or at least serious about drinking.

Eddie opens the door with one arm. His tough-guy routine was not quite answer-me-these-questions-three, but we're in.

It's night inside the bar, with the overhead lamps and bar lights shirking their illuminating duties. There's a moldy pool table in one corner, a dartboard with no players, and some wooden tables and chairs that look like black skeletons. The place is half full, which is to say it's half empty. The patrons at the bar sit huddled over their drinks, protecting them. A small group stands in a dark corner, laughing loudly and too loose with their spilling glasses. It's a place for small-timers, their small deals, and their smaller dreams. I feel right at home.

Gus and I claim two stools at the bar. He orders beers, and I add a whiskey kicker. The bartender is dressed like Eddie but is happier about it.

I say, "Do I get to meet any more of your charming friends?" Gus smiles and waves me off. "Eddie's all right. He's just, shall we say, territorial. A dog barking behind a fence, but once you're inside he's all cuddles."

There's more to it than that, and conclusions about Eddie, Gus, and the other side of the law aside, I'm going to let it all go, and dive into a couple of rounds and see if I sink or float. I say, "I'm not going to let him lick my face."

"I'd say that's wise. You might catch something."

We drink. He talks. I pretend that I do this sort of thing all the time, that a guy like me always goes to a place like this. Gus tells me that he's a bartender here a few nights a week and a bike messenger during the day. He shows me some scrapes and scars from pavement and automotive metal. I'll drink to that, and so we do. Gus keeps talking. He's spent two thousand dollars on tattoos, drinks scotch only at home, had a bout with Lyme disease a few years ago, got the tick bite while biking in some local state park. There's an overflow of information, and I'm not sure what to say, how to respond, how to act, how to be. This shouldn't be as hard as it is.

Full glasses replace the empty ones, and I don't remember making the empties. I'm winking on and off like a strobe light. Don't know if Gus can tell. His words and phrases aren't fitting together. I can nod my head and add the occasional commiserative chuckle in my sleep. I drink too fast and too much. My head slows down, gets heavy, fills with buzz and murk and anxiety, a stew that'll just about guarantee that I shut down. I try to focus on my surroundings, but there is no bar. There's no one else here. We're a two-man play. There's a spotlight on me and Gus, and everything else is black.

Gus hits me with questions. My turn to talk. I open my mouth and words sputter out like butterflies; they flitter around, so fragile. What am I saying? I might be talking about Ellen. Gus says he wants to help. I might be talking about my dead father, my dead best friend, or my dying business; everything is dying. Gus says he wants to help me. I might be talking about Dr. Who, the Red Sox, or the van accident that left me forever mangled and broken. Gus says he wants to help me out. I might be talking about how after my big case broke I thought everything would be better and easier for me, and it was for a little while, but then it wasn't, and nothing gets easier because each day stacks on top of the one before it, building a tower of days that will lean and fall eventually.

Maybe I didn't tell him any of that. Probably. Now he's laughing, shouting to the bar patrons out there who I can't see because it's too dark around us. He's clinking glasses with me, slapping my back like I'm choking and need some foreign object expelled from my throat. Maybe one of those butterflies got stuck.

Then it's later only because it has to be later. It's always later. It gets later early around here. I'm really drunk, can't keep my eyes open, and I'm stumbling out of the bar with my arm around Gus's neck.

Gus says, "No sleep till Brooklyn, my friend. Brooklyn being my couch." I didn't know he was a Beastie Boy.

The bouncer, Eddie, that fucking guy, he's still there at the door, smiling and laughing at me, and he says something about taking that shit pile out of here and dumping it out back. I try to swing and hit him, but my arm stays around Gus's neck. He must be strong to carry all my weight.

FIVE

I dream that Gus and I are walking down West Broadway, and we are the pictures we drew at the Wellness Center. We're made of paper and very fragile. Gus is already in pieces. The wind growls and threatens to tear us up. Then I'm not little Jackie Paper anymore, and I wake up on Gus's couch.

A puddle of drool sticks my cheek to his leather cushion. I sit up slowly, afraid my head might fall off and roll away. The room is too bright. I'm blinking madly, like a liar.

Gus sits in a chair by a desktop computer. He says, "Mornin', sunshine. This'll help." He tosses me a half-full pint bottle of Irish whiskey. I actually catch it.

We celebrate appropriately.

SIX

I wake up in my own apartment for the first time in two days, though still on a couch, my couch at least. Hopefully I'm working my way up to a bed soon. I'll try my best. Today is going to be about survival.

A shower that empties the hot water tank isn't enough. Clean clothes and a clean hat don't really cut it either. I eat three slices of wheat bread only because I need to line my stomach with something other than the fur of the previous two-day bender before I swallow the bottle of ibuprofen. One must medicate properly, after all.

Water. Pills. Coffee. I'm only capable of action one word at a time. On my third cup of coffee I attempt forward progress.

I move like a slow leak down the stairs and to my office. I unlock the door but leave the lights out and the blinds closed. Coffee cup and my head go down on the cluttered desk. The clutter doesn't mind, and my own lights dim. Mark Genevich, open for business.

Sometime later, it's always later but we knew that already, my front door opens with a crash and the track lights in the ceiling flash on too. Someone is treating my office very rudely.

A man struts in, walking to the beat of his own inflated ego. He announces: "Mr. Genevich, I'm Timothy Carter."

Oh, goody. The CEO's lawyer is here. I guess I'm supposed to be impressed. He pulls my wooden client chair up close to my desk, against its will; the legs scrape and complain on the hardwood floor. He says, "I'm not interrupting anything, am I?"

Carter is tall, with a medium but athletic build, and wears a dark blue suit with creases sharp enough to cut meat. He's youngish, has purposeful beard stubble and a trendy, slathered-in-gel haircut. He could be in those magazine ads with the models who look like weird mannequin/flesh hybrids, those ads that try to sexily sell vodka, perfume, jeans, and other shit we don't need. If that isn't reason enough to hate him, he adjusts his cuffs after he sits and doesn't take off his Ray Ban sunglasses. Doesn't he know that only self-important assholes wear those? Somebody should tell him.

Can't say he's at the top of the list of people I want to see right now. It's a long list. I say, "Make yourself at home. You don't mind if I sleep through this, do you? Don't worry; we'll make it work."

"I'll be quick. I have a cab out front waiting for me, and you're going to pay that fare, too, Mr. Genevich." His voice is small, rodentesque. Nobody's perfect, and I take a measure of comfort in it.

"Sorry, I'm all out of coupons."

He snorts and leans back in the chair. "It's been one of those mornings, Mr. Genevich. Cooperate and don't push me over the edge." Some high-powered lawyer he is, quick to anger and reliant upon cliché.

I say, "Right now, I'd be more than happy to shove you off that edge and watch your pretty little plummet."

"I don't think you realize how serious my client and I are about suing you for willful negligence. It's a serious charge that could bankrupt your business, Mr. Genevich. Your complete and utter botching of the contracted surveillance has publicly embarrassed my client, causing undue emotional distress, and is costing him untold dollars in damage control with his own clients and would-be clients . . ."

There's more, but I don't really want to hear the end. So boring and predictable. I wave my hand at him, shoo fly. "We all have problems, Carter. Life's about overcoming adversity. Besides, that professional lacrosse player was awful cute."

Carter laughs and leans in, putting his elbows on my desk. "You don't understand . . ."

I've had enough. Yeah, I'm in a mood. I cut him off, at the knees preferably. "I returned what you paid me and you aren't getting one fucking cent more from me."

Carter leans back, and I can see him switching gears and game plans midstream. He says, "I want to see any photos you might've taken while on surveillance. Play ball and things will go smoother for you, Mr. Genevich."

Oh, he's smooth, like chunky-style peanut butter. I say, "I only took a few shots and didn't bother downloading them off my camera because they didn't seem to be all that relevant anymore."

I find the pictures on my camera view-screen; the first few are of the apartment building, and then there are a couple shots of the woman I thought was Madison, the CEO's wife, walking out the lobby door. It's from the first night, I think. I stop, then flip back to a photo of the building, zoom in on the address numbers. I hadn't really thought about it, been a little too occupied with my repeated failures, group therapy, and then the past two lost days with Gus, but I assumed my CEO case went FUBAR because I'd written down the wrong information, presumably the wrong apartment building.

I pass the camera over and say, "That's the building where the CEO's love nest is, right? That's where you sent me?"

Carter looks at the picture and says, "Yes, of course." He's so pleasant. I wish we could hang out more often.

"I guess I followed the wrong woman, then." I take the camera back and flip ahead to a picture of the woman, zoom in a bit, then give him back the camera. It's great that we can share like this.

Carter takes the proverbial long hard look, hard enough to crack the LCD screen. Or he could be playing me. I don't know. He's still wearing those huge sunglasses, so I can't read him. I'd be surprised if he could see anything in my office through those tinted windows. Maybe seeing the pictures isn't as important as he's letting on.

I say, "I assume Madison isn't Madison."

Carter hands the camera back to me, says, "No, she isn't. Thank you, Mr. Genevich. We'll be in touch. Soon." He gets up and leaves as abruptly as he entered. His suit is loud; sounds like someone else's money. I didn't get to say goodbye, or tell him to fuck off, or ask him to turn out the lights.

My head goes back down on the desktop, and my eyelids are doing a damn fine job of dimming the room on their own. My breathing slows as my systems cool and default into hibernate mode, but I'm not asleep yet because I'm thinking about the surveillance gig and now this odd and confrontational exchange with Carter and how it all seems a little off. Maybe I should take another trip out to that apartment building. Maybe I'll figure it all out after I park my head on the desk for a little bit, but that's just the lie I tell myself, we all tell ourselves.

Sleep on it; you'll feel better in the morning.

Sleep won't solve any problems or answer any questions. My mornings are false starts, and I have them throughout the day and night. And sometimes, mornings are the promises that never come.

SEVEN

"Knock, knock. Hello, is the good doctor in?"

I open my eyes. I'm reclined in my office chair, hands folded across my lap; such a polite sleeping position. Gus stands in the doorway, lightly rapping on the door. He has a brown bag in his arms. I didn't get him anything.

Two visitors in one day. I'm a popular guy. I wipe my eyes and face, stir in my chair, pat the desktop, and mutter, "I don't make house calls." A dumb, nonsensical line, and I hope Gus doesn't hear it.

He doesn't look like I feel; he's clean-shaven, wide-eyed, and wears a new porkpie hat, this one danger red. I'm a barely there cadaver who shouldn't be donated to science. If Gus tells me he feels fine, I might have to punch him. Gus holds up the paper bag. "Do you have room on your desk for Chinese? I figured you'd be so busy playing catch-up today you'd probably forget to take care of your basic food needs. Chinese food is a basic need, my friend. Especially the day after."

I nod. He laughs nervously. Then silence. We're so awkward with each other when we're sober.

Gus dishes out veggie lo mein with some seafood medley onto paper plates. He gives me a plastic fork and he uses chopsticks. Is the fork an assumption on his part, or did we previously have a discussion about Chinese food and my inability to use chopsticks? I don't remember much from our two-day event.

I say, "This will help, especially if I can keep it down." The food is good, increasing the odds of me surviving the day.

"So, dear, busy day at the office?"

"I saved the world and got some other shit done."

He says, "I could tell." From anyone else, that would be a cheap shot, but he makes the joke seem commiserative. I could just be rationalizing of course, acting like a puppy around my new friend. I need to keep a handle on my level of desperation. I'm no one's lapdog.

Gus gulps his soda and looks disappointed that it's not something else. "Do you remember climbing into a tree on K Street and yelling at kids and the drunks like us who walked by? Ha! You were pretending to be the voice of God. Old Testament, angry kind of stuff. You were very believable."

I wipe my face and shake my head. There's nothing rattling around inside. Climbing a tree doesn't sound like something I'd do given my physical limitations. I guess the drunk, narcoleptic me wanted to impress his new BFF.

I say, "I didn't even believe in myself."

"Actually, at the end, you shouted about being the god of hellfire and then started singing some sixties tune."

"I wasn't God. I was Arthur Brown. Same thing, really."

"I knew the song but couldn't think of the guy's name." Gus slaps the table with his hand and chuckles. He pauses and gives me the look, the here-is-the-Broken-Man look. Gus puts down the chopsticks. He can't think and work them at the same time. "You don't remember any of that, do you?" When I don't respond, he adds, "I tried to talk you out of climbing the tree with your limp and everything, but you were stubborn. You insisted. Then I ended up giving you ten fingers anyway. You're heavier than you look; no offense." He laughs and shakes his head. "I'm such an enabler. And I must say, getting you out of the tree was a project. Almost had to call the Fire Department. I was going to tell them my cat was stuck in the tree." Gus laughs like everything he says is clever and doesn't hurt.

The narcoleptic me would've clawed the firemen's eyes out. I say, "There's a lot I don't remember from our night on the town. Most of it, actually."

"Correction: nights on the town." Gus performs some acrobatics with his chopsticks, before snatching a big piece of shrimp. No one likes a show-off. He says, "So you remember the guy who sang that *fire* song, but you don't remember our soon-to-be legendary domination of the bars of South Boston?"

As a drunk narcoleptic, I have short-term memory issues. As an everyday narcoleptic, I have short-and long-term memory issues, but I still remember *The Crazy World of Arthur Brown*.

I say, "Don't talk with your mouth full."

Gus leans back in the chair, puts his arms behind his head. "That's really too bad. We had a lot of fun."

"I'll read about it in the papers."

My jokes aren't all that good when I'm hungover. Gus doesn't point out my latest flaw. What a pal. We stop talking and focus on the food.

A tidal wave of fatigue rushes in, and I can't keep my eyes open. I full-body twitch, and my fork clatters to the floor it's loud and angry and my head almost bounces off the desktop. I sit up quick, and everything looks a little different than it was. A common sensation for me, but one I'll never get used to.

"Whoa. Are you okay, Mark?"

"Yeah. I'm fine."

"You just fell asleep there for a second, didn't you?" Gus has his elbows on my desk, our makeshift dining table. Such poor manners; I'm embarrassed for him.

I nod. No need to speak the words detailing the obvious, only need to acknowledge them.

I think about denying it, telling him, *No, I'm fine. Just spazzed out with my fork.* Lying about my narcolepsy is a natural impulse first, second, and third nature. I lied when Juan-Miguel and my other roommates were living with me. At first, the lies were simple, harmless denials: "I wasn't sleeping on the couch," and "I saw how the movie ended." I wouldn't admit anything, even when the outlandish became my defense: "That's not smoke, and I wasn't smoking," and "The cigarette burns in the couch aren't mine," and "I didn't piss on the goddamn couch," and then just a blanket "Fuck you, you're making it all up" to the lot of them. It all piled up so quickly, an avalanche of symptoms, and no Saint Bernard with a barrel of whiskey around its neck to save me. I'm still there, buried. I lie to my mother, Ellen, all the time, even though she knows I'm lying. Maybe I should be consistent and just tell Gus that I didn't almost fall asleep, and that I wasn't God stuck in a tree.

Gus doesn't say anything. He's not letting me off without further explanation. So I say, "You have that affect on people. Sorry, someone had to tell you."

"All right, all right, I know when I'm not wanted. I've got a couple of things for you, and then I'll go so you can continue your recovery in relative peace. I wasn't going to say anything, but you look like shit." Gus laughs, pulls a small plastic bag out of his jeans pocket, and throws it on the desk: twenty or so green pills.

"My headache isn't that bad."

"Last night we talked about your trials with prescription drugs, Desoxyn especially, and how they never really improved your symptoms." Gus pauses long enough to read the glittering neon sign that is my face. "You don't remember, do you? Wow, we talked all about the side effects: the insomnia, headaches, tremors, how it made you feel depressed. Awake but heavy in the head, was what you said."

"Sounds like something I'd say, but I don't remember rhyming."

"We were at the Playwright down on East Broadway. Oh, and you complained about raging diarrhea too."

"Wasn't I sparkling company?"

"You were a delight, as always, and it helped clear out our tidy corner of the bar. We also talked about trying amphetamines. They'd probably only handle the fatigue symptoms, but it's better than nothing, and they wouldn't have the rest of the neurological effects the Desoxyn had."

"I don't suppose you got a prescription for these."

Gus sighs, his first sign of annoyance. "It's not a big deal, Mark. It's just a bag of greenies. Easy to get. Athletes and cops use them all the time."

I lift the bag. "I'm not an athlete or a cop, or even a pretend cop."

"Just trying to help. I know you don't remember, but we talked about this."

"Where did you get these? Do you take these yourself? I'm a semiconscious slug over here, and you're . . . you're Dr. Pepper."

"Dr. Pepper?"

I wave my hands, frustrated at the words. Maybe I can swat the pesky ones away. "Christ, you know what I'm saying. I mean, Mr. Pep. Bushy eyed and bright tailed, and all that bullshit." My turn to hit my desk. It's taking a beating.

Gus shows me his pair of slow-down hands. "Hey, hey, take it easy, Mark. If in the light of this bright new dawn you're not comfortable taking them, no big deal. You can throw them away. I won't be insulted, and they're not expensive."

Gus doesn't answer my questions. I don't know if I should push him on it. He doesn't sound nervous, just very matter-of-fact. He could be talking about a terrible sweater he got for my birthday and giving me permission to take it back.

I say, "I'll think about it. I can't make any big decisions until I'm a little more than subhuman, which could be a while. I'm a slow evolver, like the Galápagos iguanas or something." Why am I so nervous around this guy? Not sure why I don't tell him to go choke on the bag of greenies instead of serving up wishy-washy maybes and the inexplicable apologies to Darwin comparison of myself to isolated marine lizards.

"I'll take your word for it, iguana-man. But that's fine. I understand. Like I said, don't worry yourself over it, one way or the other."

We stop talking and nod at each other as if we traversed some grand intellectual impasse. That, or we don't know what the hell to say to each other.

"Okay, I've got one more thing for you, Mark." Gus cringes, tucks his head between his shoulders, and says, "A job, if you want it. You'd really be helping me out."

"If it's tracking down some punk amphetamine dealer, I have a lead."

"Funny. Do you remember Eddie, the bouncer at the Abbey?"

"Him I remember."

"He's stalking my friend Ekat. She came by the Abbey a few weeks ago, and he wouldn't leave her alone despite her clear communication to the contrary. He called her at work the next day, too. She told him to fuck off, and we thought that was that. But Ekat called me this morning, woke me up, and said he called again, threatening to show up at her bar tomorrow. She works at the Pour House, which is downtown, near the Prudential. Eddie's not taking my calls yet. I checked the schedule and he has a couple of days off but I'm on tomorrow night. I tried calling the other bartenders already but none of them would take my shift. So I won't see Eddie at the Abbey and I won't be able to go to the Pour House either. It's a scary little mess. Do you think you could just go hang out at Ekat's bar tomorrow night? Maybe follow her home, make sure she's safe. She lives here in Southie, over on I Street, between Fifth and Sixth. Ekat would kill me if she knew I was doing this, but I'm worried, you know?"

That was quite the speech. Quick and well delivered, but I don't like its implications. "First, let's pretend this is all legit." I pause, and Gus does a classic double take. He really is an expressive son of a bitch. "I don't back down from anyone, but I wouldn't describe my par tic u lar skill set as including intimidation, muscle, or protection."

Gus's brow furrows; he's in thoughtful mode, choosing his words carefully. He says, "I'm hopeful that if Eddie does go to her bar, he'll see you. Knowing that she's serious enough to hire professional help should throw some cold water on Eddie, at least for one night."

"Maybe. Maybe not. Second, you heard the story about how my last surveillance gig went. It didn't exactly fare thee well."

"People make mistakes. Who knows? It might not have been your fault."

"Yet to be determined, if I'm being kind to me."

"Having spent the past couple of days with you, I know that you're hard on yourself, a little too hard on yourself."

"Are you taking over the group therapy session from Dr. Who next week? I suggest you arm wrestle him for it."

"We'll leg wrestle." Gus pulls out a couple of cigarettes and lights them. Why didn't I think of that? He says, "Now, what's with the crazy talk about pretending this is legit? What are you trying to say?"

I inhale, let the smoke do its yellow voodoo on my teeth for a bit before spitting it out. I could use some real magic. I guess I'll have to stick with blunt honesty for a change.

I say, "I feel set up. You only took me out for a drink so you could show me off to Eddie and then use me later, which is fine. I'm all grown up now, tuck myself into bed each night, tell my own bedtime stories even if they don't work. But you coming in here and acting like you're doing me a favor by offering some new gig when you wanted me for this all along doesn't sit right. Why you want me, I don't know. Maybe I'm the only PI you can afford. Maybe you think you can buy my help with cheap booze and little green pills. Can't say I like that you obviously think I'm not smart enough to connect those dots. I don't—"

"Whoa, whoa, Mark, stop, listen to yourself. I know it's your job and probably a part of your DNA to not trust the scenarios laid out in front of you, but Jesus fuck, this goes beyond a little healthy paranoia."

"Does it?"

"You can trust me. I promise. I swear it all came up this morning when Ekat called." He shrugs, looks around, and then his hands scurry into his pockets again like bugs fleeing when the lights come on. "Look, I can show you my cell call history if that'll help." He holds out his phone, but I don't take it. I clutch my cigarette instead. It feels safer.

Gus says, "We thought the Eddie thing was over. I had no idea he called her again until this morning, and then I just thought we could help each other out. That's all, Mark." Gus scratches his arms and rubs his face. He's clearly uncomfortable. So am I.

"How well do you know Eddie?"

"Not well. We work together, and that's it. We don't hang out. I never talk to him or see him outside the Abbey."

"What else does he *do* besides bouncing?" I stress the word *do* like it's a cipher to my secret code. Not that I'm speaking in secrets, but I am trying to learn a few.

"Eh, he's a small-timer. Really small-time, sells some stuff on the side, to kids at the bar mostly."

"Did you get this bag of jelly beans from him?"

"No, Mark, I didn't."

We don't talk, just share looks that we should probably just keep to ourselves. I'm getting tired again. Other people are such hard work.

He says, "There are plenty of small-timers in Southie who sell this stuff, you know. He's not the only one."

"So I've heard." I take out one of my own cigarettes and put it to work. I don't know what to think or how to think. There should be a manual or a training film. Our words are forming complicated crossing circuits in my head. I need to regroup. I need a nap. I do think he's telling the truth about the amphetamine conversation that I don't remember. The stuff about Desoxyn and the side effects, particularly the diarrhea, has the ugly ring of my truth. The Eddie connection, though, I don't know.

Gus isn't in the client chair anymore. He's standing at the side of my desk, tugging gently on my sleeve. I must've gone out for a bit, and he waited. Don't know if that counts for or against him.

"Hey, Mark." He waits until I move my arm and adjust in my seat, then he adds, "I understand everything you're saying. But I don't know what else to tell you. I didn't invite you out to set this up. There was nothing to set up. I promise."

I don't ask, *Why did you take me out?* I want to know the answer so desperately my teeth ache, but I won't ask. I'm not that needy. I say, "All right, I'll do the job." I am that needy. I don't say it aloud because I've already made my neediness quite apparent. "Write down the details for me."

Gus slaps me on the shoulder. My shoulder is going to hit back eventually. "Thanks, Mark. You're a lifesaver." Gus brightens considerably. The eclipse of my mistrust has passed. He's practically dancing in place as he pulls a folded check out of his pocket and tosses it on my desk. It lands like a betrayal.

"Not necessary. I'm not a charity."

"Stop it, Mark. Take it. You're doing work for me. Like I said, you'll be helping me and Ekat out, big-time."

I unfold the check. Five hundred bucks.

He says, "Is it enough? If it isn't, I—"

"It's plenty." I fold the check and throw it at his chest. A strong throw.

Gus tosses it back. "I'm not leaving here with this check, Mark. I mean it."

He wins. Again. I tell him, "I'll be at her bar tomorrow night."

"Great!" Gus claps his hands, then shakes one of mine and says, "All right, I'm out of here. Call me tomorrow night." Still standing, but swaying side to side, he writes down his cell number and the other details I'll need for tomorrow night.

"Thanks again, Mark. I'll talk to you soon." He backs out of my office, pointing at me like everyone should be looking here, at me, hiding behind my desk, the not-so-incredible shrinking man in his shrinking office, same as it ever was.

When the door shuts, I give the check my hairy eyeball. I might cash it, or I might lose it. I open my top drawer and put the check inside, wedge it under a cigarette lighter shaped like a handgun. It was a gag gift from my late best friend George, the one who died the night of the van accident. I don't want to think about that now, so I won't.

Instead, I think about turning on the computer and checking e-mail, but I decide to call it a day. My days usually end early anyway. The bag of amphetamines, almost forgot about the little fellas. They're still on my desk. A bag of promises. A bag of threats. I don't know which. Probably both. I pick up the amphetamines and tuck them inside my suit jacket. They make a lump on my chest.

Maybe I trust Gus. Maybe I don't. I really want to, though, and it's the want that scares me.

EIGHT

The next day comes like it was supposed to, though I suspect it won't one of these days. I sleep in, cash the check at the bank across the street, and hit the office late 1:00 p.m. late. No one visits or calls.

There's no real work to do until this evening, so I try verifying Financier CEO Wilkie Barrack's Commonwealth Avenue apartment address by calling the building's rental agency. No go there. Then I call the Boston Herald's Inside Track pretending I've just spotted Madison and her lacrosse accessory coming out of a building, and I give Madison's address. The wonderfully helpful intern with the asthmatic voice tells me that it's covered; they already have a freelance photographer stationed outside that address.

So I had the right apartment, anyway. Not sure if that's good or bad, but after experiencing a modicum of success I celebrate by sleeping.

It's 7:00 p.m., and I wake up thinking about how I'm getting to the Pour House. Transportation is always an issue, an incident waiting to happen. Instead of a cab, I could pick up the number 9 bus at the stop right across from my building, and ride the 9 all the way in to the Prudential. It'd be easy and much cheaper than a cab, but I don't do well on buses.

I take out Gus's gift bag and dry swallow an amphetamine. Yeah, just like that. There is no soul-searching or deliberation. I summarily dismiss the nagging question, *What if these aren't amphetamines?* because I can. Swallowing the pill is a complete what's-the-worst-that-could-happen gesture on my part. Amphetamines are essentially the same stuff I tried before, and probably only have a little extra hot sauce. So why am I clutching the edge of my desk, expecting a *Wolfman* soft dissolve and transformation?

While waiting for the fangs to sprout, I do a Web search on amphetamines, which is something I should've done first. Apparently amphetamines are habit forming with both physical and psychological dependence. That's nice. The drug has an impressive and familiar list of side effects that I jot down in my handy-dandy palm-sized notebook. I might need this list later. If I start freaking out, I'll know why.

The list:

- hallucinations, confusion
- anxiety, ~~restl~~ nervousness
- headache
- irregular heartbeat
- panic

- may only hide the symptoms of extreme fatigue
- diarrhea or constipation

I wonder if diarrhea or constipation is user's choice.

I close up the office and step outside. It's another scalding-hot night, but lower humidity and there's a coastal breeze. I limp across the street to the bus stop and light up a cigarette as the 9 bus surfaces and beaches itself on the corner. I make my first and only drag count before grinding it under my heel. What a waste.

Inside the bus, the lights flicker with the sputtering AC. It's cooler in the tin can, but no one feels cool. I lay claim to a seat in the back, behind a couple of giggly teenage boys wearing crooked baseball hats, listening to iPods, and carrying on a loud semiverbal conversation. They'll annoy me enough to keep me awake.

The bus rolls away from the curb, and we're off. Should be a ten-minute trip. Fifteen tops. I'm growing more nervous that I'm too trusting of Gus's little green pill. Is it too late to change my mind? I have a second pill in my pocket just in case I rechange it later. Gus never did tell me the recommended dosage. As a bike messenger/bartender, he makes a lousy pharmacist.

It's a slow ride down Broadway with too many stops. I look out the bus window, but the interior lights reflect my mug on the glass. I'm having trouble focusing, a sentiment I should have tattooed on my tongue. My heart beats louder, knocking its Morse code against my chest. I check my pulse, and it feels quicker than normal, and seems to be gaining momentum, but I don't usually check my pulse so I don't really know what is normal.

I'm multiple-shots-of-espresso wired, but I'm also withdrawn, a step back from reality, whatever that is. My field of vision has a frame on it. I'm in a window. No, I am my own window, and I'm not making any goddamn sense.

The bus hits a pothole, and I almost scream out. Wait, there is no "almost" about my scream as the two teens turn and look at me, clearly a-scared of the hairy, sweaty, screaming man on speed. At least I'm not driving.

Okay, calm down, Genevich. I think we passed over Interstate 93 and are getting closer to Copley. I pull out my collection of side effects, and it reads like a checklist. I know some of what I'm experiencing is the placebo effect, me and my damaged gray matter simply cooperating with the list of symptoms, but it doesn't make me feel any better.

I curl and pass the paper between my fingers. My fingers feel big and clumsy, and that's because they are. The "may only hide symptoms of extreme fatigue" is a particularly ominous side effect.

Ten minutes past forever the bus stops at the Prudential. My fingers are vines, choking the seat in front of me, but I made it. I step off the bus on legs that are skittish and easily spooked. The fresh night air mixed with bus exhaust is a welcome splash of cold water on my face. Released into the expanse of the city, I relax.

The walk is short, two blocks, and I'm feeling good, confident, focused, the near meltdown on the bus already forgotten. The Pour House is a big place with an upstairs and a downstairs. It's early, but most of the booths are full of late diners. Graffiti and collected kitsch cover the brick walls. The staff is dressed in black, with a few wearing neon plastic leis around their necks. I hate this place: it tries to be a dive, but it's too happy, too young. The contrived spontaneity motif rubs me all the wrong ways. I need a smoke, but if I were to light up here the kids would throw their mojitos and appletinis at the grumpy old man.

I mosey downstairs. Here, it's darker, and with less crap smeared on the walls. No crowd. The bar takes up most of the square footage with small tables for two tightly lined along the walls. TVs hang in the corners, each tuned to the Sox game, volume muted. Upstairs is the play room. This is the bar. I decide to lean on it.

Ekat works alongside a male bartender who is completely uninteresting. She's pretty in an everywoman kind of way. Her face mixes a sharp nose with rounded cheeks. No makeup and her brown hair tied up tight. She sees me, jogs to my end of the bar, and says, "What can I get you?"

I'm doing okay, but I don't know about mixing amphetamines, alcohol, and surveillance, oh my. I ask for a beer, Sam Adams. Can't exactly sit at a bar and order water, now, can I?

Ekat is a few inches shorter than I am, but moves a hell of a lot faster. She drops my full glass onto the bar without spilling and asks, "Do I know you?" She doesn't cock her head to the side or send her voice up a few unsure octaves. She says it like she's mad at herself for not knowing the answer to a stupid question. I throw a five on the bar. "Don't think so. But I get that all the time because I look like everyone else."

I went into this assuming Gus wasn't going to tell her about me. She lives in Southie, so maybe she's seen me around, or she knows of me because the DA died in my stairwell. Everyone in Southie knows who I am even if they never see me. I'm their Sasquatch, only no one collects my footprints. It's hard being so popular.

She laughs at me or with me, I don't know. "You're right. I get your types all night long, usually only on Wednesdays, though. You're off a night."

"I'm usually off." I retreat to one of the small square tables up against the wall. I'm going to be here for a while and don't want to be more conspicuous than I already am. I'm the only person in the joint not wearing a tight T-shirt and tighter jeans.

I think about calling Gus but decide against it. I poke and prod my beer through a couple of hours, then have the waitress bring me ginger ale on the rocks and without a straw. The Red Sox lose. People come and go, and Ekat and her partner serve the drinks. Nothing new, and even the randomness of who orders what and who gets served first seems regimented and predetermined if you watch for too long.

All around me there are pockets of conversations, some animated, some quiet and subdued, whispers in a crowd, but all the participants are engaged, effortlessly so. They know what to do and how to act. It has all been done and said before.

As the evening moves on past eleven, my companion fatigue returns, coming back like it's mad at me for ditching it. I hurt its feelings, and it will not be ignored. It's been four hours since I took the first amphetamine. I can't fall asleep here. Taking the other pill isn't even a choice now. This one, I swallow with ginger ale. I'm sure the carbonation will make it behave.

Ekat waves at me from the bar. She wants me to come over. Did she see me take the greenie? She's wearing an I-gotcha smile. She says, "Aren't you the private detective from Southie?"

"I'm Peter Parker, but I'm all out of special powers."

"Come on . . ."

"Okay. Don't know if I'm *the*"—and I pronounce *the* as *thee* because I'm so fancy—"PI of Southie, but I do work there."

"I knew it. You've only had the one beer since coming in. I've been watching you. You're on a case, aren't you?" She points a finger at me.

Her act tastes a little hammy. I still don't know whether Gus told her I was coming or not. Maybe now that the night's getting later, the threat of Eddie showing up seems more real and she wants her presumed protection closer. Or maybe she's just fucking with me.

I sit at the bar. There's room. I say, "You're my case."

"If that's a pick-up line, it's terrible and not funny." Ekat wipes the bar with a rag, angry at the spill that I can't see.

"All my pick-up lines are terrible and not funny, but that wasn't a pick-up line. Our mutual friend Gus . . ."

She throws her bar rag, and it bounces off my chest. I didn't deserve that. "Gus? Gus sent you here?" She swears and talks under her breath, and I'm too polite to eavesdrop.

"He didn't tell me there would be flying bar rags." I think I'm speaking louder than normal, my normal anyway. The second amphetamine has kicked in. Its charge and voltage hum through my system. I'm itching in my stool, toe tapping, both eyes dancing in their sockets. This will work as long as my blood doesn't explode from my veins.

She says, "I can take care of myself," and points at herself with that finger. I'm much more comfortable with that thing pointing away from me.

I try to sound relaxed, even if I've been deported from the island nation of Relaxed. "Gus said the same thing. He also said he thought you could use a little help tonight, that's all."

"I don't need any help." Ekat stalks to the other end of the bar, but there's no one to serve. Any customer would be scared of her anyway.

I hold up my empty glass, and she comes back with her arms folded over her chest. It'll be hard to pour drinks that way. I order another ginger ale, no ice this time. I'm so sophisticated. She puts it down in front of me, and I ask her, "How are you taking care of it?"

"Excuse me?"

"The Eddie problem. You said you could take care of yourself, and I want to know what your plan is for tonight."

Ekat pours herself a glass of water from the soda gun. It's a good way to spend a pause. "I'm leaving early tonight, before closing, soon if they'll let me."

"Good idea. Mind if I follow you home? You could help me out, make sure I don't fall asleep on the way back." Oh hell, that sounds like a line when it isn't. I shrug and hold up my empty palms as I really don't know what I'm doing or saying.

"How am I supposed to do that?"

"I don't know. But if you figure it out, please tell me."

Ekat finishes her water and throws a quick, spinning look around the bar. "Fuck it. Let's go now. You get to pay for the cab ride."

NINE

I'm suffocating. I try to cover up my gasps with some fake coughs, but I can't cover any of it up. It goes without saying I shouldn't have taken the second little pill. What a drag it is getting old.

Ekat sits pressed up against the passenger door, as far away from me as possible. I wish I could sit far away from me too. Her posture is granite hard; a statue could take lessons from her.

We're in the cab for days, and then she turns to me and asks, "What's your name again?" She's as formal as a free clinic doctor.

"Mark Genevich."

"Do you know who Eddie is, Mark Genevich?"

"He's the shady bouncer at Gus's shady bar."

"Does that make Gus shady? Or me?"

Good questions, ones that I've been too compromised to fully consider. "I think everyone is shady. Sorry, that wasn't very nice of me."

That last bit teases a smile out of her. She'll probably regret it. "How much is Gus paying you?"

"Enough."

Ekat shakes her head, expels her disappointment as a sigh through her nose. "I can't believe he did this. He should've asked me first. I'm very mad at him."

It's not my job to defend my employer, new drinking buddy or not. "How do you know Gus?"

"We're both from Hull, been friends since middle school." Hull is a coastal town on the south shore, and Hull to Southie is a common migratory path for wannabe urbanites. I say, "Isn't that sweet?"

"You're not funny."

Maybe loss of humor is a symptom of narcoleptic speed freaks. I'd write that down on my list of side effects, but my hands are shaking too much. "I was only hired for tonight. What's your plan for tomorrow?"

"You mean besides sleeping in and going to the gym?"

"What are you going to do about Eddie? You can't leave work early every night."

"I can do whatever I want." Ekat crosses and uncrosses her arms, then her legs. Her anger is making everything uncomfortable. She pivots in her seat, turning to face me head on, as in the collision. "I might look into getting a restraining order. Or I might just buy a gun and shoot him in the face if he ever comes near me." I don't know if she's giving herself a win-one-for-the-Gipper pep talk or if she's serious. I don't think it matters, because right now, when she says it, she is serious.

She turns away and asks, "Are you feeling okay?"

"I've been better. Has Eddie confronted you, in person, since that night you met him?"

"No, only the phone calls."

We don't speak for the rest of the ride. We're in Sartre's *No Exit,* only we're in a cab, which adds the elements of potholes and random acceleration and deceleration to our quaint Hell. I wish I could smoke a cigarette, even if my chest is getting tighter with each breath, each strained heartbeat.

Finally, and right before the walls implode, we stop and idle in front of her I Street apartment. Ekat jumps out. I'm blinded by the interior light but manage to scrape together twenty-five dollars of Gus's money for the cabbie.

Her building is a well-kept two-family house with yellow vinyl siding. It's between Fifth and Sixth streets, and about the halfway point between Carson Beach and East Broadway. New and trendy cars and SUVs fill the street parking spots on both sides of the one-way.

Ekat is already past a chain-link fence, the basement bulkhead, and stands on a small wooden staircase, key in the side door lock. She says, "What are you doing?"

I stand outside the fence on the sidewalk, in the shadows. "Just making sure you get inside."

"Don't be an asshole; I'm fine. Seriously, why didn't you just stay in the cab? You're not staking out my apartment. I'm dismissing you, Mark. Say goodnight, tip your hat, get a cab, go home."

I like that she used the term *staking out,* but I won't tip my hat for anyone. I don't say anything and only give a slight nod of my head. I'm too far away and out of focus for her to see it. She doesn't wait for my long slow goodbye and disappears into her apartment.

Hostile client notwithstanding, a gig successfully completed. I'll reward myself with a midnight trek home. As much as I hate walking and I'll probably hate it more in the morning the outside air cools down my melting reactor core. That's how it works, right? Simply walk off the speed like it was a big meal.

I make my way up I Street and take a left on Fifth. I turn on my cell phone, and there are no messages. Maybe I'll call Gus when I get back to the apartment. He's probably still at work. I walk behind a church, Gate of Heaven. It's a big gate, taking up most of the block, its restored spire and turrets propagating the lie that they'll forever point skyward.

Something's off, and it's not me for a change. The spire. There's a light at its base, but there's a dirty fog obscuring most of that holy pointing finger. Wait. It's smoke, and I smell it too. I turn and stumble around, an aimless weather vane, and there, up ahead, at the end of the block, on the corner of H and Fifth, is a two-family with bright orange lights dancing in its first-floor windows, smoke billowing out of the second floor, and a stick-woman staggering around the street screaming for help.

I call 911. The presumably interested operator listens to my *Timmy's in the well* spiel, then requests I stay on the phone. I hang up because I was never good at following directions.

I can't really run or jog. My best is an awkward speed-walk crossed with a follow-the-yellow-brick-road skip. I'm off to see the grand and terrible wizard. I almost fall down, my weaker right leg buckles a few times, but I stay up and make it to the corner.

The woman, she's young and skinnier than the scarecrow. Tears and mascara form twin muddy rivers on her contorted face. She bounces around like a panicky electron, all angular momentum. She peaks too fast for complete sentences. *Alone* and *just a boy* and *upstairs* are her verbal shrapnel.

I mumble something noncommittal, I think, and it works. She takes off down the street, screaming. I hope I didn't say "I can help," because that's a promise I can't make, nobody can make. Sirens harmonize with her screams, but they're still the backup singers here, and they sound Rhode Island far away.

I climb the short set of wooden front stairs, fully aware that the worst of my symptoms cataplexy and the hypnagogic hallucinations attack when my anxiety levels go toxic. The burning building in front of me is likely to present as a stressful situation.

But with the amphetamines, I'm the new me, Genevich 2.0. I've been a physical wreck at times tonight, but I've made it without any real narcolepsy symptoms, without any gaps or naps or missing time. But the list, the side effects, that bit about amphetamines only hiding or masking the symptoms. But and but and but . . . Screw it. I open the door.

A blast of heat and smoke lands a devastating one-two punch, and I have a glass chin. I swoon into a standing eight count. Goddamn, I actually feel my consciousness want to detach and hide like a turtle retreating into a hopelessly soft shell that won't save anyone.

I hike up my jacket to protect my head. Cotton is just so flame retardant. The front stairwell looks like my own brownstone's stairwell. I can't see the second-floor landing because of the smoke. I've seen this picture before. Orange flames chew their way up the left wall.

On my direct left, the front door is missing from the first-floor apartment. I shuffle by and peek inside. There's a body in the middle of the floor, on display, writhing and twisting, jointless; its movement is too fast to be natural, but it is natural because fire is the body's puppeteer. *Dance, puppet, dance*, the fire chants, and I vomit into my mouth. The body stops gyrating abruptly, and the entire apartment, the TV and furniture and rugs and floors and the discarded puppet bubble and melt, everything made of wax or some material that yields the deepest black smoke when it burns. I'm not supposed to go in there.

Then I'm halfway up the stairs, and they melt too, pool around my feet and ankles, so I climb through a bog of wood. Upstairs. The air is too hot; my lungs are quitting, shrinking away from their duties, the bastards, and after all the smoking I've done for them.

On the second-floor landing the flames talk to me, but I don't understand. They're being too loud. Their ancient roars and commands stick to the walls of my head. This time, I'll never be able to get them out.

The second-floor apartment is locked up, but my hands and body pass through the door like it's a curtain. I can do this because I know someone is keeping a precious secret in here. I ghost around the apartment so the smoke passes through me instead of into me. I can't see very well, though.

I'm in a kid's bedroom, and on his walls are the pictures of me that I drew in group therapy. I'm embarrassed at first, then relieved as the flames burn it all away. I hear the boy. He's inside some makeshift nightstand, which was made from other bits and parts of furniture that don't quite match up. He's asleep in the top drawer. Patches of his skin are charred and still burning. I blow him out like a candle, any kind of candle that is small and can break easily. I pick him up and wish I could cup him in my hands like a firefly, but that's not right. The fire isn't his fault.

The bedroom walls collapse, and now I have a perfect sightline down Fifth Street, to Gate of Heaven, which looks old and useless. The building I'm standing in is its own church with its own turrets and spires, only they're made of flames, and this building has its own gathering of folks below, watching, maybe even worshipping. I can feel them there, but I'm not the god of hellfire and I do not bring them anything.

I walk through walls of flame and down to the bottom of the stairs. The boy is now standing next to me, wearing powder blue PJs. He sits and wants me to sit next to him. That's not a good idea.

TEN

Someone shakes my shoulder, and that someone says something from a science fiction movie. She says something about Soylent Green is people. Don't know why that information is important. I'm not hungry, and besides, everyone knows that.

I think I'm still dreaming, but I open my eyes, and it's Rita, a local homeless woman who usually hangs out in the bank parking lot across from my office. Couple times a month, I share lunchtime pizza with her in the lot and talk old movies. She's anywhere between thirty-five and a hundred and five years old and is a Charlton Heston devotee. Who isn't?

She slaps my cheeks, smiles, an infectious smile even if her eyes disappear somewhere into the bag of skin that is her face, and then she takes off, leaves me alone.

I'm in a stretcher, low to the sidewalk, oxygen mask over my mouth and nose. These are important details that take some time to verify, not that I fully trust the verifier. The oxygen tastes better than the smoky film of vomit in my mouth.

I sit up and take off the mask. I lose a few beard hairs in the elastic strap. No pain, no gain. Me and the stretcher are on the corner diagonally across from the burning building. A roped-off crowd and twin fire engines, ladders extended, block my view of the first floor. Firemen aim their hoses at the roof and the second-floor windows. Everything is loud, a world of noise too big for my shrunken head. Flash floods of debris-filled water run down H Street.

I wouldn't mind curling up on the stretcher for a bit. All of which means I'm feeling back to normal, my normal. I stand slowly, making sure the earth doesn't spin too fast. All of my body parts seem to be intact, and in the right place, or, more accurately, everything is where and how it was when I started the evening.

Two people sprout up next to me, one on each side, and they both take an arm. They can't have them. The paramedic asks me politely to sit. The cop is less friendly with her invitation.

I sit and tell them that I'm fine, that I black out all the time and I keep score at home. The paramedic gives me his best professional voice: low, soothing, but insistent. I cooperate with him long enough to have my blood pressure checked and a light flashed in my eyes. I pass.

I give the cop my IDs. She writes everything down. I'm convincing enough that they let me stand again, and the paramedic says I'm okay, but gives me a list of go-to-the-hospital follow-up directions should I experience any severe symptoms of smoke inhalation. I guess it'd be a bad time to take out a cigarette. He leaves.

I ask the cop, "Is the kid okay?" I'm asking about the little boy who was in my hands. She doesn't say anything right away, and now I'm afraid I didn't make it into the building, and I didn't save anybody.

"I don't know. A neighbor found him at the bottom of the stairs, hiding behind an old coat rack, and pulled him out." The cop nods her head at the corner behind me. An older, bald, pink-skinned man draped in one of those tinfoil emergency blankets has a microphone and a camera in his face. She says, "They sent the boy right to Mass General." She clicks her pen twice on the notepad and tells me that, according to eyewitnesses, I went into the building and came stumbling out a short time later. My stumble carried me across the street, where I puked and then dropped to the sidewalk. She finishes with "That was admirable of you to run into the building. Tell me what happened in there."

I'm stuck and can't talk. I don't remember the kid hiding behind the coat rack. I don't remember a coat rack. Was the whole scene a dream? No, that doesn't feel right. I was up on that second floor. Or at the very least, the narcoleptic me was up there. I helped that kid. I had to have helped him.

I try to stick to the facts, even if I'm missing some. I say, "I was on my way home, saw the fire. There was a woman screaming about a kid on the second floor. I ran inside, upstairs, found the kid in his blue PJs in his bedroom." I pause, waiting to see if she'll verify that the kid was actually wearing blue pajamas. She doesn't give me anything. I add, "I got him out of his apartment, helped him down the stairs before succumbing to the smoke and everything else."

"Everything else?"

"Yeah, everything else. Severe stress tends to goose my narcoleptic symptoms into action. Or inaction as the case may be."

"What are those symptoms?"

I hesitate. Which means I'm lost. "Hypnagogic hallucinations. Cataplexy." Might as well tell her lycanthropy with the looks I'm getting.

She writes something down in her notebook and doesn't ask how to spell anything. "So you left the boy by the coat rack? Right near the front door?"

"I got down the stairs with him, and then it all kind of goes black. Look I did what I could, all right?"

"Okay, Mr. Genevich. Please remain calm." She says it like she has proof that what I told her didn't happen. Maybe the kid's pajamas weren't blue. The smoke was thick and the flames were bright, so the narcoleptic me got a color wrong. So fucking what? How else would the kid have gotten to the bottom of the stairs, if I didn't help him? I don't need a hero's badge or the camera in my face. A one-on-one acknowledgment of what I did would suffice.

She asks, "Why were you at the scene, Mr. Genevich?"

Her tone has gone from dismissive to accusatory. Can't say I'm shocked. The South Boston police don't like or respect me. To them, I'm a sad clown relegated to children's birthday parties compared to their big-top, big-show clowns. A pretend cop again.

I'm no longer feeling very helpful. I say, "Did you talk to Rita, ask her what she saw?"

"Who's Rita?"

I point out Rita in the crowd. She's behind everyone, looking for an opening, too short to see anything.

The cop says, "Yeah, we talked to her. She only followed the sirens here." Her answer is a shrug, brimming with impatience, and it's a lie. She hasn't talked to Rita. "Let's try again. Why were you at the scene, Mr. Genevich?"

"Like I said, I was walking home, down Fifth Street, and I just happened by it."

"Walking home from where?"

I yawn and don't cover my mouth. I'm not very polite. Mom would be mortified. "From not home. I was on a job."

"Where was that, Mr. Genevich?"

I could tell her. I could do a lot things. "Sorry, client confidentiality." I reach for my cigarettes. It's all about timing.

"You're not a lawyer, Mr. Genevich. Just a PI."

"Really? I guess I've been doing it all wrong. I'm so glad you're here to straighten me out." I'm being a jerk, and yeah, she deserves it, but I'm also frustrated with myself. It isn't so far-fetched to conclude she doesn't believe me because I don't and can't fully believe in myself.

"Have you been drinking, Mr. Genevich?"

I light up, fully aware there's already too much smoke here. "Not enough and not very well. Look, goddamn it, I'm fine, I was fine, there was just too much smoke, and I did what I could before I passed out, and . . ."

The cop flips her notebook closed. She's not waiting for me to finish. "Go home, Mr. Genevich. We may call or stop by your office tomorrow. Maybe you'll be better equipped to help us after a good night's sleep."

That hurts. The cop leaves me alone, propped up against someone's apartment building. I'm behind the crowd, which has gathered around the news crew and the hero neighbor.

I check my cell, and there are no messages. It's almost 1:30 a.m., and I think about calling Gus and asking him to come get me, to help me home, but I won't do that. It's easier to think about closing my eyes and just disappearing, even if it's only for a little while.

Ambulance lights and sirens explode, giving me a jolt. The flashing lights reflect off the huddled buildings. We're all in danger. I stub out the cigarette on my heel; maybe it'll help spur my shoes into carrying me home. I adjust my hat and coat in anticipation of my renewed journey.

I notice my stretcher is gone. I didn't see it leave. Maybe it rolled away, slinked off on its own, looking for someone to help.

ELEVEN

I wake up on the couch. Again.

I had a crazy dream about two FBI agents busting in and knocking my ass around the apartment, asking me about aliens, little green men. I had one living under my couch apparently. It said we tasted like chicken.

My heart beats hard enough to alter my chest's concavity. The sun is out, spewing its radiation through the windows. I sit up, blink, mash my hands around the mess of my face, and I might need to shave my tongue.

Where the hell did that nightmare come from? My dreams and hypnagogic hallucinations are always so vivid and real, like snippets and disjointed scenes belonging to my incredibly detailed secret life, a life usually more inhabitable than my real one. But my recent dreams seem pumped up, maybe amphetamine enhanced.

I'm wearing the same clothes I wore last night. I'm embarrassed for myself, so I take off the jacket, which feels lighter than it should. I check the pockets. My little bag of greenies isn't in there. I could've hidden them in an odd place while asleep and in the throes of automatic behavior, but I'm not getting that vibe. I'm a vibe guy, after all.

This summer, ever since Ellen left, my apartment has been a dog-eared paperback that's missing its cover, nearly unreadable. Magazines, newspapers, DVD boxes, and assorted entertainment accoutrement crowd the coffee table and leak onto the floor, adding to the musical chairs of clutter that I don't bother to rearrange after the music stops. That said, the apartment looks different. Stuff's been moved, and not necessarily by me. There's a kitchen chair on the other side of the coffee table. I know the asleep me a little bit, and he wouldn't do that. The placement of the chair is too neat, too purposeful. My apartment door isn't locked or latched. Someone was here.

Maybe it was Gus, and he showed up this morning, following up on his nocturnal surveillance investment. Maybe the asleep me accepted his bon mots on a job well done, returned the amphetamines, and sent him on his merry way. If so, the asleep me is so thoughtful.

I do a cursory search of the apartment, including the leaning tower of dishes in the sink and the butter and egg drawers of my refrigerator. No sign of the greenies. No butter or eggs either. I'll worry about it later.

My kitchen clock tells me it's 12:39 p.m. The clock is a filthy liar. After a quick dry cereal and past-the-expiration milk repast and a gallon or two of coffee, I paint on a fresh change of clothes, shuffle down to my office, and crank up the computer. I want details on that fire. I'm not disappointed.

Lead stories in all the local papers and blogs. Bold, large-font headlines at both the *Boston Globe* and *Boston Herald* Web pages; both original stories already have links to updates: Two-family town house on the corner of H and Fifth burned almost to the ground. There was one fatality the first-floor resident whom authorities would not identify yet and one critically injured eight-year-old boy who lived on the second floor with his single mother, Jody O'Malley, age twenty-four. The apartment lease lists her boyfriend, Eddie Ryan, as a cosigner. Yeah, that Eddie Ryan.

Fire Department officials suspect arson, and while no suspects have been announced, the press is clearly presenting Eddie as one.

Despite the late hour of the fire, Jody wasn't home. She was drinking at a friend's house down the street and had left her son alone. Jody O'Malley has been previously arrested a handful of times, and DSS has a file of abuse and neglect on Jody. Her son has now been removed from her custody. The updated links are about O'Malley, her documented violent relationship with Eddie, and years of oversights by the DSS concerning the well-being of her son, who had been removed from the home before, in 2006, but returned only six months later because the child's grandmother was moving in to help out. The grandmother was never listed on the lease, and neighbors claimed she hadn't lived in the apartment for over a year.

There are also stories about Fred Carroll, as well. He's the former air force lieutenant turned baker, the Good Samaritan neighbor who went into the burning building, found the O'Malley boy at the bottom of the stairs, and pulled him to safety. The cops didn't believe I could've found the boy first. My continued snubbing is not Fred's fault, but I hate him anyway.

When I look up from my computer, four hours have disappeared. I'm not doing well today. I don't know what to do or whom to blame. I get up and pace the room. I should never have taken the greenies. They hath forsaken me. But if I'm being honest with myself, which isn't often enough, I know the greenies are another crutch, one too small even for Tiny Tim, and just another place to assign the blame because this day has really been no different from all the shitty ones that came before it. My time is always unstable and breaking down.

I have a message on my cell. It's Ellen, reminding me that the group therapy session will meet earlier than usual tonight. She has the schedule printed up and magnet-stuck to her refrigerator. She says that Dr. Who reports perfect attendance. She says, *Keep it up,* but leaves out the *or else.* Love you, too, Mom.

I don't call Ellen back. I call Gus's cell twice. All I get are rings and a recorded Gus saying, "Speak and be free," then a beep. The beep freezes me. I don't know what to say. I want to talk about Ekat's night, and the fire, ask why Eddie's name is popping up everywhere, ask if he came by the apartment this morning and relieved me of the bag o' green. If he was here, do I admit I was asleep again?

I call a third time and leave the following message: "It's Mark. Call me. We need to talk." I can't decide if I sound serious and threatening, or like a moon-eyed teenager pining over someone who might have dared sharing a look with me in the hallway between classes.

Even if Gus did visit this morning, I don't like that he isn't answering his phone. I don't like any of this, and I'm not sure what to do next, besides go to mandatory group therapy and draw Ellen something pretty for her fridge.

TWELVE

This is the earliest our group has met, and it's too bright in here. I shouldn't have to squint indoors. Some shadows are okay, even necessary.

Dr. Who passes a photocopy of the collective self-portraits we drew last session. There's the doodle I drew of my head, center square. Below mine is Gus's everything-falls-apart picture. Above me is the cat guy's portrait, an anal-retentive stick figure surrounded by other, small, anal-retentive cat stick figures, with whiskers. He has whiskers too. Isn't he so clever!

There's an empty chair in our circle: Gus's. I hoped he would be here, but didn't expect it. I leave my cell phone on, violating the number one group rule of phones off.

A brief discussion ensues about the drawings, which quickly focuses on my doodle head. The agoraphobic woman in the baggy gray sweats thinks my picture is the most accurate, likes how I conveyed the height difference in my eyes, then asks me how my pulverized face happened. Cat guy cuts in and disagrees with her assessment and says there's plenty of style but no substance to my doodle.

I tell him I hate his cats, then I thank everyone for making me more self-conscious than I already am. That effectively ends the group chat for the day.

Dr. Who hands out our journals. Today's assignment is to write a sentence or two about yourself that you've never said aloud to anyone.

I write and then cross out:

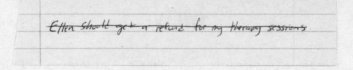

All the other points of light at the Wellness Center are in deep thought, even the cat man, and scribbling down their sentences. Apparently, those secrets are easy to give up, which means they can't be trusted. Dr. Who should know that. He hovers and gives winks and nods of encouragement.

I look at my crossed-out note and think about Ellen and the current state of our nonrelationship. Never been good at playing along, but I try again.

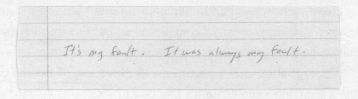

It's my fault. It was always my fault.

Not exactly a breakthrough, and too ham-fisted and teen angsty.

Dr. Who gives follow-up instructions. We can leave what we wrote hidden in our notebooks, or we can tear the page out, pass it up, and he'll read the sentences aloud for discussion, without necessarily identifying the author.

My circle mates rip and tear their journals like they're opening presents from Santa Claus, although nobody believes in him. I tear mine out, too, but just a rectangular ribbon of paper, enough to encompass what I wrote. Dr. Who walks around the circle, moving but not really going anywhere, and collects the sentences. When he gets to me, I put the piece of paper in my mouth, chew it up, and swallow. It tastes stale, but it's mine.

Dr. Who tilts his head because I'm tilted. He says, "I don't know if that was necessary, Mark."

I say, "Sorry, I slept through lunch."

Dr. Who reads what everyone else wrote, and I can't pay attention. The anonymous secrets aren't exactly helping my focus. I nod in and out of sleep, my head bobbing up and down in rhythm with my consciousness. I don't participate in any discussion, and for once Dr. Who doesn't prod me. Today I'm the kid in the back everyone ignores, and that's fine.

After the session ends, Dr. Who shepherds me aside. He has the journals stacked in his left arm, and his right hand rests on my elbow, gently holding on like it's a rare musical instrument. He says, "Mark, you can of course say no, but I'm wondering if you'd consider sharing with me, just me, what you wrote today."

"Regurgitation isn't a part of my skill set, doc. I bet the cat guy could cough you up a nice hair ball to interpret, though."

"Not quite what I had in mind, Mark. I was hoping you might just tell me what you wrote."

I can't believe I'm the one he's holding after class. And Christ, he's leaning on me in his own wishy-washy way. I'm too aggravated to continue being a smart-ass or resist. I say, "How about I write it down again, doc? Don't worry, I'm not hungry anymore." I pull my journal out of the stack and rewrite the screed that sits in the bottom of my stomach. I close the book, put it back in the middle of his stack, and say, "Have at it," then head out the door.

I take the long cut home and walk by Gus's East Second Street apartment. He lives in a run-down three-family. Its forest green paint sheds in giant flakes, falling green leaves from a sick tree. The other houses around him aren't faring much better. I ring the bell and then press my face against his first-floor front window. The curtains are open, but it's too dark inside and I can't see anything. I knock on the glass, and it's thin, brittle.

I want to believe Gus came by my apartment this morning while I was indisposed, and don't know what to believe if he didn't. I sit on the warped and slanted porch stairs, cheek resting on fist, pouting. I think about leaving a where-are-you-where-have-you-been? note under his door but, feeling more angry than pathetic, I call the Abbey instead and ask if Gus is bartending tonight.

"No." The answer is a quick jab or a rabbit punch.

"Can you check the schedule, tell me what night Gus will be there?"

Mr. Happy says, "We're too busy, call back later," then hangs up.

I light a cigarette and attack my lungs. The sun is setting, hiding behind the city somewhere. A cool breeze kicks up, but it's a lie. It'll be world-melting hot again tomorrow. I finish my smoke quick, the only thing I can do quick, and leave the stub on the porch. As my calling card, it's perfect: bent, broken, and all used up.

On the walk up Dorchester, I sneak a peak at the Abbey as I pass East Third. There's a cop car parked out front, real cozy with the sidewalk. No bouncer at the door. Everyone's playing Go Fish inside. I wonder where Eddie is right now. I wonder where everyone is.

A few more tortured steps and I'm through the nexus of Dorchester and Broadway and to my building. As I unlock my door, a guy who isn't Gus appears to my left and leans on the building like he won't tip it over. A practiced posture, and he's good at it. He might be too relaxed, though. It could get him into trouble.

I say, "Hey."

He says, "Hello, Mr. Genevich."

We're communicating. He presses a button on his key ring, and the blue Crown Vic parked right in front of my place chirps and blinks. Nice spot. If I had a car, I'd be jealous.

My key and lock cooperate finally, and I say, "The door is opened, but I'm closed. Come back tomorrow morning, and bring donuts, preferably honey-dipped."

The guy who isn't Gus laughs loudly; it's high-pitched and sounds like a call from one of those almost-extinct New England birds that spends too much time alone on a frigid lake. I guess I'm a funny guy.

He asks, "Given any thought to our conversation this morning?"

That, however, is decidedly not funny.

THIRTEEN

A narcoleptic is the ultimate cynic, left with nothing to believe in, least of all himself, because everything could simply be a dream, and a lousy, meaningless one at that. Have at it, Freud.

The alien dream from this morning has retreated to the shadows, a vampire hiding from the daylight, but I still remember its fangs. The man who isn't Gus doesn't look like either of the FBI agents who burst through my dream door. He's African American, a few inches shorter than I am, and likely a few years younger too. Thick through the shoulders and chest. He wears a Red Sox hat, jeans, a white dress shirt, untucked, and a blue sports jacket, the color a little faded, a badge hanging out of the side pocket.

I don't recognize this man at all. I recognize the badge, though. He's a Boston Police detective.

I say, "No, I haven't thought about our conversation." He probably doesn't want to hear that, even if it's the truth. I don't remember any of our conversation, assuming one did take place. I doubt it was about aliens.

"I thought our chat was riveting, and I've been thinking about it all day. Mind if I come in?"

I don't think that's a question upon which I can drop a no, like an anvil on a coyote. "My office is your office, Detective . . . sorry, I forgot your name already. I've never been good with details." If I play nice, maybe he'll give me the highlights.

I fiddle with the office door. The detective moves in, stands behind me. I hear his pause but don't see his is-he-serious? facial contortions. "Bayo Owolewa. You spent the morning calling me the Big O." Sounds like something the asleep me would do. He's a rascal, that one. I finally get the door open, and we enter the magic chamber. After last year's ransacking, fire, and rebuild of my office, I haven't added any personal touches. Don't see that much sense in adorning what has been made painfully clear to be nonpermanent. The walls are split, the lower half is wood paneling that matches the hardwood floor, and the upper half is wallpapered, some shade of light maroon Ellen picked out. Apparently it's soft and nonthreatening, just like me. Nothing else on the walls other than some brass light fixtures. I turn them on. It's show time.

We sit, take our positions. "Apologies, Detective Owolewa. I wasn't exactly myself this morning. Never am before my first vat of coffee."

"Is that so? Who was it that I talked to this morning, then?" He smiles. I'm treating his question as rhetorical, even if it isn't.

I take a shot in my proverbial dark and say, "Going solo tonight, Detective? Where's your partner from this morning? He didn't want a return engagement? Was it something I said?" I keep talking because I already know the shot missed and missed bad, and the only way to prevent the uncomfortable conversation that is sure to follow is to go defensive and box it out with my misguided words.

Detective Owolewa takes off his Sox hat and rubs his shaved bald head. "I don't have a partner, Mr. Genevich." He doesn't raise his voice, and I appreciate his patience with me, but his calm is probably much more dangerous.

Maybe I should take off my hat too, but I'm afraid he'd somehow see how much I'm panicking inside my head. I scratch the side of my face, and like the majority of lottery scratch tickets it's a loser. I say, "I don't remember meeting you or talking to you this morning, Detective." I'm not quite sure how to continue, how to explain, so I blurt out, "I have narcolepsy," as if narcolepsy was a thing, something I could cup in my hand, show it off, and then coo, *Look, isn't the narcolepsy adorable?*

"I know that, Mr. Genevich, and I know who you are."

"That makes one of us."

"I spent part of my afternoon reading up on you, familiarizing myself with narcolepsy."

Yeah, because all it takes to know narcolepsy is an hour or two in the afternoon, or, more likely, a coffee break spent on a cursory Web search. I say, "Great, then, and since you're a self-appointed narcolepsy expert, you won't have any trouble believing that I was asleep for the duration of your a.m. personal appearance. Or asleep enough that I don't remember you."

There are shades and hues of my sleeps that I discover every day. A panoply of consciousness levels that are complex and fickle, and they can't be codified by the WebMD, and they can't be learned by someone who isn't me, because I'm alone being me, and I always sleep alone.

Dammit. I'm getting too worked up over a throwaway comment by a detective simply doing his job.

He says, "I never claimed to be an expert, Mr. Genevich. I won't pretend to know what you're going through."

I take out a cigarette and offer him one by pointing it at him. He declines. I say, "You're too calm and reasonable to be a police detective. I'm guessing no one likes you at the station because you're overly productive and efficient."

There's that bird-call laugh of his he gave me out front. Can't describe it as infectious, but it tugs a half smile out of me. He says, "Just to be clear, you're claiming that your end of our previous conversation was performed while in the throws of automatic behavior."

I guess he did some familiarizing. I'm impressed but won't admit it. "Yeah, sometimes I carry on conversations and other simple tasks while asleep. I'm fun at parties."

He says, "Are you awake now, Mr. Genevich?"

A fair question, but nobody gets to ask it. My tugged-out smile retreats into the forest of my facial hair. "I think so. Unless you're another unpleasant dream. I could be Jacob Marley, and you could be the undigested bit of beef, the crumb of cheese."

"I'm not into role playing."

"Your loss." I pause and give some brief attention to my cigarette. "Let's get to it, Detective. Never keep a narcoleptic waiting, or is it don't feed him after midnight? I get the rules mixed up."

"I hope you're aware that the amphetamines I found in your possession this morning are enough to warrant an arrest."

I almost swallow my cigarette. I'm sure he notices. I would've preferred the missing bag of greenies stayed missing. Everyone would've been happier. I talk slowly, wanting to believe my own lie, "They're not mine."

"That's what you said this morning when you were asleep. At least you and yourself have that part of the story straight."

"We make a good team."

Detective Owolewa pulls a gray piece of paper from his sports coat. "I suppose this handwritten list of side effects wasn't yours either, Mr. Genevich."

I should just give in to despair now and get it over with. I completely forgot about the list, didn't realize it was missing. I take it out on my cigarette and mash it into an ashtray.

"That's my list. But it's research. Information. Data points. Just, you know, familiarizing myself with the side effects of the drug like a good detective would." My traitorous hands hold themselves out palms up, a supplicating pose that says, *Might as well put the cuffs on me now.*

"Multiple witnesses placed you at the Abbey four nights ago, Mr. Genevich. Were you at the bar?"

Why are we going to the Abbey? This is going south too fast; we'll be in Patagonia soon. It's clear Gus did not visit me this morning, and now I'm wondering if he's being lumped into the witness pile.

"I was, and had a few drinks too many. My apologies if you find the evils of drink offensive."

"Temperance isn't my concern, Mr. Genevich." Detective Owolewa is so relaxed he should be asleep. It'd only be fair. "How well do you know the bouncer, Eddie Ryan?" He takes out a little black notebook. He's not going to ask for my phone number.

Whoa. Don't like where he's making connections. If I was nervous before, I'm facing a China Syndrome scenario now. "I know of him. I know he's a scumbag. That night at the bar we exchanged unpleasantries. He called me a pretend cop, I told him to kiss my hairy foot, and we went about our merry ways."

"Did you refer to Eddie as a scumbag because he's a small-time drug dealer, dealing almost exclusively in speed and meth, or because he simply called you names?"

Well played by Detective Owolewa, and there's no winning answer to that question. I say, "I was working on a case involving Eddie." Here comes a whopper. I pause to yawn and barely cover it up with my dead-weight hand. "I went to the Abbey to put a face to the name of Eddie Ryan. A friend of a friend was being stalked by him."

"Jody O'Malley?"

"No, another woman. Eddie had seen this woman once at the Abbey, wouldn't accept her 'fuck off' to his dating game invitation. He called her work and threatened he'd show up, pull a *Here's Johnny*. The night of the fire, I was at the woman's downtown bar, watching and waiting for Eddie, who never showed. Then I followed her home, to her apartment on I Street. I was walking home and ran into the fire. Literally."

Detective Owolewa sighs. I share the sentiment. He asks for Ekat's name and her home and work addresses. I give him the information and tell him that a concerned friend hired me, not Ekat, a detail that I'm sure Ekat will provide the detective. My story sounds good, and it's almost true, but the timeline of the Abbey visit and Eddie's harassing call to Ekat doesn't fit together. Details schmetails.

He says, "How about the name of the friend who hired you?"

"I'm keeping that."

"Why?"

"I don't give out info on who hired me."

"You do realize I'll be able to get that name from"—he pauses and looks at his notebook—"Ekat, right?"

"As long as it doesn't come from me."

"Why would this friend hire you, and not Ekat?"

The case was a favor, right? Gus's words. We'd both be helping each other. It isn't exactly working out that way. I'm not getting by with a little help from my friend. I say, "Ekat didn't know of me and my services. The friend did."

"Sounds like the friend might know Eddie, too, Mr. Genevich. Are you sure you don't want to give me a name?"

I'm not sure. Withholding Gus's name could be putting him in more trouble than he already is, assuming there is trouble. Then again my performance here isn't helping Gus out either. Or helping me.

"I'm sure."

Detective Owolewa writes something lengthy into his notebook. I won't ask him if it's a self-portrait. He looks up, passes his pen between his fingers, which still want something to do, and says, "Did you purchase the amphetamines from Eddie Ryan?"

"No. I didn't buy the drugs from anyone. They were given to me by a client. The client was misguided but was trying to help me and my narcolepsy."

"A client or a friend, Mr. Genevich?"

Good question. "Does it matter?"

"I'm getting the feeling it might."

"You can't rely on feelings, Detective. Trust me, they're as unreliable as I am."

"Thanks for the tip. I could insist that you tell me who gave you the amphetamines, Mr. Genevich."

My cell phone rings. I shrug and say, "Sorry. So very popular these days," and pull it out of my pocket to shut the ringer off. The call is from Ellen, not Gus, as I'd hoped. I let it go to voice mail. She has impeccable timing, at least.

"Is the person who hired you to watch Ekat the same person who gave you the amphetamines?"

"No." The word comes out structurally intact with the *n* before the *o*. It's an easy word, the one we all learn when we're cute and everyone loves us. But I say it wrong. There's no power of authority behind it, no conviction, no strength. It's a request or a plea, and one that won't be granted.

Detective Owolewa closes his notebook and leans in, hovering his head over the table. "Between you and me, Mr. Genevich, did the amphetamines work? Did they help you with your condition?"

I don't think I can tell him that I didn't take the amphetamines. I've lost control of a conversation that I never had in control. I say, "No," again, but this one is real, and then I get stuck on the phrase *your condition*. It sounds like a rash that simply needs cream, a little dab will do ya. Or the opposite: *your condition* is expansive, like he's asking about the state of the union of me, something I'm not prepared to address.

My head snaps up from the pillow that is my chest. I was out, but not for long. Detective Owolewa is sitting in the same position, watching. Familiarizing.

"Are you back, Mr. Genevich?"

I nod. Too embarrassed to be pithy, I finish what I started and say, "I took two pills last night, and it made everything worse. Still is making everything worse, by the looks of it."

He says, "I'm going to be straight with you, Mr. Genevich. I don't think you've done anything intentionally wrong, but I also don't know exactly what to think here. It seems more than a little odd that you'd show up at the fire that wipes out Eddie's girlfriend's apartment building, odd that you told the on-scene officer that you saved the O'Malley kid when a crowd saw the neighbor taking him out of the building."

I interrupt. "I never said I saved the kid. I helped him get off the second floor, to the bottom of the stairs."

"Regardless, then I find you this morning with a stash of amphetamines, the exact stuff that Eddie sells, and now you give me this stalking case involving Eddie."

"You're right. It is more than a little odd. Tell me what you find out. You have my permission to wake me up, if you need to."

Detective Owolewa stands up and adjusts his coat. I stay seated because standing is overrated. He says, "Oh, we're going to talk again soon, Mr. Genevich. Mind if I take a business card?" I surrender it.

I imagine Detective Owolewa talking to Ekat and hearing about Gus, whose employment status at the Abbey probably won't ease the detective's oddness vibe. It's certainly not easing mine. Part of me is screaming to give him everything I know about Gus, and not just to keep his foot out of my ass. Maybe I can't get a hold of Gus because something happened to him. It's hard not to think that way, especially when I'm so desperate to give Gus the benefit of the doubt, one he hasn't earned. But he's only been missing, or missing from me, for less than a day. I'll keep him mum for now.

Let Detective Owolewa talk to Ekat, and then I'll talk to her, too.

I say, "One question: is Eddie your only suspect for the fire?"

"Goodnight, Mr. Genevich. Stay local."

"I'll cancel my trip to Lithuania."

Detective Owolewa shakes his head and laughs. I'm not too stubborn or thick to realize that he's giving me the benefit of the doubt, one that I haven't earned. Where have I heard that before?

On the way out the door, he says, "Check that call you missed first."

I almost forgot that Ellen called. It's a good suggestion and it's nice he's thinking of me, but I'm calling Gus first. No answer. I check my messages next. Ellen left one, just checking in, wanting to see how everything is going. What she really wants to know are details about the therapy group but won't come right out and say it.

Calling Ellen back is not on option as I need to focus on the swirling mess around me, a hurricane quickly gaining strength, and the goddamn hatches need some battening. I go outside, grab a coffee, extra black, from the chain donut place three doors down. I burn my lips on the first sip, but it's all right because I meant to do that. Next, I flag a cab from the stand across from my place. Gus's apartment is only a handful of blocks away, but it's too nice a night to waste on walking.

FOURTEEN

Parked cars choke both sides of West Second Street. There are too many of them, and even the newer ones have an abandoned look. All those darkened headlights and stilled engines are spooky. It's a little after eight o'clock, and streetlights buzz and hum, the sorry-ass stand-ins for sunlight that they are.

My cigarette stub isn't on Gus's porch anymore. It made the great escape. So I light a new one in its honor. I hear the tenants on the second and third floors, residential sounds falling out of their windows. Someone's stereo plays a seventies tune about a captain and his mystery ship. Gus's apartment is dark; the only lights in the place are the digital clocks on various appliances, keeping time, green digits glowing their messages for no one.

I call Gus's cell again. Nothing. I call the Abbey from the porch, even though I already called the bar an hour ago. Someone else answers, and she is just as helpful.

My meeting with Detective Owolewa has all my strings tangled. I planned to watch Gus's place for a few hours if he wasn't home because I couldn't think of anything else to do. Now waiting here seems like a colossal waste of time, like a dying man deciding to spend his final hours watching a movie he'd already seen before, one he didn't like the first time around.

I ease down the porch stairs. The railing quivers under my weight like a fault line. There's a rush of footsteps close by, but my hearing is too slow. The footsteps happen before I hear them, and I can't react. A blur hits me hard in the stomach. Maybe it's a sledgehammer. I go down, landing on my ass. The cowardly wind leaves when I need it the most. I suck in and can't breathe, but my cigarette fills the vacuum of my mouth, rolls up against the back of my throat look out teeth, look out gums and I gag and swallow. The back of my throat hurts, scorched by the lit cigarette. Maybe the little firebug has introduced itself to my strip of group therapy snack paper. They probably won't get along too well. It's so hard to meet new people.

White stars and their long dead light fill the city sky, but I don't think they're real. Someone dressed in black, grunting and swearing, grabs my left arm, which has gone all lead on me. That someone yanks me up and leads me into a small alley between Gus's apartment building and his neighbor's.

"You talkin' shit about me to the cops?" He spins me around, tries to punch me in the gut again. I drop my arms in front, and they absorb the blow. An unorthodox block, but effective.

My stomach hides somewhere in my chest, and I can't stand up straight because of the spleen-splitting pain, but other than that I'm fine. The white stars have followed me into the alley. Need to be careful not to stare at them too long.

Through finely gritted teeth, I say, "Why would I do that, Eddie? I hold you in the highest regard."

Eddie sways on his feet, like a boxer, a real one, someone who has taken his share of knockout punches but doesn't care because nothing can hurt him more than he's already been hurt. He wears a black hooded sweatshirt, black baggie jeans, and a high-brimmed baseball hat with script letters flowing into an abstract design. The hat rests carefully askew. My new short-term goal in life is to knock that thing off his head.

"You tellin' the cops I sold you my bees? You're a fuckin' liar, pretend cop, just like the real ones." His Boston accent is thick, honed by years of practice and indifference. Say *chowder*.

My white stars become swollen bees of light, fuzzy and buzzing. I have a rare moment of clarity where I think that I'm asleep, so I close my eyes and shake my head, try and take some breaths but only manage shallow, painful ones.

I say, "Didn't know you were an apiarist."

"What?"

"A beekeeper. Sorry, just trying to keep up with the lingo."

He spits on the ground, next to my feet. I need to be careful; he's spitting mad, and his desperation is physical, emanating off him in waves strong enough to be picked up by a Geiger counter. He wears violence and ignorance like a badge, the only badge he's ever been offered.

He says, "You ain't funny, bitch. I didn't sell you shit, and you know it."

I'm getting used to the dark of the alley. Eddie isn't looking too good. His thin mustache and Vandyke are unruly, the patches of stubble on his cheeks are more than a few hours past the shadow stage, and he has a fresh outbreak of whiteheads near his mouth and nose. He hasn't showered for a couple days, maybe more. His eyes look drawn in, exaggerated. He's probably been sampling his own bees. Whatever that means.

I say, "I didn't tell the police anything." Not exactly true. Another lie that won't keep me up at night.

"Bullshit, you . . ."

"No bullshit."

He says, "Aw, fuck. What, did fuckin' Gus give you some of my bees? And then you point the finger at me?" His hands lash out, punching and slapping the air around me. I don't flinch, not because I'm tough, but I'm too slow to keep up.

I say, "He didn't give me any bees. I don't like honey. And I didn't tell the police anything. The cops probably were throwing shit against you to see if it would stick. You panicked, and the shit stuck, like it always does."

"Fuck you." Eddie wipes his face and whimpers. He's not in pain, but it's a the-tears-are-a-omin' sound. It's the scariest thing he's done tonight. "You don't understand, fuckin' cops tryin' to set me up. I didn't burn Jody's place up." He pauses, sways hard to the left and then right, a bellows filling himself up with air. "That was my place too! I pay for half of it. Fuck. I wasn't anywhere near the place. I wasn't. I was . . . I was shootin' pool at Murphy's Law, didn't leave until one. I was too far away to start the fire, man; it wasn't me."

Murphy's Law is a bar just off L Street, heading toward Summer, more than a quick handful of blocks away from the fire. He sounds believable. He probably was at that bar. It'd be easy enough to verify. His being there doesn't prove anything, but it might explain why he isn't already under arrest. Can't decide if he's a little too eager in his own defense. I'm not his accuser.

He says, "Fuckin' cops know it, too, but don't care. They tell me it don't matter none. They say they got shit on me but won't tell me what. The only shit they tell me is lies. I didn't sell you fuckin' nothin'." He swings at me for emphasis. It's a wild, arcing swing, starting in his shoes. It's only for show, and it misses. I sidestep it, but clumsily, and almost collapse to my knees. I'm London Bridge, always falling down.

Eddie laughs at me, and he sounds like the world. I somehow stay on my feet, but the referee should stop the fight. Eddie's voice goes soft, like a rotten fruit. "Jody's my girl, and JT, he's my boy." He taps his chest with his fist, a simple hand gesture usurped and corrupted by pop culture that I might believe is sincere if it wasn't so pathetic, part of the act. "I wouldn't do anything to hurt them, man."

I say, "Where's Gus, Eddie?"

Eddie jab-steps forward, and unlike the haymaker this move is focused, sharp enough to cut me in half. I stumble back into a racked set of garbage cans and fall down. A seven-ten split.

He kneels next to me, then grabs fistfuls of my jacket, holding me down. At least my hat didn't fall off. He says, "What, you think I know? I came here lookin' for that bitch. Don't try and get me thinkin' it all backward, asshole. You tell me. Where's Gus? Where's that little bitch? I wanna talk. He's gonna wanna talk to me too."

Lying on my back is my natural state, but it's not the best of positions considering my current location and predicament. I'm about to make everything worse, too. I say, "I think you know where Gus is. I think you made him disappear."

Eddie goes feral, lifting my torso off the cement, thrashing me around. "Fuck you!" His voice bounces off the alley walls, a ricocheting bullet. "You're makin' shit up. You liar. Fuckin' liar. Maybe it was you. They told me you were at the fire, you know. I know that shit. What the fuck were you doin' there?"

"I was trying to save your boy, JT. And I did save him, mostly."

"You fuckin' liar. Freddie saved him. Everyone knows that. Maybe you burned up my girlfriend's place, my place, and tryin' to set me up? I'm gonna fuckin' burn you up if I find out you did this to me, you and Gus, you and Gus settin' me up . . ."

Nice. Seems everyone wants to burn me up like I'm a fossil fuel. I'm not a renewable resource. I've about had enough. While he's still in raving-lunatic mode, I prop myself up and land a punch, pushing the reset button of his nose. There's not a lot behind it as I don't have any leverage, and I don't think I actually hurt him, but he's surprised enough that he lets go of my jacket and wipes his nose. More surprising, I have enough time to sit up and throw a kitchen-sink punch landing below his equator. Down goes Frazier. I stand up, fulfill a dream by knocking off his baseball hat, and kick him in the groin again, injury added to injury.

I leave Eddie facedown in the alley, inhaling concrete and spitting broken glass. I limp-jog out onto East Second, cell phone in hand and ready to call a cab. I know better than to stand there and spin some clever closing argument line. I'm not that clever, and I need the head start. One has to know one's limitations.

FIFTEEN

I ignore Satchel Paige's advice and look back whenever I can. Eddie isn't gaining on me. No sign that he's even emerged from the alley, which in the immediate present is a very good thing. Even better, I get a cab only a block away from Gus's apartment.

I give the cabby Ekat's I Street address instead of my own, then sink into the seat. I need to talk to her, face-to-broken-face, and find out what she knows about the new men in my life.

The cabbie taps my shoulder, being gentle with me, and says, "Wake up, please. Please, wake up." He must want a big tip. I open my eyes and can't lift my head. I'll need to carry it in a wheelbarrow. I rumble and groan myself back into animation, back to a semblance of life.

I open the door, and my cab is in front of Ekat's apartment, double-parked next to a blue Crown Vic, the one that belongs to Detective Owolewa. He gets around. My cab idles a bit too long and loudly, announcing to the neighborhood that it's dropping someone off. I hope the detective isn't standing near Ekat's front bay window and seeing me, the lumpy man with a fedora and a trench coat but without that head-toting wheelbarrow he needs.

I leak out of the cab, backpedal across the street, and duck down behind a parked car. I've always been subtle. Not the best hiding spot, so I find a better one.

A few doors down, there's a brick building full of overpriced condos that aren't selling. The building used to be a parochial elementary school. I duck inside another alley, one without Eddie. Not an alley really, but a small pedestrian walkway between a three-family and the condo lot, its perimeter ringed by wrought-iron fence and trees. Good sight lines for me, bad for the detective. Even though my throat still burns and my stomach isn't right, I light up a cigarette to commemorate the occasion.

I wait and attempt to focus solely on eyeballing Ekat's front door. Hard to do when thoughts of Gus and Eddie and all the possibilities are poltergeists in my head, moving stuff around, toppling the furniture and making a mess. Me and the ghosts, we have so much in common.

Couples with hands in each other's ass pockets and small groups of annoying people pleased with the other's company walk past my hiding spot and give me, the man in the shadows, a nervous glance. I flick ash at them. My first cigarette is still dutifully chugging along when Detective Owolewa opens the front door, disappears into his Crown Vic, then plows through the Fifth Street intersection toward Broadway. I like a short wait.

I walk back up the street and put finger to the apartment buzzer. Ekat is quick to answer the call, wearing a white T-shirt and red nylon shorts.

She says, "Mark?" I'm a question, one without an answer.

"Good guess. I only have a thousand and one questions for you. Mind inviting me in?"

"Yeah, okay. Please ignore the mess." She's sheepish and quiet about the decision. Her front door opens into her bedroom. Sparsely decorated, the bed unmade, the blanket and sheets twisted and piled and spilling onto the floor. The linen disaster partially obscures a blue suitcase leaning against the bed; its corner and a black wheel stick out from beneath the pile.

We pass through the bedroom and into a small living room with white stucco walls and a high ceiling. The fan above rotates its blades but doesn't have its heart in the job.

"I hate to impose, but could I have a drink? My throat's burning like I swallowed a cigarette."

Ekat says, "Okay," with a long *o*, then goes into the kitchen and grabs two beer bottles. She passes one to me, then sits on a futon couch and kicks off her sneakers. I'm left with few sitting options, relegated to a papasan chair, which is like sitting in a creaky cereal bowl.

I say, "Thanks." The first sip cools my throat, but the pain echoes back. "How'd it go with Detective Owolewa?"

"You saw him? Are you still watching me?" She unties and then reties her hair up, pulling her sweaty bangs off her forehead.

"No. I was watching the detective. Aren't we a little self-centered this fine evening?"

She says, "He was out front waiting for me when I got back from my jog. I probably came off sounding like an idiot, I was so nervous. Being interviewed by a police detective is not something that happens to me every day, you know."

I nod but am too busy losing to the papasan chair. The bamboo frame digs into my ass and back. I scoot backward, lifting myself up and dropping like a bomb. I land too heavy, tilt the chair frame to the left, and spill a little beer on my pants. I squirm some more, grinding bamboo against the wall, and pull my legs under me so I can sit up taller. I'm a kindergartner who can't sit still for duck-duck-goose.

"You all right over there? Want to switch seats?"

"No. I worked too hard to get here." I drink half my beer in one gulp. She hasn't touched hers. "So what did the detective have to say?"

"Why would I tell you, Mark?" She peels the label from her beer but still doesn't take a drink. Fingers tap on the bottle, and eyes crawl around the room. She's frazzled or spooked. Less confident and confrontational than she was last night, even if her words aren't.

"Because, I'm assuming, you have nothing to hide."

"Are you here to make sure our 'stories' match up?" She uses quote fingers for the word *stories*. I hate that.

"I didn't know we had any stories."

Ekat tilts her head and narrows her eyes as if it just got brighter in here. "He made some connections between you and Eddie that I'm not wild about."

"Why'd you let me in your apartment, then?"

"I didn't say I believed they were true."

"All right. How was I connected to Eddie?"

"The detective said that you or a friend bought drugs from Eddie."

"Might be true. Might not. I don't know."

"What does that mean?"

"It means I don't know where Gus got or bought the amphetamines he gave me."

"He's such an idiot. Why would he buy you that shit?" She stands up and paces. I'd join her, but my legs have gone numb.

"He thought the amphetamines would improve my narcolepsy. He was trying to help. Not so famous last words."

"Did they help?"

"No. I mean, I don't know if they would've. I didn't take any."

"Right." She gives me a half sneer, half smile. It's a look that doesn't have a very high opinion of me. "So you told the police that Gus was buying drugs even though he was just trying to help you? Some friend you are."

J'accuse! "Slow down. I didn't ask Gus to buy me anything." I'll never know if that's true, not that it matters. "And, I only told the detective that I didn't buy the amphetamines from anyone, that some nameless client of mine did. I never told him Gus's name. I keep all my clients confidential."

"How did the police find out about the amphetamines, then?"

I sigh. That never works. "It's complicated, unflattering, and not all that important." Having had the weight of my dignity removed, I feel lighter in the papasan chair.

Ekat returns the sigh, pumps it up with some extra juice,

throws her hands up, and sits back down on the futon couch. She finds her beer and attends to it, finally.

I say, "How well does Gus know Eddie?"

"You know Gus. He's friends with everyone. Never says no to a favor or an odd job. He's been working with Eddie at the Abbey for about a year now. I guess he knows Eddie as well as he needs to."

I yawn but cover it up with another sip of beer. Falling asleep, in this position, has great appeal, more appeal than continuing this interview. I guess the papasan chair is comfortable despite its thoroughly designed attempts to be otherwise.

I say, "How about you? Did you give Detective Owolewa Gus's name?"

"What? No. Why would I?"

"Detective Owolewa didn't ask you who hired me to watch you last night?"

She looks away, down into her bottle. "He did. And I told him I hired you."

Interesting lie, one that'll impact my relationship with Detective Owolewa seeing as I told him my friend hired me, not Ekat. We were only in the get-to-know-me phase, too. I say, "What exactly did you tell the good detective?"

"I talked about the Eddie story . . ."

"You and your stories. What's the Eddie story?"

"You already know it. I went to the Abbey with friends for a few drinks. Eddie was the bouncer and wouldn't leave me alone until I poured a beer on his head. Then Eddie left me threatening phone messages at work. I told the detective that I hired you to watch me at the Pour House last night and then follow me home." Ekat talks with a calm and even rhythm. It's natural or practiced to the point of being rote.

"You're protecting Gus or trying to. Why?"

"I could ask you the same question, Mark."

"You're right, but I asked first."

"Obviously I'd heard about the fire and that Eddie was a suspect. The detective told me about you and a so-called friend and Eddie and drugs. I didn't know what to think, and I just panicked, and decided not to tell him about Gus. I didn't want Gus to be in any trouble or get him into trouble." She pauses. Silence always has meaning. "He's not exactly new to drugs. He's been selling joints to friends, same shit he did in high school, but that's just a stupid, little, juvenile thing, you know. Something to brag about, make him look cool. But he'd never do anything big stupid."

Sounds fishy. Or maybe it doesn't. My sincerity radar is off tonight as both Eddie and Ekat seem to be telling me the truth when both can't be. I know which person I want to believe, though.

Ekat piles onto my hesitation with "I mean, come on. Gus has been my best friend since middle school. I'm not going to do or say anything that gets him in trouble. You'd have said the same thing for a friend if you were in my shoes."

I did do the same thing for the same person, but I can't explain why. I say, "Style's okay, but my feet are too small for your shoes."

She ignores my attempt at the funny. "Gus does well enough finding trouble on his own, anyway."

"Have you talked to Gus since last night?"

"No. Have you?"

I shake my head, and there isn't anything in it. "Eddie says he's looking for Gus too."

"You talked to Eddie?"

"Not voluntarily." I give her a brief account of slamming into Eddie outside of Gus's empty apartment, his denials and alibi and threats to me and Gus.

Ekat holds her head in her hands. She doesn't want it to fall off. "Wow. I called Gus three times today, and nothing. I'm really getting worried now. I never realized how dangerous Eddie was. What do you think, Mark?"

I don't say anything and just stare. My stare turns into another yawn. The yawn could continue down the darkening path if I'm not careful.

She says, "Maybe Gus and Eddie had a falling-out because of the whole stalking-me thing. Gus said he was going to talk to Eddie last night, tell him to leave me alone." Ekat chews her nails. "You said Eddie threatened Gus too, right? Maybe Gus somehow found out or knew Eddie was going to set that fire, and now he's laying low, hiding out."

I say, "Gus never struck me as the type who sleeps with his head under the covers."

"You might be right. I don't know. There're a thousand places he could stay in Boston, and he's pulled disappearing acts before with angry girlfriends." Ekat's legs bounce up and down.

There's no air-conditioning in the apartment; the ceiling fan is threatening to go on strike. She says, "Something must've happened to him. Maybe Eddie or one of Eddie's lowlife friends did something to him."

I'm getting the sense that Gus was closer to Eddie than he'd let on. I have an idea, and it's a pretty good one if I don't say so myself. "Mind if I call Gus?"

"Please do. Call him."

"How about with your phone?"

"What?" Ekat's brow knots up and mutates into a question mark, then she says, "Oh, sure."

Ekat returns to the kitchen, comes back with her phone, and hands it to me. It's sleek and black, a piece of the future. I find Gus's name in her contacts list and dial him up. Four rings and straight to voice mail. I'm a little surprised and disappointed. My considerable gut was telling me that he's ignoring my calls, but hers he'd answer.

"No go, but let's try again." Not ready to give up on her phone. Maybe she and Gus have a pick-up-on-the-second-call system. There's no answer to call number two. "Mind if I have a peek at your incoming and outgoing calls list?"

"You think I'm lying to you about Gus?"

"I think everyone lies to me."

"Go ahead."

I check. In the last twenty-four hours the only incoming calls were from Mom and her bar. There were three outgoing calls to Gus's number, but she'd told me that. There's no way to tell how long she was on the phone with Gus as it's just a list of numbers and times, a call log. I fold the glowing flower of her phone back up and toss it to her.

She says, "Am I all clean?"

"For the moment."

"Wonderful. What do we do now, Mr. PI? Are we worried

that something happened to him? Should we call the police and tell them Gus is missing?"

I can't tell if she's serious about involving the police, or if it's some kind of call to my bluff. I say, "We're going to have another beer and see if Gus calls you back. I have a feeling he might." The waiting game isn't a real strength of mine, but I don't have a whole lot of other options. That, and I can't get out of the papasan chair.

"Fine by me." She goes to the kitchen and comes back with two more bottles.

"Mind if I smoke?"

"It's a nonsmoking apartment, stipulated in the lease."

"Don't you just hate overbearing, manipulative, I'm-gonna-rule-your-life landlords? Maybe it's just me."

"Maybe you need a new landlord." Ekat opens the beers and spreads the wealth. "How'd you meet Gus? Wait, let me guess: a bar."

I'm too tired to put up a front. I can only muster the ability to answer her with ugly, unprotected truth. Hope no one gets hurt. I say, "Our first date was at a bar, and he even bought me breakfast the next morning. But we met at group therapy down on D Street."

"That's right. I almost forgot he'd joined another group. Which one of you is getting the lobotomy?"

"We're going to flip for it."

"Sorry, that wasn't very nice of me." She says it, but I don't think she means it.

"Do you know why Gus sought out the group?"

"He likes to share his deepest and darkest with strangers. He's needy and an extrovert. He had a tough childhood, like everyone else. Who knows? I'm his friend, not his shrink." She laughs, at me, I think. "Why do you go? Why does anyone go?"

"I go because my mother makes me."

Ekat covers her mouth with the back of one hand and laughs all over it. She thinks I'm joking, but the joke is on me. There's a big difference between the two.

We go back to our corners and our beers, waiting to hear her ring tone. I'm still surprised that Gus hasn't called back. If pressed to choose, I'd now place his folder in the something-happened-to-him file.

The weight of my fatigue is increasing. The fatigue, it's always there, like walking around in wet clothes that don't dry. Need to keep talking if I'm going to stay awake. I say, "So. Seeing anyone, Ekat?"

"You're not good at small talk, are you, Mark?"

"No such thing as small talk. Just details." Wow, even I have to admit that sounds as lame as I feel.

I didn't notice before, Ekat has multiple thin rubber bands on her wrist. She picks at them, absently, and says, "No one at the moment. Been on a bad luck streak, thanks for asking. Anything else you want to know about me?"

"Sure. What's life after bartending going to look like?"

"I don't know. I thought I wanted to be a lawyer, but I dropped out of Suffolk Law School like five years ago, been bartending ever since. I'm waiting for a spark, something to excite me, I guess. I'd make a great writer or an artist if I was creative."

I try to smile politely. It's what I'm supposed to do. I can't say what I really think: that an early-thirties bartender who drops out of law school doesn't have an apartment in Southie like this unless she's living off Mommy and Daddy's trust fund. Might be an accurate assessment, might not be, and never mind being fair. And I think it like I'm some working-class hero who isn't living off his own mother. My situation, my case is different. It just is.

She says, "Every once and a while I think about going back to school or going off in some whole other direction, like living in the Ca rib be an or Mexico or something, but I'm not there yet. Not really motivated for some big jump. I like what I'm doing, who I work with. It's easy, and I'm mostly happy."

"You could always become a private investigator. The pay sucks, but the respect the occupation engenders is worth all the toil."

"I bet." Our second beers are quickly becoming thirds and more.

It's probably rude of me now that we're chummy, but I've got another curveball to throw a twelve-to-six bender. I ask, "Did Detective Owolewa see the suitcase?"

"What suitcase? Oh, you mean the one next to my bed." She doesn't hesitate, and her answer is no quick and easy denial. My curve didn't have as much break in it as I thought.

"Yeah, that suitcase. The one cowering under your covers."

"I don't know if he saw it. He didn't ask about it."

"I'll ask. Why's it out?"

"I was sitting here alone last night, and Eddie and his call to my work was really getting to me, scaring me, and I started thinking about calling in sick to work, then staying at my parents' house in Hull for a few days. I got as far as taking the thing out of my closet, but staying at home would've been too much of a headache."

"Sounds like it would've been a good plan."

"I know, but I didn't do it. It probably sounds silly, but I didn't want that fucker to think he could change how I lived my life with a phone call."

"That's not silly."

"Cheers, then." She drinks and says, "So let's hear it, how did you become a PI? Me and my stories, right? What's the Mark Genevich story?"

I'm learning to hate the word *story*, especially when applied to someone's life, especially my own. There isn't enough gravity, not enough weight to the word. It's disrespectful, borderline demeaning. Stories are simple, silly, for bedtime. Stories aren't reality. Stories have good guys and bad guys, morals, inspiring plots. Stories are what you tell kids because they don't know any better. Stories are what you tell kids because you don't want them to know any better. Stories hide the truth. Stories . . .

"Yo, Mark, you still there?"

Ekat is standing, bent over, and snaps her fingers in my face. She tries hard not to laugh. I don't know if I should be mad at her or thank her.

I say, "I'm fine. Just a quick recharge of the batteries."

"Good. Let's hear it, then." She sits back down on the futon and holds her beer up in a silent toast, presumably to me.

Here's mud in her eye. Mud being my story, the highlights and lowlights. I find it less inspiring in the retelling and rehashing. I tell her that my father died when I was five, and Ellen and I stayed on the Cape. I tell her that I was beautiful and everyone loved me. I tell her that, somewhat like her, I left school. After three semesters at Curry College, my best friend, George, and I left to start our little businesses. I tell her about the van accident. George was driving us back from the Foxwoods casino. I don't know how it happened exactly, but the van found a drainage ditch and rolled all around in it. George died, and I was left broken on the outside and the inside. I tell her about the arrival of my narcoleptic symptoms shortly thereafter, the stork dropping the cute, fuzzy bundle into my unsuspecting lap. It all happened millions of years ago, the Jurassic age of me, but the expanse of time doesn't make talking about it any easier.

She says, "That's terrible." What happened to me is terrible, or my story is terrible. There's no difference, really.

"I'm sorry about your friend."

I could tell her more about George. I could tell her the worst part is that he has ceased being a person and become an unattainable ideal of "friend," as if our relationship had never had an uncomfortable moment and we were always good to each other.

I say, "So am I."

"So you didn't start experiencing your narcoleptic symptoms until after the van accident? Huh. I didn't think it would work like that."

And just like that, she questions who I am. But I know who I am. I do. I'm Mark Genevich, the one who lived, he who emerged from the van wreckage as the monster, the misfit, he who sleeps alone, and my clock always strikes twelve. But is that right? Thinking back to preaccident and postaccident is suddenly difficult, almost impossible to remember. My Jurassic age has giant gaps in the fossil record. Am I remembering what actually happened or remembering some previous retelling or reshaping of what actually happened? My life as a game of telephone where the original message was lost and screwed up eons ago.

I think I've had too many beers. I say, "It does work like that. Trust me. I'm an expert." My words come out loud and dangerous.

"Whoa, big fella, I didn't mean anything by it." She stretches a leg out, kicks the base of my chair, and laughs.

I don't laugh. I pout. It's my narcolepsy, and I can cry if I want to.

"I'm sorry. That was rude of me. Hey, I don't know anything about narcolepsy; I was just asking. I believe you, Mark."

She believes me. Do I? Doesn't matter, ultimately. I'm done with the past. There's nothing left there for me. My here and now is already confusing and surreal enough. Who I am now is who I'm stuck with.

I say something like "No worries," then add a flurry of words, some joke about her running the group therapy circle, but it makes no sense, so I mumble and trail off, fade out. I cover it up with a yawn and stretch as big as the room.

She asks, "Am I boring you?"

"That's an awful line." I check my watch. Quarter of eleven. Gus hasn't called back.

"Shut up. It wasn't a line." Ekat chucks a throw pillow and connects, mashing into my face and hat, and everything goes dark. I take the pillow off my face, fix my hat, and when I look up Ekat stands in front of me and the papasan chair. Her arms are out in front of her chest, and it looks like she's shaking hands with herself, but she's not. She fidgets with the rubber bands on her wrists. She smiles an odd smile, one I haven't seen in a long time, so long as to be unrecognizable. Some PI I am.

I ask, "What's with the rubber bands?"

"Oh, you finally noticed. It's my thing." She sounds a little tipsy; the *s* in *it's* blends into the rest of the sentence. Ekat takes the rubber bands off her wrist, one at a time, and snaps them audibly. "I've been collecting them since I was a kid." She grabs my right hand and holds it up. Her fingers are cold and strong. She molds and kneads my flatbread skin and slowly rolls a rubber band over my fingers and onto my wrist.

"What am I, a lobster? Ow!" I flinch as the tight band yanks out some hairs, but I don't take my hand away.

She laughs at my pain. Someone else's pain is always funny. "The fun part about my rubber band collection is that I leave them in odd places, places where people wouldn't find them." She does the same to my left hand and wrist. Her fingers are still cold, but I'm warming up. This second rubber band she puts on me is thick and green. I don't match and am off balance. "Or if someone does find them, they'll wonder how the hell the rubber bands got there." She alternates putting each of her rubber bands on my wrists. "I've put one inside a concert piano, on the back leg of my old neighbor's annoying dog, buried one in some random apartment's flower box on K Street."

I say, "And now my wrists."

"Right. It's as good a spot as any." Ekat pulls the bands, intertwines them tightly around each of my wrists and hands, locking them together. The thin rubber is surprisingly strong. The accumulated bands pinch and pull at my skin. She lifts my arms and pushes my bound hands behind my head. "Sometimes I forget where I put them and find them all over again. Last week, I took one off the toilet handle at work."

"It's my sincerest hope none of these were on that toilet."

Ekat pulls my fedora over my eyes; everything goes dark against my will, as is usually the case. Her hands are insects crawling over my body; they caress and tickle but make me nervous too. I wonder if they'll bite.

She pulls my legs out from under my ass, which takes some doing. My legs eventually cooperate and hang off the chair frame. I sink deeper into the half-shell bowl of the chair. My back bends and chest contorts, folding in half, folding into myself, a flawed pearl in a giant oyster.

My wrists are bound but my fingers are free, and I'm able to pinch the brim of my hat, slide it up off my eyes, and back onto my head. Proper appearances must be maintained.

The lights aren't on in the apartment, but there are candles. Everywhere candles, and of every size. She should know me and fire don't mix. Ekat is naked from the waist down and straddles my lap. She's lighter than a daydream. I'm naked from the waist down too. A show of support.

My skin is hypersensitive, her slightest touch a detonation. It's too much. I feel everything and nothing at once.

There's music coming from somewhere. It has an odd rhythm, is psychedelic, and not all that appropriate for the moment. The moment is something that hasn't happened to me in a very long time. She quickens her pace with the music.

The candle flames brighten even as the wicks burn down, and I'm disappearing into the light. Her arms extend above her head and across the room, across the whole apartment. Her T-shirt and then bra melt off her body as if made out of wax.

I'm made of wax too, and I'm melting.

SIXTEEN

The cab dumps me in front of my building. I didn't leave the lights on. The office windows are dark, and I walk upstairs in the dark to my dark apartment. The dark; it's where I'm normal.

I shed my sports coat, hat, tie, shirt, my outer skin, onto the couch. The skin bit is a metaphor, though sometimes I don't know the difference. I don't turn on a light until I enter the bathroom.

I blink and adjust, which takes time. Everything has a price paid in time. I brush my teeth, and my visible world is still blurry, still fetal. Things take their shape and form, and I stop and stare at the face in the mirror. It's the same jumbled one I had when I left. I could draw another picture.

Further inventory: My wrists aren't red or raw; they aren't sore. No rubber bands. My belt is still buckled, and the button of my pants is still there. I can't remember if that button was supposed to be there or not. Ain't life a mystery? I decide to take a shower, even though I don't think I need one.

I turn on the water and let the steam billow and roll over the mirror glass. I slip off my shoes, kick them up against the back of the bathroom door. The heavy thud they make is deeply satisfying.

Next come the pants, and I take them off like everyone else; they fall down in their hurry to meet the floor. I step out of them, my socks still on. There's a rubber band around my left ankle. It's so thin I don't even feel it there. I reach down and take off the rubber band, then aim and shoot it at the steamed-up mirror. I catch it on the rebound and put it on my wrist. I've never done this before.

Inside the shower, under falling water, I close my eyes and replay the end of the evening in Ekat's apartment; the disjointed and fading scenes are still with me, those dream scenes that are both inspiring and frustrating. I'd try to convince myself that those scenes are enough for me, but I'm too tired. So tired that I can't sleep.

I dry off and collapse into my bed. Only problem is that my bed isn't working. It has performance anxiety. No matter how much I flip and flop around, changing positions, I can't get comfortable and I don't sleep. I relocate to where I tend to spend most nights anyway, the couch. The couch doesn't reject me even if I continue to callously scar it with cigarette burns.

The cruelest irony of narcolepsy is that sleep won't always be there when you need it. And so tonight, I briefly change identities. I'm my own odd couple. I'm Mr. Hyde's Hyde. I'm the insomniac me, a completely irrational and infuriating being.

I lie on the couch, thinking about everything, and hope a runaway train of thought will take me away like it usually does. I try to trigger and invite the narcoleptic symptoms against which I spend my days battling. Nothing works. I yawn and my eyes water and want to close but won't. Sleep as the wish that won't ever come true.

I turn the TV on and off. Late-night talk shows do nothing for me, and the infomercials are more than depressing; they're harbingers of the end. I'm on the couch and wide awake in America, where my every thought falls apart and dovetails into dire scenarios and conspiracies.

The minutes and seconds are glaciers, but night eventually becomes morning. I'm witness to the painfully slow transformation. And my transformation back to the narcoleptic me is as painful. Not exactly a here-comes-the-sun moment. I know I'll spend the rest of my day fighting and losing to the many-tentacled beast that is sleep.

The sun is up, but it's too early to do any real work. I try to watch the vapid a.m. morning news shows, but I nod off and wake up and nod off and rinse and repeat. Eventually, I detach from the couch, emerge from the cocoon, but I'm no butterfly. I apply coffee and cigarettes liberally before descending to my office. I check my messages and e-mails. There aren't any. It's too early to call Ekat, but I try Gus again. He's a hard habit to break, and he doesn't answer.

I browse and read local news sites and blogs. The fire is still the lead, as are the puff pieces on Fred Carroll, the hero. Good for him. No named arson suspects yet, though one member of the Police Department who spoke on the condition of anonymity said a suspect was interviewed and released.

There are more articles on Jody O'Malley and her troubles and history with the DSS. Her son is in critical but stable condition. There are op-ed pieces demanding renewed DSS oversight and regulation.

And I almost miss it. There, on the *Boston Herald*'s site, is a link tucked away from the bright lights of the block letter, sans serif font of the lead headlines. A digital afterthought, an article on the fire's lone fatality: Aleksandar Antonov, a Bulgarian man who had an expired work visa. In the opening sentence the *Boston Herald* describes the man as an illegal alien, of course. Journalism at its finest. His most recent employer, Financier CEO Wilkie Barrack, issued a statement via his lawyer saying that he and his staff mourn the loss of such a hardworking and good man. They empathize with Antonov's friends and family, while Barrack regrets the innocent but unfortunate oversight of the expired visa. His personal employment practices are something he'll attend to with greater vigilance in the future. Blah blah blah.

I lean back in my chair, the jackpot almost too much to take in at once. My alien dream now has context. I slept and dreamed through Detective Owolewa's a.m. interview, and he asked if I knew anything about the man who died on the first floor, Aleksandar Antonov, the erstwhile illegal alien, to quote the *Herald.* And the CEO is suddenly back in my life. The reappearance is ominous, unpredictable, a tornado warning.

I search for more stories and find a blog linked to Nantucket's *Inquirer and Mirror* newspaper. A former employer of Antonov's, Midge Peterson, says that Aleksandar was her custodian for eleven summers. He was kind, friendly, and the victim of the current immigration squabble and impasse in Congress. Peterson, an owner of a small hotel on Nantucket, relies on seasonal employees from Jamaica, the Dominican Republic, Poland, Bulgaria, and other countries to fill her summer needs, as do many of the local seasonal businesses. Congress has yet to renew the program that grants work visas to the large numbers of foreigners who enter the United States legally, so Peterson and the hundreds of other businesses have had to scramble to find employees. She's running her hotel at only half the normal staff, and, consequently, at half capacity. Peterson lost contact with Aleksandar Antonov after he was denied his usual visa. She said Aleksandar, like most of the seasonal workers, could not accept an offer of H-2B status (and be allowed to stay continuously in the country for thirty-six months) as he had to go home every fall. Peterson is planning a fund-raiser to help Antonov's family in Bulgaria.

My to-do list is suddenly as tall as the Empire State Building. I guess that makes me the doomed giant ape with a cool name and no girlfriend.

First, I call Midge Peterson's hotel, but she's not available and won't be for a few days, so claims the clerk. I find an address for Jody O'Malley's friend Rachel Stanton, the one she was with on the night of the fire. I let a call from Detective Owolewa ring out and go to voice mail. I find a phone number for O'Malley's and Antonov's landlord. She answers and tells me that Antonov was renting month-to-month, but she didn't really know anything about him. I call Ekat. She's at the gym and in midworkout on the elliptical. She hasn't heard from Gus yet, and she'll call me when she gets back. I try not to sound too desperate to hear her voice.

I nap and smoke and make phone calls, and not in that order. Still, I'm on a roll for me anyway but I need to get out, move around, or I'll lose the rest of the day to my fully fatigued system, and then I won't be able to sleep again tonight. I stand up, stretch, try a couple jumping jacks, but they're more like gyrating jacks.

All right, before stepping out the door and making a little trip back to H Street, I commit to one more phone call.

Timothy Carter answers after one ring and grunts his name. Someone's tightly wound. Or just an asshole.

"Timothy, your good friend Mark Genevich here."

"Oh, goody. I thought today couldn't suck more balls than it already has. I was wrong. What do you want?"

Charming. His voice jogs the too-clear memory of him strutting into my office wearing his two-month-salary suit, those big sunglasses, and his avarice. Carter oozes the same arrogance and privilege, even on the phone. I say, "World peace and just to hear your sweet, sweet voice. But what I really want is for you to pretend you're human for a second, and tell me all you know about the unfortunate late Mr. Aleksandar Antonov."

"Why do you care about Mr. Antonov?"

"I'm a people person. And I've been hired to investigate the fire that killed him."

There's the briefest of pauses on his end. So brief that I might be imagining it. He says, "Mr. Barrack released a statement to the press concerning Mr. Antonov, and we're fully cooperating with immigration officials."

I don't say anything. Let's see if it makes him uncomfortable. Let's see if it makes him want to say something more.

"Is that it, Mr. Genevich? I've got more important things to do, like clip my toenails."

"Ew. TMI, Carter. Though I am surprised you'd deign to even touch your toes, like the rest of us."

"What are you talking about? If you have something to say—" I interrupt, "Yeah, yeah, yeah." I wave my hand in the air, even though he can't see it. "I've been saying it, Carter, you're just not listening. Don't bust a pretty cuticle. A few more questions before you hang up in a tizzy. First, forgive the cliché, but I find it odd that our paths would cross again so soon."

"That's not a question, Mr. Genevich." "You're right. How's this: isn't it odd that our paths . . ."

"Very odd. Truly, a most unfortunate and cruel fate for me."

"Come on. It's fun."

"Anything else? I'm giving you thirty more seconds of my time." I know he wants to punctuate that statement with "which you can't afford."

"Did you know Mr. Antonov?"

"Not well, no."

"What does that mean?"

"That means he was summer help, a driver. We chatted, but never for long and nothing more than destination and directions. Nice guy. Always clean. English was good."

"That's lovely, Carter. You should give his eulogy. So who hired him?"

"I think I'm done with your shtick. Our statement to the press should be sufficient for your needs."

I haven't even started my shtick yet. So I hit him with it. "Did you ever find out who the other Madison was in my surveillance photos?"

"What? No. And why the fuck would I care? Shouldn't I be asking you that? Have you found out, Mr. Screwup? Are you daring me to sue you, Mr. Genevich?" He's shouting. His words are clumsy, have two left feet. The earlier pause might've been an audio mirage, but this is legit. He's way past the city limits of annoyed and entering bothered and concerned.

Something's going on here, so I'm going to push him some

more. Keep jabbing him in the chest with my big fucking finger. I say, "I'm triple-dog daring you to sue me, Carter."

Carter laughs, an ugly sound, capable of killing flowers and other pretty things. "As you wish, Mr. Genevich. Expect some paperwork within a week."

"Fuck you, too."

I hang up and stomp over to the coat rack by the door. I want to pick it up and break it over my knee, but it's a good coat rack, loyal like my couch. I spin it, instead, and watch my sports coat billow out toward me. My anger feels good and the temporary adrenaline rush feeds my energy-starved furnace, but I have to be careful to not overload. Mine's an ecosystem always at the tipping point.

It's pushing the midnineties again out there, so I'm going to H Street sans jacket. I adjust my hat and tie, roll up my sleeves. I say to the rack, "He's bluffing about suing. I know he is."

The coat rack, smartly, doesn't say a thing back.

SEVENTEEN

It's worse than I thought it would be out here. There's no breeze even though I'm only a half mile from the water, and the sun glowers down at the city like it has a vendetta. It's too goddamn hot for the old door-to-door, so I head directly to Rachel Stanton's apartment. Her place is down the hill and about a block and a half away from the fire.

The two-story town house fits in with the other houses in her row like a Lego piece. Its exterior is light gray with white trim; both could use a fresh coat. A rusty, waist-high, chain-link fence carves out a small rectangular alley with its garbage cans and debris. Tufts of yellow and dead grass vainly poke through the cracked pavement and have nowhere to go.

I buzz the second-floor apartment, and a familiar woman opens the front door to the building. She's the scarecrow I saw the night of the fire, the one who grabbed me and begged me to save the kid on the second floor. Maybe I should tell her that I did save him, and then she'd trust me. Or, like the cops who don't believe me, she'd want nothing to do with me.

She says, "Hi," and it's clear she recognizes me too. I'm just so memorable.

I extend my hand and say, "Hi, I'm Mark Genevich, private investigator. Are you Rachel Stanton?"

Rachel has dyed black hair, chop-cut short to uneven length. Thick black mascara rims her paperweight eyes, which are sunk deep into her face. Her look comes from so far away, it might get lost. Dim lights in a cave. She's wearing a tight black, logoless T-shirt, gray jeans, and large black plugs in her earlobes. She says, "What's this about?" The black plugs stretching out her flesh are the monstrous periods of leviathan sentences.

"I'm working on my own search for the arsonist who set your friend Jody O'Malley's building on fire. Mind if I ask you a few questions?"

Rachel is too skinny. She could use a sandwich. Instead she folds her pale arms over her thin chest and she chews on a fingernail. "Jody is here. Upstairs. She doesn't want to talk to anyone." Rachel is a recording. No inflection, no life, all static. I wonder if she's on something right now, or maybe she's just sleepwalking through this.

I hoped and had a hunch that Jody would be here, but fear of success fills my gut with poisonous winged insects, too ugly to be butterflies. I say, "Can I come in? I think you and she and we know some of the same people. I want to make sure I have all the dancing partners straight."

Rachel doesn't say anything. I'm greedy, and asking to see Jody is too much. She unfolds her pop-up-book arms and is going to shut the door on me. But she doesn't. She hides her hands in her pockets, which is a neat trick, because I thought the jeans were too tight for empty pockets.

"I won't say anything to upset Jody. I want to help."

Rachel's bony-shouldered shrug is an anatomy lesson. She turns and walks up the white stairs without me but doesn't shut the front door. Follow the leader.

I need to acknowledge my entrance. I say to her back, "Are you doing okay?"

Rachel doesn't turn around. The plugs shake her ears like little earthquakes. "I've been better."

She waits for me on the second-floor landing, and her hands are rocks in those pockets, all inert. The walk up the stairs leaves me winded and tired, my legs heavy and outmoded machinery that I shouldn't be operating.

I hear the TV through the closed apartment door. If it isn't turned up as loud as it can go, it's at least turned to eleven. People talk and yell, begging for attention and self-worth, in their tinny, one-speaker voices, and a crowd cheers and jeers, filling the background with American white noise.

Rachel says, "Don't step on anything," and opens the door, then slides inside and ahead of me, moving like a river. A blast of air-conditioning is a welcome temporary respite from the heat. The TV goes quiet, but I know the quiet won't last. I'm right. Their quick and harsh whispers fill the void. I shut the door, its ability to mark boundaries suddenly very questionable.

The apartment is in a state of recent neglect. The hardwood floors and various pieces of furniture support only a few days' worth of laundry, magazines, dirty dishes, take-out food bags and cardboard containers.

Jody and Rachel sit on a couch in the middle of the living room. The couch is askew. No one has cared enough to adjust it. A dingy white sheet covers the cushions; two pillows are smooshed into the armrest. The couch as a makeshift bed reminds me that I didn't sleep at all last night. Not that I need any reminding.

Jody wears cutoff sweatpants and a white T-shirt. She rewraps herself in a blanket, cold when the outside world is cooking. There's wisdom in there somewhere. Jody stares at the TV screen, at the muted daytime talk show. She stares at it like she's looking at the future. Rachel stares at me like there is no future.

Rachel says, "Jody, this is Mark. He's the first guy who ran into the building."

Jody looks up and says, "What happened in there?" Her voice is ragged, broken, a scratchy record continuously ignored in a world of digital recordings.

I tell her what happened in there. I tell her I did what I could, which was helping her son down the stairs before stumbling out of the building empty-handed and passing out. At least, that's how I remember it.

Jody says, "Is this true? No one told me that."

Rachel says, "No one told me that either."

I adjust my hat. "Yeah, it's true." I try to adjust my beard by rubbing my face. "Sorry I wasn't able get him all the way out of the house."

Jody pulls the blanket tighter around her and says, "Thanks for doing that, then. Thanks for trying."

Her uncertain, pseudo-acknowledgment will have to do for now. I say, "Is it all right if I ask you a few questions?"

"Don't think I can help you any."

That's not a no, so I start off slow by asking each woman what she does. Jody works at the chain supermarket on Broadway, in the deli. The managers give her only thirty-two hours per week, and she's currently on unpaid leave. Rachel washes hair at a salon and takes classes at Bunker Hill Community College. Not quite sure how either supplements her income for the luxuries of food and rent, and I don't ask.

Instead it's time to get more personal. I ask, "How's your son doing, Jody?"

"Aw, fuck, I don't know. They tell me how he's doing, but I can't go see him, won't even let me talk to him until after the hearing, maybe, so I don't really know."

"Has he said anything to the cops? Did he see anything?"

"No, they told me he won't talk about the fire."

I say, "I'm sorry that this all happened, Jody." And I am. Despite spending the better part of two afternoons reading about her and the DSS, about her utter and spectacular failings as a mother, I am sorry. No one deserves this.

"Yeah." Jody's in her midtwenties, but her extra weight makes her look older, carrying the pounds like outed secrets or sadness. Maybe there's no difference. She has a small silver ball stud that pokes out just below her bottom lip, not centered, but on the left side. A robo-dimple. The stud is too small and is being swallowed by her skin. Her face is red and puffy and breaking out. She's been crying, and I'm guessing she's on Valium or using antidepressants, prescribed or not. Her hair is dark brown, almost black, and greasy. Like the apartment, she's in a similar state of fresh neglect. Her nose is short and squat, pushed in, a button that doesn't work. Her eyes are a bright, severe blue. Her stare is a challenge, one that I can't meet.

I'm too nervous for my own good, and I'm getting a bad feeling. The kind of feeling that might grow into a sweep-the-leg moment. Eventually always becoming inevitably.

I have so many questions to ask. I'm just going to let them loose and hope order sorts itself out, my personal chaos theory. I say, "The night of the fire, what time did you leave your apartment to come here?"

Jody tilts her head to her left, half a shrug. "Ten. Ish. It doesn't matter. It was way past JT's bedtime. He's a heavy sleeper, never wakes up for nothing once he's out. Doesn't matter if someone's yelling or poking him. I left him like that all the time, and he was fine; nothing ever happened. It wasn't a big deal. Nothing should've happened to him. It wasn't my fault. Me being in the apartment wouldn't have changed anything . . ."

Jody trails off, talking into her blanket, smothering her quiet words of regret. Rachel grabs the faltering baton and says, "It wasn't a big deal. JT would've been fine."

I can't tell if she believes that or if she's acting as Jody's chorus. I'm not here to contradict her. I'm not here to tell her the truth, only to find it. There's a difference.

"How come Rachel was at the fire before you were?"

Jody covers her head and growls. Rachel clucks her tongue. Then the women speak at the same time, voices and words overlapping.

Jody says, "I've already answered these fucking questions a million times."

Rachel says, "I was just running to Jody's apartment to get my iPod that she forgot, left on the kitchen table. The building was burning when I got there. I panicked and just started screaming for help."

I remember her screaming and grabbing me. Her emotions from that night are so alien to her flatline response to my question. Sounds like she's giving me an excuse. I don't trust the scarecrow anymore.

I say, "And you didn't see anyone coming out of the building? Anyone there?"

"Just you. Then Fred, the neighbor who saved JT."

I say, "Of course. Fred." I have a bad feeling that is getting worse, bullying me around, kicking Mr. Sandman sand in my face. I push a small stack of magazines off a wooden chair that doesn't seem to be part of a set, and say, "Tell me about Aleksandar Antonov."

Jody says, "Nothing to tell. He'd only been living there for a few months. Kept to himself. Quiet guy. I hardly saw him. Sorry he died. Sorry he died like that."

Jody sinks deeper into her blanket. Her body language isn't good. But neither is mine. I slouch and slide into the chair, my skin and bones wanting to weave into the fiber of the wood. I sit up too quickly and almost topple over.

I ask Jody if she ever saw or heard any of Aleksandar's friends or anyone who might've visited his apartment, and Jody shakes her head no and stares at the muted TV. I turn and watch the pointing fingers and wide silent mouths and clapping hands and know that everyone is only pretending to be angry or righteous, or pretending to be laughing. They're all just scared because no one knows what the hell is going on.

I ask Rachel the same questions about Aleksandar. She gives me the same *no* answers, then gets up, leaves the couch, and disappears into a bedroom. I'm losing both of them. I'm losing myself too.

It's too cold in here. My damp shirt is a clammy fish on my skin. Wish I had my jacket, should've been prepared for anything. I say, "How long have you known Eddie Ryan?"

"Just about all my life. Unfortunately. We're both from here. Grew up together. Same project." She's giving me the typical Southie story, although I've never understood it: proximity and place as a badge, as an identity that determines loyalties, relationships, and destinies. So kiss me; I'm from Southie, where friends protect friends and sometimes fuck them over too. Yeah, everyone's friends here, friends of convenience, as if there were any other kind.

Time to shake things up. I twist and lean back in my chair and paw at the TV's power button. I hit it, but there's also a loud crack coming from behind me. Nothing falls off the chair, but I think I'm dealing with a stool now.

I know the answer to my next question, and I know the

question will be as comfortable as this broken chair. "Is Eddie the father of your son?"

Jody looks at me like I tried to throw a punch at her but missed and now she's going to hit me back. One for flinching. She says, "No! Is that what he's saying? Is he telling people that so they'll think he didn't do it?"

I shrug, and it's a lie, but I don't care. It's clear she needs and wants to hate Eddie.

"That motherfucking son of . . ." Jody growls out obscenities, squeezes out some tears, and it's all too much of a reaction. I wanted to push her but not get an eruption.

I say, "Slow down. He didn't exactly tell me he was the father, but that he was like a father to your son."

Rachel comes running out the bedroom. She's a wisp and might be incinerated by Jody's volcano. "Just tell him to leave, Jody. You don't have to talk to him."

I shoot Rachel my that's-bad-advice look. A look that is often confused with I'm-goddamned-tired look.

Jody says, "What, are you and Eddie friends? You can go fuck yourself."

"Would that I could, but I'm not Eddie's friend. I asked him some questions last night, that's all. Like we're doing now. He wasn't exactly cooperative. For what it's worth, I kicked him in the balls at the end of the interview. He wasn't singing 'That's What Friends Are For' when I left him."

The women look at each other, look at me, and I look at them. We don't want to believe in our own eyes.

Jody smiles, but it goes away, like hope. She says, "Good. Even if you're lying to me."

"When was the last time you saw Eddie?"

"The goddamn night before the fire. I went down to the Abbey. We got into a big fight. Didn't like the way he was talking and looking at some little red-headed bitch. And I told him all about it."

"You guys are always fighting," Rachel says. She adjusts her earplugs. They're big enough to be plates for Mrs. Tittlemouse. I can't help but stare and wonder what it feels like to actively change your skin like that. If only . . .

Jody says, "It's his fault. He treats me like shit, like I'm nothing. Worse than nothing, like I'm a pet, need to be kept and told what to do all the time. You should hear how he talks to me in front of JT, like I'm dumber than a plant. JT has started mouthing off to me just like Eddie does. Eddie's teaching him to do that shit. I fucking hate it." She pauses, then adds, "Should've burned down Eddie's place a long time ago."

Her last sentence is a direct challenge to me, to see what I'll say. I'm not going to say anything. It's an easy answer for me, but I don't know if it's the right one.

I take out my pocket notebook and flip it open to an empty page, which isn't difficult to do as all the pages are empty. Maybe I should keep a journal. I pretend to read my staggering list of clues and information.

I say, "Do you know a guy named Gus, works at Eddie's bar?"

"Yeah, I know Gus." Jody pokes more of her head out from underneath her blanket, but the sky is still falling. "Can you turn the TV back on? It makes my head hurt less."

"I'd rather not. I think we need a little focus here. Tell me what you know about Gus."

"He's like everyone who lives in Southie. He talks too much. He's full of himself. A smart-ass, smartest-ass-in-the-room type of guy."

"Did Gus help Eddie sell drugs?"

Jody coughs, and it sounds purposeful. She says, "I'm not saying anything about that. Don't know nothing about that."

"And you wouldn't tell me if you did know anything about that, right?"

Rachel laughs. The outburst of merriment so unexpected, it's hard for me to not take it personally. I'm so sensitive. Rachel says through lingering giggles, "I'm done. I'm taking a shower, Jode. Come get me if you need me."

Jody says, "I won't need you."

Great, we've established no one needs anyone. I ask, "Did Gus know Aleksandar?"

"I have no idea. Never saw Gus anywhere near my building. Only saw him at the Abbey. And like I said, never really saw Aleksandar either."

"I don't buy it."

"I don't really care if you do."

I ask the next question while she's in mid-denial. "Do you know a woman named Ekat?"

"Never heard of her."

"You sure? She's a good friend of Gus's, and from what I gather"—I make a show of flipping pages in my handy-dandy notebook—"a real good friend of Eddie's."

Yeah, I'm lying again. It's not that I think I can push her or manipulate her because she's dumb. She's not dumb. She's smart, too smart to be hopeful. She knows exactly what's in store for her with the DSS and the custody of her kid. She knows who and what Eddie really is, and who and what I am for all I know. I can push her only because she wants to be pushed, wants to be manipulated, and expects it. It's what she's used to, and despite the bluster she needs it. She'll go back to Eddie to get it. Wouldn't be surprised if she calls him right after I leave.

"So what? I'm supposed to know all of his girlfriends? I know I'm not the only one. Fuck him and fuck her and fuck you." Jody is done crying and has been done for a while.

Maybe I'm wrong. Maybe I'm projecting her into the role of hapless victim because I'm conditioned to think that way. I'm as weak and easily manipulated as anybody else.

I stand up too quick and hello dizziness, my old friend. I recalibrate but still feel like I could end up with my nose pinned to the floor at any moment. The back of the chair falls off and dies angrily on the hardwood. "Sorry about that." Then I mumble something about knowing a guy who can fix it when it's obvious I don't. I turn the TV back on but leave it muted. It's a commercial. Some group of people wants me and Jody to buy a product that'll make us as happy as they are. I'll take my crooked face over their smiles.

I say, "Last question, and then I'll leave you alone."

"Promise?"

"Do you think Eddie was the arsonist?"

"Yes, definitely." Jody is quick to follow up her thumbs-down verdict with "No. I don't know. I don't know what to fucking think. He says he was at Murphy's Law, but I haven't talked to anyone who saw him there yet. But he hasn't been arrested yet, either. They've been trying."

She's not telling me the whole deal. Her raw deal with Eddie. I could stay and push some more, but I'm already spent. The overwhelming tide of tiredness is rushing back in, and no Dutch kid with a magic digit is going to keep it all behind that rickety dam, keep it from sweeping me off my feet.

"Thanks for talking to me, Jody. I know it wasn't easy."

She says, "Thanks for trying to help JT, Mark. Really."

I turn and walk toward the front door, stepping past the pieces of her previous days. Everything recently broken, and broken beyond repair. The TV volume explodes back on, the noise as regimented and relentless as time.

I'm at the door, and I'm not sure why, but I have the urge to put my fist through it. If not my fist, then maybe my face. I turn the cold knob and open the door. Nothing but stale warm air in the stairwell. Jody calls out to me before I step out, yelling to be heard over the TV.

"What about you? Do you think Eddie did it?"

I stop and hover in the doorway like doubt, like suspicion. The easiest thing to do would be physical, take a step forward, out the door, and start sweating almost instantly, as if the sweat is out there waiting to jump me in the stairwell.

I throw a "Yes" over my shoulder. It's casual, irresponsible, and I don't know where it lands. Then I close the door behind me.

EIGHTEEN

Back in my office I have a fist full of cigarette, burning up time. A quick check of my various communication systems yields no return calls, e-mails, or messages. I'm starting to feel forgotten.

I call the Abbey to ask again for Gus, but no one answers. I try three local bike messenger companies I find in the phone book, but no one admits to having Gus, or any Gus for that matter, on the payroll.

Next up, I think about calling the Nantucket hotel again to ask about Aleksandar, but I call Ekat instead.

She says, "Hi, Mark, how are you doing?" Her voice is inflected, the words delivered sing-song. Was she waiting for my call? Is she annoyed because I called her only a couple of hours ago? Is she being ironic, playful, or familiar? Is she flirting? I'm a barely functional illiterate desperate to read too much into how she answered the phone.

Her rubber band is still on my wrist. I pluck it, and it snaps back, biting my skin. It beats pinching myself to see if I'm dreaming. I say, "Like always, I'm peachy."

"So, you're like a fruit?"

I struggle to find clever. What I come up with isn't it. I say, "Yeah, I'm seasonal."

"Who isn't?" Ekat laughs, and it's breathless, manic in its euphoria. She's too happy to be talking to the peach on the phone.

I tap ash off the glowing tip, and my cigarette plumes smoke and crumbles away like a dying building.

"You still there, Mark?"

"Oh, yeah. Still here. Always here."

"Aren't you going to ask me if Gus called?"

"Did Gus call?"

"No."

"You don't sound worried."

"You can get that from a 'no'?"

"I'm that good."

"I'm very worried."

"So am I."

I wipe the back of my hand across my forehead. I tap more ash into an old paper coffee cup. The cup doesn't mind. Yeah, I'm stalling because I'm not ready to ask her what I really want to ask her. I say, "I was out earlier, digging up some dirt on Eddie."

"I'm sure that wasn't hard to achieve."

"Trying to figure out what his role was in the fire." I stop and start, *um* and *ah*, and my words are obstacles I can't traverse. "He's not a good guy, Ekat. He's dangerous. And I was thinking. Thinking maybe I should take you out to dinner or something. Or you could come to my office and eat. Food. And I'd make sure that you're okay. That everything is okay." My soliloquy is as awkward and desperate as I feel. Christ, maybe I should've waited until I was asleep to make this call, and let the narcoleptic me act as a built-in Cyrano de Bergerac.

"Are you asking me out on a date, Mark?"

Is that what I wanted to do? I can neither confirm nor deny. I mumble something noncommittal but incredulous into the phone. I have the ability to grunt and stutter in a manner that subtly communicates my complex thoughts and emotions. Everyone wishes they were like me.

"I'm just giving you a hard time. I know you're a professional." She laughs, and my life's number one regret has become this phone call. She adds, "I actually think dinner is a great idea, but I can't tonight. I'm not even in Southie right now. I'm still at the gym, and I'm about to head over to work. Maybe later this week?"

"That's fine. Just trying to, you know, help you out, with your situation." I really need to stop talking, as in give up talking, and for an extended period of time, but I'm too stubborn. "Has Eddie or the police tried contacting you again?"

"No. Should they have?"

I shrug, but you can't hear that over the phone.

Ekat says, "Hey, did you find one of my rubber bands in a strange place?"

"Oh, yeah. A very strange place. I found it while standing in my bathroom."

Ekat laughs. "Very funny. When you fell asleep, I couldn't resist your ankle."

"My ankles get that all the time."

"It is a nice ankle, and it kept me entertained while you were asleep." There's a pause. I hear her waiting. "Hey, are you okay, Mark? You seem a little off."

"Not much of a phone guy. I present much better in person. The Mark Genevich Experience. I'm going to take it out on tour soon."

"I didn't mean to embarrass you with the rubber band thing. That's it, isn't it? I didn't mean anything by it."

I have an idea of how much did and didn't happen last night at Ekat's apartment, and it's a lousy idea. I say, "No, I'm fine."

"Now I've embarrassed you just by asking. God, sorry, I always put my foot in mouth."

I snap the rubber band back against my wrist again. It hurts. I say, "Shut up and don't worry about it." I'm louder than I intend, and we grudgingly share the silence of the aftermath.

Ekat says, "Okay. All right. I have to go to work, Mark. I'll call you as soon as I know something. I promise."

"That would be peachy." Peaches again.

"And you call me if you hear from Gus, okay?"

"I will." I don't know how or why, but I screwed something up. I hurry to add, "Thanks for the rubber band."

She hangs up, and I'm hung up. I should make a few more calls, but I'm done with the phone.

Okay. I have a new plan. I look at my watch, and there are still a few hours of daylight left. I'm going to waste those hours, throw them way like the lima beans I refused to eat as a kid. I'm waiting until it's dark. Then I'll go back to Gus's apartment and invite myself inside. I'm so rude, the guest who only shows up when nobody's home.

I close up my office and drift upstairs. My apartment is just as I left it, a scene from a postapocalyptic movie. I'm seeing it with new but tired eyes, and it's never been this bad, this far gone. If Ellen Genevich were to come by, make her first visit of the summer, first visit post–group therapy, she'd explode, and then everything would be a mess, as if everything wasn't a mess already.

The decrepit state of my apartment is more than an act of rebellion toward dear old Mom and the therapy. It says something about my inability to live on my own. Yeah, my apartment is talking to me. My hands are over my ears, but I still hear it. It says what I wrote at group therapy: *It's my fault. It was always my fault.*

I really should do something about this. I should do a lot things. Instead of cleaning or doing, I crash-land on my desert island couch. Hands fold behind my head like they know what's best for me, and I close my eyes. During my waking hours, I don't allow myself to daydream, as entering that unfocused state is tantamount to ringing narcolepsy's dinner bell. I indulge in a daydream now, though. Come and get it, big boy.

I imagine that Ekat accepted my dinner invite, and we decided to eat at my apartment. I imagine rushing out and getting some groceries. I have a brown bag full of meat and vegetables, all her favorites. Next up is the frenzied cleanup and preparation of my apartment. I wouldn't have gotten the place clean in time, but I would've tried. I'm wearing my best suit, but no tie, one or two of the top buttons undone. Prior to her arrival, I would've obsessed over the one-or two-button decision like it would determine the future. The doorbell rings, and she's standing on my doorstep, smiling, bottle of wine cradled in her arms. She's wearing a sleeveless, black dress. Her hair is down, bangs partially obscuring her suddenly shy eyes. She's also wearing a smile of hers I've never seen before. We've dropped into a scene from a generic romantic comedy or a beer commercial, but I won't let myself dwell on the negatives. My groceries have become something good cooking in the kitchen. I hear the sizzle of meat and low rumble of boiling water, and the air smells perfect. She tells me the place looks great, and I tell her not to open or look in any of the closets. We laugh. I'm funny, and she's delightful. She hasn't come in yet, but we'll eat well and have a magically predictable time. No surprises, no disappointments.

I fall asleep, and I dream my impossible dreams.

NINETEEN

It's after 2:00 a.m., and the thrill is gone. I'm standing in the alley next to Gus's apartment building. It's warm and humid, but I'm shivering in a light breeze that doesn't whisper anything. Breaking and entering Gus's darkened apartment doesn't seem like such a great idea anymore. I'm afraid of what I might find. I've always been a buyer's-remorse kind of guy.

I have the tools of the trade with me: a set of picks and a tension wrench. The set was part of a business-warming gift from my old chums George and Juan-Miguel. The other part of the gift was my gun-shaped cigarette lighter. Bang, bang. I thought the whole package was a gag gift until they started locking me in rooms and stealing my apartment and office keys to force me to practice lock picking. My friends, they always knew what was best for me. I got to be okay at it, but I haven't tried picking a lock since before the van accident.

The motion-detecting light is on, shining above me and the side door like an accusation. Can't say I want to be in the spotlight, so I pry off the outer casing and unscrew the lightbulb. Great idea, right? Now I can't see a thing. I blink away the afterimages of light, my private sunspots.

Gus's building is old and hopefully not all that updated. The side-entrance door rattles a bit in the frame. There's no deadbolt, just a simple door handle lock, and a loose one at that. I could probably push on the door and pop it open, but I can't risk making too much noise. Instead, I pull out the plastic.

I slip the credit card between the door and the frame, adjacent to the doorknob, and it slides in easy. I tilt the plastic while pulling and pushing on the doorknob. The card slides in a little deeper, kicks the lock to the side, and the door opens. Transaction complete, and I don't need a receipt.

I shut the door behind me and stand in the dark. I grope the walls for a light switch, find one, and flick it on. A dewdrop of a light fixture hangs in the small hallway; below the fixture are two doors. One goes to the basement, the other to Gus's apartment.

The air in here is hot and stale, like a lunch bag full of breath. God, I want a cigarette. I'm still shivering, but that's the aftereffects of waking out of a deep sleep and then animating against my body's dearest wishes. I shuffle past a stairwell and into a smaller, secondary hallway with white stucco walls stained with black smears and streaks, about waist high. I'm guessing handlebars made these and that Gus keeps his bike out here. It isn't here now.

Gus's door is purple with black polka dots. It's a door that should only be used by clowns, supervillains, or diminutive musicians from Minneapolis. It's recently painted by the feel of it.

I call Gus's cell one more time. No ring tone comes from the other side of the purple door.

I twist the knob freely, but the purple door doesn't open, and I don't know why until I see the deadbolt is one of the black polka dots. Cute. It's hard to tell in the dirty yellow light of the dusty hallway, but I think it's an older lock and hopefully a simple pin-and-tumbler setup. I take out my set of picks and open the box. The collection of odd-shaped metal is pitted, discolored, and smells like a jar of old pennies, the years long rubbed or worn off.

I insert the tension wrench and twist the lock in both directions, looking for give. Next I try one of the picks, its head bent and wavy. My hands shake, and I grope for my creaky and warped memories of how to pick locks. George and Juan-Miguel aren't behind the purple polka-dotted door, ready with a mock cheer once I finally get it open.

I have no feel. I'm flailing, scraping around the inside of the lock instead of reading it. The pick catches on a couple of the pins, and I try to force them up, but my fingers are clumsy and blind. Like me, they changed a lifetime ago. I am that jar of old pennies.

I make another run at the lock with a second pick. The end of this one is more rounded and smooth. No go, and my sweaty fingers slip and I pinch my skin between the pick and wrench. Ow!

I suck on my pinched finger and empty the box of picks; their not-so-delicate meeting with the floor makes more noise that I thought they would. I'm too frustrated to care. There, in the bottom of a small pile is the rake pick, a piece of metal with a cascading set of jigsaw bends. I forgot I'm supposed to try this one first.

The rake pick feels too light and brittle for the job. A hummingbird instead of an eagle. I jam the rake in as far as it'll go and pull it out quick, raking upward against the pins and applying torque with the wrench. You can never have enough torque.

There is some movement, so I try it again, pushing up hard enough on the rake pick to bow it out. I pull and turn. The metal digs into my skin; my skin goes both red and white around the metal. The tension wrench turns the lock one-eighty, and the deadbolt slides back, a raspberry tongue going back into a mouth. The purple polka-dotted door opens, and I didn't know the magic word.

I shake out my cranky fingers and gather my box of picks. The box is as heavy as a weapon inside my coat. I ease inside, a vine growing into Gus's apartment. The linoleum in the kitchen creaks under my Sasquatch feet, and his fridge hums like an industrial nation. My heartbeat is still louder. The air in the apartment is as stale and still as the back hallway. No one's been in here for days.

Progress is slow and painful and irreparable. I make it to his bay windows without tripping or breaking anything. My not-so-secret view of the porch and street disappears as I pull the curtains and blinds across the glass, strengthening the interior darkness.

I have a flashlight and turn it on, but it's too small and cheap. The beam is weak and limps around the apartment, illuminating nothing. Rage against the dying of the light. Me and my weak beam sulk back to the kitchen and turn on the lights. Honey, I'm home.

Not really sure what I'm looking for. I operate under the edict of I'll know it when I see it. The cleanliness of his apartment screams at me. There's an initial rush of guilt and shame when I think of my apartment by comparison. Mostly I'm struck by the oddness. It's too eat-off-the-floors clean.

The floors and molding are hardwood and stained dark. The walls are a deep blue, the color of distant oceans. The kitchen is a set piece in a museum. Counter and tabletops are spotless, chairs pushed in, everything in its place. Utensils sparkle in their racks. The sink is clear of dishes. Even the cabinets are stacked and ordered. Goldilocks is here, and everything is too just-right.

Didn't realize that Gus the bartender/bike messenger is a type A, OCD personality. And I thought I sort of knew him.

I wander through the rest of his place, look in closets and dressers, peek under beds, and it's all just as clean and orderly as his kitchen. Nothing seems to be missing. There's certainly no sign of a panicked flight or a struggle/rough visit from Eddie or someone else, unless the sterilized apartment is a sign of poststruggle cleanup. Eddie doesn't strike me as a clean-up-after-yourself type of guy, though. I'm so judgmental.

It was only a handful of days ago that I coma-ed on Gus's couch, but I didn't store any scenes or images from waking that morning, only a memory of a black hole of a headache and vague impressions of his apartment, which are being corrupted by the new-and-improved images. His apartment could've been in this condition days ago. I don't remember. I feel like it wasn't, but that could be a perception clouded by the thunderhead hangover I had. I'm my own unreliable witness. Story of my life.

I settle back in the living room like dust. While his place isn't on the East Broadway side of Southie like Ekat's apartment, Gus's interior is nice, as are his accoutrements. Flat screen TV, shelves full of DVDs, and new computer system complete with a high-end laser printer, photo quality. I recognize the make, and it's an upgrade over what Ellen uses in her photography studio.

Is Gus's rent that much cheaper than Ekat's because of the locale? I doubt it. More likely, Gus is living beyond his means. Wouldn't be a shock. Why should he be any different from the millions who are brainwashed into believing they are a part of the disappearing middle class, own everything on credit, and are one paycheck away from being homeless? So says someone who's subsidized by his mom.

Maybe Gus creatively supplements his hardest-working-guy-in-Southie income. Jody's no-comment answer to my Eddie-plus-Gus-equals-drugs question seems more revealing in the face of his closet consumerism.

I've sweat through my jacket, so I take it off and throw it on the couch. It's a wet dog that should know better than to lie there, but I'm a softie. I let that jacket get away with murder.

Next to the sprawling couch is Gus's computer desk. It's black and funky, ergonomic, but not all that practical. It's a cubist's wet dream, with the computer screen and components fitting flush inside the varied rectangular parts of the desk, the wood acting as a protective skin. There's no one unifying desktop, but multiple and separate plateaus at different heights for the keyboard, mouse, and a writing area. Maybe the desk is art. Maybe I'm dreaming, and it's a giant bug, Gregor Samsa made into furniture. The desk chair is a misshapen torture device, and I refuse to sit in it.

I turn on the computer, and I'm jealous with how silent it is and how quickly it boots up. The operating system is password protected, and after three quick and futile attempts at cracking the code I give up. I poke and paw around the desk, into the overdesigned nooks and crannies. Wedged next to the hard drive are a sheet of half-used labels and a partially melted sheet of laminate.

What does Gus do with laminate? Who is this guy, really? What would he think if he found me snooping around? Maybe I should just wait him out, assume my default position on his couch, grow roots, and stay put until he comes home.

I'm broken out of the me-as-a-couch-tree reverie when the

alley door slams shut and artillery-loud footsteps fill the rear hallway. My cultivated silence is shattered, along with my calm and confidence because I don't remember if I locked the doors behind me. I step away from the desk on wet spaghetti legs.

The kitchen door opens, and Eddie shambles inside like a zombie. Not a slow *braiiiins*-zombie, but one of the new fast ones. We make everything even zombies meaner and faster and more violent now. I grab my coat off the couch and put it on like it will protect me. It's still wet.

Eddie walks across the valley of the apartment, pointing at me. It's not polite. "You!" He stops at the couch that's between us, a leather moat. I hope he can't swim. "The fuck are you doing here?" Eddie's chest heaves, a growling engine, filling and emptying, so inefficient and greedy.

"I'm not really here, Eddie. I'm a ghost. You don't believe in ghosts, so go home." The front door is a few paces behind me. I could reach it if my feet would move. I'm not sure they will. Those strange little bastards at the end of my legs are just so unpredictable.

I don't like the look of Eddie. That's a general mission statement of mine, but it applies to the here and par tic u lar. He's a smudge on a window. His clothes are dirty and don't fit, and that makes him the bad guy. His eyes are dark, red wounds, and he blinks constantly with eyelids made of sandpaper.

He says, "Where's Gus?" but it's not a demand. It's a whisper. Suddenly, he's the kid afraid to earn the attention of the boogeyman in the closet.

Either Eddie knows where Gus is or he's scared of the answer. I say, "He's in my pocket. I only take him out at parties."

"How the fuck did you get in here? Do you have a key? Gus give you a key? Why's he fuckin' me like this?" Eddie goes loud again, and his wild shifts in volume and mood are concerning.

He grips the couch like he wants to tear it down the middle. His knuckles grind and roll over each other. "Why are you doin' me like this? Huh? I never did nothin' to you." He talks fast, too fast for his own tongue. He wipes his mouth, then looks at the back of his hand like he expects to see what he's going to say next written in blood. Eddie's in rough shape, but he's gearing up for an offensive.

I say, "I'm just looking for Gus. He didn't return the two cups of sugar he borrowed from me last week."

"You went to Rachel's place today."

That was fast. I knew he and Jody would coffee-talk about my visit. I hoped their chat wouldn't happen for a couple of days, not a couple of hours. There's no reason to be angry about it, but I am. I briefly indulge in an image of Jody, Rachel, and Eddie as the Three Neros, dancing and fiddling away while all of Southie burns.

I say, "I went to a lot of places today, Eddie."

"Shut your fuckin' mouth. You went to Rachel's, and you told Jody that you saved JT. The fuck is that about? You fuckin' liar, man. You fillin' her head with shit so she believes you about me. That's it, isn't it? Then you tell her I was the one who burned up her fuckin' place. Now she won't let me in, won't talk to me, won't listen to me. She called the cops on me, you fucker. I just wanted to talk. She locked the door. She thinks it's me. This is all your fault, pretend cop. All your fault. I didn't do nothin'."

I don't believe his denial. He's sticking to a plan, a strategy, like a desperate and sleazy politician losing his district. His guilt is physical. I see it on him, as plain as the black veins of tattoos on his arms. The circles or bruises under his eyes are dark plumbs.

I think I can get a confession if I push. I say, "Why'd you set the fire, Eddie?"

Eddie springs over the couch, turning himself into a projectile with fists. I don't have a chance. I duck and twist, but he lands a stunner of a shot onto the left side of my head, near the temple. Then he buries his shoulder into my kidneys and takes me to the floor. Too many direct hits to absorb at once, and my systems are hurrying to fail.

I try to wrap my head inside my arms. He hits me in the nose and everything goes white. The pain is bright and sharp and won't quit. I roll over, prop up on my hands and knees, and crawl toward the front door. Breathing and seeing hurt, and I'm not really moving anywhere. Eddie kicks me in the ribs twice; the tip of his boot is a crowbar trying to separate the bone and cartilage. I go down again and become a stain on the floor.

The kicking and punching stops but the pain doesn't. My mustache and beard are wet and warm. The curtains of my eyelids are ready to fall. Eddie knocks my hat off, grabs a fist full of my hair, and yanks me up. We go nose to nose. His mouth is open. His breath is a truck full of roadkill, and his teeth are blackened stumps, burned-out buildings. Eddie is a zombie. A real one. Just because he doesn't know it doesn't mean he isn't one.

He shakes my head, slaps my face a couple times. I don't see him anymore, but the wet sound on my cheeks is discouraging. He says, "No goin' out on me, you fuckin' pussy. Get up. Hey, ho, let's go. Let's go. Letsgoletsgoletsgo!" He expects me to dance without a beat.

Eddie has gone all caveman, dragging me out the front door and onto the porch by my thinning hair. My feet scrabble on the wooden floors and doorways, and they keep slipping out from under me. I swipe at Eddie's stomach and legs, but there's no force behind the blows. Outside, the heavy apartment door swings and knocks me in the head. What little reserves of energy I have to keep me conscious are ebbing away, a faucet left running.

Eddie tosses me down the porch stairs, and I fall forever in a barrel over Niagara Falls. I finally land. The world stops moving, and I lie on the sidewalk, on my back. It's snowing out. Only the snow is gray, not white. Wait, it's not snow. Chunks of the haze hanging above the city are falling. The sky is falling. Someone go tell Chicken Little he was right. He was always right.

Eddie stands over me, as large and terrible as a skyscraper. He steps on my chest, and his footprint will be fossilized. He walks over me like I'm the chivalrous jacket covering the puddle of blood.

Eddie stalks up and down the street, punching out the driver's-side windows of the parked cars. Glass explodes, and the shards turn into hundreds of small, screaming birds. They fly away even though the sky is still falling on Eddie and me, filling the sidewalk and streets with its broken parts.

TWENTY

I dream of riding down a dark highway in a white van as large as a whale, a van I've been in before. Although I'm inside the beast, sitting in the passenger seat, I feel more like Ahab than Jonah, but I really want to be Queequeg. It's all so confusing. Don't call me Ishmael.

My group therapy journal is on my lap. I fill the pages with pictures of me. They're supposed to be pictures of me, but the heads are eggs, and they're all cracked. The radio is on, someone talking, talking, but I'm not listening.

George isn't driving the van. There's no one driving. This makes sense because I know the driver has been dead for over ten years. What doesn't make sense, though, is the ten years.

The van drives itself into uncharted depths of highway, and nothing happens; it doesn't veer or wobble. Still, I'm download-in-my-pants scared because the only thing in the world I want to do right now is flip the van. Make it roll and dance in the drainage ditches and dry brush. I want to reach over and spin the steering wheel like I'm playing roulette, ten bucks on black.

I wake up, slowly, my consciousness returning from the yawning highway distance. Upon my less than triumphant return, pain cranks up its volume, frequency, and pitch. My head is a bruised fruit, a reject from the produce department, which was true before Eddie's assault. My eyes are still closed. My ribs don't take well to breathing. I'll try to cut back on that.

Eddie is on my left, talking in a low, fast monotone. Talking like a junkie. He remains background noise because I can't focus on him or his individual words.

I open my eyes and emerge from my latest and greatest cocoon. I don't have beautiful wings, but I am transformed. My clothes are stained red.

". . . been easy. I've always done good by her, done what I

can, always tried to help her and JT, aw man, JT, he's my boy, I didn't do nothin' to him, never would do anythin' to him, I tried, I tried to help him, I wouldn't hurt her neither, she's crazy and I'm crazy, but that's not what I'm about, no, no none of it is fuckin' right, no, this whole fire thing has her all fucked up, all fuckin' fucked up, she'll listen . . ."

Eddie talks to himself and grips the steering wheel with both hands. He has the thing in a chokehold, or he's hanging off the edge of a cliff by his fingers; there's no in between. His head hangs lower than his shoulders. I know the feeling.

He and I sit in an idling car. The ignition hangs by a clump of wire from the steering column, condemned to swing for someone's sins. The car is compact and at least ten years old. I could write *Mark Genevich was here* in the dashboard dust if I was able to move an arm, any arm.

"Thanks for the ride," I say. Can't really form the *th* or *s* sound in *thanks* too well with my busted lip. Talking isn't good for me anyway. The words tear down walls in my head. I try to move around in my seat, but my body is a bag full of sand and broken glass. My nose and lips are balloons, and they throb along with my skittering heart. I've got rhythm.

Eddie stops talking and grips the wheel tighter. The pleather complains to his deaf fingers. He says, "The fuck is wrong with you? I thought you were out, but your eyes were openin' and closin', and you were talking all kinds of weird shit."

His concern is touching. "It's not polite to eavesdrop."

"You got some crazy disease, right?"

"There's nothing wrong with me. I'm a model of good health and clean living."

"What happened to your face?"

"What do you mean? Ain't I pretty?" I'm not telling him about George and the van accident. He hasn't earned that privilege.

Outside the windshield is a highway, but not the one from my dream. This sea of blacktop is well lit. I have to squint against the onslaught of streetlight wattage. The four-lane-wide road is empty of cars, but giant buildings loom ahead, looking like the cardboard set of a Godzilla flick. Some guy in a lizard suit is going to knock it all down.

Just ahead is the Boston Garden and its green and yellow sign. To my direct right are thick white cables growing out of the concrete like Jack's bean stalks. I could use some magic beans.

I turn my head to say something to Eddie, and a supernova of light, sound, and unseen force blasts our little car. The apocalypse is right outside my thin and flimsy door. We shake and shimmy, worms trapped inside the jumping bean. The piercing wail from the air horn trails behind the eighteen-wheeler that rockets past us. The truck harmlessly disappears into a tunnel at the bottom of the hill.

We're idling in the middle of I-93 South on the Zakim Bridge. The car is straddling two lanes of the four. I say, "Nice view, but I think you've parked in an illegal spot. Don't want you to get a ticket." The dash clock reads 3:13 in green letters. We won't get caught in rush-hour interstate traffic, but it'll take only one truck or car to pancake us.

Eddie shoots an arm across me. I flinch, thinking he's going to hit me again. My flinch doesn't amount to anything. He opens my car door, and there's nothing I can do about it. Sometime during Eddie's assault, I must've had a cataplexy attack. Cataplexy is the booby prize in the grab bag that is narcolepsy. It's a temporary but full-on paralysis, and for me it's generally triggered by heaping gobs of stress.

I can turn my head and talk, but the rest of my body is stuck in quicksand. It'll take time to recover, too. I won't be able to skip to my Lou for at least fifteen minutes. That's an estimate that doesn't take into account any of my just-driven-off-the-lot physical injuries either. The cherry on top of a shit sundae. Yeah, I have Eddie right where I want him.

He says, "Jody never listened to the fuckin' cops, didn't listen to the shit in the papers, didn't listen to nobody. But she listened to you. She believed you when you said that I fuckin' did it."

I eyeball the open car door next to me and can't decide if it's a threat or a promise. Maybe Eddie isn't sure either.

I say, "That makes one of us."

"The fuck is that supposed to mean?"

"She asked me what I thought, and I was just telling her what she wanted me to say."

"Why would you fuckin' say that?" Eddie shakes his head. Tapping fingers and shaking legs join his head in a symphony of jitters. Another car beeps as it swerves past us. Eddie doesn't react. He's the boy without fear. He says, "Tell me where Gus is."

"I broke into his empty apartment tonight, Eddie. I wasn't looking for his library card. I was looking for him. I have no goddamn idea where he is."

Eddie laughs, and it sounds like a test from the emergency broadcast system. "If that's true, we're both fucked."

Sometimes the truth is more desperate than lies. Eddie's

desperation feels, tastes, smells genuine. I say, "Tell me something, then, Eddie. What do you know—"

Eddie interrupts and yells, "I don't know anything! I didn't do anything! Wouldn't do anything to Jody! We fight and we fuck, and that's it!" He punches his steering wheel and yelps. Maybe he damaged his hand on my head and body. Good. Then I see the blood and some shattered glass on his side of the dash. His driver's-side window is broken.

He says, "Jody and me, we grew up in the Ninth Street projects. Shitty fuckin' place that I ain't never going back to. Fuckin' never. Neither is she." Eddie pauses for the moment of his life, and I try to make a fist and wiggle my toes. "When I was a little kid, I wasn't always good to her. If it was just me and her, we were fine. When I was with my friends, we'd make fun of her, throw shit at her and her friends, chase 'em, tackle 'em, twist their arms, flip their skirts over their heads. I was just a stupid kid. A stupid little shit."

"That's great, Eddie, but I ain't Father Flanagan waiting to hear your Boys Town confessional." I regret it as soon as I say it. While stationary in the middle of a metropolitan highway probably isn't the best place for a conversation, the longer Eddie talks, the more I have a chance of recovering. I should be goosing the gander. Maybe I should invite him to come with me to group therapy, have him draw a picture. Have him write down the lines *It's my fault. It was always my fault.*

Luckily, Eddie ignores me. His eyes are almost shut, and I wish I could hit him or at least close my door. He says, "I was nine years old, and I ran away. I just got up one mornin', no one was home, and maybe there wasn't any fuckin' Froot Loops left; I don't know. It wasn't any one thing. I remember thinkin' I was done, man. I was sick of everythin'. I was definitely fuckin' sick of getting the bag beat out of me by the older kids. I was sick of it all, and I upped and walked out of my apartment and over to Jody's. I knocked on her door, she opened it, and we didn't say nothin' to each other. I walked past her, into her room, and crawled into her closet and closed the door. When she asked what I was doing, I told her nothin'. And I was doin' nothin'. And that was enough. She didn't talk to me or bother me, didn't ask why I was there.

"She brought me food when it was time to eat. Kept watch when I had to go to the bathroom. That first night she cried herself to sleep. I stayed in the closet and pretended not to hear. Her mother came in and asked her what she was fuckin' whinin' about. Jody didn't say nothin' but stopped cryin'. I stayed in her closet for three days. It was great. I was okay, no one buggin' me, yellin' at me, and I slept a lot. It was *fuckin'* great. I wasn't bored. I wasn't. I could've stayed there forever.

"Jody never told on me. I only got found out when her mother followed Jody and the plate of food to her room."

Eddie stops and stuffs his palms into his eyes, and says, "Fuck me."

I say, "So that pocket-sized scene from this-is-my-life is supposed to convince me that you couldn't have possibly lit Jody's apartment on fire? I know better. Just because you love someone doesn't mean you won't hurt them. You know better, too."

Eddie stares at me and vibrates in his seat. He's a live wire covered in skin.

I take a quick physical inventory of myself. I can move a hand and maybe perform a "Where Is Thumbkin?" routine, but that's about it. Wind whistles through the open passenger door and through my hair. I miss my goddamn hat. I feel exposed and powerless.

Can't let our date end early. I say, "What kind of work does Gus do for you? Besides selling drugs, if I may be so bold."

Eddie gives me a wry, aren't-you-silly smile. I wish I could give it back.

I say, "I know I have a dry sense of humor, but I didn't think I said something funny."

He says, "You don't know nothin' about Gus, do you?"

Who am I to argue? "Enlighten me."

"You talk to Gus's girl?"

I don't answer, not sure of what to say, and I know the hesitation is a fatal mistake while I'm making it. The true curse of a cerebral cortex: knowing you're fucking up as you're doing it. I say, "I've checked everywhere for Gus." And I say it lamely.

"Fuck, you don't even know who she is." He laughs, and his lungs are made of paper. "Fuckin' guy doesn't wipe his ass without checkin' with her first."

Wallowing in my stubbornness when I can't afford it, I say, "I know who she is."

Eddie keeps on laughing. Send in the clown.

I say, "I know she's the one you were stalking and threatening the night before the fire."

He says, "You don't know shit about what happened, or who anyone is. I thought you were fuckin' it all up on purpose, out to get me, frame me. Now I don't know. Maybe you're just a fuckin' stumble-bum runnin' head first into a mess. Or you were led into it all, by the scruff, like me. Doesn't really matter. You showed up, and you ruined everything. Jody'll never believe me because of you. Never." He fills his hands with my left arm.

"Let go of me, put the car in drive, take me back to Southie, and I won't make you eat the steering wheel." My tough-talk threat is emptier than a church on a Friday night.

Eddie weighs my arm in his hands like a fishmonger sizing up the big catch. He says, "You haven't moved the whole time we've been here. You can't move, can you?"

"I can move." My lies don't work often enough to warrant their continued use.

Eddie lifts my left arm up, down, whichever way he wants. He puts it between my legs, my hand over my crotch, and he laughs hard once, a percussive grunt that's more shock and surprise than mirth. He watches my hand, still vibrating in his seat but he's trying to stay still, like my paw is a squirrel he doesn't want to scare away.

Eddie takes my hand away when he believes I can't move it. He's embarrassed for both of us.

He says, "You ruined me and Jody. I can't let that go. You stay away from her and me. Just fuckin' stay away." He puts both hands on my left shoulder. "We're gonna find out if you can move, and how fast." He smiles like a bully, gives me that mix of sadism, schadenfreude, and need. The smile is a lit match in a dark closet. After it burns out, he makes hard lines with his eyebrows and his mouth. He's pensive as pensive as a dyed-in-the-wool junkie can get.

"You better move quick."

Eddie lifts my arm and pushes under my shoulder. I'm a tilting lever, my head and torso leaning outside of the car. The highway cement is too close and too far away.

I yell, "Eddie, stop!" but his hands walk down my shoulder onto my side, still pushing, and I can't do anything to resist. I become the tipping point, and momentum takes over. I tuck my head into my chest and fall out of the car and onto the highway. I don't land hard, making first contact with my shoulder. On the road again. I spill out like a poured glass of water, rolling onto my back; the rest of my body pours out and pools on the cool, uncaring pavement.

I yell, "Eddie," again, but he drives away. I crane and tilt my head back to see him. Everything is upside down. The gray slab of highway is the sky. His passenger-side door is still open. His upside-down car disappears into the tunnel.

I try to roll over but can't. I'm lying on my back in lane three of four. I bellow for help. This is too much. This is too much like the Foxwoods night with George, my best friend, my dead best friend, and the van accident. George was driving, and the van flipped. He was thrown out, but I stayed in until the ride was over. Please remain in your seats until we come to a complete stop. I opened the door, had to go look for George because he wasn't anywhere. I jumped down from my seat, out of the van, but I couldn't walk on my broken leg and I fell. Bloodied and lying on the side of the road, I was as helpless as an infant. I was born again and born broken.

Fresh waves of panic and fear surge over my levees. I won't be able to recover. There're too many thoughts of *get up! run! crawl!* stampeding into each other, creating logjams in my neurons and synapses, shutting everything down again. I'll be the possum playing dead in the road. I'm not playing.

A car swerves past me on the left, tires squealing, and the smell of burning rubber is close and hot, singeing my sinuses. I scream for help again. I scream at myself to move. I lift my right hand and hover it over my face. The fingers are pink with my blood. My hand trembles, and I'm not strong enough to hold it up there, way up above my face.

The bridge under me shakes like a by-the-hour motel's vibrating bed working on a fistful of quarters. A distant roar is becoming not-so-distant. I manage to lift my head up, and the scene rushes back together. I'm staring at the gleaming grille of an eighteen-wheeler, and it's almost on top of me. Its twin-sun headlights are already shining their dirty light past me on the road ahead. The truck dives downhill, a great white shark with chrome teeth rushing to a feeding frenzy. My legs are almost in its gaping maw.

It's going to drive right over me. I pull my arms against my side and my legs together, turning into a lowercase *l* or a sardine. I think flat-as-a-tortilla thoughts and try not to move. Need to keep away from the tires, somehow. My eyes won't close, and the truck's engine, that smog-spewing, great-grandchild of the industrial revolution, is infinitely sized as it passes over my head. Below the undercarriage, everything is heat and noise and wind and metal and rubber, then smoke as the wheels to either side of me spin and burn, and the bulk above me drifts left. The idiot is breaking. He can't break now; he'll fishtail, and if he freaks out and cuts the wheel I won't even register as a speed bump as the tires chew a path through me.

Days pass, and I'm still here beneath the truck. I understand the yawning horror that is eternity. I can't see the end of the truck through the smoke. I can't see anything. Every molecule in my body wants to go away, to move-move-move. I hold steady, wishing to dissolve and diffuse into the pavement and become part of the road.

The sensory assault ends abruptly, and the truck is past me. I close my eyes and could give in to sleep right now so easily. Sleep is holding its jacket open, and it'd take no effort to slip my arms inside and button up.

Approaching cars make their gluttonous sounds. I can't get up and walk, or even crawl, but I can pendulum my hips, turning them left and right. I push and strain and swear, until I build up enough momentum to roll on my right side, toward the passing lane. The first roll is always the hardest. I momentarily teeter and almost fall into my original turtle-on-its-back position. My left shoulder pistons forward, and I roll over onto my stomach, then flip up onto my left side. My husky build and the grade and pitch of the highway help to facilitate my roll-out-the-barrel progress. I traverse the passing lane and roll up against the median, leaning facedown.

I close my eyes and listen to cars and their horns, brakes, and sirens. I close my eyes and listen to the shouting. It's all over, but they're still shouting.

And I lie there, wondering where Gus is. And I lie there, wondering where George is. Wondering why he left me in the van by myself. Wondering why he disappeared and left me alone to deal with all this.

TWENTY-ONE

The sun cuts through the window and blinds, leaving pieces of itself on the linoleum, the dead TV screen, and the breakfast tray littered with crushed-up balls of cellophane. I didn't eat the scrambled eggs because they melted, filling my green plate with yellow water.

Detective Owolewa sits in a chair next to my bed. I catch him in midyawn and stretch. I'm rubbing off on him. He says, "Are you awake, Mr. Genevich?"

"Maybe. Are you?"

I'm awake enough to know I slept through Sunday. I sit upright with my legs stretched out on the bed. Swaddled in a Johnny and tucked under a thin, noisy sheet as rough as shark skin, I'm in Mass General hospital. No private room for me.

He says, "You're due to be discharged within the hour."

"I thought I had this bed booked for the whole week." Various aches and pains report from the different precincts of my body. My face is a mask, two sizes too big. I need a hat and a cigarette. "I know I look like I was entered in a demolition derby, but they tell me nothing is broken. Shows what they know."

"Your toxicology screen came back clean, as well, which was a surprise."

"Don't be surprised. My body is a temple."

Detective Owolewa wears a white buttoned shirt, sleeves rolled up. He has work to do. He says, "We have surveillance video of Eddie Ryan leaving you on the Zakim."

I shouldn't be surprised, but I am. "I hope you got my good side." He has a surveillance video, and all I have is the Andre the

Giant of headaches.

"You appeared to be unconscious when you were falling out of the car to the road. Then, before the truck passed over you, you were twitching around like you were having a seizure. Do you remember any of that?"

"The truck I'll remember most of all," I say, then describe cataplexy and narcolepsy and the big bang theory. It's all about mass, gravity, and black holes, and none of it seems to make an impression.

"We picked up Eddie only an hour after he left you. We found him passed out in the same stolen car, which he parked down by Carson Beach. He was initially nonresponsive, and he had methamphetamines in his possession."

"He's a reprobate, that one."

"Did you know the car was stolen?" He's reading off a pre-planned script of plays. His cool and collected is more like a simmer, though. He's not pleased.

I say, "Yes and no. But mostly yes." If I was interviewing me, I'd hate me too.

"Allow me to rephrase the question. How did you end up in the stolen car with a local meth dealer?"

"The short answer is that me as the late-night bridge delivery wasn't voluntary. You'd think that'd be clear from the video."

"Eddie forced you into the car as well as out of the car, then?"

"Beaten, carried, and dragged would be more accurate, but we can go with forced."

"Did you two gentlemen have a dispute over the purchase or disbursement past, present, or future of amphetamines or any of its derivatives?"

I laugh. A garbage can rolling down an alley. "Hardly. Eddie thinks I'm responsible for putting him on your arson suspect short list."

"I didn't know I had a short list. Why would he think that?"

"I don't know. Ask Eddie. Conspiracy theories really aren't my bag."

"Where did Eddie pick you up?"

"I don't remember. I think I was asleep. You know how that is."

"Here's what I know, besides you not being truthful with me from the get-go." Detective Owolewa leans and picks up something from under his chair, and he throws it to me like a Frisbee. My hat lands on my chest.

I say, "You know my hat?" I put it on, and know I'm making a terrible mistake.

The detective says, "The owner had parked the car in front of 74 West Second Street. Does that address mean anything to you? It should. I found your hat in the first-floor apartment. The door was open."

I sink into the quicksand of my adjustable bed. Suddenly my johnny is too tight. "Maybe it isn't my hat. Though it does look nice on me."

"A local resident reported a disturbance in that same apartment and witnessed two men fighting on the sidewalk in front of the building."

"To be fair, I wasn't fighting. I was getting my ass handed to me."

"I don't know what to do with you, Mr. Genevich."

"That makes two of us."

"Who's apartment is it?"

"A friend's."

"Name."

"Gus."

"Why were you there?"

"I've crashed there before. Sometimes I need to get away from my place, from the rut, the routine. It's a sleep strategy. Might be hard to believe, but I have trouble sleeping at night, and getting out and going to his place helps sometimes. Change of scenery, greener grass, and all that." I'm believable, and so is Gus, my good friend who's close by and takes me in when I'm feeling lonely.

"What time did you go to the apartment?"

"Around two a.m."

"Was Gus home?"

"No. I assume he was at his girlfriend's place."

"Does Eddie know Gus?"

I should just tell the detective everything. I don't know why I'm resisting, holding back. I don't know why I continue to protect Gus, if that is what I'm doing. Gus isn't even real anymore. Maybe he never was. He's a Snuffleupagus, a secret I keep while continually molding his image to fit a need, fill a purpose. Yeah, I'm saying he's my imaginary friend.

I say, "I don't know who Eddie knows."

"You think Eddie followed you to the apartment."

"Seems like the likeliest scenario."

"Is Gus the client who gave you the amphetamines?"

"No."

The detective shakes his head. "I don't know what to do with you."

"You said that already."

"It's still true. You're simultaneously on the outskirts and in the middle of the whole mess. I don't think you've purposefully done anything wrong. I also don't think whatever it is you're trying to do is helping anyone. Yourself included. But you're too stubborn to tell me everything I need to hear."

His outskirts/middle of the mess spiel is a more than apt description of me. It's frustrating to be reduced to fifty words or less. I say, "I refuse to accept that I'm stubborn." His insight is impressive and more than a little scary. Or maybe I'm just that obvious. "What has Eddie told you?"

"Eddie thinks that everyone is out to get him, that he's done nothing wrong, and that he's depressed. He admitted to drinking and doing a lot of meth but claims to remember nothing about the time he spent with you."

Is there a chance that Eddie is telling the truth? The meth would explain his zombie pallor, the ragged speech pattern and behavior. If fully rational, he'd have to understand that dumping me on the highway would not serve his long-term goals.

I say, "He said all that?"

"And more. He was surprisingly compliant." The detective smiles. He knows more than I'll ever know.

How long before Eddie will tell him about his relationship with Gus or my visit to Jody, if he hasn't told him already? I'm digging a hole where no one really needs one, and I'm more than likely going to be the only one to fall in and have dirt kicked over me.

I nod out, lose more time that I can't ever get back. Detective Owolewa stands in front of his chair, arms across his chest. Maybe I should worry about what was said while I was out, but it couldn't be any worse than what I said while I was in.

I say, "I wasn't sleeping."

"Eddie is going to be charged with possession of a controlled substance, aggravated assault, kidnapping, and perhaps attempted murder."

"I noticed you didn't say arson."

"No, I didn't say arson, Mr. Genevich."

"I don't suppose you'd tell me about your investigation. How the fire was started, for instance."

"We haven't decided what you're going to be charged with yet, Mr. Genevich."

"I guess that's a no," I say and smooth out the lumps in the bedsheet with my hands. It doesn't work. "I hate Eddie like poisoned poison, and maybe this doesn't make sense, but I don't think he was trying to kill me. He was frustrated, angry, and scared. Not in control. Not methodically taking out a perceived threat or loose end. I might be projecting my issues with discerning reality on a meth addict, but I'm not convinced he started the fire on H Street either, at least not consciously."

I blink my eyes, and he's not in my room anymore, the quantum detective. I don't know if Detective Owolewa heard my closing remarks or if he offered a rebuttal. I could lie here and fret about how he left, if he said anything, what he thinks of me, what kind of expression he had on his face, if he looked over his right or left shoulder before leaving, if he walked backward, skipped, crawled, or floated out the goddamn door.

Ultimately, his mode of exit doesn't really matter. The result is the same: he's gone, and I'm alone.

TWENTY-TWO

That night the ER hospital staff resuscitated and saved my sports jacket and its contents, namely my wallet and cell phone, but they cut up my shirt and pants and peeled me like a banana. Now I'm stuck leaving the place wearing mismatching scrubs, sports coat, and my fedora. Dressed for success on a Monday.

The cab ride back to my building is not good for my health. It's violent and herky-jerky, a mechanical bull ride. The driver doesn't believe in smooth acceleration or stops, bouncing me around the backseat like a ball bearing in a spray paint can. My kingdom for inertia. I think about going home and crawling into my bed, or better yet, seeking a safe port on my couch for a few weeks, go all Rip Van Winkle until people forget my name.

The cabbie leaves me and a hubcap on my corner. The bright midmorning sun is an insult, and I scurry inside, a vampire Jonesing for his coffin or a cup of black coffee. Instead of going directly upstairs, I circulate the air in my office.

Let's take inventory. Eddie is in custody, Gus is in Narnia, and Ekat is probably still sleeping or at the gym. Jody and Rachel are hiding in plain view, no one in Southie knows who Aleksandar Antonov was, Timothy Carter wants to sue me, and Detective Owolewa wants to arrest me.

I run through some investigative calisthenics. I check both phones, no messages, and no e-mails that I want to read. Maybe *no messages* is a message. Being paranoid is a given, but it's hard not to be a narcissist as a detective, attributing weight and meaning to the meaningless. Maybe someday, if I work hard and I'm lucky, I'll achieve irony and paradox.

On the local news Web sites there's no word of Eddie's arrest, but there are brief reports about a yet-to-be-named schmuck being dropped, middle lane, on the Zakim Bridge. The stories refer to the existence of a surveillance video, but there's no sign of it online yet. Something to look forward to.

I call the Nantucket hotel owner, Midge Peterson, again and actually get her on the phone. She talks softly, like the world is a library. She doesn't have any new information for me. No names or addresses of Boston-area friends or acquaintances of Aleksandar and no knowledge of how Wilkie Barrack went about obtaining his services.

The phone call ends, and I intend to creep upstairs to the bat cave, hang upside down for a few hours. As I'm shuttering up and locking the office, I look out my front door and across the street. Sitting on a cement bench is the first person I saw when I came to after the fire: my occasional lunch date, Rita.

She's wearing a green baseball hat, a black sweatshirt with the sleeves cut at her forearms, and acid-washed jeans. Her head falls forward and body leans to the left. She catches and corrects her posture, but the cycle repeats. She's nodding off, falling asleep. I'm familiar with the process.

She and I need to trade notes about the night of the fire. I dash into the Greek pizza joint next door and pick up a couple of slices. Cheese, no pepperoni. I part a sea of pedestrians and wade across the parked cars and traffic of West Broadway. Everyone lets me pass. The power of my hospital scrubs compels them.

"Hope you like pizza, Rita."

I sometimes imagine Rita's previous lives. She was a laid-off bus driver and an undiagnosed schizophrenic. She suffered serial physical and mental abuse at the hands of emotionally barren men. She was a runaway from the western, nowhere part of Massachusetts and quickly succumbed to heroin and a bipolar disorder. The past lives I conjure, those caricatures of a twenty-first-century victim, are supposed to be reassuring because it couldn't possibly happen to me.

I sit next to her and give her a slice. A brittle, papier-mâché tree shades our bench. Rita nods and says, "Pizza doesn't suck. Nice pants." She eats her slice dutifully, and I feel guilty inhaling mine.

I ask, "Where'd you stay last night?"

Rita finishes her pizza and wipes the grease on her pants. Her painted-line thin legs are hidden somewhere inside the faded denim. I'm not sure if Rita approves of my deviating from our usual topic of Charlton Heston movies. We have an unspoken deal. I don't ask for details about her everyday hell. I can't handle it, and she won't have to relive it; her suffering is a safe abstraction for me and a recurring bad dream for her.

She talks softly, and I have to lean in so she isn't buried beneath the avalanche of lunch hour on West Broadway. "I have a new spot. It's been safe. It's been good. So far, so far. No one trying to take my stuff or rubbing their dirty cocks on my face when I'm sleeping. Over by Gate of Heaven, in the back, facing Fifth Street. Between the Dumpster and a stairwell. Don't go telling anybody."

I hate myself for asking her about where she stayed, and I hate myself for not asking her about it before today. I say, "I won't tell anyone, Rita."

Okay, she's been sleeping at Gate of Heaven. I know that

Dumpster, too. Jody's burned-down H Street apartment is visible from it. I ask, "The night of the fire on H Street, were you staying at your usual spot?"

"I was making my way there when I saw the fire. Smelled it before I saw it." Rita pauses, cranes her head in real close to mine. That dry laugh of hers plumes out, and she says, "You know, everyone knows it was you."

I say, "It wasn't me. You can't prove it." My denial is rote, something I do on autopilot, but as I pull a cigarette out of my coat like it's a passport, what she said sneaks up on me and flicks the panic switch. "Wait. What are you talking about?" Is she talking about the fire? Was Detective Owolewa telling me not so cryptically that I was the arson suspect?

"Give me one of those." She grabs my hand and takes the cigarette. Her skin is an autumn leaf. "The word is out. That was you lying in the middle of the Zakim Bridge the other night."

My color-coded alert system changes colors and mixes them together, going chameleon. How the hell does she know? Who did she talk to? I check myself; maybe I did pull a Rip Van Winkle. I've emerged weeks later and with everyone laughing at me.

"It wasn't me. It was Charlton Heston."

"He's dead. I know it was you."

I know when I'm had. "All right. I'm guilty. How did you know?"

"I see things. I hear things." Rita pauses to blow a cloud of burned air into my face. "I know things."

Great. Somebody told her, and I'm sure she's hardly the only person swinging on that grapevine. The half gainer onto the bridge isn't going to win me the respect and admiration of the locals, who are already abuzz with the news apparently. So Fred the friendly neighbor gets newspaper credit for saving Jody's JT from the fire, and I'll be a back-page joke and a YouTube legend.

I say, "What do you know? Besides Soylent Green is people." Everyone walking by our bench looks at me and knows what happened and knows who I am.

Rita absorbs my bitchy verbal jab with remarkable dignity. A dignity I clearly lack. She pats my shoulder, which aches and is made of cracked balsa wood. There, there.

She says, "There's something seriously wrong with you, my friend."

"Can't argue with that. Let's get back on topic."

"Didn't know we were off topic."

"We were. Trust me."

"If you say so."

"The night of the fire, who did you see there?"

"I saw you run in and then stumble out a little later, then timber! to the sidewalk." Rita stretches our her *timber* call like a lumberjack. "That was real good of you to try and help those people."

"I did help. I got the kid off the second floor before the smoke got to be too much, but no one will listen . . ."

Rita nods, then says, "Other than you and the hero guy who went in after you, I didn't see anyone else go in or go out. I already told this to the cops. I only got there when you did."

I try not to let toxic disappointment ooze out of my pores. "Did you know the guy who was killed? He lived on the first floor. His name was Aleksandar."

Rita fiddles with her cigarette and her baseball hat. Leftover pizza grease darkens the brim. "Saw him around town but didn't really know him or talk to him."

She is as patient and gentle smoking as she was with the pizza. I have no patience and want to empty my pack, stack each cigarette on the bench like kindling, light a fire, and thrash around in the smoke like a greedy parasite in blood.

Rita passes and twirls the lit cigarette between her fingers. The pinwheeling ember is hypnotic. Then she switches hands. It's a trick I've never seen before. I don't know how she's doing it. She starts talking without dropping the minibaton made out of tobacco.

She says, "What'd you say his name was, again? Didn't know that. Didn't see him around all that much. Seen him walk to a Laundromat maybe, or to the Hub, not that I followed him around, right?" The spinning cigarette is a turbine on her fingers. It's a blur. "Used to see this well-dressed guy going into that first-floor apartment. I saw him like three times, a month ago, maybe less, walking down H, always walking real fast. Young, good-looking guy, never stayed for more than a few minutes, always dressed in a suit, shiny black hair, wearing big, fat, dark sunglasses."

I see Timothy Carter's face, the face that filled my office once, and I want to take a swing at him; I see myself throwing a compact, three-inch punch. Then I'm falling from a great height, from the top of the Tower of Babel, and my arms flail and spin like her cigarette. I land in a tree. The thin trunk is a fist between my shoulder blades, all knuckles. The shaking leaves complain and let scalding sunlight pass through the canopy to punish me.

My legs are still in contact with the concrete bench, and my ass hangs a few inches above the ground. I figure out my previous few moments even though I wasn't there. Yeah, I'm an instant archaeologist or an archaeologist of instants. My findings: I passed out, fell backward into our shady tree, and the Mayan calendar has doomed us all. The spindly little tree will never be the same.

Rita paces in front of the bench, wearing out the sidewalk. She yells, "What's going on? What the hell, Mark?" She's looking around for help, for someone to commiserate with, but the people walking by are doing their best to ignore her. They don't have to try that hard.

I say, "Easy, easy, Rita. I fell off. I'm clumsy. I'm fine. I'm sorry. Help me up, will ya? I smacked the back of my head again. I'm seeing stars right now."

She's scared and won't look at my face. I don't blame her on either count. She crouches next to me and grabs an arm. I push off the tree and, with her help, wiggle back up onto the bench.

"Thanks, and I'm sorry about that, Rita. Didn't mean to scare you." The apology disappears into my lower register, where words go to die.

Rita stands next to the bench, arms folded across her chest. She's host to a raging internal debate; the pro and con arguments about her continued association with me bubble underneath her skin.

I don't know how much of what I remember her saying about a well-dressed man was real or a dream. Was she telling me about seeing Timothy Carter visiting Aleksandar? And holy shit, I'm in a lot of pain again and don't think I'll be able to move for a day or so.

Not sure of what tack to take, I throw out some phrases decorated with question marks. "You were saying? Young guy? Well dressed? Big sunglasses, too? At that apartment?" I light two cigarettes, keep both for myself, and give her the rest of the pack.

She says, "Yeah. That's what I said. Saw him a bunch of times."

I need time to process this. Maybe she saw Timothy Carter, and maybe she didn't. And Timothy Carter visiting Aleskandar by himself, in and of itself, proves nothing. Nothing except that I really want him to be the person to take the blame for the fire, take the blame for everything that's ever gone wrong anywhere, to be the mythical bad guy we all need and maybe even deserve.

I ask, "Did you tell the police about the well-dressed man?"

"I told them everything I know. Why wouldn't I? I'm not stupid."

"Right. Of course. That's very sensible of you." I bring both burning cigarettes to my lips. In with the bad and out with "Thanks, Rita. That helps me out a lot."

Rita says, "I was lying."

I look up, and she's covering a smile with a shaking hand. The smile repairs me, but her shaking hand tears me back down. I say, "Lying about what, Rita?"

She says, "I didn't know that was you who fell on the bridge. No one's talking. I guessed."

"You guessed?"

"Yeah. I saw your hospital scrubs, and you looked like you got the shit beat out of you. Flopping around the bridge sounded like something you'd do."

I laugh, but Rita stops laughing. We weren't supposed to share that. I stand up, and my body, that flawed bag of meat and bones stuck carrying around my consciousness, doesn't like the standing. Tough shit.

I say, "All right, Rita. Sorry again for the scare. I gotta go. Next lunch we'll take it easy and swap *Planet of the Apes* lines. Okay?"

Rita nods, and neither of us knows what I meant by *we'll take it easy*. She hitches up her pants and says, "My favorite line is, 'It's a mad house. A mad house,'" and walks away, into the bank lot behind our bench and loses herself in the maze of gleaming metal and glass of the cars parked tightly together.

TWENTY-THREE

I call Ekat's cell and leave a message. I tell her that Eddie Ryan has been arrested (but not for what) and maybe we should consider reporting Gus missing. I tell her that Owolewa interviewed me again but not why. I wish her a happy birthday even if it isn't happy or her birthday, and then I hang up.

Expecting an instantaneous return call that doesn't come, I sit and stare at the phone like it's the magic mirror on the wall, waiting for it to lie through its glass teeth and tell me I'm the fairest of all, like it's supposed to. There's no such thing as magic.

Maybe I don't need magic, and it's all as simple as a high or drunk or sober Eddie trying to burn up his estranged girlfriend and her son, with the unfortunate Aleksandar Antonov, the forgotten man, as an unintended casualty. But I don't believe that. I don't think Detective Owolewa believes it either. The list of people who are connected to me and the fire spreads. I can't help but feel there's a terrible balance to it all, it's about to be upset, and everything will fall apart. Maybe I should go to group therapy tonight.

I leave the bench, determined to walk past my brownstone. I could go upstairs and change my jacket and out of my scrubs, but the escapee-from-an-institution look is edgy and hip and surprisingly comfortable. Besides, I need to avoid my apartment now. It's the rabbit hole, and it leads down into a deep, dark, and empty warren. I'd get lost and never be found.

I cross Dorchester Street against the advice of the traffic lights and the red don't-walk hand. A bus driver and an idiot in a Hummer express dissatisfaction with my chicken crossing the road. I tell them I think they're number one. Glad we got that off our chests.

It's the ten-thousandth consecutive day of ninety-plus-degree heat, and the city is withering, drying up, turning to bonemeal. I stick with the long walk and pass on a cab ride, even if the not-so-complex movements of right-foot-left-foot and inflating my chest with air result in spectacular fireworks of pain. Ooos and ahhs, indeed. It's a collective and collaborative pain that's keeping me awake and upright for the moment. Me and time, we're marching on.

I mosey up East Broadway, past more brownstones, darkened and taped-up real estate offices, a Laundromat, court house, and bowling alley. Then I take a right at the Store 24 and onto H Street. Time to canvass the neighborhood. I'm convinced that knowing more about Aleksandar is the key to what happened the night of the fire. He's a secret that somebody is keeping.

I ring bells and knock on doors up and down H Street. I get an answer on maybe one out of four apartments. Those who do answer their doors aren't impressed by me or my PI ID badge. I don't know their language or the Southie handshake. My ID photo is cracked and faded, and I'm not wearing a hat. Maybe I should replace it with the picture I drew at group therapy.

The mini-interviews are microscopic. No one knew or talked to Aleksandar. Only one old man the size of Jiminy Cricket, wearing flannel pajamas and wisps of white cotton-candy hair clinging to the top of his head, wants to chat for more than ten seconds. He recognizes me from last year's DA case. He tells me he knew the DA wasn't a good guy. I yawn. He tells me I should be looking into the kook who got dumped onto the Zakim Bridge. I tell him he's right, I should. He doesn't let me leave until I give him a sweat-damped calling card from my wallet. I sign it upon his insistence. Give the people what they want.

I try a few more buildings on H Street, but I don't get anywhere. I limp down one more set of wooden front stairs of another swing and miss, straining the rotting handrail with my weight until I crash onto the sidewalk like an asteroid. I sit on the stairs, take off my hat, and wipe the flop sweat off my face and forehead.

I scan H Street, trying to recall which places I've been to already, and Jody O'Malley creeps into my vision like a forgotten memory. She's a block away, walking down East Sixth, probably coming from Rachel's place. She wears cutoff gray sweatpants and a white T-shirt. Same T-shirt she had on yesterday. The exposed skin of her thick arms and legs is pale, sun-starved, Transylvanian. Hubble telescope–sized sunglasses cover most of her face, and she looks like a wingless dragonfly.

Jody stops at the corner, sways a little, feels the world turning and tumbling under her. She roots through a black handbag slung over her shoulder, then puts her arms behind her head and wrestles with her hair. She loses the match, barks out a monosyllable, and throws a black hair elastic onto the curb. She slowly crosses H, walking like she might step into an open sewer at any moment, and continues down East Sixth.

I wonder if she knows about Eddie's arrest, if despite everything, she was his one phone call. I wait until she's out of sight, and I get up and follow the leader. When I hit East Sixth, I peek around the corner, and she's there. We've managed to maintain our one-block distance. Like me, she isn't walking very well.

Jody lists to the right, toward the street, and almost stumbles off the curb. She manages to correct herself, but it's an overcorrection, and she walks into a chain-link fence on her right. She's drunk, and by the looks of it, it's been a long, hard drunk, the kind of drunk that's supposed to act like sleep, a dimming or dulling of the lights until you can't feel anything.

She turns left, onto I Street. We walk, slow and deliberate, and when we pass Ekat's apartment I can't help but throw a glance at her front window. The blinds are down. Then it's past Gate of Heaven and up toward East Broadway. Jody stops at the corner of I and East Broadway and ducks into a little place called the Hub, a catchall convenience store that also sells liquor, Keno, and lottery tickets.

I don't know if I should go inside, talk to her, confront her because she told Eddie about my appearance at Rachel's, tell her what Eddie did to me and where he is now, maybe even mention their childhood hiding-in-the-closet story. While any sort of discussion like that wouldn't go over well in a small public venue, I'm too fucking sore and hot to stand out here with a metaphorical thumb up my ass. I enter the Hub.

Through the door, and I'm welcomed by a blast of chilled air. I exhale for what feels like the first time since leaving the hospital. I could stand beneath the manufactured cold all day and contemplate the existential implications of air-conditioning. The rapid change in temperature also brings on a flash-flood headache. Seems I can't win, but I knew that already.

Off to my right, there's a group of people, almost exclusively gray-hairs, all bundled up and braced for the store's canned winter. They're rooted in the gambling nook, filling out their Keno cards and watching the TVs that hang from the dropped ceiling. They stare at the noiseless screens, the blue backgrounds with ordered rows of white numbers. That order belies the hidden and stacked-against-us laws of statistics and chance. No one will get lucky.

I pull my hat lower over my eyes. That way no one can see me. I head deeper into the store. Toward the back, I catch a glimpse of Jody near the refrigerated section micro wave dinners, Push Pops, and twelve-packs of beer. She still wears the sunglasses, and she fills her arms with bags of chips and bottles of vodka. I'm now of the professional opinion that chatting with her here would not be the best way to go.

She floats toward the front of the store, and I drift back and grab something cold and loaded with caffeine. I don't think she has seen me hiding in the stacks yet, and I keep watch from the periphery. There's no line at the register. A large older woman is sunken in behind the counter.

Jody dumps her haul next to the register and dives into the

bag slung on her shoulder. Receipts and gum wrappers spill out and flutter to the floor, a pocketbook autumn. She mutters and swears, and her hands are lost in a bog.

With Jody's items processed and brown bagged already, the woman behind the counter stands but doesn't increase her height by more than a few inches. She adjusts her waistband and has a go at some serious eye rolling.

This might be an in for me. I could offer to pay for the stuff, win her trust, and maybe Jody would tell me more about Aleksandar, about the night of the fire. I don't walk. I sidle toward the counter and behind Jody, but I don't get there in time. She pulls out the Excalibur credit card from the stone of her bag and flings it onto the counter.

Opportunity lost, I creep back, the blob shrinking away from the cold. Maybe I can lose myself among the Stonehenge of Keno players to my left, and I start to lean that way.

The woman at the register runs the card through the magic bean-counting machine that no one ever questions. She glances at the card and starts to give it back to Jody in a practiced yet indifferent motion, but she stops, swapping cartoon-eyed looks between the card in her hand and Jody. The woman's arm recoils into her chest quicker than a cord returning to a vacuum cleaner. She brings the card up to her face, lifts her glasses, and inspects it, a jeweler appraising a flawed pearl.

She announces, "I'm not taking that; I know who you are," and aims the card at Jody like it's loaded.

Jody shakes her head, laughs, and wipes her face. She says, "You don't know me." Her voice is a desperate growl, an SOS signal with fuck-you attitude.

"I'm not taking this card."

The barometric pressure inside the store plummets, and a blizzard warning should be issued. Even the folks blinded by Keno electric-slide away from Jody and the front register. Not sure what I should do. I don't like confrontation.

"Fine." Jody smacks the counter with an open hand and says, "Give it back."

The woman behind the counter clutches it to her chest, shakes her head, and asks Jody to leave before she calls the police.

"Gimme the fuckin' card!" Jody reaches across and rips it out of the woman's grasp, then lumbers to the entrance/exit, head down, breathing heavy. She rips the door open and leaves. The sing-song, two-note, electronic customer-left-the-building blat echoes gently through the Hub.

The woman behind the counter is shaking, talking to herself, and dialing. I step up, flash my PI badge, the kind you can get if you send the state a check and Frosted Flakes box tops.

"I'll take care of it. No worries." I drop a twenty and a ten on the counter and add, "Keep the change," without being sure that I've covered Jody's tab. Doesn't matter. The woman puts the phone down and stares at me like I'm a mirage, like she won't believe that I was really there until after I'm gone. It's a stare I get a lot. I snatch up the brown bag and follow Jody out the door.

She's already a half block ahead of me, and I can't run on my lactic acid legs to catch up. I call out, yell her name three times. Bad idea. My headache goes supernova, and white stars of varying sizes and mass invade my vision, bending time and space. I stumble and lean against the brick outer wall of the Hub.

Hopefully, it's strong enough to hold me up.

I try to put myself back together, but the pieces of me are getting more difficult to find and match. I'm afraid I'm losing pieces now, too, spreading myself thinner than skim milk.

"What? What do you want? What do you want now?" She repeats herself, as if offering an answer for each of my multiple calls of her name.

I push off the wall, desperate to escape from the Hub's gravitational pull. I get a walking start and take a peek down I Street. Jody slowly edges back toward me, hands on her hips. She wants something, maybe the brown bag and its liquid contents, or she wants to punch me in the face like Eddie did.

"It's me, Mark Genevich. I have your stuff." I hold out the bag, a convenience store peace offering or a sacrifice to a pissed-off god. I say, "Can I get a little help? Your boyfriend sucker punched me a few hundred times the other night, and I'm a little sore," which is a nice segue, I think.

Jody lunges down the street like she's going to tackle me. "That piece of shit isn't my boyfriend."

"Who is he, then? Besides a piece of shit."

She shrugs, stumbles, and knocks me up against the brick wall. She says, "Just a guy I've known forever." The *er* at the end of *forever* is mugged by an *ah*.

"He's in custody right now."

"Fuck 'im." Jody looks away, toward the front of the store. Maybe she's waiting to see if the woman behind the counter is going to come out and chase us off. And maybe she isn't.

I say, "Hold this for a sec? I need to adjust." I give her the goody bag even though she's unsteady on her feet. I'm afraid the added weight is going to tip her over and she'll shatter on the pavement like the vodka bottles would.

She doesn't fall, and she says, "What'd you do, just take the bag?"

The heat crawls inside my shirt and dies. I reapply the hat to my head and retie the belt string of my scrubs, making a pretty, showy bow that hangs limp below my navel. I reach inside the bag and take out the rapidly warming energy drink and pour half of it down my throat. It tastes terrible. I say, "No. I paid for it all. I'm a responsible guy."

Jody laughs, and it's messy. (I don't laugh. That means I'm serious.) She says, "Thanks for the stuff," and starts off, slow to gain any consistent forward momentum.

I struggle to keep up. I say, "It's a beautiful day for a walk, and I want to ask you some more questions."

She says, "Whatever," and dumps the bag into my arms again, then slaps me on the shoulder twice.

"Ow. I didn't know we were playing hot potato."

"Stop being a pussy and carry this shit back to Rachel's. I'll buy you a drink, all right." I can't see her eyes through the sunglasses. Her head moves, almost imperceptibly, from side to side, as if she's continually scanning for an improved state of equilibrium. She's much drunker than I thought she was.

"Do you want to tell me why the Hub wouldn't accept your credit card?"

"Not now. Need to drink more, then maybe. Let's just walk."

I don't ask her any more questions, and she doesn't say anything else. We walk past the hulking Gate of Heaven church, and instead of taking a shortcut down East Fifth, onto H Street, and walking past her ruined apartment building, we continue down I Street whistling past the hidden-from-view graveyard.

We're awkward together. We bump into each other and take turns acting as obstacles in our own paths. My limp doesn't mesh with her crooked-mile. We're grinding and dulled gears in a dying machine. By the time we get to Rachel's apartment building, my arms shake and quiver. The brown bag weighs as much as a small car. My eyelids are just as heavy despite the energy drink.

The front door is unlocked. I don't know what that means. Up the stairs and through another unlocked door and into the apartment. Inside, there's a stale smell of sweat and accumulating laundry. I drop the bag on the kitchen table and take off my jacket. I'm breathing heavy, and I might be whimpering out loud.

"You okay?"

"Nothing a bottle or two of ibuprofen wouldn't take care of."

Jody takes off her sunglasses and throws them onto the counter behind her. Like a plane crashing in a cornfield, they don't land well, clattering and plinking off a ceramic jar. She says, "You pretending to be a doctor today, or something?" Jody rips the brown bag, a lion tearing open a kill. The bags of chips and bottles of vodka spill out on the table.

I say, "I play one on TV."

Jody goes more than half full with vodka in a jumbo, not-so-clean plastic cup. She adds two scoops of lemonade mix, a fistful of ice cubes (she drops two on the floor and kicks them under the table), and a splash of water. Homemade hard lemonade. Hard enough to crack rocks.

I say, "Is that for me? If it is, I'm going to need more ice."

"This is mine." Jody takes a deep drink of the grog, then exhales sharply enough to blow out hundreds of birthday candles. "Help yourself."

If it was only that easy. "Tell me about that credit card."

Jody grabs a bag of chips and turns away. With her back to me she says, "Go find it and take a look. It's in my bag somewhere." She stomps into the living room, falls onto the couch, and turns on the TV. It's loud but doesn't say anything.

My head gets heavier, filling with too many thoughts, and it all churns up the murk. Since she didn't take my ibuprofen cue, the doctor heals thyself with a couple of pulls from the vodka bottle. It burns my teeth. Take two and call me in the morning. The vodka is awful, cheap stuff, not that I know any better. The drinks might've been a mistake, but I won't dwell on it.

Jody's black bag is on the kitchen counter, next to the open container of lemonade mix. There's a dusting of yellow snow on her bag. No sugar was added. I unzip it, and my hands do their thieves-in-the-night routine, crawling around inside. Among other debris, I find three almost-empty prescription bottles (one with the label torn off), a cell phone, an iPod, a pack of gum with only two thin pieces left, a pack of cigarettes with only a few smokes missing, three two-dollar winning scratch tickets and one loser, and a fistful of tampons instead of dollars. I also find a credit card and two fake Massachusetts driver's licenses.

The name on the credit card is Fiona Langan. One of the fake licenses matches the name with Jody's picture and a Framingham street address. She doesn't look like a Fiona. The other license also features Jody's not-smiling mug but with the name Sue Booth. Sue lives in the swanky suburb of Weston. Sue is doing well, and maybe she owns a mansion and a yacht.

I take another pull off the vodka bottle, although I know better. The heat expands in my belly, and I imagine it diffusing directly into my sore and battered muscles. It's the least I can do to help them out. After the not-so-wee nip for courage, I stroll into the living room, cradling the precious and fragile vodka bottle in the crook of my left arm and carrying the credit card and IDs in my right hand. Pick a card, any card.

I ask, "Where's Rachel?" The living room is in the same condition that it was yesterday, with the couch as a makeshift empty nest, wrapped in a white bedsheet.

"Out. At work, I think."

I turn the TV off and sit on the opposite end of the couch. Jody grips her jumbo cup with both hands, face buried inside. She could be little orphan Oliver, contemplating the risks of asking some miserable, terrible person for a spot more gruel.

I hold up the fake IDs and say, "I didn't know you had twin sisters."

She speaks into the cup, into the plastic. There's an outline of a faded logo on the cup's side, but it has been long since rubbed away. "Look. You can't tell anyone. You can't tell 'em. I can't get caught again. They find out, they'll take JT away from me. Forever. I mean it. I'll never see him again. That can't happen. He's mine. I can't let that happen. I don't know what to do. We're so fucked."

Part of me thinks that she talks about JT like he's a repossessed car and that's her ultimate problem. I know that par tic u lar conclusion isn't quite fair.

"Where did you get the IDs and credit cards? Did you get them from Eddie?" I take another sip from the vodka bottle, then put it down next to the couch before I do some real damage.

"Eddie didn't know nothing about this. I never told him nothing. This was my thing, not his. It was the only way I was gonna pay off all the bills, get JT new clothes, get him the stuff he deserved, you know, without none of Eddie's help. JT's a good kid. A great kid."

"I'm sure he is."

Jody stands up and drinks a heroic amount of her drink, although there are no heroes here. She puts the sweating cup on top of the TV, then returns to the couch and sits next to me. Her legs touch mine, and I feel the heat of her skin through the thin green cloth of my scrubs. I wonder how many people before me have worn these same pants.

I say, "All right. It wasn't Eddie. Where'd you get the fake IDs?"

"You can't tell anyone."

"I can't make that promise."

Jody repeats herself. "You can't tell anyone."

"I'm not here to get you into trouble or report you to anyone."

"Why are you here?"

"I'm trying to figure out what happened the night of the fire. I'm trying to figure out why it happened."

"You were there, and I wasn't."

It's an accusation. One that's true. And it's meant to sting both of us. "I know."

"My IDs have nothing to do with the fire or with Eddie."

"Do you know that for sure?"

Jody fiddles with the stud below her lip. She says, "Your

buddy Gus gave me the IDs." She laughs and runs a clumsy, heavy hand up and down my right thigh.

I spasm and rise up from my seat like a bee stung me. I settle back down, a layer of sediment, and push her hand away. I say, "Let's stay friends, Jody."

She smacks the back of my hand, the violence and urgency are more than a little intimidating. My hand retreats. The coward. She crushes my already weakening resistance movement with one swift blow.

Jody smiles, and the smile might slide off her face, fall to the couch, and disappear between the cushions. She'll find it later, flattened and smooshed up against some loose change, pens, and the other forgotten debris of her daily existence. Or she'll never find it again.

Jody says, "Gus recruited me. That's how he put it. I was his recruit."

My buddy Gus, Jody, and identity theft. I remember Gus's apartment with the high-end, photo-quality printer and the sheet of laminate wedged next to his hard drive, and there was Eddie in his apartment, too, eagerly waiting to leave his indelible mark on Mark. I think about grabbing the vodka bottle off the floor. I might need to hurt myself a little.

Jody edges closer, draping one of her legs across my lap. Like her hand, the leg is drunk heavy, and it falls on me like a tree in the forest nobody hears.

She says, "He gave me credit cards and matching IDs every couple of weeks. I could use them wherever, but I'd have to run some errands for him, too. I got nothing for free."

Her eyes are half closed, and her hands resume the Genevich

exploration, rubbing my body while in contempt of gentleness. It's like she's waxing a car and can't get me to shine or can't buff out all the scratches. That's not to say to my utter shame and excitement that I'm not having any physical response to her handling.

"Stop. Please, stop. You don't need to do this, Jody." My voice goes small, and my conviction is smaller. I'm the junkie uttering a breathy, anticipatory, and completely fraudulent no. Unlike the night at Ekat's apartment, where reality was as thin as toilet paper and my senses clearly addled, every sensation is mine right now: the weight of her palm, the stubble of her legs, the smell of her lighter fluid breath and the smell of her hair, the taste of the cheap vodka coating my drying mouth, the prickly wet of my ass sweating through the scrubs. Unlike the night at Ekat's apartment, there are no cute stories or rubber bands or dreams. I am awake.

Jody doesn't listen to me. She doesn't stop. She puts a hand under my chin, pushes my head back, and licks my unshaven neck. Her lips are wet and sloppy, and my skin is hypersensitive. I'm at the edge of being ticklish and feral. I'm so easy. My pulsing and guiltless erection presses against her leg, and her leg presses back.

I have to say something, to slow it all down, if not stop it. "What errands would you run for Gus?" I'm so polite. I try to envision Gus as a Robin Hood, stealing credit cards from the rich and giving to the poor, but I'm distracted.

"Once a month or so he'd send me to the Connecticut casinos or to one of the dog tracks around here and get big cash advances on the cards. And Gus took half." Jody sticks her tongue in my right ear, and I let her. I'm all ears, closing my eyes, and I continue to press against her leg. Her fingers go almost delicate on my face, tracing the cracks and lines of my brow and cheeks, tracing my history. Maybe I should ask her to rub it all away. I know I've tried.

What are the implications of our continued and increased physical contact? Am I taking advantage of her? Is she too drunk or too desperate, or not desperate enough? What will she expect of me after? What do I expect of her after? Will there be an after? The cheesy and regrettable pick-up line *How can it be so wrong when it feels so right?* runs through my crowded head, and it makes me feel worse. I'm sinking lower than the subbasement that I usually inhabit.

I try to push Jody away again. She says, "Stop fucking doing that." She doesn't say, *Let's just feel good, feel something for one lousy fleeting fucking moment, all right?* But it's what she means.

"Where did Gus get the credit cards?"

"I don't know. Never told me." Her hand snakes inside my shirt, and she pinches my left nipple. I yelp, but not because it hurts. Nothing hurts right now.

"Did Gus recruit anyone else?"

"Don't know. But I got caught with a card, like three weeks back, at the Hub. No big deal."

"What happened?"

"Nothing. Nothing really happened to me, and I told Gus about it. He kinda shrugged it off but said something about his partner wouldn't be happy."

"Who's the partner?"

"I don't know."

Jody grabs my right hand by the scruff and sticks it between her open legs. The thin material of her shorts is damp and warm. She closes her legs on my hand and presses my fingers against herself.

I say, "Do you know who Timothy Carter is?"

"Never heard of him."

My fingers pulse between her legs, and she rocks back and forth in a rhythm upon which we agree. I say, "Holy shit."

Jody laughs, pushes my head back, and grinds her face into my neck again. Teeth or her stud piercing pinches my skin.

"Did Eddie find out? Does he know?"

Jody climbs up over my neck and pushes her face into mine. We smash our mouths together, sealing tight. We lick and bite each other's lips and share the secrets of our tongues. We separate, holding our mouths an infinitely small space apart from each other, and we try to hover there because we believe in that place like we've believed in nothing else in our flawed lives, but we can't stay. The distance is too much. We kiss again, even harder, knocking our teeth together, drawing blood. We wordlessly argue over who will swallow the other first.

Jody breaks our clinch, bites my bottom lip, and stretches it out, then lets me go. I didn't want her to. She says, "Eddie didn't know nothing. I didn't tell him nothing."

The lizard part of my brain, one that I assumed had atrophied because of disuse, fills with an irrational jealousy of Eddie that I have no right to, and I think about saying something smart and cruel about how she ratted me out to him. Instead, I pull my hand out from between her legs and fill my fist with hair from the back of her head. I pull her farther away and then back, pressing her into my imperfect face. I want her to pass through me and come out the other side.

I say, "Eddie didn't know or he didn't say anything to you?" talking out of the side of my occupied mouth.

"Same thing."

We stop talking into each other. It isn't anything we said. Our mouths become tight seals again, tight enough to block our bottled-up screams. I reach to put my hand back between her legs, but she's coiled and twisted, and my wrist doesn't bend that way. She shifts, aching to comply, but there's no leverage and my angle is awkward.

Jody grunts. I grunt back. We communicate shared frustration. She rolls off me and says, "Stand up."

I'm too slow to put my ass under my feet and clumsily paw at her right breast instead. She grabs my arm, yanks it, and yells, "Fucking stand up!"

I jump up and almost fall but manage another small step for man. Standing is a good position. We kiss more, playing a game of push-hands with only our mouths; we bend and sway, no other body parts make contact. She's only two inches shorter than me, but the slight uptilt of her head fills me with an odd mix of gratitude and someone-tear-my-clothes-off lust.

Jody unties her shorts, then shimmies as they slide past her hips and knees and pool around her feet. She hooks her thumbs in the waistband of her underwear, but I interrupt by sliding my left hand inside the lower elastic between her thighs. I pull the curtain of her underwear aside and hold it there while my right hand slides two fingers inside her. Jody gasps into my mouth and grabs two fistfuls of my shirt. I slowly take my fingers out and then quickly rub and press her clitoris. Jody's legs go jointless, knees bending in all directions.

Her hands rappel down my chest and undo the pretty bow I'd made of the scrub's string tie. There's no shimmy necessary. The scrubs fall like clown pants. I'm not wearing underwear, and I get a brief but appalling waft of my own underwearless-in-July undercarriage. Jody doesn't seem to notice my musk, or care if she does. She briefly tickles my erection with her fingertips before taking me fully in her hand. I lose my breath, can't find it anywhere. She rubs the length of my penis, taking her time initially, then changing speeds and the heaviness of her touch.

We both move our hands faster and we're clumsy about it, missing our marks on occasion, but we're still effective. Jody pulls me toward her thighs, and my orgasm starts in my toes, and I want to stop it but can't. It's beyond me, and there's a deep disappointment in my inability to last longer underneath the current of ecstasy that ends in small lights exploding in my head. I shake and groan and come all over her hand, her shirt and thighs, my shirt, my legs, the floor, the apartment.

I turn my head away from her mouth and mutter "I'm sorry" repeatedly into her ear.

"Ssshh, it's okay. It's all right. Just keep going."

Jody keeps squeezing and pumping with her hand, sending aftershocks through my already crumbling body. My lights are dimming, and I'm really sorry. I stumble forward and lean into her, my head resting on her shoulder. Maybe I could close just my eyes and imagine and dream . . .

"Please, don't stop." She twitches her shoulder and bounces my head upright. Her right hand readjusts my hand between her legs. She doesn't want me inside her anymore. "Come on. Just move your fingers. Right there!" There's no more *please*.

We sway like it's the last dance of the night. Her eyes are closed, and she's concentrating. I'm blinking, trying to stay awake, wanting to stay awake. She says, "Almost there, almost there, almost there," but I don't know if she's telling the truth or trying to convince herself. She continues to pull and tug on me like my penis is a piece of gum stuck in someone's hair.

Yeah, she's hurting me, but I laugh a little because it's funny. And I laugh a little because it's sad. If we were a new couple, or even an old one, we'd hold each other after and giggle uncontrollably about her almost ripping my penis off. It'd become our little private joke (though I'd maintain no pun intended with the *little private* crack), the kind of intimate secret that I imagine lovers keep to themselves, cherish through the years, to use as winks and nods in mixed company or just before they go to bed at night.

"Mark, come on, don't stop!"

Goddamn it, stay awake. Her thigh muscles clench around my hand, her breathing increases, then stops, and her mouth drops open, a trap door. Color rushes into her face, and she comes. She's quiet and reserved compared to my outburst, but her legs give out and I hold her up with my other hand until she pushes all of me away.

Jody lets go of me too, finally, and we kiss one last time, a chaste kiss, two teens on a doorstep just touching lips, or two people saying an awkward goodbye. Jody pulls up her shorts and takes the sheet off the couch and wipes her hands, thighs, and stomach.

"You need this?"

Feeling more than a little ridiculous, standing in front of her TV with my pants down, on display, I take the sheet and wipe my crotch and my legs. The sheet isn't very absorbent, and I'm just spreading wetness around. I give up, ball up the sheet, and toss it to the floor. I bend to grab my scrub pants, and my head goes anvil-heavy. I fall to my knees, ass in the air, waving it like I just don't care.

Jody says, "Whoa. You okay?" She loops one of my arms around her shoulder.

"I'm fine. Just a little dizzy." I'm not fine. I'm far from fine. My voice is coming from another room somehow. Dark spots fill my vision, and my nervous system hums and pulses. I'm about to go out, and hard.

Jody helps me and my pants up. We shuffle over to the couch. She and I sit together, and she guides my head into her lap. The skin of her thighs is cool against my cheek.

I say, "Tell me something, anything. Just talk, please." I close my eyes, and I'm falling down a well, not a rabbit hole.

Jody strokes my hair and starts to talk, telling me a story about her and her son JT. Or I might be dreaming the whole goddamn thing. The truth is somewhere in the middle, the mean, the median, all places foreign to me, the outlier.

There was this time when JT was only a toddler, maybe two years old. He was old enough to have a few sentences in his pocket, all beginning and ending with the word *Mommy*. Jody was working two jobs, cashier at the local supermarket and part-time, seasonal telemarketer for a heating oil company. Both gigs were minimum wage, and both gigs were never enough. Jody was just another Bob Cratchit, and everyone else was an Ebenezer.

JT didn't need a crutch but had a nasty case of conjunctivitis diagnosed by the free clinic. Jody was supposed to put an antibiotic ointment in his eyes. Her insurance paid for only half the prescription.

She thought administering it was going to be easy. She was Mommy, and he would trust her. She would explain to him that he needed the medicine to get rid of the red and itch and sick, and his eyes would be all better and she wouldn't have to take any more shifts off work, wouldn't have to stay home another night.

JT didn't listen, didn't trust her. He shouted, "Nononono!" and he screamed and cried, gumming up his eyes worse. He kicked and punched, and he blocked his eyes with his pebble-sized fists.

I'm falling deeper into the well, but I'm still listening to her story. I hate that word, *story*. But we knew that already. So this is Jody's story that is not a story, and during the telling, Jody's voice changes into my voice briefly, and then changes back to her voice, and then a child's voice. It's the kid's voice that frightens me, fills me with dread, as if nothing is scarier than a child.

Jody tried bringing JT into his bedroom. She had him watch her patiently put the medicine into a stuffed animal's eyes. Jody tried consoling and soothing and hugging and petting and kissing. At least, that's what she remembers happening before the drinking, before the inevitable shame and regret. She remembers the trying.

She tried and failed. It was the failure that egged her on. If she couldn't even get her kid to take this most benign of medicines, how could she possibly do this doomed kid any good?

She took a break, had a few drinks, and then a few more. She tried giving the medicine to JT again, and he still resisted with tantrums. Jody yelled at JT. Told him to stop it. Stop the crying. Stop the fucking crying! Stop moving! She scooped up her wailing son, the one with the brown straight hair just like hers, and laid him on his back, on the rug that needed to be vacuumed. Stop it, JT! Listen to me! I am your mother! She sat over him, on him, holding his squirmy arms against his sides with her knees. She was trying. And yelling. Still she couldn't get the medicine in his eyes. JT squeezed and clamped his eyes closed, and they wouldn't open. The medicine smeared all over his cheeks. She only had enough ointment, the minimum for his proper dosage. She couldn't waste any, couldn't afford to pay for another prescription. She couldn't miss any more work this week.

Jody's hand gently strokes my head. And I'm still here, or there, at the bottom of the well, but I can see everything. JT's bedroom scene plays out in front of my closed eyes. I see everything and know everything, and everything is happening right now.

Right now, Jody picks JT off the floor and places him into his crib with a gentleness that she's not feeling. JT is in a time-out. Jody throws the small and expensive medicine into and through the wall. The hole in the sky-blue paint bleeds red. Jody swears and yells and bellows and pulls out her hair. He's going to take the medicine, and he's not leaving the room or eating or playing or fucking doing anything ever again until he does. Jody yells louder than she thought possible. She knows she's out of control and that she's not a good person; she's not Bob Cratchit. She wants another drink. The yelling isn't working; it's only making her hate herself more, if that's possible, but there's some part of her that has to yell more, to make him cry, to make him know she's serious, to make him listen even if he'll hate her for the rest of his life (why should she be the only one?). So she yells and screams, and JT isn't crying anymore. He stands in his crib, wide eyes and blank expression, a small totem to silence.

If this were a story, it'd be the worst kind, the one without an end. We're all there in that bedroom, the one with baby blue walls. Jody cries until the paint and plaster peel away, exposing the studs, the rotting skeleton of the apartment building. JT stares out at no one, at everyone, at me, and he doesn't blink and he won't blink.

We're all there, in that room. A fire erupts, and the remorseless orange flames will burn everything. Me. And you too.

TWENTY-FOUR

I woke up in Jody's lap. She was asleep too, slouched and head slumped into her chest, hair fallen in front of her face, a sleeping position right out of the narcoleptic's handbook, a position I like to think I've perfected. She gave it an amateur's attempt. She'll wake later with a crick in her neck and a laundry list of regrets.

I stood up without disturbing her, without wiping my drool off her thigh, and I watched her breathe. If she had woken up before I left, I don't know what I would've said. Leaving was so much easier without having to say anything.

I say I woke up, but even when fleeing the apartment I wasn't fully awake. The fog hadn't burned off. My thoughts and decisions occurred at a Bronze Age pace. I called a cab and came straight here, to the Wellness Center, instead of going home and cleaning myself up. For some reason, not wanting to be late for my therapy appointment was the highest priority for the foggy me.

I am late, though, and coming here was a mistake, a mistake I keep repeating. I carry with me an aura of stench, a potent mix of vodka, sweat, and sex. But, hey, we're all friends here. My compadres are already seated in the circle (minus one Gus, of course), journals on their laps and pens in hand, so eager to please someone else in the name of self-improvement.

I pull up a chair. The circle widens around the force of my antigravity, and they curl their collective noses at me. It wasn't something I said.

Dr. Who gives me my journal, and the circle pretends not to watch. The weight of the notebook in my hands is oppressive. It's a B-grade responsibility that I no longer want. He tells me that today's journal assignment is open-ended, to do or write or draw whatever I want, but I'll have to explain whatever it is I chose to do.

Nice. The lazy quack isn't even giving the directionless a direction today. I think about drawing the good doctor's violent demise at the hands of a zombie horde, but that's too obvious and campy.

Not in the mood or condition for deep thought, I think about settling for a catchphrase. I open the notebook, and my words from last week, the ones I ate, the ones I rewrote at the doc's request are still there. *It's my fault. It was always my fault.* They've been circled in red ink. Dr. Who and his frigging circles.

I turn pages quickly, letting my fingers do the running. On the top of a clean white page, I write in large block letters:

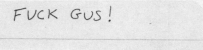

I scribble it out, turning the angry letters into unrecognizable loops and blobs of ink, my personal Rorschach test. Instead of filling the page with my signature or the names and symbols of my favorite punk bands like I did when I was in high school, I continue the scribble-doodle on the perimeter of the page. I stay outside the margins. The living sum of the chaotic swoops and swirls is an ink frame for a blank page. That's probably appropriate and as meaningful as can be expected.

Of course, I'm going to ruin it by writing something inside the frame.

I try this:

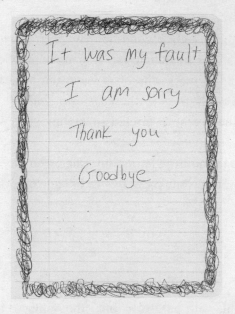

I center everything in the scribble-frame. The new words have built off the old ones. These words are pins waiting to be knocked down. But those phrases, the ones I would've lamely offered Jody were she awake when I left, they decrease by one word. Four, three, two, one. Zero. I didn't do that purposefully. I'm a poet, and I didn't know it.

I can't show this to anyone, but I want to know what the loss of words represents. Am I losing something more with each guess? Does it mean I would've said all four phrases in descending order, or am I just supposed to choose one, an either-or situation?

Maybe those phrases, or the choice of phrases, are what Gus would say to me if he were here. Maybe it's what he'll say to me when I find him. I stare at the words and marvel at their secret double life, at how they exist in my maybe-past and my maybe-future.

"Mark? Hey, Mark? Are you awake?"

Dr. Who taps my shoulder like a woodpecker. Those birds have always creeped me out with how they maniacally smash their faces into trees.

I brush his hand off my shoulder, swivel my head like I'm an owl, which is a proper bird, and Christ, I'm caught midsnore. It's a loud, uvula-rattling snore too, like I'm choking on my own esophagus. There're few things more embarrassing than being caught snoring. The snoring fool always gets the cheap laughs. The snoring fool is always vulnerable.

"Yeah, doc, I'm awake. I'm practicing my Bigfoot call, using my sinus cavity."

No one in the room laughs at Sir Snore-a-lot. No one else is in the room. Is there anything lonelier than a room full of empty chairs? The circle is empty. There is no circle. The chairs lost their shape, and it feels like an indignity. I try connecting those chair-dots and get lost in an amoeba. I'm still groggy, and the shades of my eyes are slanted and uneven.

"You fell asleep, Mark, and we thought it best not to wake you up."

Can't help but feel like my trusted circle mates abandoned my sinking and snoring ship. The rats!

I opt for the antacid of projected guilt. I say, "You should've got me up. I'm totally embarrassed and can't face those people anymore. So I don't think I can come back here again." I almost ruin it by smiling. Although, the idea of the cat man thinking he is in any way superior makes me want to rip out fistfuls of my beard.

"I'm sorry, Mark. That was inconsiderate of me."

I still have my notebook. It's in my lap and open to a blank page. I lift it and flip through it, and all but one of the pages is blank. The words from last week are still there, inside the red circle. I could ask Dr. Who if he tore out the new page, collected my framed assignment, but I don't think I want to know.

Dr. Who prods with an elongated "Mark" and tries to drag us into the pit of a conversation about me. I stand up on cartoon legs, drawn too skinny, and push my empty journal into his chest.

I say, "I need to change. I need to shower. I need to do both, in any order."

"Do you need to change, Mark? I can't help but notice you said that first."

"I wasn't trying to be deep, doc."

"I'm not saying you were." He stops there. It's an effective technique. I have to fill the negative space with something.

I say, "Well, doc, sure. Change is why I'm here."

Dr. Who takes my notebook and opens it. "I also can't help but think about what you wrote in here last week. About it always being your fault. Do you want to talk about what's your fault, Mark?"

Not really, but I might as well make this, my last night at the opera, a bravura performance. "It was an off-the-cuff thing, doc. Didn't put too much thought into it, really, which was why I crumbled it up."

"You put it in your mouth and swallowed it, too, Mark. That's going a step beyond crumpling."

"Eh, it's crumpling with style."

Dr. Who doesn't say anything, just stares. It's kind of rude.

I say, "Look, I didn't want you to see what I wrote because it was too melodramatic. I only wrote it down the second time because you asked so nicely. When I first wrote it, I guess I was mostly thinking about my on-the-skids relationship with Ellen. How it didn't need to come to this. And yeah, how it was mostly my fault."

"You wrote, 'It was always my fault.' That's a strong statement."

"I only meant it about Ellen. And about this place. Me being here isn't exactly voluntary. If I didn't come to these sessions, Ellen was going to pull the plug on my business."

"She told me her contract idea to get you to come see me, and I advised against it. I'd hoped she didn't go through with it and that you came here on your own."

"What else did she tell you?"

"She loves you and is very concerned about you, Mark. With your business not doing well, she thought you were spending too much time alone, getting depressed, and that you needed some help, or least some people to talk to. How she went about presenting you the idea of group therapy was wrong, but . . ."

"If you say her heart was in the right place, I might rip yours out of your chest." I try to say it like it's an edgy joke between friends, but he winces. "I won't make you talk about it anymore, Mark. I do think you should ask yourself why you wrote it, that second sentence in par tic u lar. I also think you need to accept yourself, the way you are now, and accept that it isn't always your fault. It's not your fault for having narcolepsy, Mark, nor is it your fault for having to experience the difficulties associated with the disorder."

I wonder how much Ellen has told him about my past. Did she tell him about the van accident? Did she tell him about my roommates leaving because of me? Did she tell him about all of my symptoms? Did she tell him about the giant fucking mess the narcoleptic me always makes?

I say, "I know that."

Dr. Who nods, resigned to our finish, then says, "Your cell phone rang while you were asleep."

Happy to be done with the two-bit analysis, I'm ready to focus on who called. Could've been anyone, Detective Owolewa or Ellen, but I know it's Gus just like I know I'm not coming back to the Wellness Center next week or the week after. My hand is afraid to go into my pocket, but I pull it out and bathe in the radioactive glow of the LCD screen.

Okay, it wasn't Gus. I missed a call from Ekat thirty-five minutes ago. She left a message.

I say, "Sorry to be rude, doc, but I need to check this."

"Be my guest, Mark. I'm just going to tidy up." Dr. Who picks up the chairs, rearranges them. I resist the urge to watch and see what he decides is their preternatural shape.

I take a few steps away from the center of the room, toward the hallway door that leads to another, unchartered part of the building. My left leg is asleep and fills with pins and needles, voicing its displeasure at being woken up.

Voice mail. Ekat says, "Hi, Mark. Just checking in, seeing how you're doing, seeing if you heard anything or learned anything more." (I like how she leaves that open-ended, like I'm some half-assed student of what's-going-on?)

"I'm at the gym and going straight into work again, but

let's meet for lunch at the L Street Diner tomorrow at twelve. Okay? Aw, shit, my phone's dying. I'll see you tomorrow. Noon! Okay? Bye!"

Maybe it just feels like everything has changed because of my afternoon with Jody and what she said about Gus, but Ekat sounded measured, rehearsed. A bad actor on a worse soap opera.

I call her back, and her voice mail picks up after four rings. I leave a message: "We need to talk. Preferably before noon tomorrow."

I call her bar, the Pour House. I tell the hostess a quick and hokey sob story. I'm Ekat's brother, back in town for a couple of days, and I want to surprise her tonight. I'm so caring and fun. I ask what shift she's working, and I ask her to keep my arrival hush-hush. The hostess has a voice filled with helium. She laughs and says that she didn't know Ekat had a brother. I tell her I know, people are funny with the secrets they keep. She goes away, then comes back quickly and tells me that Ekat isn't scheduled to work tonight and doesn't think she switched with anyone as the downstairs bar is already covered. I thank her and hang up.

Behind me, Dr. Who takes my old chair. I think of it as mine although I can make no proprietary claim on it. My chair is the last one to be placed and stacked with the others, up against the far wall.

Dr. Who surveys his chair monument and claps his hands. Another job well done. He turns to me and says, "So, Mark, I'm probably not going to see you next week, am I?"

I have to hand it to him. He's a perceptive son of a bitch. I pull out a cigarette and put the stick in my mouth, between my teeth like it's a cigar, only it's not a cigar.

I fade across the room to the front door, thinking my broken-glass smile is enough of an answer for him. But then I stop at the door. I do have something to say to Dr. Who, even if all the words aren't really meant for him. I need the practice, because I'm so far from perfect.

"This isn't your fault, doc." I'm careful to enunciate and project. We all want to be so goddamned dramatic and important. We all want the long, slow goodbyes. "It was my fault. I am sorry. Thank you. Goodbye." I don't stumble over any of the words, but I sound like I'm reading unpleasant news.

TWENTY-FIVE

I leave the Wellness Center with a false sense of dignity and hangover intact. I apply inhaled tobacco and feel worse, but at least I'm feeling something. A dying bumblebee of a taxi stops for my flailing hand, the hand with a plan: home and then to Ekat's. The cab sulks down D Street, quick detour onto West Second, then onto Broadway and to my building, where it abandons me.

I'm not on speaking terms with my office, and I head directly upstairs. The walk through my living room is a horror movie, and I watch it through my fingers, hiding my eyes from the scary and icky scenes. The kitchen isn't any better, but I'm hungry, and I eat a can of beef ravioli. The pasta pockets of processed meat taste like cigarettes.

I add the red-stained bowl to the slag heap in the sink.

Tomorrow, I promise myself, there'll be a big clean. Or maybe the day after tomorrow. It'll get done someday. Procrastination is a form of optimism. That's me, Mr. Sunshine and Lollypops.

This is only supposed to be a pit stop, but I'm winding down, Pavlov's reaction to my environment. Turning on the TV and getting lost on my couch is a concept rapidly gaining appeal. I can't let that happen. I flee into the bathroom and shut the door. The couch is the real boogeyman in my living room.

I peel out of my clothes, the scrub pants sticking to hair and other more fleshy parts of my lower half. I shower with the water scalding hot. Hot enough to melt the layers of sweat and stink off me, too hot to just stand there and fall asleep. Postshower, the razor sprints a few laps around my neck, tripping when I nod out for a microsecond and cutting the skin on the lower left side of my Adam's apple. Blood bullies through the toilet paper patch, but I'll live.

I dig out a mostly clean set of shirt/pant/tie combo. I cut off my hospital bracelet but leave on the rubber band Ekat gave me. I don't usually accessorize. I'm all dressed up with nowhere to go, and it's dark outside, darker than I expected.

Before leaving I do stop in my office. In the top drawer of my desk is the gun-shaped cigarette lighter. Now that it has long out-lived my friend George's gag, and George himself, the novelty gun doesn't seem so funny. It's ugly and dangerous even if it isn't the real thing. But Eddie's attack leaves me feeling like I need some form of protection, even if it's a placebo.

I jump into another cab for a quick ride to Ekat's. The cabbie is in no rush. I'm anxious because I'm running out of time. He drives and talks and breathes slowly, a tree sloth with a license.

It gets worse with buses beaching themselves in our path and people dripping off curbs and wandering into the street like some mutant breed of pedestrian lemmings. It's a goddamn animal kingdom out here when I just want to go five quick blocks. Everyone needs to be faster and more efficient. Don't they realize we're all running out of time?

After the epic half mile, I get out on the corner of I and Fifth. It's considerably cooler out, but I'm still sweating. I limp to Ekat's building. Her lights are on. Front windows are open and the blinds down. She must be home.

If nothing else, I have a new apartment to haunt. My cell phone is a dead weight in my jacket pocket. Instead of being the someone knocking at the door, I crouch under her front window and call her cell. It rings from somewhere inside her apartment, and she's not answering it.

Soon after her phone quits its digitized blats, there's a rush of commotion, focused and ambitious footsteps and the jingle of a fistful of keys. Her soundtrack moves toward the front window, toward me, and mixes with the opening and closing of her interior door.

I back away from her window and duck into the alley. Not a very good hiding spot if she happens to walk in this direction. Someone flip a coin. The front door closes, and the aural specter of her footsteps float up I Street, away from me. I've always been lucky.

I poke my head out of the alley and watch her walk away. Ekat wears tight jeans with an iPod tucked into her back pocket, a dark (maybe black) T-shirt, and a baseball hat. Her wooden-heeled shoes clack against the pavement. She has a large black bag slung over her shoulder.

I stretch out the rubber band on my wrist, momentarily savoring and teasing a memory that I know isn't real. Then I follow her.

She walks like she doesn't want to look back, only forward, so I'm not too concerned about being spotted. She won't hear me with those earphones taking root. Despite my earlier success with tracking Jody, walking in pursuit of someone isn't exactly my forte. Walking isn't my forte. The thing is, I'm still sore all over, one big bruise, grinding through every step.

I push my pace to where it can go, which isn't very far. I've dropped back more than a block now. Slow and steady won't win this race. My knees are swelling, and tight bands of pain constrict and squeeze, yielding less flexibility. The popping noises don't fill me with confidence either.

Maybe the Pour House hostess was wrong about tonight's work schedule. Maybe Ekat forgot something at home, didn't have time to answer her phone, and is going to catch the 9 bus and head into work. The unlikely scenario becomes less likely as she hits the corner of I and East Broadway. Instead of waiting at the bus stop, she takes a right and disappears.

I'm light-years behind her, warpless, and without any wormholes or loose change in my pockets. This is a mistake. I should've knocked on her door, confronted her. If she jumps into a cab or ducks into a store while I'm still stuck snail-trailing toward Broadway, I'll have no idea where she went or whom she's meeting. All I know is that I have the not-so-subtle feeling our cute lunch-to-be at the L Street Diner is a fantasy, one that was supposed to be easy for me to believe.

I climb Kilimanjaro, and I'm finally around the corner onto

Broadway. I turn right at the Hub and try to see everything at once but see nothing instead. Too many cars and people and buildings. I get a touch of vertigo, which is enough to twist my feet and spiral my head. I stumble into a parked car, then lean against it with my head covered like I'm counting in a game of hide-and-seek. It's so easy to get lost in the great wide open.

Ready or not, I pick up my too-heavy head and push off the car, leaving handprints on the roof. Mark was here. And Ekat's still there, walking down East Broadway, only half a block away. I didn't lose her, not yet. She has slowed from her previous Olympic record pace, floating along, looking left, toward the street or across the street. I look too, although I won't know what it is when I'll see it.

Ekat stops and turns around. I keep walking, but my heart loses its rhythm, switching to some experimental beat John Cage might dig. Ekat jogs quickly up the sidewalk but isn't looking ahead, isn't looking at me. Her view is fixed low and toward the street. Did she drop something?

She stops and opens a door belonging to a car that I can't see because it's just one of a long line of parked cars, each bumper growing and attaching to the next, a segmented snake of chrome and glass. Ekat disappears into the snake.

The car she climbs into has its lights on and attempts to break free from the curb and pull out onto East Broadway. I can't tell the make. It's a sedan, maybe Japanese. I step off the sidewalk and detour between the parked cars.

The traffic light behind me is a confident and regimented green. A steady stream of cars splits the rows of brownstones and spills downhill, through the I Street intersection. The collected wattage of the passing headlights only illuminates the rears of other cars and leaves me in the dark.

Whoever is driving Ekat won't be able to pull out and join the club right away, but they won't be stuck there forever. I need a ride.

I'm in the street now, walking along the row of parked cars, heading back toward the intersection and away from Ekat, hoping she or her driver doesn't see me. My big paw is out and up, begging for one more cab ride. I try to watch her car inching out of its spot and the passing traffic at the same time. I can't lose sight of either. Two days later a cab pulls over for me. I crash-land into its backseat. The cab rocks and sways with my aftershocks.

"Easy, fella," the cabbie says, and he's the same mound of polyester who dropped me off on I Street ten minutes ago. He doesn't say anything, is too polite to point it out. I'm sure he's happy to see me.

I say, "Follow that car."

"I'm not supposed to do that." His voice is small and light, coming through too many soft filters. Hc talks like he's talking to himself. Maybe he is.

"I'm a private investigator and follow that car," I say, mustering as much authority as I can. The baggage of the line's history weighs me down.

He sighs. I've ruined his evening. "What car? There're millions of them out here."

I've lost sight of Ekat's ride. I didn't see it pull out. Shit. I jam my head, shoulder, and arm through the opening in the Plexiglas partition that separates the front seat from the back. Through his scratched and dirty windshield is a night sky of brake lights, the red refracting through the imperfect glass, twinkling auras that aren't really there.

There's the empty spot in the row of parked cars. Then, up ahead, one-two-three four cars away is the sedan. I think that's it. It is. It has to be.

I say, "That car! The Lexus. It just pulled out. See it?"

He turns his head left, away from the jackpot car, and says, "I see it. I see it."

"Tell me: which car am I talking about? I want to make sure you and me are crystal, as in clear."

He says, "That one," and waves his hand noncommittally at the windshield. Of course, it's that one. "Sit down, now, please. Sit down."

I don't know if he's following the right car, but I don't want to press my luck so hard that I stub it out in the ashtray. I give up on further verification attempts. As recompense, there are complications. I might be stuck here, in the Plexiglas partition. Actually, there's no might-be about it.

"You sit back down, or I'm stopping this cab." He rapidly repeats the sentence under his breath. Everything needs to be said twice.

"I'm stuck, chief, but I'll get out. You just keep watch on that car." I pull back, and there's no budging. The partition framing is wedged under a shoulder blade on one side and a sore rib on the other. I lean forward, bury my palm in the marsh of the front bench seat, push, and sink up to my wrist in damp pleather and foam. With what little leverage I can manage, I twist my head and shoulder, adding some torque. Torque is good until the pressure on my neck and across my shoulders rapidly climbs into a shrieking-pain range, but then I pop out and land on the backseat.

He says, "Stop doing that! Stop moving around!"

I say, "It's okay. I'm all right."

The cabbie waves me off again, then his hand panics and quickly returns to a ten o'clock position on the steering wheel. He says something else, out of one of the sides of his mouth, but I don't hear it.

I say, "So what's your name?"

The cabbie grunts, but I don't hear a name. He keeps it to himself, hoards it like his name is the last piece of gum in the pack.

My vantage point sunk down in the backseat is terrible, and I can't really see anything out of that windshield. I don't see Ekat's car, assuming the car I pointed out is hers. We turn left down L Street and head toward the waterfront area.

He says, "Do you know where they're going?"

"If I knew that—"

He interrupts, his voice as shrill as a whistling teakettle. "I know that. I mean, do you know if they're going far?"

I say, "Not far," although it should be clear to all involved that I have no idea.

I sit back. Fatigue rushes in. It's a gas that forever expands and fills my vacuum. I think the sleeps have been occurring more frequently today because of the beating I took the other night. My body is pleading with me to stop, to reboot, to heel, to quit, to do the time warp again.

The cabbie says, "I'm not supposed to leave Boston."

I look out my window, and I'm not on L Street anymore. I

must've winked out like the flickering light in the dashboard. He's about to pay a toll at the Ted Williams Tunnel. The tunnel mouth is up ahead, bright, open wide, and no cavities. Is Ekat going to Logan Airport? East Boston?

I say, "I've got enough cash on me to make it worth your while. I promise."

The cabbie talks under his breath again, running through his personal list of worst-case scenarios: I'm a psycho or a stalker and I'm going to kill everyone, or I am who I say I am and I'm following the psycho stalker who is going to kill everyone, or me and the folks in the other car are all psychos and we're going to make him pull over in some secret lair of psychos and we'll all kill him over and over again. He fixates on this last possibility. He doesn't feel very safe.

And I agree, he shouldn't be feeling safe. Safety is the big lie. I'm not going to tell him that, though. Instead, in an effort to alleviate some of his agita, I pull out my PI license and drop it onto the front seat.

I say, "You'll be fine, pal. I think." I have to laugh at that. He doesn't, so I continue, veering into cab-as-confessional mode. "Now, listen. I have narcolepsy, which means I can fall asleep at any moment and usually do. It's generally a given that I'll nod off in a car. Just wake me up when we get there, all right? I won't be cranky, I promise."

While waiting for his response, I lean back on the seat and imagine all manner of drivers for Ekat's mystery ride. Every mystery driver has Gus's face.

While waiting for his response, I lean back on the seat, and the passing tunnel lights strobe across my face, push against my closed eyelids. I'm in and out of the light and dark so quickly I wonder if I look different, if I change under the passing lights. I need to change.

While waiting for his response, I lean back on the seat and notice that the cab is stopped. I look out the windows. A mostly flat and empty space with some scattered tall and skinny poles dangling weak dewdrop lights. There are no buildings because they uprooted and left, running away with someone, maybe even the spoon. Never did like the spoon. Always doing shit behind my back.

Wait, wait. I shake my head, yawn, and scratch my beard. Sometimes waking is as complex as a Rube Goldberg machine, one with too many unpredictable and moving parts, and a mouse-trap that never seems to work. I press my forehead against the cool glass of the cab window and look outside again. Upon further inspection, I realize we're idling in a sprawling parking lot that has more white lines and empty spaces than cars. It doesn't look like a Logan Airport lot or terminal.

I say, "Where the hell are we?"

"Wonderland."

He says it again, presumably to ensure that at least one of us is listening.

TWENTY-SIX

Wonderland. I'm a dreaming and damaged Alice and the Mad Hatter at the same time. Off with my head, please.

I roll down my window, smell a different-yet-familiar mix

of low tide and exhaust, and I believe the cabbie. We're at Wonderland, the dog-racing track in Revere. A couple hundred or so feet away is the red, white, and blue club house signage for the track, with its sleek, muscular, and muzzled dog floodlit and flanked by American flags.

Wonderland's days are numbered, just like its dogs. The voters of Massachusetts passed a referendum banning greyhound racing. The track is in its seventy-fifth and final season of operation.

The track and the city of Revere are just five miles north and east of downtown Boston, but it might as well be five thousand. While Revere is almost as old as Boston, it has none of the fabled charm or cachet of Ye Olde Town. Revere's reputation fair or not is of blight, sprawl, and decay. For many Bostonians, Revere and the whole East Boston area is an urban caricature that never fails to make us feel better by comparison. A mythical place of exaggerated crime where the people have accents worse than ours. A place most of us see only from the window of an airplane landing at Logan.

The cabbie rolls my window back up for me. What a guy.

I say, "I haven't been here in over a de cade. Me and my buddy George would come here when we didn't have enough money or gas to drive down to Foxwoods. We'd always pick the long shots and lose." I don't know why I'm reminiscing with the cabbie. For some reason, it feels like it was important enough to say out loud: the old-and-improved me was once here, and he had a real live friend named George.

"There's your car, Mr. PI. You can reach out and touch it if you want."

What an odd thing to say. I pry my stare away from the club-house entrance and its glowing Americana and wearily survey the row of parked cars to our left. Just outside my door is the Lexus. We're parked perpendicular to it, and we make a bulky *T* together. This is good news, and I might celebrate by making *T* the letter of the day. It might not be Ekat's car, but it is the one I wanted him to follow.

I say, "Don't need to touch it, but that's the one. Well done, my good man."

Buoyed by my praise, he says, "I hung back a few rows until they walked inside."

"How long ago was that? How many is they?"

The cabbie's hands still grip the wheel, and he doesn't turn around to talk. "Ten minutes ago. There were two people: a man and a woman." His voice is a breathy sigh, like he's angry or disappointed with me. Like I'm not giving him enough credit or enough attention. You can't please everyone.

"What'd the man look like?"

"Didn't get a great look. I was too far away. But I thought he looked younger."

"Younger?"

"Younger than you."

Gus looks younger than me. Him being Ekat's mystery driver is a notion that has progressed past the hunch stage. I say, "Aren't we all." The words aren't right, but the sentiment is legit. I add, "All right, good to know, chum. Thanks. Really, I appreciate it." I slide across the bench seat, ready to duck out.

He says, "When I first pulled in, I thought you were awake." He stops there, at a place where neither of us is comfortable.

I shrug my shoulders and say, "Sorry?" A one-word question and apology.

"You asked if I was married and if I had any friends." He doesn't turn around to talk to me. His words bounce off the windshield and never fully recover their volume.

"I must've been asleep. I don't remember asking that. Happens to me all the time, unfortunately."

The cabbie nearly yells, "I know! I know you were asleep. I turned around and saw your eyes closed. I snapped my fingers in front of your face, and you kept talking. It was weird. I didn't like it. You said we should go inside, hang out, have a few drinks, have some fun or something."

The narcoleptic me is as lonely and hard up for companionship as the awake me. I say, "I'm a little busy tonight. How about a rain check on the boys' night out?"

With his right hand, the cabbie taps and touches the dashboard instruments in a completely random yet orderly manner. He shifts from park into drive and then goes through the touching ritual again before stopping and flexing his fingers around the wheel. We all have our problems.

He says, "No. I don't want to anymore."

Did I hurt his feelings, or did I give him the willies? Which one of us is the lonely freak here?

Time to move. I hop out of the cab. His front tinted window opens only a couple of inches. I can't see his face. I slide him forty dollars, which includes one hell of a tip. He gives me my PI license back. I have a business card palmed, and I think about flicking it into his cab and insisting that he and I go out for the drinks that the narcoleptic me promised. But I don't.

I'm too slow or too something, and he drives away.

I'm alone in the parking lot. Used betting slips and wrappers scuttle over the pavement like crabs. I run my hand along the cool metal of the Lexus. It's real. Touching it isn't a bad suggestion after all.

TWENTY-SEVEN

It only costs me two of my crumpled and dwindling dollars to get into Wonderland. What a bargain.

There's a bar on my right when I first walk in, with a track-level viewing area that's mostly empty. I walk up a cement ramp to the main concourse. ATM machines and concession stands flank the row of betting windows. Two out of every three windows are open and occupied. There're enough people here to designate them a crowd.

A couple of retirees wearing faded and threadbare Wonderland jackets hand out free racing programs and personal observations on your chances of getting all kinds of lucky. The observations are free too.

Smoking isn't allowed, but the place smells like stale tobacco. Old betting slips, the dead skin of the afternoon races, are everywhere. The remnants of the ticker-tape parade for the desperate cover the counters, the concourse floor, and the ramps. A group of loud teens trades shoulder punches and picks through the discarded slips, looking for winners. They won't find any. The speakers crackle with a voice from out of time and out of place, announcing to everyone that the next race starts in ten minutes. He says it like the next race might be the last.

I pull my hat over my eyes, not wanting to be seen by Ekat or Gus before I see them. Where do I look first? There's club house and grandstand track seating. TV carrel seating as well. I'm going to try the grandstand first. Popcorn and peanut shells crunch under my feet.

It's an overcast night, and the grandstand is only a quarter full. Everything is different than it was when I was last here. Private tables, each with its own hanging television. The people already seated drink and eat and stare at the TVs, although there's only a white text scroll on a blue background of the next race listing being broadcast.

There's a small stir in the grandstand as handlers lead the greyhounds down the track. The dogs' legs are as thin as knives. Their skin stretches across overbred muscles and tendons like drum heads wound too tightly. The dogs have their heads down looking disappointed, defeated already. Maybe running all that distance and ending up in the same damned spot brings them down. Maybe someone told them that the rabbit they chase every night is a fraud.

I leave the grandstand and head into the concourse again, planning on cutting through and wading into the club house. Then I see him. I stutter-step and plow into one of the retirees handing out the racing programs, the one with the Clementine-sized goiter in his neck. He doesn't drop any programs. He says, "You're gonna be the big loser tonight if you don't watch where you're fuckin' goin'."

"I read that in a fortune cookie once."

He laughs, slaps my back, which echoes hollow, and tells me to get the fuck outta here. We're buddies now. I resist the urge to rub his goiter for better luck, and I hide behind the popcorn guy's cart.

Okay. Him. I almost didn't recognize him without his sunglasses. Timothy Carter. I wish I could say he looked nervous, like the dogs were going to be chasing him instead of Frankenstein's rabbit, but he still has that my-shit-tastes-better-than-yours grin, big and bright as a center-stage spotlight. His eyes are little black rocks, like bird's eyes. Twitchy and all iris. Windows to his soullessness. He should've kept the sunglasses on.

Carter wears a white button-down shirt, sleeves rolled over his pampered forearms. The shirt is tucked into disco-tight khaki pants. He's a goddamn walking mannequin with a beer in each hand.

Hanging off his shoulder is Madison Hall, the wife of the CEO Wilkie Barrack. Hanging off his shoulder is my previous case, the woman I was supposed to follow, the platinum blonde with a thing for lacrosse players.

I look away. I'm staring at an eclipse, and I'm afraid I'll do serious damage if I don't protect myself. I scan the crowd again quickly. Seeing Carter and Hall is an unexpected treat, but where're Ekat and Gus?

The power couple saunters through the concourse, and I stare at her. She isn't the real Madison Hall. She's the other woman that I mistakenly followed. Or the other woman that someone wanted me to follow. It's suddenly hot in here. My heart goes all rubber ball inside the cement walls of my chest.

Carter and faux-Hall stop walking in front of the ramp. She pulls him down to size and says something into the satellite dish of his ear. His awful but younger-than-mine face splits open to let out a wild impersonation of a laugh. He goes down the ramp toward the club house, gliding like the unclean wraith that he is. She struts to a customer service window, hips swinging like a metronome and heels clacking out a message on the concourse cement.

I swap my popcorn man hideout for the hot dog man. Everyone knows you can't trust the hot dog man, so I hide behind a couple of middle-aged women in leather biker jackets who read their race forms and argue about a dog assigned the number five. I follow faux-Hall to the customer service window, and it feels okay because I've had practice following her.

The blonde wears black horn-rimmed glasses that are shaped like the eyes of a cat although we're at a dog track. Her little canary yellow short-sleeved dress ends above the waterline of her knees, and her black shoes have finger-length heels sharp enough to pop balloons upon sight. She opens her black purse and slides something under the customer service window.

The man behind the glass is blurry in the booth's amber lighting. He hesitates to accept whatever she slid under the window, like he's looking at the subject of some fifties B horror movie *It Came from Her Purse!* He does finally pick it up, inspecting her gift and her. He asks a question that I can't hear. She holds up two fingers and grinds the toe of her right foot into the cement.

My human shields leave me, and I don't know if they resolved the great debate over dog number five. I'm not a betting man, anyway.

The customer service agent counts out a seemingly endless stack of bills, then slides the bounty under the glass. Faux-Hall folds the windfall, and I swear that it's too big for her purse, but she fits it all inside and clasps it shut. Maybe it's a circus purse, and I'm the clown who's supposed to crawl inside too.

I teeter, blink, and shake my head, and she's already walking away from the window to the ramp. All right, new plan. I dig into my jacket pocket and make sure my cigarette-lighter gun is still there. Another wave of fatigue threatens to sweep me under. My legs are made out of oatmeal, and my hands tremor and shake, nervous about what I might do or say. I ignore it all and cut her off at the top of the ramp.

She sees me. She adjusts her cat glasses, which I now notice are broken. The left temple is tied to the frame with a wound-up rubber band. She turns, twists on her heels, looking back at the milling and droning crowd of the concourse, surprised that everyone else in the place doesn't share her displeasure that I am here. She's taller than I remember.

I make a gun-tent with the cigarette lighter in my jacket pocket and point it at her. Yeah, like the gun and the rabbit and woman in the blonde wig, I'm a fraud too, pretending to be the hardest of hard guys.

She says, "Is that a gun?"

With my voice coming out from the land of the lost, I say, "Hi, Ekat. It's a gun, and I'm not all that happy to see you. I dig the wig and glasses, though."

TWENTY-EIGHT

We're outside, walking across the parking lot like we're the only two people left in the world. Just us and greyhounds. We phantom away from the club house entrance, away from any windows, she in her blonde wig and me in my hat. I have the urge to pluck and snap the rubber band on my wrist. I keep my hand on the fake gun instead.

My feet are afraid to lose contact with terra firma, so I scrape their bottoms on the gritty blacktop until they throw sparks. Ekat is on my left. She's quiet, only looking ahead. She rubs her arms like she's cold, but she's not cold. It's just something for her to do to pass the time. Time is distance tonight.

We dock underneath one of the giraffe-tall lampposts with a dying bulb that flickers. It uses us to make shadows, but we don't mind. I pull my fake-gun hand out of my pocket and fill it with something truly lethal: a cigarette. The rush of tobacco and nicotine gives me a quick but powerful buzz. Maybe that's just the hum of faulty wiring above or the faulty wiring within.

Ekat leans her back against the light post, and she glows like a blinking traffic light. Yellow. A warning to slow down. I don't need the warning. I know only slow.

"I lied about liking your wig. It couldn't be more obvious. Might as well be wearing a flashing siren on your head."

She says, "As obvious as that lump in your coat pocket? I know it's not a real gun. You hate guns. You told me that night in my apartment."

I go back to my pocket, but my hand and cigarette lighter are clumsy and forget who is supposed to lead. They've lost the motivation for the scene.

Ekat continues, "Don't you remember? We talked about your job, and I asked if you carried a gun. You said other than the cigarette lighter your friend gave you, you've never owned one, never used one, never even held one."

Don't remember saying it, naturally, but it's the truth. Nothing like a little gun talk among friends. I say, "I lied. I'm so untrustworthy. I have lots of guns. Big nasty ones that'd chew a hole through your lamppost."

"You don't have a gun, and I just want you to know that I came out here with you anyway." Ekat talks in a quavering, the-jig-is-up voice. "So how much do you know?"

"Enough to be here, out in the parking lot of Wonderland with you, Marilyn." She doesn't say anything. Goodbye, Norma Jean. I try a couple more prompts. "Enough to know you're responsible for the fire and that you guys played me like the long-shot fleabag in the sixth race."

"Oh, that's not it, Mark, and it's so much more complicated than that. I am sorry, Mark, so sorry, but I can explain everything."

"Don't know what name is on your fake license and credit card, but the rubber band on your glasses is a nice touch. You're incognito, but with that dash of perky personality. You're a reckless renegade, but endearing too, right?"

She doesn't hear my last bit as she talks over me, burying me in words. She says, "It was never supposed to be like this, get to this point, get to any point. We didn't know what to do. Timothy was out of control, and I wanted out. Me and Gus, we set up the whole cheating-wife surveillance thing with you, but not to purposefully embarrass or harm you. I mean, we didn't really know you then, but it wasn't ever about you, I swear. It was about him. About Timothy. It was a kind of . . . I don't know; I'm not saying any of this right." Ekat pauses, rubs her forehead, looks away, at her feet, and talks to her shoes. They won't talk back. "We were desperate, and we thought we could get something on him, blackmail him, get some leverage, or just get his attention at least, get him to listen to us and to show he wasn't totally in control of everything, that he definitely wasn't in control of us, but it didn't work. It wasn't smart, and we didn't think it out. We made it all worse, I know. We screwed up. It was a panic move, but we had to try something. We didn't want anyone to get . . ."

Her words are moving at the speed of light when I'm still stuck in the dark. Need to try and organize things a little. "How do you know Carter?"

It should be an easy question to answer. She looks back up at me, her face hiding in the wig's schizophrenic, on-again-off-again shadow. She says, "He went to high school with Gus and me."

Her answer ignites an irrational and complex mushroom cloud of rage. I don't know if I'm Mr. Boiling Point because of how they're using me, or if I'm school-yard jealous because the cool kids, Ekat and Gus, choose an ass-hat like Carter as a friend over me. Whatever. I'm usually such an easygoing cat, too, but now I'm ready and willing to go all lake-of-fire, see red, crack the earth, and spit blood. Yell, bellow, froth at thine mouth. I am the god of hellfire.

"Fuck me! And you! Fucking unbelievable! Getting owned by a goddamned high school clique. A mini–class reunion."

mark

"So let me get this straight; you three amigos had your cute little identity fraud game going, using people like Jody and Aleksandar . . ."

mark listen to me

". . . giving them fake IDs and stolen cards because they're not from the south shore, they're more suited for the dirty work, right?"

no mark that's not it really it isn't

"So you kept such good mules, they'd get big cash advances, you guys got your cut, and you got your adventure, your fucking jollies and goose bumps, and if your bagmen were ever caught, who would believe them over you, right?"

please stop and listen to me stop it

"Then you guys decided it was over, maybe you got bored with it, thought identity theft was too bourgeois, and then it was burning-down-the-house time . . ."

stop it stop it stop it

". . . you know that song, sung by that guy with the big white jacket with big white shoulders, and he also sang something about asking yourself how you got here or how you go there howyougothere . . ."

"Stop it!" Ekat has my lapels wrapped inside her fists. She shakes me like a burned-out lightbulb, listening for the filament, testing to see if I'm broken. She's strong, and the wig remains on her head despite the violence.

I pry her hands off me and gently push her away, back to the safety of the lamppost. I say, "I stopped it."

I feel like low tide, so far from shore and with nothing ebbing or flowing, dead water. My hat and half-spent cigarette are on the ground next to my feet. I didn't see them get there. I pick both up and try to remember everything I said. I hope it was good.

"Where'd you get the credit cards?"

Ekat leaves the post and stands close enough to slap me. She puts her hands across her chest, instead, holding herself back. She says, "Timothy and I stole the cards from health clubs and hotel gyms and bars. It was always so quick and easy. We'd pluck them from wallets and purses left in open lockers. Most of the time the marks wouldn't know the cards were gone until days, sometimes weeks, later."

"And Gus made the fake IDs to match the credit cards, then."

"Right. He'd been making fake IDs for people since high school."

"He's so talented."

"We were smart with the cards. Didn't mess around online or too close to home. We went to racetracks and casinos, all on the East Coast, and only used the cards to get cash advances."

I say, "Like tonight."

"Gus made me a new fake ID for each card, using a different picture, each with a slightly different look."

She pauses. She primps her wig, then sighs again, dropping her arms to her sides, hands slapping against her legs. And I know that being a different person each month, making up stories for the women in the IDs and living in those stories, was the thrill, was why she did it.

This is the part where I'm supposed to commiserate, to say that I understand, that I'm like her, that I want to be somebody else too. But I'm not giving in. Not this time.

She says, "The system was foolproof. We'd be practically anonymous in the big casinos and racetracks, especially the old racetracks. You'd be surprised how many don't even have security cameras.

"And I assumed it was just us the whole time. I had no reason to think otherwise. I had no idea that Gus was outsourcing, as he called it, giving cards and IDs to Jody and Aleksandar. I didn't find out about them until a few months ago, at the beginning of this summer.

"I was in Gus's apartment, just having a few beers with him after work, and I saw an ID he'd messed up lying on the top of his trash can. The picture wasn't mine. It was of some woman I'd seen hanging out at Gus's bar. I thought maybe he was just practicing new IDs or something, but when I confronted him about it, he told me who Jody was and what he was doing. He tried to laugh and shrug it off, of course. He's always gotten his way because everyone loves him, but I was having none of it. I lost it, threw the ID at his face, took off, and didn't answer his phone calls.

"A couple days later, Gus came back to my apartment and apologized for not telling either me or Timothy about his outsourcing. He said that he only picked Jody and Aleksandar because he knew them, they were good guys who were struggling, and he wanted to help them out. He figured they would be easy to keep track of because they lived in the same building. But he agreed that getting the other two involved was a bad idea; the extra profits weren't ever going to amount to more than a supplement to our incomes, and it wasn't worth the added risk of them being caught and pointing their fingers at us. All of which should've been obvious from the get-go. But you know Gus, Mr. Social Butterfly, has to be friends and doing deals with everyone.

"Then Gus told me about his first conversation with Timothy and how he promised that he wouldn't make any more IDs for them. Timothy didn't take it well; he exploded and said that Gus had doomed us all, ruined our lives. He even accused Gus of being jealous of his new career, even of trying to set him up because he was using Aleksandar his boss's driver."

"New career?"

"It took Timothy countless tries to pass the bar, and he's only been working for Financier and the CEO for less than a year. This was his big break."

"What'd he do before that?"

"Odd jobs. Stuff to the pay the law school bills."

"And by *odd* you mean *illegal,* I assume. Did he sell drugs like Gus?"

"No, his thing was gambling, running some books for local college kids and law school students. He'd been doing that since we graduated high school, really."

"Right. Okay, to sum up: onetime bookie turned high-powered lawyer was miffed at Gus about Jody and Aleksandar."

"Yes. And after Gus left my apartment, Timothy called Gus back. He was slurring drunk, and he went off on a rant about how his career would be over if anyone found out about this stuff, saying his life would be over. He started talking about doing more than cutting the others loose and that Gus had to help, had to make up for his mistake and show who he was loyal to. Timothy was talking crazy, actually talking about killing those guys. Gus was shocked and horrified and refused to even listen to it.

"Timothy was drunk and upset, and we didn't want to take the threats seriously. But even just to hear him talk about stuff like that had me and Gus completely freaked out."

I say, "I still don't understand where I come in." I look down. Ekat has my jacket's lapels in her hands again. The material is irresistible.

"Gus was a part-time personal assistant for Timothy, one of his many side gigs. Timothy's boss wanted someone to watch his wife for a few nights while he was out of town. The CEO had been hearing rumors about her cheating on him. Gus was going to watch her for Timothy. Keep in mind, this was set up before all the Jody/Aleksandar stuff came out."

Ekat's hands are gone. Her arms are sunken up to the wrist in my jacket, missing and stuck somewhere inside. She says, "Like I said earlier, we didn't know what to do about Timothy's wild threats. We couldn't go to the police. We weren't about to do anything that would get us arrested. So we came up with the fake surveillance idea to blackmail him. Gus knew about you from group therapy. He canceled the surveillance gig with Timothy but recommended you for the job instead, and he went for it."

I say, "You're still not making a whole lot of sense."

She shrugs. It's an honest shrug, too. Her arching shoulders might as well be a big middle finger. And it's now that I know how much trouble, how much danger we're all in. It's worse than that they don't know what they're doing, which is clear. The amazing Technicolor dream-wig, the scams and schemes, the pretending, the lying, all of it means it was never real to them. It was just something to do, something to pass the time. They never thought any of this through. Their getting caught always was (and is) a given, and whom they take down with them, and how, are the only variables.

Her arms sink deeper into my jacket, halfway up her forearms. My jacket is made of quicksand. We're both sinking, and we'll never get out of it. Ekat's face is only a few inches from mine. The brim of my hat tickles her wig.

She says, "Gus pretty much knew the wife was cheating on Timothy's boss. He'd seen other men's clothes in her apartment when picking up and dropping off dry cleaning. So while you were watching me doing nothing out on Newbury Street, Gus was going to tail the CEO's wife and get pictures of her out on the town. You were going to report to Timothy that nothing happened, and Timothy would forward your all's-well report along to the boss.

"Gus was then going to tell Timothy that you'd followed the wrong woman me and show him the pictures he'd taken of Barrack's wife, and then threaten Timothy with going straight to Barrack with his photos and a detailed story about how Timothy, his *new* personal attorney, was actively covering up his wife's infidelities. All of which meant Timothy would lose his precious cushy job and likely his career as his name would be mud in local professional circles if he didn't stop the crazy talk about killing Jody and Aleksandar."

"That almost makes sense."

"It didn't work out that way, though. Obviously. We never dreamed the *Herald* would get and print shots of the CEO's wife out with someone else, and everything blew up in our faces.

"The *Herald* pictures on the heels of your report already put Timothy in hot water with his boss, so we had no leverage to present our blackmail scenario. Gus and I decided not to tell him anything about it. Then after Timothy saw your pictures of me dressed as the wife, he really lost it, called and threatened the both of us. God, the whole blackmail thing, I think it made everything worse."

I say, "Eddie never stalked or threatened you, did he?"

"No. Gus hired you that night to watch me because of Timothy. We were afraid he might try something and figured if Timothy saw you, he might think that you, the PI, knew about him, knew what he was up to, and it would scare him off."

My hands are missing, have sunk inside the sleeves of my jacket as well. It's only fitting. I say, "Gus lied to me." I try not to sound like a hurt lover.

"He had to lie and tell you it was Eddie who threatened me because he didn't want you finding out about the three of us. We didn't mean to do any of this to you, Mark. Really. We both like you, and we're so sorry that you got caught up in everything we did."

We talk faster like it'll help us avoid true contact. Our noses are almost touching. I say, "The fire was set by Carter."

"Yes. Yes."

"How'd he do it?"

"I don't know. I have no idea."

We both sink deeper into my jacket. We'll be part of a fossil site eons from now, and whoever finds us will dream about what it was we said to each other.

"Why are you here with Carter now?"

"He wanted me to come with him. Make sure that I wouldn't talk, that we were still good, that I was still loyal. He wanted to make that one last score; then we'd be done. I was too afraid to say no, afraid of what he might do to me. I had to play along.

When we got here I had to pretend I wasn't scared of him and I was having a good time. I just have to get through this night and figure out what to do next."

"Where's Gus?"

"I don't know."

The lamppost light flickers faster. It has lost patience with us. When the bulb is on, it glows brighter and whiter, and when it's off, the darkness is total. My eyes are starved and greedy for the light.

I ask, "He hasn't contacted you at all?"

"No. Not since the fire."

She's lying. There's some truth mixed in with the lies. There always is. I ask her where Gus is again. Where is he?

She says,

   "I

     don't

       know,

         Mark."

Her sentence stretches out, thins, and fades toward the edges. There's nothing for me to grab on to, and I stumble, waving my arms like no one is paying enough attention to me, then fall. I splash into the empty sea of the parking lot. I'm lost, and I thrash about with arms and legs as dead as wishes that never come true.

Okay, the parking-lot sea is not so empty. Nightmarish leviathans live in these waters, shaking the cowering earth with their tidal movements.

Those goddamn monsters, they swim and fuck and eat and shit in the depths below me; they're always below me, down in the deep, black, and terrible sea.

And those goddamn monsters, they're arguing about me. They whisper through machete-sized teeth because they know I'm listening. I don't speak their language, but I understand they can't decide what to do with me. They weren't expecting me even though I always show up. I'm always here, right here.

Without a consensus, and almost as an afterthought, they open their deep, black, and terrible mouths. Say ahhh. I'm going to be swallowed. It won't be my first time, but someday there will be a last.

Yeah, I'm their Jonah again, but the joke is on them because I don't believe in them or in anything else.

TWENTY-NINE

The leviathans are picky bastards. They chew me up and spit me out again. I don't taste very good.

I lean against the lamppost. I need the support, but I hate this goddamn lamppost and its epileptic bulb, and want to see it all razed and run into the ground. There're no bulldozers lying about, but there is a man standing in front of me with his hands in his pockets. I'm seeing myself through Ekat's eyes. I didn't realize I was losing so much weight. I never realize how much I'm losing.

But that's not right. I'm me. I'm awake enough to know that much. The other me is another guy. He's wearing a similar quicksand jacket, white shirt, loosened tie, and not quite permanently pressed pants. All that stuff could've come out of my closet, except for his lid. On his head is that red-nosed-reindeer porkpie hat of his. It's not the red breast on a robin. It's the piece that doesn't fit the ensemble. Too showy. I'm a fashion expert.

Gus says, "No worries. I've got you covered."

He pulls something out of his pocket. It's not a bag of amphetamines. Part of me wishes it were. He has a cigarette, cradled delicately between two fingers, and he lights its short fuse. He dangles it between us, a stolen watch he wants to sell me.

He can't tease me like that. I'm weak, and I'm buying. Smoke pounds its dirty fists on the walls of my lungs. It's a clove cigarette, and it waters my eyes and corrodes my delicate system. Just what I need.

I say, "I know you and Ekat are the same person. Case solved."

"Well done, Mark. You can go home and get some rest then, right? Give yourself a gold star." Gus laughs, and at me. He's always been laughing at me.

I say, "Or I can go home and give that gold star to Detective Owolewa." Yeah, that makes a bucketful of sense. Christ, I need a rewind button sometimes.

I open my mouth to try and correct myself, but I cough instead. I double over, and my lungs turn inside out. My tenderized ribs make an official declaration of hate for me and threaten to leave their post.

I drop the hipster's clove cigarette to the pavement and don't bother grinding it under my flat foot. Not sure I can lift my leg that high. I croak something that might sound like "Where have you been?" It's not easy turning green.

"I wasn't anywhere, really. In hiding. And sorry I couldn't contact you or . . ."

I walk away from Gus. I have nowhere to go, but I feel better already. I check my watch. It's ten after ten. I don't know how long I was out here talking with Ekat, but I'm missing at least twenty minutes from my evening. I'll never find those minutes either.

Gus nips at my heels. He's simultaneously on my left and right. He says, "I know you're mad at me, and you have every right to be mad at me, Mark. I've screwed up so much, and I know that, and I know that I'm going to pay for it. I've put you in harm's way and I can't make everything perfect, but I can make it better, I promise. But I need a favor. I need your help. I need you to wait until the morning before you go to the police."

It's my turn to laugh at someone. "What happens in the morning?"

"I have a new plan, all right? I'm improvising."

"I'm guessing you do that a lot."

"It's a good plan, simple, not a lot of moving parts, and it's my last plan." Gus grabs my arm, and I stop rolling down the hill.

He holds his hands out in front of him, framing the discussion. He's a frustrated mime. "Ekat and I are going to leave Boston and disappear." He opens his hands with a magician's flourish. Houdini without the chains and appendicitis. "I've got some places we can go to for six months to a year, maybe longer." Gus pauses, waves his magic hands, turning that last sentence into a flock of doves. "It doesn't matter where we go, but we'll leave tonight as soon as she's away from Carter. And then you and the cops can have him." Gus pats my chest twice with the back of his hand. "You'll look like a hero."

"Or an accomplice."

"No, that's not how it'll work." Gus shakes his head. His porkpie hat is a red light. I'm supposed to stop. He says, "Come on, Mark. Follow me." Gus backs away, toward a pod of parked cars. Or is it a gaggle?

I say, "I already have, and got nowhere."

Not sure if he heard me. Maybe I wasn't loud enough. Maybe I didn't want him to hear me. Maybe, even after everything that's happened, I still want to follow him for one more night.

Gus fiddles with his keys while standing next to a yellow vintage car. It's a compact but has long front and back ends. Canvas topped, but I don't think it's a convertible. The make is familiar. I might've owned the Matchbox version when I was a kid. That's assuming I played with Matchbox cars.

"Climb in." He's an action hero sliding into the front seat. The chrome, glass, and steel is a prefitted body glove. I'm not as graceful upon entrance. I groan and creak as I duck my head and bend my arms and legs, like a retired contortionist who was never any good, even in his prime. Me and cars have never quite worked it out.

He says, "What do you think?"

"Of what?"

"The car. Just picked it up. It's a '73 Dodge Dart. Come on, what do you think? I joined an antique auto club too. I couldn't resist. Supposed to go for a group ride next Wednesday. But I'll probably miss it." He runs his hands over the black leather interior and a faded decal of Jesus pasted on the dashboard.

"So far we have Ekat and her wig, you and your seventies mobile and auto club, and your plan to snap your fingers and disappear, and then what? Dine on happiness and shit sunshine for the rest of your lives? What I think is that you every last one of you live in fantasyland, or Wonderland as the case may be.

"But don't mind me. Your car is sweet, man. Did it come with that pack of clove cigarettes?"

Gus laughs, adjusts his hat, then strikes a pose with his arm across the bench seat. "You're a funny guy, Mark."

"Yeah. Hilarious. So what are we and your cherry ride doing now, Fonzie? You gonna take me to the hop, then maybe to Inspiration Point for a little necking?"

"I wish, big fella. We have more pressing matters to attend to." He points out the windshield, and there's Carter's Lexus, three rows away. "We're going to follow Ekat, make sure she gets home safe. For obvious reasons, I don't trust Carter."

"I heard it as he can't trust you. Ekat says you hired Jody and Aleksandar without either of your two high school sweethearts knowing."

I'm real interested to hear Gus's response as I'm thinking about my time sitting on a Broadway bench next to Charlton Heston-loving Rita. As long as her well-dressed man in the big sunglasses is who I think he is, then Carter had been visiting Aleksandar's apartment prior to my fraud surveillance and the fire. Which means Ekat's timeline doesn't jibe with Rita seeing Carter entering Aleksandar's apartment. Something tells me his visits weren't just teatime social calls, either. If Rita is right, Carter knew about the bagmen, Aleksandar at least, all along.

Gus says, "I didn't think it was a big deal. I was just trying to make us a little more money and help a couple of people who were really struggling."

I say, "You're a regular Robin Hood," but he isn't listening to me.

"It was a risk, but I certainly didn't think it was anything sinister, like Carter did. He really thought I was trying to set him up. I had to grovel, get on my knees and kiss his Italian loafers before he would even listen to me. Then all of a sudden he hits me with a crazy scheme to burn down the building and take those guys out."

All right, so Gus and Ekat are both lying to me. I think. It's possible that they're telling the truth, and maybe Carter knew about the bagmen and was completely playing them. Maybe Rita was wrong in her month timeline, and Carter's visits to the apartment occurred only after Gus confessed to using bagmen. Maybe the person Rita saw wasn't Carter. I assumed Carter by her description. Could've been anyone. Could've been Gus.

I say, "You could've stopped Carter, but you didn't."

"We tried, Mark." Gus sings their song about the failed blackmail scheme, hitting all the same notes that Ekat did. I'm getting sick of that tune. He adds, "I screwed up, Mark. What can I say? I fucked up, big time. I never thought Carter would really do it. Why would I ever think he'd go through with something like that? I mean, shit, I've known him forever. To be honest, initially I was more worried he would do something to hurt himself with all of the talk about his new career being his life."

"You could've gone to the police. Aleksandar would still be alive if you did."

Gus drops his head into his chest, soul searching. I don't think he'll find one. His voice goes soft, presumably in honor of the dead. "If I had known any of this was going to actually happen, I would've. I'm going to make it up to Aleksandar's family, somehow."

I laugh. I don't think he takes it well. "You almost believe your own bullshit, don't you?"

Gus wisely doesn't respond.

I say, "You thought Carter was enough of a threat to have me follow Ekat home."

Gus shakes his head. "Well, yeah, in the aftermath of our botched blackmail scheme and Carter's phoned-in threats to knock out our teeth, I thought Carter might be a threat to me or Ekat. I know it'll sound corny, but I also felt really guilty about using you the way we did, and I wanted to make a restitution payment of sorts. Give you an easy, paying gig to ease my conscience and help your wallet. You don't know how close I came to telling you everything about Carter and the fake surveillance that morning in your office, but you seemed a little on edge and I chickened out."

"I'm not buying any of it. Including your putting a price tag on pity."

"What do you think we were doing, then? Really, Mark, why would I have continued to involve you if I actually thought Carter would set the fire? It makes no sense."

"A lot of stuff you and Ekat have done so far makes no sense."

"Touché."

"Why not go to the cops after the fire?"

"Would going to the cops after the fact have changed any of it? I wasn't about to send me and Ekat to jail for Carter."

"But you could let the fire be pinned on an innocent man, right?"

"We're going to fix that, Mark. You tell the cops everything tomorrow. Give them Carter on a platter. And not for nothing, Eddie is a lot of things, but innocent isn't one of them. He'll be fine."

"Eddie isn't fine, won't be fine, never was fine." I pause to breathe and pull the plug on my *fine* perseveration. "Eddie's in jail right now. Did you know—"

Gus interrupts and points out the windshield. "Hey, here they come."

The king and queen of Wonderland promenade arm in arm across the lot. Their smiles sparkle like shattered glass on asphalt.

I say, "They seem to be getting along swimmingly." I watch Gus and wait to see if that designer coolness of his is ever going to melt away.

He says, "She's doing fine, supersleuth."

Carter and Ekat untangle and separate when they reach the Lexus, but no one bows to their left. Ekat pulls a black bag out of the trunk, ducks inside the already started car, and they're off.

Gus starts his obnoxious engine but leaves the headlights off. He says, "Let's give them a twenty-second head start. Do you want to count?"

I don't say anything. That'll learn him.

Gus leans across my chest and opens the door. The déjà vu makes my muscles hurt all over again. He says, "You can leave and go to the police now, if you really want to. I won't stop you. Or you can stay with me and we'll make sure our friend Ekat is okay, and if nothing else you get a ride back to Southie."

I dig under my shirt sleeve and find *our friend*'s rubber band and snap it. Then I shut the passenger door. I say, "Drive. You'll talk about me behind my back if I don't come with you."

We've established that he and Ekat are lying to me, but I don't know to what extent. I'm staying to find out. I'm not staying because he said the word *friend*. Really, I'm not.

Gus rolls across the lot, lagging a few hundred yards behind the Lexus. Optimum distance achieved, Gus turns into a narrator. "I don't need to be right on his tail. He's just going to drop her off at her apartment." He looks at me, and his confident veneer cracks momentarily, showing off a worried, oh-shit-I-can't-stop-what-was-started face. It's the first time tonight that I can almost believe any of what he said might be true.

I relaunch into the ballad of Eddie. I tell him about Detective Owolewa finding my amphetamines and concluding that I was a drug-buying client of Eddie's. I tell him about Eddie staking out Gus's place, Eddie thinking the two of us were somehow setting him up to take the fall for the fire, and Eddie pounding me into shape with a few well-placed but lucky sucker punches and then dumping me on the Zakim Bridge like I was pothole filler.

"Jesus, Mark. I had no idea." Gus takes off his hat and runs his fingers through his not-thinning hair. I could say that I hate him, but I'd be lying to myself again. "I couldn't be sorrier about what he did to you. But I don't care about Eddie. I'm sorry if that sounds callous or if I'm rationalizing, but he isn't a good guy. He's dangerous. Clearly, he's always been dangerous. He treats Jody like shit. I've seen him hit her in the middle of the bar, man. He's no good. It was why I was trying to help her out financially and let her use the cards and IDs. She kept all that ID stuff from Eddie, too. She never told him."

"I know. I already got all that good stuff from Jody." I blush even though Gus has no idea why I would.

"Did you? Nice show. Man, you're good." He laughs, and goddamn me, now I might be blushing at his praise. He adds, "What Eddie did to you is further proof of how dangerous he is."

Gus pays a toll, and the Dart descends into the gullet of the Ted Williams Tunnel. The engine roar echoes off the walls, and it sounds like the tunnel clearing its deep throat. Carter's Lexus is about a quarter mile ahead of us. We're all headed back to Southie. Wonderland is already a million miles behind us.

Gus says, "I know that I've been saying Carter started the fire this whole time, but I don't really know that. He's responsible, don't get me wrong, but who knows? Maybe he went and actually paid Eddie to do it. Carter knew Eddie, talked to him a few times at my bar. Carter knows what Eddie is. For all I know he paid off Jody's crazy friend Rachel. I remember reading somewhere that she was first at the scene, right? Fuck, I don't know. I wouldn't put it past any of them. But that's not up to me to figure it all out. Give the cops Carter, and let them sort out the rest when we're long gone."

Gus's story is evolving, growing, getting harder to keep track of, the words mixing and meshing with what Ekat, Eddie, Jody, Rita, and everyone else said and with what I thought I knew. I'm a sap because it's working. I remember how I felt when operating under my earlier assumption that Eddie lit the fire. I remember the safety of righteousness, and I want it back. So okay, maybe Carter paid Eddie to light the fire and Jody survived because he knew she was at Rachel's place. He got cold feet, he couldn't go through with killing her, but what about her son, JT?

I shake my head and pull out of the tailspin. I say, "It wasn't Eddie. There's no way."

"You're probably right. I don't know; I'm just so scared, to be honest. After it happened, I thought that Carter would've been caught within twenty-four hours and that he would take me down with him. I didn't know what to do, and I needed to figure a way out, so I went hedgehog."

"Hedgehog?"

"Yes, a member of the rodent family. I'm not familiar with the scientific name of their phylum, but, you know, they live underground."

"I thought they lived in hedges."

"Regardless, I found out I was pretty good at being gone. I could've stayed gone, too. I didn't have to come back, Mark."

I say, "I believe you," which is a lie. I don't feel bad about it either.

The Dart emerges from the tunnel, and we navigate an on-ramp labyrinth no minotaurs and head toward the developing waterfront area and South Boston. We stop at the D Street intersection light.

There's a new and giant hotel on the corner of Summer Street, all lights and glass. I wonder if anyone is looking out one of those windows and sees me in this car. I slide into a comfortable slouch in my seat, roll down the window, and let a cool breeze play with my beard. An embarrassingly large part of me wants to indulge in a fantasy where Gus and I are just cruising in his Dart, with no particular place to go.

Gus says, "Hey, see their car anywhere?"

I fix my slouch. "No."

"I didn't think I was that far behind them. No biggie. We all know how to get to Ekat's place, right?"

I whistle "Do You Know the Way to San Jose?" Sitting in the seventies car, wind blowing in my face, I think it's appropriate.

The light goes green. Gus starts straight onto D Street but changes his mind, squealing wheels left and onto Summer Street. He doesn't use his blinker. He says, "Like I said, I could've stayed gone, but I had come back to help Ekat and you."

"You're a regular Albert Schweitzer." I rub my eyes and try to remember more of my parking lot conversation with Ekat. It's an itch between my shoulder blades, and I'm having a hard time reaching it. "How did you know Ekat and Carter would be at Wonderland?" Now that we're moving, the wind is too much, threatens to steal my hat, so I roll up the window. The fast lane isn't for me.

"Ekat left voice-mail messages and texts, telling me some of what was going on with the both of you, but I didn't return any of those messages until today. She texted me this morning that Carter wanted her to go with him to Wonderland for one last score. I broke my radio silence. We decided that she'd go with Carter, that I'd be there too and would be watching just in case, and then we'd go away for a long while."

"She told me that she hadn't heard from you."

"She was trying to protect me, I guess. You surprised her, and she panicked. I wasn't surprised, though, pal. You're good at what you do, and that you somehow found your way to Wonderland tonight isn't the upset of the century as far as I'm concerned."

"Aw, shucks. You sure got a pretty mouth."

Summer Street is now L Street, and we pass through the East Broadway intersection. We're only a cupful of blocks away from Ekat's apartment, but it doesn't feel like we're any closer to the end of this. Whatever this is.

Gus says, "All that said, to be brutally honest with you, buddy, maybe Ekat didn't lie to you. You might not have heard her right. You might not have been all there. I know you pretty well, Mark. It happened during our magnificent bender, right? Maybe you were asleep while you were talking to Ekat. Your first-hand accounts aren't exactly reliable. When I found the two of you, Ekat was pacing, wearing out a patch of the parking lot, and you were snoozing up against the post with your big hairy gob drawing flies."

"Keep it up, and I'm gonna smack you in that pretty mouth."

"I'm not saying any of that to be mean. I'm just trying to be straight with you."

"That would be a first."

It's our first fight, and I don't think we'll ever be the same. We don't speak during the final leg of our jaunt. Gus turns right onto East Sixth, and we park at the corner of I instead of in front of Ekat's place.

I say, "You're really going to make me walk?"

Gus shuts the car off and says, "Carter could still be hanging around. He shouldn't be, but you never know. We need to play this safe."

We creep up I Street like a couple of creeps. If Ekat is home alone and if this is really the end, I don't know what I'm going to do. Will I call the police and have the wonder twins picked up, or will I do nothing, stand on her doorstep, get pats on the head, then blow kisses and breathlessly scream, *Bye-bye, bon voyage, don't forget to write*?

Looks like I don't need to know the answer to that question just yet. The outdoor lights (both front door and back door) are on, but the interior is dark and lonely. Her apartment is in mourning. Gus peeks in the front window, roughs up the glass with his knuckles, and nothing. No one's home.

The Lexus isn't parked out front, and there are plenty of open spots up and down I Street. Carter and Ekat are not here. I pull out one of my own cigarettes, no cloves or other nonprocessed ingredients, the way nature intended.

Gus takes off his hat and looks around. He wears incredulousness quite well. He says, "There's no way I beat them here, is there?"

"Maybe Carter took her on the scenic route, the long-cut. Maybe they stopped at a bar first. Maybe they wanted to play Keno, pick up a few scratch tickets."

"No, no, no. She was going to have him drive her straight home. We must've beat them here. Maybe they went down D Street." Gus spins around three times, a dog looking for a spot to lie down, and then jogs across the street and back toward the Dart.

Down on the corner instead of out in the street, we wait. Gus leans on a city-planned tree with his arms outstretched, palms flat against the bark, like he's trying to push it over and block off the road. I stand behind him, relegated to the background, a lowly subordinate to his commander. I tend to my personal fire and smoke. A few cars go up I Street. The cars don't stop and they don't drop off passengers wearing blond wigs.

I decide to throw something out there at Gus and see what sticks to his slick old self. I say, "You know what else Ekat told me?"

"What did she tell you?"

"She said that you were in on it. That you helped Carter plan and set the fire. Tonight was her last score, and then she was running away from the both of you. Maybe she's on her way to some remote island right now. She'll build a house on the beach with teakwood and live off coconuts, fish, and clams. I like her plan better than yours."

Gus keeps watch on I Street, like it might run away. He says, "Not funny, Mark," but there's something there, a microsecond of hesitation and doubt, and if I were able to pick up that moment and stretch it out like pizza dough, I'd find the holes.

"You said I was funny earlier."

"I was wrong. You need to work on delivery and timing." Gus still hasn't turned his head, talks in a monotone, and keeps contact with his tree. He doesn't look like a man happy with the way things are working out. That makes two of us.

I throw my dead and used smoke at his foot. I have good aim. "Why did you get mixed up in any of this?" It's a painfully earnest question, one I don't expect will be answered.

"You mean: What's a sweet boy like me doing in a place like this? Well, I'll tell you, but only because it's you, Mark. It's because my parents were just awful to me, didn't kiss me enough, and they yelled at me when I wet the bed." Gus laughs, and it goes on for far too long. Nothing is that funny. He says, "Come on, what do you want me to say? I stole credit cards and made the IDs because I could. It was easy in a very casual way, and I was good at it. Because getting away with it was a rush. Because the money was real good. There are no deep dark secrets here. You know me, Mark."

I do know him, now. We wait another few minutes. A cab and a lopsided minivan drive by, and that's it.

"Shit, shit, shit . . ." Gus stands up and stretches his arms out wide to give the world a hug. "They're not coming here. Something happened. What are we going to do?"

I say, "Call her. Ask her what's taking so long. Have her pick up a pizza, with sausage. I'm hungry."

Gus takes out his phone, then stops. "I-I can't. I can't risk Carter knowing that I'm back and that she and I have been communicating."

"I'll call."

"You can't call her either. He doesn't know that you know about any of this."

"I'm calling." I take out my phone. It needs to be charged and is almost dead.

Gus reaches for my phone, but I dodge him. He says, "We can't. Either of us calling could put her in danger, Mark. Carter . . ."

Gus stops, looks up and down I Street again, eyes spinning free in his head. He says, "All right. Let's think. We lost their car coming out of the tunnel, right? I didn't see them on D Street or on Summer." He pauses, rubs his chin like there's a genie in it. "Did they go onto 93? There's a ramp there, right at the end of the tunnel. They did. Fuck, Carter took her to his house."

I say, "They could be anywhere."

"I know, I know, but his house is the only other place that makes sense. It's the only other place we can check." He runs the short distance to his car. "You coming or staying?"

Gus is smooth. Even when he appears to be flustered, he does it with style, panache with a soft, drawn-out *che*. He's a walking and talking wink, a come-hither look, and I can't help but follow even when every ounce of my being knows to stay away from him and his Dart, to go home and call Detective Owolewa, and drop this hot and messy fondue in his lap.

I limp to his car, dragging my lazier-by-the-minute left leg behind me. Looks like he and I get to take a joyride after all. I'll try not to let it go to my head.

Gus starts the car and says, "Carter lives in Milton. We'll jump on the highway real quick. Fifteen-minute ride, tops." He pulls out of the parking spot, shaking his head. He says, "This isn't good."

"I know."

THIRTY

The Dart's front end is an elongated snout, rooting through the dips and potholes of the southeast expressway. There aren't any truffles. We don't feel the bumps as much as we glide over them, cresting the waves, a boat on water. It's a sea-sickening feeling. With every swell the tires strain to keep contact with the road, and we could go careening into the median at the slightest breeze or driver misstep.

Gus talks because he has to. He doesn't know what else to do with his mouth. I can't hear him over the engine. My window is open, filling the old car with new air. But the air isn't new. It's unaccountably ancient and used.

I turn my head, and Gus isn't driving anymore. It's my old roommate Juan-Miguel. He looks small with the Dart's Conestoga-wagon-sized steering wheel in his hands. He wears a black T-shirt over a white T-shirt, like he always did. I send him a smile, and I'm as nervous as a middle schooler at his first dance. Juan-Miguel yells at me about what I did to the couch, and he yells at me about what I did, about the lies I told him, but he won't look at me, can't look at me, and I can't remember when he could.

I turn my head, and Gus isn't driving anymore. It's my mother, Ellen. She calmly explains why she's relocating me back to the Cape and our old family bungalow. She tells me that I'm not doing well on my own and that I need help. She can look at me, but she won't.

I turn my head, and Gus isn't driving anymore. It's Dr. Who. He has a stack of notebooks on his lap, and Jesus is still on the dashboard. I reach across the canyon of the bench seat to grab the notebooks. I need to leaf through them and find pictures of me, find one that I like, or at least one that I can live with.

I turn my head, and Gus isn't driving anymore. It's my old friend George. I'd like to say that he never left, that he's always with me it's the sugar-sweet culturally approved sentiment but it'd be a lie. He's been gone for ten years. He's a fading memory, a shrinking part of the story-of-me that I tell occasionally. George is here now, though, and he's finishing a laugh about something. He always finished after me. I loved that about him.

I turn my head, and now I'm driving the van. This isn't right. The van is too big for me to control. Too big for me to handle. George is in the passenger seat. He finishes the laugh that wouldn't end, shaking it out like he's emptying his shoe of sand.

He slumps against the passenger door and rests his head on the glass. I shouldn't be watching him instead of the road, but I am. This isn't how it happened.

I blink, wiggle my nose, try to Bewitch him back into the driver's seat. It doesn't work. I'm driving. My hands are too sweaty and treacherous. I can't trust them, the saboteurs, and I can't stop them from pulling right.

Our seats in the van are too high up. Our falling down is an inevitability.

I turn my head, and Gus isn't driving. Neither is George. I'm driving. George is asleep. This isn't how it was supposed to happen. George promised to help keep me awake. George is asleep. And I am too.

THIRTY-ONE

The Dart rolls onto the grass shoulder of a narrow, wooded street. Just outside my door is a stone fence with gaps, missing pieces, and it's not tall enough to stop anybody. Behind the crumbling fence is a thicket of trees, putting a mighty lean on the remaining stones.

Gus shuts off the car, taps my arm, and says, "We're here. You awake?"

"Always." I have a crick in my neck and in the rest of my body.

"I drove up and down the road a couple of times but couldn't really see anything, couldn't tell if they're here. The house is set too far back and up that big hill," Gus whispers.

Orderly lines of trees act as the honor guards on both sides of the road. There is a gated driveway entrance across the street, but no homes are visible through the surrounding woods. We're neck-deep in quaint New England charm and misanthropic privacy. Although I haven't seen Carter's bachelor pad, it's a safe bet that it must've cost him a medium-sized fortune, one that was credit card aided.

I say, "Any reason as to why you're whispering? I won't tell anyone."

Gus opens his door, and the interior dome light flashes on, blinding the blind. He says, "Come on. We hoof it on the driveway. Try and be quiet."

"I'll be a delicate ballerina. What are we going to do when we get there?"

"I'm not sure."

We're both on the same page. And we both climb out of the car.

The starry-starry-night sky is cloudless and filled with pinprick holes of light, light that took too long to get here, just like us. A soundtrack of crickets featuring the *Into the Woods* orchestra is undercut with the familiar Sturm und Drang of not-so-distant interstate highway traffic.

On our right, the weathered and rolling stone fence parts for Carter's driveway. We follow the one-lane private road, which is canopied by more trees that crowd and elbow each other, fighting for the right to blot out the night sky. Gus has his hands in his pockets. We don't talk. There isn't anything left to say.

We climb and come around a bend, and then a few more bends, until finally we spill out of the copse of trees, to the top of the hill and onto a gravel path that splits an open field of tall grass. Twenty yards ahead is Oz, a large, white, well-kept colonial farmhouse with a wraparound porch, two-story barn attached, and maybe a man behind a curtain inside. A lone lamp hanging off the barn spotlights the parked Lexus. They're here.

Gus crouches and jogs ahead of me. I can't keep up, never could. He waves his hand. I'm supposed to follow him. Luckily, I walk in a permanent crouch. Not so luckily, it's almost impossible for me to traverse this last bit of the driveway quietly. While I'm doing my baby elephant walk on the gravel, Gus glides like the hot coals under his feet don't bother him.

There's a light on in only one room of the house, first floor, its window adjacent to a side door near the barn and Lexus. The blue curtains are drawn.

We stalk to the car and hide behind its back end. My heart is in my collar, and my head fills with fuzz, like I've been holding my breath too long. I breathe, and too loudly for Gus's taste, apparently, as he shushes me.

We watch for a shadow to appear in the window or for the side door to open. Neither happens. Gus tilts his head toward the other end of the house. We duckwalk off the gravel, onto the grass, and to the front yard, which slopes away from us steeply. Nice view of west Milton and the highway. Below us, a stream of headlights moves slowly but inexorably, fish in a thickening river.

Gus pulls me onto the porch, but it's a mistake. We should've avoided the porch, no matter how nice the swing seat and matching rocking chairs looked. The boards creak, an alarm of dead wood under my feet. I try to walk lighter, but I can only do so much. Goosed by my bull-on-a-porch routine, Gus skips ahead and peeks into the lit window. I lean on the porch railing, which groans under my weight. I can't catch a break.

Gus bolts upright, firing like an engine piston. He spies in the window again but not for as long or as deeply. Then he looks at me. I can't tell if he's hesitant or determined. He says, "Come on. Quick."

I follow him to the door, and inside, past a mudroom that's too clean maybe I'm supposed to take my shoes off and then a doorway to a bright country kitchen with its one-thousand-watt bulbs and Day-Glo colors, including red on the white ceramic tile. A step ahead of me, Gus swears and dry-heaves, blocking his mouth with his hand, then skitters off to the left like a house spider.

From somewhere out there, Ekat says, "What took you so long?" She sounds like a child whose parents forgot to pick her up at soccer practice.

Timothy Carter lies on the floor, facedown and sprawled, arms and legs pointing in directions that aren't on a compass. What's left of his Humpty Dumpty head is aimed at me and the doorway. The back of his skull is deflated, and his scalp doesn't fit right anymore. A pool of red and other dark matter slowly expands in a timely fashion, sands leaking through a horrific hourglass. There's more blood misted on the tile beneath my feet and on the blue wallpaper next to me and on the door frame.

My olfactory imagination might be running away with me. I smell blood, piss, and burned meat. My gorge rises along with my stress level, which is about to go Vesuvius. Puking wouldn't be the worst thing in the world, but going out now would. My patchwork neurons sputter and fail. Limbs get shaking in rhythm to a song I can't hear, and I lose feeling in my extremities. My fingers and toes are made out of light.

If I don't keep moving, keep a focus, I'm going to suffer a cataplexy attack. A big one. All systems point to go-out, but I pretend that I can hold it off.

Ekat is on the other side of the kitchen. She's gone all fetus, huddled in a corner, propped against mahogany pantry cabinets. She still wears the wig and yellow dress. There are fine red dots that once intimately belonged to Carter coloring the dress and the wig's blond hairs. The dots form a pattern I'm unable to read. Her arms are wrapped tightly around her knees, which might run away without her.

A handgun sits at her feet, its proud black eye pointed this way, like I won spin the bottle. I don't know what kind of gun it is, but it's big and nasty and I get woozy just looking at it.

Ekat lifts her head and sees me. Her eyes are stained-glass windows, and recognition is a process that might take a week or two. She blinks a few times until it's clear that I'm in her scene.

She says, "What is *he* doing here, Gus?" Her voice cracks and eyes well up. Her face momentarily landslides into a look of utter sorrow, but she recovers. She stands up and wipes her cheeks on the short sleeves of her dress. The gun stays and heels at her feet, a well-trained dog with bite worse than its bark.

Gus is on my left, hand over his mouth, speaking no evil, until he says, "Shh. It's okay. Are you all right?" He tiptoes around Carter and his broken levee, avoiding the mess like it's a freshly seeded flower bed.

"No. I'm not all right. Why is Mark here?" Ekat shivers but not because it's cold in here.

Gus isn't listening to her or watching her. He only has eyes for the gun at her feet. He bends, hand outstretched, fingers twitching.

I'm not all right either. All this is happening too fast. I pull out my cigarette-lighter gun and point it at them although nobody wants to smoke. I call my own bluff.

"Stop! You touch that gun and—" I cut the line's cord, not sure if I need to finish the sentiment. My new headache doesn't agree with the yelling. The unfinished sentence vandalizes my head.

No one says anything. It's too quiet here. It's too everything here. I finish the old thought anyway; never too late to play it safe. "You touch that gun and I'll shoot. You. I'll shoot you, Gus. Stand up. Now."

I hope they don't see my hand and arm shaking. They're so excited and they just can't hide it. The gun lighter rattles in my hand. The sound could be authentic. I have no idea. I look at Ekat, waiting for her to share the old punch line of my fake-gun joke. She doesn't say anything yet. She looks back at me, maybe waiting to see if there's a new punch line.

Gus does stand, slowly. I'm sure he's always played well with others. He says, "Mark. Take it easy. What are you doing?" His voice drips soothing and calm and relaxed. He's a snake charmer and a barroom hypnotist, and it still kills me to know the truth about him.

I say, "Christ. I almost deserve it. I stepped on every one of the banana peels you assholes left out for me."

Gus starts in again with, "Mark, wait, you don't know what you're doing."

"Shut up. You two were lying about Carter the whole time. You both knew about the fire. You're both trying to set me up, pin the Carter-tail on the donkey me."

Gus says, "Whoa, Mark. No, no way, you're wrong, listen to me for second."

Ekat joins in: "Everything I told you tonight was true, Mark."

I yell again. "Shut up! Fucking listen to me!" This time I get as loud as I'm physically capable. I usually don't have the energy to get this angry, and it almost ruins me. I keep my feet, though, even if I don't feel them under me.

The exploding Mark yields two results. Gus and Ekat both stop talking, which is good. Not so good, I'm running out of me-being-upright time. I say, "You both lied about Carter not knowing your bagmen. Carter had been stopping by Aleksandar's apartment throughout the summer, exchanging money and credit cards, and maybe Christmas cards too."

Ekat looks at me and Gus. The real gun is between Gus's feet. Ekat stares hard at my cigarette lighter, and we both know she could take me out with one phrase, but she doesn't. She says, "That's not true, Mark."

I say, "I have a witness who places Carter at his apartment. Multiple times."

The three of us get lockjaw and share an eternal instant. We'll never forget it because, crazy as it sounds, there's a weird vibe in the farm house air. It's almost as if one of us buddies could break the tension by giggling and we'd all crack up into tear-pulling, gut-busting laughs; then someone would suggest we go to the nearest bar for some shots, and we'd cheer and leave the house and body behind, and we'd be all smiles, slapping each other on the back, secret handshakes, fist pounds, and at the bar clinking glasses and obnoxious platitudes in honor of each other's names.

All right, so no one laughs. I'll always miss my would-be life with my youthful imaginary friends. My hand sweats on the butt on my lighter, which is gaining mass despite not moving anywhere near the speed of light.

Gus opens his hands, presenting some sort of offering, but they're empty. He finally says, "Okay, Mark. You're right. You're right."

"What?" Ekat turns to look at him. Part of her wig falls in front of her eyes.

"Mark, listen, that is the only lie I told you tonight. I swear."

Ekat says, "What do you mean?"

Gus's hands move fast when he talks, and now he's talking even faster, in a hurry to get somewhere. "Look, Ekat, we wanted to expand a little and knew you wouldn't go for it. So Jody and Aleksandar were our experiment, and we were going to tell you about it after it had gone well, but you found that ID in my trash, which you didn't take so well, and Carter and I and remember, this was all before he went off the deep end, all right? we decided we couldn't tell you, not then anyway, and shit, then everything blew up and . . . I'm sorry. I should've told you earlier, and . . . I'm sorry. That's all I can say. I'm sorry, Ekat, I'm sorry."

Ekat shakes her head, and the wig doesn't look real anymore. It's hard to believe that anyone ever thought it was real. She gives me a look, but when I accept it she hides her eyes under the wig. This isn't an act, can't be an act. She didn't know that Carter knew about Jody and Aleksandar.

I say, "Everything blew up because Jody got caught at the Hub with one of your stolen cards and you found out about it. You and Carter weren't too happy about that, were you, Gus?"

Gus says, "Yes," pauses, then adds, "I mean, yeah, after Jody got caught, that's when Timothy started panicking, getting so goddamn paranoid and unreasonable about everything. That's when he started talking about killing those guys."

"Unreasonable is an interesting way to put it."

Gus says, "But Jesus, Mark. The rest of it is true. It was all his idea, and we tried to stop Carter. We—"

I interrupt. "Where'd you get the gun, Ekat?"

"It's Timothy's. I got it out of his game room while he was getting us drinks."

And that's it. I wait for more: explanation, recrimination. But I get nothing. She's as matter-of-fact as the two untouched glasses of wine on the marble countertop behind Gus. The wine is a dark red. I don't and won't know if the stuff is any good.

Gus sighs deep as a canyon, and he sways on his feet, left to right, midtempo. He doesn't like her answer. He says, "Mark just put down the gun, all right? We're talking. We're good, okay? We're all going to get out of here. I'll make it better."

I say, "I think you should answer one of Ekat's questions."

"What questions?"

"Short-term memory issues, good buddy? I sympathize, I really do. So let me help you out a little. Way back when we first crashed the little kitchen party, Ekat wanted to know what took you so long to get here. It sounds to me like you were expected, like Ekat being here instead of her place wasn't a surprise to you. I could be wrong. It's happened before.

"Then there's the follow-up: she asked what I was doing here. I'm guessing both questions are related to each other, part B to a part A, so feel free to address either. No partial credit awarded."

I already know the answers. They had already planned Carter's murder, but when I showed up at Wonderland tonight, Gus decided to bring me along to be the suicide half of that act. Cops find me and Carter dead tomorrow, or if Gus is lucky a few days later. Carter and I share a brief, convenient, and what-I-hate-about-you recent history, with me screwing up his surveillance case as a matter of phone records and office visits, so the cops might buy that I was Carter's killer for a day, maybe two. It wouldn't stick but would give Gus and Ekat more than enough time to disappear, to find their own rabbit hole.

"Mark, come on. Put the gun down; let's get out of here." That's all Gus has to say, his voice flatter than Stanley.

Ekat covers her face with her hands. She can't believe how quickly she and her friends sank so far over their heads. Maybe I'm projecting. Yeah, they planned to kill Carter tonight, and here at his house, but Ekat wasn't planning on the second act featuring Gus's improv. She wasn't planning on killing me. It has to be the reason why she hasn't told Gus that my gun is a fake.

I say, "One more try, Gus. Why am I here?"

"Mark . . ." He shakes his head, lifts his eyebrows, shrugs, holds up surrender hands, might as well throw in a tap dance, back flip, and a split.

I think I shined too much light on him. He's not an ant under a magnifying glass. He's bigger, and he's going to mount a counterattack that I'm not currently equipped to defend.

"That's what I thought," I say and extend my cigarette-lighter gun, point it at Gus's chest. "Both of you, put it in reverse." They slowly back away. The real gun is alone on the floor. I need to get to it and put that ugly goddamn thing in my hand before something worse happens. Something like my heart popping like a zit. I walk the impossibly thin line of clean tile around Carter's body. It's a ledge above a gorge, and I'm going to fall. It's not a matter of if but when. I breathe faster, and the muscles in my arms and legs pulse and spasm. The wattage my body generates is too much for my outdated and faulty grid.

I'm past Carter and standing above the gun, sweating like my skin knows it's not bulletproof. Gus and Ekat are a few steps away, huddled under the doorjamb between the kitchen and some other darkened room of the house.

I lick my lips with a dried-out tongue. The gun in my hand shakes. I could be the maraca player in our merry mariachi band.

I bend and reach down with my left hand. Knees crackle and pop like breakfast cereal in milk. I'm going down and I might not come back up. The closer I get to the gun, the farther away my body feels from me. My reaching left hand is a distant outpost, and we're having difficulty communicating. The hand moves slower than I want it to, need it to. The hand doesn't trust the information I send. The hand knows I'm a liar, and it reacts like I'm asking it to put its palm print on a hot stove.

I'm reaching, still reaching, when I see the attack mapped out on Gus's face before it happens. I can't stop him with a cigarette lighter. He's quick, fluid, no wasted movement. He skips forward and round house kicks my gun hand with his left foot. My arm slingshots across my body, and the lighter flies away, crashing into the cabinets to the left. Gus lands, plants, and dives, dipping his shoulder and plowing it into my chest. I lose my air and everything else, driven backward, my head, neck, and back bounce off the cabinets behind me, my vision goes center-stage bright, and then I'm sliding to the tile, trapped inside a body welcoming cataplexy, welcoming its total shutdown.

I'm awake, but I can't move or speak. Gus lifts me up by the lapels of my jacket and leans me against the cabinets, a piece of furniture being moved to a more convenient spot. Or maybe the feng shui is better with me here, near the dead feet of Carter's body.

Crouched next to me, Gus picks up my hat, twirls it on his fist for two or three times the merry-go-round, then fits it back on my head, pulling it down tight and patting it like he's afraid a wind gust might come and steal it away. Then he picks up the cigarette lighter. That's mine too, and he can't have it.

Gus adjusts his own obnoxiously red hat. He says, "This is all so fucked up, isn't it? I didn't mean for any of this to happen. I'm sorry, mate, I really am." He puts my cigarette-lighter gun under my chin. I don't need a light. The nozzle is cool against my defective skin. "You didn't have to come with me, tonight, you know. I gave you a choice at just about every turn. Remember?" His voice is weak and might break. He's no pro. Which makes it all worse.

"Nothing personal, Mark. It never was." He grimaces and squints, then pulls the trigger on my lighter. There's a bright but brief spark of pain under my chin as the flame licks my skin, but my head is still intact, as it were.

Gus doesn't know why there wasn't an earth-shattering kaboom. He pulls the gun out from under my chin and inspects it. He might not like what he'll find. He points it away from his body and pulls the trigger again. The half-inch novelty flame is orange and cute. I'd say, "Smoke 'em if you've got 'em," if I was able to talk.

Gus giggles nervously, and the left side of his face disintegrates into a red cloud, one that instantly becomes a terrible storm raining and hailing on my arms and legs. A light mist dampens my face as well, and I need to find some shelter. The storm finishes almost before it began, and in the instant aftermath Gus's body lies crumpled and discarded at my feet, his right arm pinned behind his head and up against the cabinets. I get a front-row view of the black hole that used to be the lower half of his face. No light escapes it. Fleshy stalactites hang above his jagged, broken teeth. His two intact eyes stare out at me. I'm the final image to be burned upside down onto his retinas.

Gus's facial detonation was horrifyingly quiet. So quiet I'm still shocked to see Ekat standing there holding the gun, the one that doesn't fuck around, pointed where Gus's head used to be. Ekat's yellow dress is a sunset turning red. Red skies at night.

She whispers, "This was all your fault," repeatedly. It's her mantra. She should write it down. She hovers over Gus's body and drops the gun on his torso. It lands with a thud but never makes contact with the tile. It sticks somewhere within the folds of his clothes or in some new nook or cranny of his bent body.

Ekat steps toward me and lowers herself, straddling my legs just above my knees, sitting on my thighs. The skin of her bare legs feels cold through my pants. She cries, but not loudly. No wall-rattling moans and wails. She's composed, a model of melancholy restraint, yet it all sounds like dying to me.

Her eyes are made out of glass again. She wipes her face with her shaky hands and says, "Are you all right? Can you hear me?" I want to say that yeah, I'm great, I'm just taking a little nap, but I can only manage the slight flex of an eyelid. Maybe I'm breathing through my eyelids. I'm so Zen.

Ekat says, "I didn't know he was bringing you here, Mark."

Gus says, "Don't listen to her, buddy. Check her pants. Wait, she has no pants. Check her metaphorical pants, then. They might be on fire because she's a liar liar." His voice is a mouth full of bubble gum and a throat gargling saltwater. Him talking is a neat trick. His mouth isn't moving. He has no mouth, and he can't scream. His dead slug tongue isn't moving either. I'm watching. There's no ventriloquist to this dummy. I'm hallucinating again.

Ekat says, "Back at Wonderland, after you fell asleep against the lamppost, we argued about what we should do with you."

He says, "No. We talked and joked about what we were going to do to you. We made fun of your sorry ass. We were going to put your hand in a glass of warm water and laugh when you pissed yourself. I know that you've pissed yourself before."

Ekat says, "I had to get back inside, or Timothy would've known something was wrong, so we left it as Gus was just going to do whatever he could to ditch you at Wonderland, make sure that you didn't follow us here to Timothy's house."

Gus says, "I call bullshit. You coming here was her idea, man. All hers. I just did what she told me to do. I ain't the brains of this outfit. I ain't got none anymore, see? Ha, made you look!"

I know he's lying because I didn't look. I didn't want to look, anyway. I can't even move enough to close my eyes.

Ekat keeps talking. She either doesn't hear Gus or is ignoring him. She says, "After the whole blackmail scheme fell apart, I didn't want you to be in any part of this. Remember that night you came back with me from the Pour House? I was angry that Gus had hired you. That wasn't an act. I didn't want you getting hurt. You didn't deserve to get hurt."

He says, "Pfft. Tell it to Dr. Who and the losers at our group therapy. They might believe you." Gus has an abrasive edge that he didn't have in life. Maybe getting shot in the face will do that to a person. Maybe it's the real him, operating without his charm filter. The filter that I knew and loved so well.

Ekat looks over her shoulder, and Gus stares back. Caught, he goes silent, quietly bleeding out.

She says, "I didn't know Carter knew and that Jody was caught. I didn't know that Gus was bringing you here. That's why I did what I did." Ekat picks up my left hand and notices the rubber band on my wrist.

I want to say, "Yeah, that's yours but it doesn't mean anything," but I can only think it.

Ekat stretches it out. She teases the rubber band to its breaking point, then double and triple loops it around my wrist. She twists my hand gently, turning my palm facedown, then up, and my hand comes off. There's no pain or blood. This isn't messy.

She says, "I didn't know that Gus planned to kill you. That's why I shot him. I had to stop him. I had to."

"Poor little me," Gus says and laughs. The laughter quickly turns into tears, into melodramatic, convulsing sobs. He's a howling, blubbering mess.

"Mark, I need an hour before you call the police. That's it, just one hour." Ekat unwinds the rubber band and slides it up my arm, relooping it at my elbow. She takes away my forearm, sliding it out from inside my shirt sleeve. Following the same process, Ekat removes my bicep and the rest of my arm up to the shoulder. She builds a neat little pile on the kitchen floor with the random pieces of me. Maybe I won't miss them.

Gus is lost somewhere in his overchoreographed death throes, moaning about his lost youth. The act lacks sincerity and dignity. It's hard to believe I ever thought he was cool.

With the help of her rubber band, she takes apart my other arm. She's disassembling a faded and out-of-style decoration to be packed and put away in the basement and forgotten. I'll be left to lie moldering in a box, dreaming my private dreams.

She says, "I know I don't deserve it, but just one hour. Please." She has at least twenty minutes before I recover from the cataplexy attack. I can't tell her that even if I want to.

With my arms separated into parts and piled high, she climbs off my legs, slides the rubber band onto my ankle, and pulls off my right foot. Then the same with my left. Right foot, left foot.

Gus says, "Hey! She's turning you into that picture I drew at group therapy. You know, that self-portrait, the one with me falling apart, arms and legs in pieces and the whole bit. That was a picture of *me*, not you. It's not always about you, Mark."

Ekat says, "Just one hour, okay? Do you want to know something? I haven't even decided what I would do with the hour. I might drive south, or north, or some made-up direction. I might go home, sit in my apartment, call Mom, and wait for the police to pick me up. I might go home and go to sleep. I might just go away. I might drive Timothy's car headfirst into a highway median or nosedive with it off a bridge and into the ocean. If I did that, you could dream about me falling off the bridge, and the splash, and watch as my car slowly fills up with water. You won't want to finish the dream and would wake up before you see how long I can hold my breath.

"I don't know what I'm going to do, Mark, but I need that hour to do whatever it is I decide to do. Please, Mark. One hour." In her hands my cranky legs come apart easily at their rusted hinges. It feels good, but I'm worried that no one will ever be able to put me back together again.

"One hour. Please." Ekat kneels and puts her face in mine. The golden strands of her wig become Gorgon, moving and writhing around her head. I've already turned to stone.

I try to talk even if I don't know what I will to say to her. Open my mouth and see what words might spill out. I can't open my mouth very wide, and what comes out is a heavy, protracted sigh.

"I should've done something to stop this from happening earlier, I know." She rests her lips over mine, gently holding both of our mouths open. She says, speaking inside of me, "It was my fault. I'm sorry. Thank you. Goodbye."

She kisses me once, and the red sunset stands and then walks out the kitchen door.

The door shuts. I close and open my eyes. I'm still here, sitting on the floor, blood claiming most of the kitchen tile.

I try to wiggle my fingers and toes, and good news manage some movement. Bad news: my fingers and toes are still over there, in the pile of me next to Gus. This is going to make getting the cell phone out of my pocket difficult.

"Finally, we're alone. We can dish," Gus says. He's speaking to me again. I thought I was going to get the silent treatment. "Between me and you, before everyone else shows up to our little circus tent, tell me the truth, Mark. We're still friends, aren't we?"

"Sorry if this is awkward, but we're kind of all done. And it's not me; it's you." Apparently I can speak now. My voice is a slight rustle of curtains, but he can hear me.

He says, "I know you, Mark. I fucking *know* you. And I'm trying to help you. Really, I am. So tell me the truth. Just like the night you got drunk and finally told Juan-Miguel the truth. It was your fault. Right, Mark? You even told Dr. Who it was your fault."

"What are you talking about?"

"I'm talking about what you said to Juan-Miguel. You remember him; he was driving the Dart earlier. You remember him, don't you? He was your old roommate, the dude who moved out because he couldn't handle living with your narcolepsy. No, wait a minute. Juan-Miguel didn't stop living with you because of your narcolepsy. He stopped living with you because you lied to him about who was driving the van and he couldn't deal with it when you finally told him the truth, finally told him it was your fault. And you couldn't deal with anything when he left. You still can't."

I can't listen to this, and I won't. He's a liar. He's been lying to me since I met him. He's a liar lying on the floor.

"It was your fault. You were driving the van, not George. You fell asleep at the wheel. You were having narcoleptic symptoms for almost a year before the trip to Foxwoods and the van accident, and you didn't tell anyone."

I'm not listening to him.

"You were too embarrassed to ask for help. You were too scared that something terrible was wrong with you. You tried to ignore it. You closed your eyes and wished the bad stuff away.

You didn't tell anyone, not even your best-est buddy George."

Shut up.

"You didn't tell him that you'd been falling asleep on the train and the bus and at work. You didn't tell him, and you drove the van that night."

Shut up!

"You killed your best friend."

No, I didn't. It was an accident.

"The irony is that I was your friend, Mark, that I am your friend, and I tried to kill you. See how that all kinda worked itself out? I think that makes things all square, now."

"Shut up

shut up

shut up!"

I take my hands away from my face because I'm screaming into them, but not at them. My fingers are wet with blood, sweat, and tears. It was my fault. No, it was an accident. I cry some more. It doesn't make me feel any better.

Carter and Gus are dead on the kitchen floor. Gus is done talking. Enough has finally been said.

I slowly stand up because I can. The room shakes and

499

sways under my jelly legs. My clothes are heavy with other people's blood.

I need to get out. I leave the kitchen and walk outside, onto the porch. Carter's Lexus is gone. Gus's Dart is somewhere at the bottom of the hill. The night is empty.

I pull my cell phone out of my jacket pocket and stare at it. The push buttons glow a phosphorescent blue. I hover my finger over the numbered buttons, and the blue light somehow curls around my fingertip. I haven't pressed anything yet.

Oh, I will use the phone at some point. I don't know if Ekat's precious hour is up, and I haven't yet decided if I care.

THIRTY-TWO

"Hey."

I'm more nervous than I should be. I'm perched on the front stoop, standing as straight as a barber pole, sans stripes, and sweating like a rain forest. It's too warm for September, and I'm dressed for winter. I shouldn't have worn my wool sports coat, but it's my favorite. It helps to give my lumpy shoulders some definition while camouflaging my gut. Image is everything.

I say, "Hey," back. My conversational prowess is a gift.

Jody wears faded jeans and a tight green Celtics V-neck T-shirt. The collar trim is frayed and stretched out. She doesn't wear any makeup, and she has taken out the stud from below her lip. Her brown hair is black because it's still wet. Loose strands cling to her round cheeks. She's just out of the shower, and she doesn't look as nervous as I feel.

She says, "Come on up, but watch where you're walking. The hall light burned out a couple of weeks ago, and the landlord hasn't dragged his ass down here to change it. It's like one of those bad jokes: how many assholes does it take to change a lightbulb?"

I say, "I don't know. How many assholes does it take? Two?" I try to play along, build on her joke, but it's a house made of straw that crumbles and blows away by the hair on my chinny-chin-chins. I'm the wolf and the pigs at the same time. Jesus, I need to try to relax a little.

Jody says, "Huh? Oh, yeah, maybe. I just know there's one asshole not getting the job done."

The front door shuts behind me, and it's dark, below-deck-on-a-pirate-ship dark. I should've brought a parrot and taken my citrus pill. Getting scurvy would suck. Above us, the apartment door is open, our navigating star. I make it up the stairs without falling.

Jody says, "Have a seat," and points at the kitchen table. I assume she means for me to sit in a chair. "Don't mind me if I'm a little cranky. I haven't, you know, drank anything for twenty-four days. That's a big deal for me. I've been drinking since I was eleven."

I say, "Good for you, Jody. I . . . uh . . . don't mean good for you for the drinking-since-you-were-eleven part. I meant good for you for not drinking. You probably knew that." Nice. I'm tripping over myself trying to play it cool when I don't have that setting. It's hard to be cool when you're sweating more than Marlon Brando in *Apocalypse Now*.

"Yeah. Good for me. I'm trying to do better, you know? After everything that's happened, I don't have much of a choice. I have to do better."

"Are you feeling okay?"

"Yeah. Yeah, I'm starting to feel pretty good. But I've gained fifteen pounds. I'm blowin' up."

"I think you look great." I'm telling the truth, but I don't know if it sounds right and don't know if it's what she wants to hear. No one ever knows the right thing to say. We're always guessing, and either we have the courage to say something or we don't.

Jody laughs and says, "You're such a bad liar, but I'll take it." The kitchen has been recently cleaned and smells of mass-produced chemicals. I sit at the table and fiddle with the salt and pepper shakers shaped like gingerbread men. The gingerbread men don't know they are out of season. I accidentally knock over the salt, the shaker with the red scarf around its cookie neck. I sweep up the granules and pocket them instead of throwing them over my shoulder. I'm not some superstitious fob.

"Do you want anything?" Jody stands in front of the open refrigerator. There aren't a whole lot of choices inside the metal box.

I say, "Water is fine, thanks."

She pours us both a glass of soda water instead. I don't like soda water. The carbonation without the caffeine gives me a headache.

"My JT calls soda water garbage juice." Jody brings our angry, frothing glasses to the table. She sits on top of a folded leg. It doesn't look like a very comfortable position. "He's a funny kid."

I wasn't planning on asking about her son. I tell myself that doesn't make me a coward. I say, "How's he doing?"

Jody looks out the window behind me. Maybe she sees something. She says, "Okay, I guess. He's out of the hospital but scarred up pretty bad. Might need some skin grafts and some other procedures later. He's staying with a foster family in Quincy." She pulls her leg out from underneath her butt, and she sinks lower into the chair. "They seem nice, but they have like eight other kids they're watching, so I don't know how much attention he gets. I get one supervised visit a month. I saw him last weekend. Didn't ask too much about his new family. He didn't say much about them neither. I don't know; it's hard, and it sucks. I can petition or reapply for custody, or whatever they call the flaming hoops of shit I have to jump through, in a year, maybe."

Jody cut a deal with the DA, cooperating fully with the ID theft, arson, and now double-murder investigations. No jail time, but probation and a parole officer, and I gather that her being granted full custody again is the longest of long shots. She knows this.

She says, "Oh hey, I almost forgot. Jesus, my head spinning with AA meetings and everything else, I almost forgot." Stops and gives me a smile. "JT said something else that was kinda funny."

"He likes garbage juice now."

"No, not funny ha-ha. He says he dreams about the fire a lot, and, um, he dreams about a big, hairy guy in a hat carrying him out of his bedroom, walking him down our old stairs, saving him. Isn't that something else?"

I say, "That is funny, not ha-ha," and pretend that there was never any doubt that I'd saved the kid. I hold in the soul-deep sigh of relief and resist the urge to pull out my cell phone and have Jody relate that story to Detective Owolewa or anyone else who'll listen. Maybe I'll tattoo *him-I-saved* on my forearm instead. It'd be more subtle.

Jody smiles at me and says, "I hope you get to meet JT someday. He's a great kid." She tucks her wet hair behind her ears. Her cheeks and the skin around her eyes are splotchy red. "So are you gonna tell me what you know, or what? Spill it." She's practically yelling at me, overcompensating for everything.

The kitchen floor is warped and pitches slightly left. I try to lean away from the subtle slant, but balance is impossible. I sip the garbage juice, and I tell her what I know, which isn't much.

The Boston police investigated me thoroughly in the month-plus since the night at Carter's house, stopping just short of a full body cavity search. While they've concluded that I am mostly clean, they haven't been exactly forthright in providing me with further details about everything that happened. I do know Carter is their number one suspect for the fire, but short of my testimony, they don't have any court-worthy physical evidence. Carter's Lexus was abandoned in Stamford, Connecticut, found in a train station parking lot. Ekat is still missing. Detective Owolewa, who still checks in with me (or is he checking up on me?), doesn't say if there are any leads.

I don't tell Jody that for the first two weeks after the shoot-out at the not-okay corral, I didn't leave my apartment. I sat on my couch in the dark and stewed about George, the van accident, and the fractured time before it and that has since passed. I stewed about Ekat, where she went, what she was doing. I stewed about Gus, playing and replaying everything he said and didn't say, connecting and reconnecting the events, trying to figure out exactly when Gus decided he could and would kill me, as if knowing that impossible precise moment would somehow redefine me or represent a measure of my worth.

I don't tell Jody that after those two weeks of self-flagellation were over, I took five hundred bucks the same amount Gus paid me to watch Ekat and sent it to the hotel manager down in Nantucket, the one who used to be Aleksandar's boss. I asked her to pretty-please pass the money along to Aleksandar's family.

I don't tell Jody that I've spent last month cleaning and redecorating my apartment. I threw out half and scrubbed the other half, focusing the bulk of my efforts in the living room. I went hazmat on that disaster. I junked the crumbling CD and DVD towers and shelves and the coffee table. I peeled away the dust-encrusted blinds and curtains, rods and all. I washed the hardwood floors by hand, twice. Throwing away my old couch was the most difficult part. It had been my only roommate for almost ten years. I tried throwing a white sheet over it so it was disguised as the ghost of my old couch, but it didn't work. I couldn't just cover up that corpse. I needed that sucker buried and gone. So I dragged it down the stairs and to the curb. After that, and a long nap, the rest was easy. I painted the walls a light shade of sky blue. It's kind of goofy, and my mother, Ellen, pretended not to approve of it, but I like it. I still might paint on some clouds or buy large cloud stickers that I can peel off and put back on, depending upon what kind of day it is.

I don't tell Jody I salvaged a bookshelf that someone left out on Gold Street, but I don't have any books on it yet. I haven't put up new curtains or bought a new couch either. Part of me likes the room the way it is: clean but unfinished. Part of me likes the possibilities more than whatever the finished product will be. That and I'm short on funds. I don't tell Jody that I'm considering putting out an ad (with Ellen's blessing) for a roommate.

I don't tell Jody that Ellen and I have patched things up and are back on speaking and visiting terms. I also don't have to go to group therapy anymore to keep the place.

Jody asks, "You hear anything about how Eddie's doing?"

Eddie pleaded no contest to a host of charges related to his stealing a car and the Zakim Bridge dumping of my pretty ass. He's being held without bail, but he's no longer an arson suspect. I say, "No. You probably know more than I do."

"I guess so. He wrote me a letter, got it last week, but I didn't open it. I know he didn't start that fire, but . . . I don't know. Opening that letter would be like going backward, or something. I just want to go forward now." Jody points somewhere behind me. I presume that's where forward is.

I concur with my silence.

Jody and I stop talking and not talking about the case, which means we're done talking, and there isn't much garbage juice left in our glasses. Ending the conversation with talk of Eddie is the worst possible lead-in to what I want to ask her, to what I was planning on asking her, but I forge ahead anyway.

"Would you like to go out to dinner some night this week? Maybe Friday night?" My hands tap out a rhythm on the kitchen table. I'm a one-man act: spoken word accompanied with free-form jazz percussion. I keep the gig going. "We could go out, or we could go more simple, more low-key. You could come over to my place. I'm teaching myself to cook now."

"Oh yeah?"

"Yeah. I'm terrible at it. I burned cold cereal yesterday morning, but I'll get better. I should be decent by Friday night."

She says, "Sounds like fun, Mark, and I'll do it on one condition."

"Okay."

"As long as it isn't a date. Call it we're hanging out."

"I never said date, did I?"

"No, not exactly."

"Let's hang out on Friday night, then."

Jody stands up and takes my glass and puts it in the sink even though it isn't quite empty. Her hands are shaking a little, too. She says, "Yeah, okay. Just keep in mind I'm still new to my AA experience, and I'm feeling good now, but I still have bad days. I might have to cancel last minute if it's a bad day, you know?"

I do know.

ACKNOWLEDGMENTS

Thank you to Lisa, Cole, and Emma, and the rest of my amazing family and friends who've been so supportive of me and the books. I'd be dead or crazy or crazy-dead without them. Thank you to my agent, Stephen Barbara, whom we all love despite his two first names. Thank you to my editor, Helen Atsma, who really went above and beyond the call of duty for me and the book(s).

And thank you Laird Barron, Books on the Square (Providence), BPL Copley and South Boston branches, Raymond Chandler, F. Brett Cox, JoAnn Cox, Bill Crider, Nick Curtis, Dave Daley, Ellen Datlow, Kurt Dinan, the Elitist Horror Cabal, Steve Eller, Steve Fisher, Michele Foschini, Lisa Fyfe, Geoffrey H. Goodwin, Jack Haringa, Ron Hogan, Stephen Graham Jones, Brian Keene, Sarah Knight, Matt Kressel, John Langan, Sarah Langan, Joe R. Lansdale, Jason Leibman, lokilokust, Chastity Lovely, Louis Maistros, Newtonville Bookstore, Stewart O'Nan, Tom Piccirilli, the qwee, Jody Rose, Brett Savory, the Secret Group, Charles Tan, Jeffrey Thomas, M. Thomas, Jeff Vandermeer, Your Pretty Name.

ABOUT THE AUTHOR

Paul Tremblay has won the Bram Stoker, British Fantasy, and Massachusetts Book awards and is the author of *Survivor Song, Growing Things, The Cabin at the End of the World, Disappearance at Devil's Rock, A Head Full of Ghosts*, and the crime novels *The Little Sleep* and *No Sleep Till Wonderland*. His essays and short fiction have appeared in the *New York Times, Los Angeles Times, Entertainment Weekly* online, and numerous year's-best anthologies. He has a master's degree in mathematics and lives outside Boston with his family.

For more fantastic fiction, author events,
exclusive excerpts, competitions, limited editions and more

VISIT OUR WEBSITE
titanbooks.com

LIKE US ON FACEBOOK
facebook.com/titanbooks

FOLLOW US ON TWITTER AND INSTAGRAM
@TitanBooks

EMAIL US
readerfeedback@titanemail.com